THE SCHOOL OF NIGHT

THE SCHOOL OF NIGHT

LOUIS BAYARD

WHEELER
WINDSOR
PARAGON

LIBRARY OF CONGRESS CATALOGING-IN-PUBLICATION DATA

Bayard, Louis.
   The school of night / by Louis Bayard.
     p. cm.
   ISBN-13: 978-1-4104-3860-7 (hardcover)
   ISBN-10: 1-4104-3860-0 (hardcover)
   1. Collectors and collecting—Washington (D.C.)—Fiction.
2. Historians—Washington (D.C.)—Fiction. 3. Secret societies—
England—History—16th century—Fiction. 4. Large type books.
I. Title.
PS3552.A85864S35 2011b
813'.54—dc22   2011011084

BRITISH LIBRARY CATALOGUING-IN-PUBLICATION DATA AVAILABLE

Published in 2011 in the U.S. by arrangement with Henry Holt and Company, LLC.
Published in 2011 in the U.K. by arrangement with John Murray (Publishers).

U.K. Hardcover: 978 1 445 85850 0 (Windsor Large Print)
U.K. Softcover: 978 1 445 85851 7 (Paragon Large Print)

For Mark H.
Now quit bugging me

PROLOGUE

Three or four times a week, it comes.

Not a dream: closer to a vision, *apart* from her but obscurely meant for her, too.

And each time the vision converges on a man. Working late into the evening. Streaks of sweat across his brow and neck. His head bowed — in prayer, she thinks, except she has never heard a prayer quite like this.

"Ex nihilo . . ."

Lapis stones clatter in a copper pan.

". . . nihil . . ."

Beneath the copper, a tallow flame crackles into life.

". . . fit."

A pewter mist billows up, then resolves into a powder. The air grows heavy with current. The man thrusts up his hands and roars. Four centuries later, she can still hear him.

"Long live the School of Night!"

■ ■ ■ ■

PART ONE

■ ■ ■ ■

Three new marriadges here are made
One of the staffe and sea Astrolabe
Of the Sonne & Starre is an other
Which now agree like sister & brother
And charde and compasse which were at
   bate,
Will now agree like a master & mate.

            — THOMAS HARRIOT,
              "Three Sea Marriages"

1

Against all odds, against my own wishes, this is a love story. And it began, of all places, at Alonzo Wax's funeral.

Now I'd known Alonzo pretty much all my adult life, but in the months after his death, I learned a surprising number of things about him. For instance, he chased his morning shots of Grey Goose with Rocky Road. He had never read a word of Alexander Pope — too modern — but he followed every single comic strip in *The Washington Post* (even "Family Circus"). He was a sneak and a liar and a thief and would have slain every grandmother he had for an original edition of *Bussy d'Ambois*. And he loved me.

But in those early months of mourning — or whatever it was we were doing about Alonzo — the biggest surprise was this: He had become Catholic. And had never gotten around to telling his parents, loosely

11

observant Rockville Jews who found the baptism certificate while sorting through his filing cabinets. After some family debate, Alonzo's sister Shayla began shaking the trees for priests, until a friend told her that suicide was a mortal sin for the Church. So she opted to hold the memorial service at the Folger Shakespeare Library, which, in addition to being marble, was home to the world's largest collection of printed Shakespearean works and to a small mountain of preserved and cataloged Elizabethiana. The Folger, in other words, was engaged in roughly the same business as Alonzo had been: ransacking boxes and chests for centuries-old documents that were, in most cases, considered highly disposable by the original writers.

Shayla was glad to have missed the incense, but something else struck her as she stood greeting mourners at the entrance to the great hall.

"Henry," she whispered. "I forgot. I hate lutes."

It could have been worse, I reminded her. The last memorial service I'd attended at the Folger was for a Buddhist restaurateur, and we were subjected to an hour of Tibetan music: finger cymbals and skull drums and, glowering over everything, a massively built throat singer, swaddled in goatskin, belching up chord after chord.

"And besides," I added, "the lute quartet was your idea."

"You know, I thought maybe they'd bring a viol. Or an hautboy."

"That's how it works. An Elizabethan collector dies, out come the lutes."

More than lutes. Significant People had come to pay respects to Alonzo, and here and there, framed by long swords and halberds, one could make out the graven profiles of More Than Usually Significant People. An assistant librarian of Congress, a Smithsonian undersecretary, an ambassador from Mauritius . . . even a U.S. senator, longtime friend and beneficiary of the Wax family, who worked the room as deftly as if it were a PAC breakfast. Alonzo, I thought, would have been appalled and flattered all at once.

"Did I mention you're his executor?" Shayla said.

She turned just in time to catch the look on my face.

"If you want to pass," she said, "I'll understand."

"No. I'm honored."

"There's some money in it, I think. Not a lot . . ."

13

"Does it matter if I don't know what I'm doing?"

"No," she said. "Your remarks — that's all you need to worry about today."

She narrowed her eyes at me. The stripe of unretouched hair along her scalp shone like war paint.

"You *did* prepare, right, Henry? Alonzo hated stammering; you know that."

For that very reason, I had written my remarks on index cards, but as I laid them in ranks across the podium, they filled me with a strange revulsion. And so, at the last instant, I decided to wing it. I gazed out across those three-hundred-plus mourners, spread across nearly three thousand square feet of terra-cotta tile, under a massively vaulted strapwork ceiling . . . and I went deliberately small. Which is to say, I spoke about meeting Alonzo Wax.

It was the first day of our freshman year, and Alonzo was the very first student I met, and because I didn't know any better, I thought all students were like him. ("I'm sorry now they weren't," I said.) The first thing Alonzo did was to offer me a tumbler of Pimm's — he kept it in a tiny cut-glass container in his hip pocket. And when he found out I was planning to major in English, he demanded my opinion of *A Winter's*

14

Tale. I got out maybe three sentences before he cut me off and told me how benighted I was. (" 'Benighted' was the exact word.") And when I told him I'd never read Chapman — well, I thought he was going to wash his hands of me then and there. Instead, he invited me to dinner.

"It was a *real* dinner," I said. "With courses. He explained to me that university food was a known carcinogen. 'Of course, the science has been suppressed,' he said, 'but the findings are unanimous. That shit will kill you.' "

Before I could retrieve them, the words — *kill you* — went shivering through the climate-controlled air. And in that moment, yes, I wished I could turn the clock back to Elizabethan days, when this great hall would have been a hive of distraction. Masques and plays and dances. Rushes covering the floor, dogs roaming free, a smell of agriculture everywhere. My voice just one thread among many.

Alonzo, I hurried on, paid for our meal, as he usually did. The tip was about the same size as the bill. And he allowed as how my ideas on *Winter's Tale* weren't quite so daft as he first thought. But I should still read Chapman.

" 'You'll never get anywhere,' he said,

'until you find a nice minor poet.' "

I stacked my unused index cards in a nice little pile. I squinted down at the finish line.

"Alonzo's self-assurance seemed to me something colossal. I was just this kid from the burbs, and here was this guy my own age carrying himself like a professor. And the *real* professors, they were as scared of him as I was, and why wouldn't they be, he was —"

He was what? I can't now remember what I was going to say because she, in effect, finished the sentence for me. Or began another one altogether. Just by walking into the great hall.

At least forty minutes late.

To this day I'm not sure I would have noticed her if she'd dressed properly. Like the rest of us, I mean, in our black wool and crepe. She was wearing an old-fashioned A-line dress, cotton — scarlet! — tight in the bust, loose and jovial in the skirt. She walked like somebody who was used to wearing such a dress. She looked more comfortable than anyone else in the room.

Nobody said a word to her. We were all probably just waiting for her to see her error. *Oh, the wedding's across the street! At the Congregational church!*

But she gave no sign of having come to the wrong place. She took a seat at the end of the third row and, without embarrassment, turned her attention on the speaker.

Who was me.

I had briefly forgotten this.

"Alonzo," I said, "was a — a great *collector*, we all know that. That's why there are . . . so many of us *here,* right? But to me, nothing in his collection was . . . ever as unique as he was. So . . ." — Finish. *Finish* — "so that's what I'll remember."

Who spoke after me? I couldn't tell you. By the time I sat down, I was gathering data. A tough job, because she was two rows behind me and slightly northward, which meant I had to wheel about in my seat at regular intervals and pretend I wasn't being the most irksome guy in the room. Somehow, through the heads and hats, sections of her came back to me. A profusion of dark hair. A creamy arm, draped across the back of her chair. And, most enticing of all, a ledge of collarbone, striking a note of pioneer resilience against the slenderness of her neck.

And then, from the podium, came the throbbing contralto of Alonzo's mother.

"My heart is so full," she said. "So very *full* to see all these people gathered to honor my son."

You might suppose I felt guilt. Given that, in this moment, I wasn't honoring her son. You would be half right. But here's the thing. You can get just as lucky at a funeral as at a wedding. In fact, luckier. Someone always needs to be comforted.

And Alonzo, more than anyone else, would have guessed how complicated the act of grieving him would be. He'd left behind no children. He'd never courted sentiment, he'd never courted anything — or anybody. But all the same he understood me. *Just come back when you're done,* I could hear him saying. *There's a letter I want to show you in the Maggs and Quaritch catalog. Written to the Laird of Craighall . . .*

And so, by the time the service was over, I believed I had his full dispensation to proceed. But as I stood up, another woman's voice rang after me.

"Henry!"

Lily Pentzler. Short-waisted and long-abiding. Braced like a professional wrestler, tufts of gray hair straggling over carob eyes, a stack of cocktail napkins in each hand. An air of harassed charity, not specific to this occasion.

"Do you need help?" I asked.

"Do I need help?"

Lily was Alonzo's amanuensis. I use that word because that's how it was printed on her business cards. "It means picking up the master's scraps," she once explained. Exactly what she was doing now.

"The security kept us waiting for nearly an hour," she told me. "The florist screwed up and sent lilies. Alonzo hated lilies. The caterer just got here. Just. Got. Here. *People,* before they go and, you know, harm themselves in some definitive way, should be required — and I'm talking beyond congressional mandate, Henry, a level of *divine* mandate that says, 'Know what? Before you do it, organize your own memorial service, 'kay? Buy the wreath, set up the open bar. *Hire* the fucking caterers and *then* kill yourself.' "

"I can see your point."

"This" — the piles of napkins began to teeter — "this will have the effect of ending suicide as we know it."

"Do you need any help?" I asked again.

She looked at me.

"We've missed you, Henry. You haven't been by to see us lately."

"Oh, yeah. Kinda busy. Teaching gig. The freelance thing. This, that . . ."

"The next thing," she said, eyeing me closely.

19

"Yep."

"Well, come by later, anyway. There's a wake at five. We're taking over the top floor of the Pour House, and Bridget is going to sing something mawkish and out of period. 'Last Rose of Summer,' I think. On second thought, save yourself."

She smiled then, just a little bit, and, pivoting slowly, labored toward the banquet table, which was nearly as tall as she was.

By now, no more than a minute had passed, but it was enough. The woman in scarlet was nowhere to be found. Through the great hall I wandered, half inspecting the crossbow bolts and the digitalized First Folio with the touch screen that made the pages turn like magic, and I was aware only of my own defeat, growing around me.

Until at my eastern periphery, like dawn, a long pale arm materialized, pushing against the oaken entrance door.

She was leaving. As quietly as she had come.

And here again fate intervened. Not Lily Pentzler this time but Alonzo's grandfather, ninety-eight, who believed I was his great-nephew and couldn't be told otherwise. Loosening his ancient-mariner grip required the intervention of the actual great-nephew, a pet insurance salesman from Centerville,

Virginia. I took three long strides into the entry hall, I shoved open the door, stood there in the blinding heat. . . .

She was gone.

No one but me standing on those marble steps in the early-September blast. Sweat tickled through my collar, and around me rose a smell like burning tires. Magnolias were growing, crape myrtles, and not much else.

Hard to explain the dejection that swept over me. I was a man in my midforties, wasn't I? Disappointment was my daily gruel. Back on the wheel, Henry.

And then I heard someone call after me: "Well, there you are!"

So much familiarity in the tone that I braced myself for another of Alonzo's relations. (The Waxes were a mighty tribe in their day.) This was someone else, a man in early winter: silver-haired, handsome and rawboned, and erect. Hale with a vengeance: his skin looked like someone had gone at it with pumice. He took my hand and held it for perhaps a second too long, but his smile was benign and vaguely dithering. In a BBC sitcom, he'd have been the vicar. He'd have ridden in on a bike with big panniers.

"Mr. Cavendish," he said (and indeed the accent was British), "I wonder if I might have a word with you."

"What about?"

This is where my little track of linearity breaks down. Because when he next spoke, it was as if he'd already spoken. And it was as if Alonzo was speaking, too, from his watery grave. And maybe some part of me was chiming in. All of us in the same helpless chord, not quite in tune but impossible to disaggregate.

"The School of Night."

2

"Have I said anything wrong?" asked the old man. His gaze was no longer quite so dithery.

"No."

"I only ask because you seem to have taken a fright."

"Oh, no, it's just —" I ran a hand down my scalp. "It's been a long — the whole day has been . . . for a second there, it was like Alonzo's ghost was passing by."

"And who says it wasn't?"

Humming to himself, the old man reached inside his suit jacket and brought out an umbrella, black and utilitarian, that exploded open at a touch of the thumb.

"The sun disagrees with me," he said.

"Excuse me, I don't think I caught your name."

"Bernard Styles," he said.

There lay, beneath his expensive accent, the faintest traces of Celtic, like tobacco fumes clinging to a reformed smoker's clothes.

"Very nice to meet you," I said.

"You've heard of me, perhaps?"

"I don't get out much."

"Well, then," he said easily, "I should tell you I'm in the same collecting line as poor Alonzo. Only in a different sphere of influence."

"As in England?"

"Buckinghamshire. Not so very far from Waddesdon Manor."

"Well, in that case, it's very kind of you to come all this way."

"Oh," said Bernard Styles. "I wouldn't have missed it."

No obvious change in his tone or demeanor. The change was all in my skin — a barometric tickle.

"Can you believe it?" he said, giving his umbrella a slow twirl. "This is my very first time in your nation's capital. Everything looks quite fantastical to me."

I thought he was overdoing it with the "fantastical," but then I turned to my left and saw the Washington Monument emerging like a thought cloud from the Capitol's brain.

"Oh," I said. "I see what you mean. Sorry about the heat."

24

"Yes, it's quite wretched. One can't altogether breathe. Perhaps we might go inside, after all."

The way was blocked, though, by a tall man with a brow like a fender.

"This is Halldor," said Bernard Styles.

A Scandinavian name but no clear race. His once-tawny skin had peeled away into islets of beige, and his neck looked almost ivory against the black of his vicuña coat. The coat hung loosely off a T-shirt that read, in large cherry lettering: I ♡ DC. It was frightening to think T-shirts came in that size.

"Halldor, I fear, is the only one who thrives in this sort of miasma. Myself, I prefer your highly efficient American air-conditioning. Shall we, Mr. Cavendish?"

Some of the heat came in with us, and for a second or two the air seemed to be ionizing around us. Halfway down the hall, I could see Lily Pentzler going head-to-head with the caterer. Pausing to reload, she flicked her eyes toward me — and then toward Styles. A crease bisected her forehead, and then she began muttering into her sleeve, like a madwoman.

"Perhaps we might talk in the theater," the old man said. "The upper gallery, I think. More private." His step was sure and even as he climbed the carpeted steps, talking as he went.

"Such a nice little pastiche. Of course, a true Elizabethan theater wouldn't have a roof, would it? Or such comfortable chairs. All the same, quite charming. I wonder what play they're putting on now."

"Oh, it's . . . *Love's Labour's Lost.*"

"Well, isn't that apropos?"

"Is it?"

"I wonder if it's modern-dress. No, I don't wonder at all. On that particular question, I have been quite driven from the field. Everywhere one goes now it's Uzis at Agincourt, Imogen in jeans, the Thane of Cawdor in a three-button suit. Next thing you know, Romeo and Juliet will simply *text* each other. Damn the balcony. OMG, Romeo. LOL. ILY 24–7. Oh, *chacun à son goût,* that's what I hear you saying, but does it rise even to the level of *goût?* I consider it, on the contrary, mere squeamishness. I have seen far more fearful things in my life than a doublet and hose. The sooner we inoculate our children against these terrors, the stronger we will make them."

Seating himself in the gallery's front row, he raised his eyes to the ceiling, where a blue Elizabethan sky had been meticulously painted — far lovelier than the sky outside.

A dusky silence fell over him. He laced his hands over the balcony rail.

"You've known Alonzo quite a long time," he said at last.

"*Knew* him, yes."

"I believe you also have the honor of being his executor."

I looked at him.

"Apparently so," I said.

"In that case, I think you might be of great use in resolving a little problem I have."

"That would depend on the problem."

Wrinkles fanned out from his eyes and mouth as he began to polish the balcony rail.

"A document," he said, "recently left my possession."

"I'm sorry to hear that."

"It's a document I'm rather keen on recovering."

"All right."

Silence grew around us until at last, in my politest tone, I asked:

"And you're coming to me because . . . ?"

"Oh! Because Alonzo was the one who borrowed it, you see."

I stared at him. "Borrowed it?"

"Well, generally speaking, I prefer to take charitable constructions of men's acts. I'm sure that poor Alonzo, had he lived, would have returned the document to me in due time. Now, of course, he's shuffled off this mortal coil." He waved softly at the ceiling. "Such a loss."

"Was the document valuable?" I asked.

"Only to an old sentimentalist like me. Although it does have a certain historical piquancy. As you might appreciate better than most, Mr. Cavendish." He leaned over and, in a conspiratorial tone, added, "You were a redoubtable Elizabethan scholar in your day, were you not?"

The air grew significantly cooler in that moment, or maybe my face was just getting warmer.

"I'm flattered you think so," I said. "I'm flattered you even remember my name."

"Confound the man's modesty! How could I fail to recall the paper you read at Oriel College back in 'ninety-two? 'Empire and the Silver Poet.' "

"You were there?"

"Oh, yes, I found it quite a welcome blow against the idea of Ralegh as dabbler. And chauvinist that I am, I was surprised that an American such as yourself could grasp the true Englishness of Ralegh's character. Only Shakespeare, I think, was more English." He clucked his tongue. "All in all, a charming — a comprehensive lecture. I'm sure I wasn't alone in expecting great things of you."

"Then I'm sorry to have disappointed you."

"Oh, but you haven't," he answered. "Not *yet,* anyway. But given your background and your *long* friendship with Alonzo — well, I can't think of a fellow better suited to help me find my little document."

Still he kept polishing that rail. Back and forth, back and forth.

"But what is it?" I asked. "A deed? A tradesman's bill?"

"A letter, that's all."

"Who received it?"

"Unclear. Only the second page survives."

"Okay, who *wrote* it?"

He said nothing at first. Only a slight trembling in his hands showed he had even heard the question. He turned to me at last with a smile broad as a river.

"Oh, God," I murmured. "Ralegh."

"The very man!" he said, clapping his hands in delight. "And imagine. The letter turned up just nine months ago. A solicitor's office in Gray's Inn Road was clearing out its archives — several centuries' worth; you know how far back these things can go. Having heard something of my reputation, they called me in to appraise its contents and to see if I might be willing to offer them anything for it. Of course, they had no inkling of what they had, so I was able to acquire the letter for quite a reasonable sum."

No mistaking the satisfaction in his voice. Some collectors spend money like oxygen — Alonzo was one. Others hoard every last atom.

"Mr. Styles," I said. "You'll forgive me, but I've learned to distrust any document with Ralegh's name on it. Having been burned before . . ."

"I should be wary, too, if I were you. In this case, I can assure you it's authentic."

"And you can assure me Alonzo took it?"

"Oh, yes." A slow bobbing of his silver head. "He hid his tracks beautifully, I'll give him that. For several weeks, we didn't even know the thing was missing. And then, when we spotted the substitution, we had to dig very deeply into our security archives before we found the — the exculpatory evidence." He smiled. "Even on grainy security video, there's no mistaking such a distinct figure as Alonzo's."

"But there are other Ralegh letters already in circulation. Why would Alonzo go to such trouble to steal this one?"

"I would guess he was intrigued by this

particular letter's content."

Styles let that settle in for a while and then, in a fit of mock astonishment, smacked his brow.

"Oh, but I quite forgot! I've a copy to show you."

The barest flutter of his fingers, and Halldor was standing over us, paper in one hand, flashlight in the other.

"When I first acquired the document, I took the precaution of having it digitized. I assume, Mr. Cavendish, you have no objection to reading it yourself?"

"None."

"Then by all means," said Bernard Styles, unfolding the paper.

It was absolutely quiet in that balcony, and yet everything around me registered with the force of sound. The poplarlike altitude of Halldor. The slight inclination that Styles's head made toward mine. My own hand, bathed in the flashlight's puddle. The words themselves, which seemed to be scratching across the paper as I read them.

Hee wold not be the first louer so to be served by Kit, who wold burn Hotte and Cold in the space of but one breth and who cold conjure up proofs for the Deuil or our Savior, howsoever the winde tourned him. Many was the time Chapman grew most greeued at some heresie, only to bee asured that Kit spoke but in jeste, as was his wont.

Yew will excuse mee, I trust, for laboring in this veyne. I cold faynde noe bettere plaster for my woundes than memorie. In parlous Times, it is grete joye to thincke vppon our homelie Schoole, where wee were glad to gathere, and where your tvtelarie Genius outsvnned ever Star.

Accompanyed with my best wishes, from

And even before I got to the closing, I could see that all-too familiar signature:

Your most asured frinde and humbell sarvant,
W Rawley
Derum Howse
This 27 of March

"Walter Ralegh," I said faintly.

I looked up. In the half-light, the old man's eyes glittered like fish scales.

"Oh, it's much more, Mr. Cavendish. It's what you and Alonzo have been searching for all your lives."

"Ah, well, as to that —"

"My dear boy, there's no need to take that

air with me. I've just shown you definitive proof that the School of Night existed."

"So it would seem," I allowed. "On first inspection."

"And tenth and twentieth inspection, too, I assure you. Say what you like, Mr. Cavendish, this is an exceptional historical find. I suspect it might form the springboard for quite a — quite a *splendid* academic treatise. Such as might restore a man's career."

He paused, before carrying on in a breezier vein.

"Unfortunately, neither you nor I can restore anything with a mere digitized copy. A nine-year-old could produce the same thing on his family's computer. No, to forward our joint purposes, we *will*, I'm afraid, require the original."

I stared down at that paper, checkered with creases. The digitized words rose up once more: *Our homelie Schoole, where wee were glad to gathere.*

And then again I remembered Alonzo's last message to me.

"May I keep this?" I asked faintly.

"Of course."

It went straight into the pocket of my jacket. I gave it two quick pats; I almost thought I heard it coo.

"Well, Mr. Styles, I can promise you this.

Over the next few days, as you know, I'll be sorting through Alonzo's papers. If your document is there — well, let's just say I'll keep a weather eye out. How does that sound?"

"Weather eye," he said, musingly. "That's a lovely expression. To my ear, it lacks urgency."

"I could be more urgent," I said. "If the situation called for it."

A brief pause. And then a laugh, bounding across the Tudor beams.

"With the right incentive, is that what you mean, Mr. Cavendish? I should have thought an entrée back into academia was incentive enough."

"Who says I want to go back?"

He grinned at me, frankly admiring. "So academia's loss is commerce's gain. Very well, I shall offer you a retainer of ten thousand dollars. Another ninety thousand dollars when you return the document to me. Or perhaps, in light of the prevailing exchange rates, you'd prefer euros?"

But once I heard those numbers, I was beyond considering exchange rates — or even Walter Ralegh. In no particular order, I was thinking about the rather terse letter from my landlord's attorney; my '95 Toyota Corolla, which needed a new belt transpon-

der and which was not strictly speaking mine; the glove compartment of said car, currently crammed with overdraft notices. (In certain moods, I used them for Kleenex.)

"Dollars will do," I said.

He leaned toward me.

"And you're sure you don't have *weightier* projects to command your attention?"

This was my first taste of Bernard Styles's savagery.

"Nothing that won't keep," I said.

Another fluttering of his fingers, and Halldor was there with a leather-bound checkbook and a Cross pen. The greater you are, they say, the smaller your signature. The old man's, at any rate, was a couple of Japanese strokes. In the very next moment, the check was resting in my hand.

"Chemical Bank," he told me, rising to his feet. "It should clear instantly. The rest, as I've said, will be yours when you deliver the document. In person."

"Where will you be staying?"

"With friends," he said simply, "for another week or so. I assume that will give you sufficient time to finish the job."

"How do I reach you?"

He tucked his umbrella under his arm. "I'll reach *you.* And now I must be off, I'm afraid. I've been promised a private tour of the archives. If it's not too much trouble, please do convey my deepest sympathies to Alonzo's family. Such a loss to the world. And now" — he rose in a straight line — "at the risk of sounding tasteless, Mr. Cavendish, it's been a pleasure doing business with you."

"And with you," I said.

No final handshake. He sealed our compact with a nod and an almost bashful smile. Only in the act of leaving did a new thought strike him.

"Do you know, I've carried off some of my best transactions at funerals? From death springs life, I always say."

3

My introduction to the School of Night I owe to Alonzo Wax's elbow.

It came at me in the winter of our freshman year, about two hours and twenty minutes into a student production of *Love's Labour's Lost,* which he and I were attending for entirely different reasons. Alonzo was testing his theory that the American dialect was better suited to Shakespearean English. ("Elizabethans loved their consonants, Henry.") I was warm for the junior playing the Princess of France. Once, in the act of asking me for my Chaucer notes, she had smiled at me, and in this smile lay such a world of promise that I honestly wasn't listening to the King of Navarre confess his love for the Princess. I was just waiting for the Princess to come back.

For this reason, I missed the crucial moment altogether. And would never have known what I'd missed had it not been for

Alonzo's elbow, gouging out a uniquely tender spot between my fourth and fifth ribs.

"What the fuck?" I gasped back.

There was a pause of maybe two or three seconds, in which all my unworthiness gathered and mounted toward the heavens.

"Never mind," he muttered.

Through the rest of the play he was silent, and for a good time afterward. But later that night, over gimlets at the Annex, he agreed to give me another chance. Walking his fingers across the sticky tabletop, he re-created the exact moment in Act IV, Scene 3, when the King's men, having sworn off the company of women, must now confess themselves foresworn. They are men in love.

Having made a clean breast of it, they are now free to criticize one another's taste — which they do, with a will. The King, in particular, taunts his buddy Berowne for craving dark-haired Rosaline. *Black as ebony,* the King calls her. *No face is fair that is not full so black,* Berowne retorts. To which the King replies — and here you must imagine every last beer mug in the Annex buzzing with Alonzo's declamation:

O paradox! Black is the badge of hell,
The hue of dungeons and the
    SCHOOL . . . OF . . . NIGHT. . . .

Ellipses, his. Capital letters, too.

"So what?" I answered. "It's a passing metaphor. The sonnets are full of them. The dark lady — my mistress's eyes — nothing like the sun . . ."

Cheap gin always made Alonzo magnanimous. Which is why he just fussed with his napkin.

"I can't really blame you, Henry, for missing it. The audiences of 1594 or '95 or whenever it was, they would have missed it, too. Only a handful of spectators, I think, would have known what was going on. And in that moment, Henry!" He smiled blearily. "I like to think their gasps would have carried all the way to Shakespeare himself. Waiting in the wings."

Alonzo began to massage the air around us until I began to feel, yes, something like a stir along my hairline.

"Why were they so shocked?" I asked.

"Because this little northern upstart, this son of a Stratford glover, was mocking some of the greatest men England had ever known. No, it's true. Walter Ralegh. Christopher Marlowe. A good half dozen others.

Love's Labour's Lost is nothing more than a satire of these great men and their pretensions. With that one phrase — *the School of Night* — Shakespeare was hauling them into the light of day, leaving them naked for all to see."

"And for evidence you have . . . ?"

"Oh, for God's sake, read Bradbrook. Read Tannenbaum. Read Shakespeare's goddamned plays, if you don't believe me. The King of Navarre and his court. The Duke of Arden and *his* court. Prospero. Hamlet! Again and again, Shakespeare came back to that same theme. Scholars — men of real *originality,* Henry — working in isolation from the world. Banished, basically, for their very thoughts. And they're all just variations on Ralegh's original school."

Here was one of the differences between us. Alcohol made him more expansive. The cheaper the booze, the louder he grew.

"I still don't get it," I said. "What *was* this school?"

"Only the most secretive, the most brilliant — God, the most *daring* — of all Elizabethan societies."

He lowered his head toward the table, eyeing me as though I were a cue ball.

"Are you ready, Henry?"

Without any more preamble, he took me

40

back. To 1592.

Walter Ralegh, the great courtier of his time, has incurred the queen's wrath for secretly marrying one of her attendants. Exiled to his estate in Dorset, he comes up with a characteristically ambitious way of passing the time. He will gather the greatest intellects of his generation and give them the freedom they have been seeking all their lives, the freedom to speak their minds.

"It was going to be — Christ, how did Shakespeare put it? In the play we just saw? *A little academe —*"

"Still and contemplative in living art."

"Just so."

Well, who could turn down such an invitation? Not Marlowe.

Not Henry Percy, the "Wizard Earl" of Northumberland.

Not George Chapman or his fellow poets Matthew Roydon and William Warner. One by one, they flocked to Dorset.

From the start, the school's members understood the risks they ran. They met exclusively in private, exclusively at night. As far as we know, they kept no record of their conversations. They published none of their findings. Until Shakespeare gave them a name, they had none.

"And *yet*" — Alonzo's index finger dug

41

into the table like an awl — "they were one of the greatest threats to the Elizabethan establishment."

"Why?"

"Because they talked about things no one could talk about. They questioned Jesus' divinity. They questioned God's very existence. They practiced dark arts. Alchemy, astrology, paganism . . . *satanism* . . . nothing was off the table, Henry. They dared to — to imagine a world without creed, without monarchy. With only the human mind as anchor. They were this quiet little *knife* in the heart of Elizabethan orthodoxy." His eyes gleamed; his voice darkened. "And they all paid dearly for it."

With unmistakable relish, he outlined their various ends. Marlowe, murdered in a saloon. ("Over a bill? I think not, Henry.") Ralegh executed. Warner, dead under mysterious circumstances. The Wizard Earl, shut away in the Tower for seventeen years. Roydon, reduced to abject poverty.

"And the only one standing at the end," I said, half dazed, "was the outsider. Shakespeare."

For the first time in our acquaintance, I think, Alonzo's eyes glowed with fellow feeling.

"You've hit on it! The sweetest, the bitterest irony of all. This hayseed *actor* with the grammar-school education, the guy who couldn't have gotten in Ralegh's school even if he'd wanted to (and he probably did) was the one who weathered every change of ministry, from Elizabeth the First to James the First. The School of Night had to close its doors, but Shakespeare lived on."

"His own little academe," I murmured.

Slowly, Alonzo sank back in his seat.

"Exactly," he said, a long stream of Dunhill smoke forking from his nostrils. "The School of Night gives way to Shakespeare. The School of Day."

I'd guess it was two in the morning when we finally settled our bill. Alonzo paid, as usual, and for a tip he left behind a neat little pile of bills. God knows how many, but the bartender was smiling.

"Henry," said Alonzo. "I believe I'm snockered."

Now I'm convinced that *snockered* is, by its nature, a funny word. Coming from Alonzo Wax's mouth, it became quite exorbitantly funny. He couldn't understand why this was, any more than I could explain it, but he came around to my way of thinking.

"Snockered!" he shrieked. *"Shhhh-nockered!"*

The bartender was no longer smiling by the time we left. Stepping with great care, Alonzo and I filed down the pavement and then, by common impulse, dashed across the street, our arms windmilling. We paused before the gates of Nassau Hall and stared up at its white tower, which held a special terror against the night's black purple. A mass of blue clouds was sweeping in from the south, and a hush lay upon every casement window, every arch, and every gargoyle.

"Henry."

Alonzo's voice came at me from a vast distance.

"What?"

"Let's have our own school."

"We're already in school."

Never before, never since, have I seen him grin like that. His mouth pulled open like a sluice gate, and an entirely new Alonzo came flooding through.

"A School of *Night*," he said. "Our very own. Let's begin."

4

The day after Alonzo's funeral service, I deposited Bernard Styles's check in what was left of my bank account. As promised, it cleared the next day. A good thing, because that morning I paid my landlord three months in back rent and took out two hundred dollars in good hard cash, which felt like Christmas *and* Easter in my jeans pocket as I strolled to Union Station to meet Lily Pentzler for lunch.

Lily had chosen a multilevel restaurant called America, which, in addition to having a big name, has a big menu, the size of an exit sign. It has to be, I guess, to hold all that Cajun dirty rice and Navajo fry bread and Idaho shoestring fries and New England pot roast, and yet the menu was nothing beneath the weight of Lily's stack of accordion files, which rose between us like Hadrian's Wall. High enough to block Lily from view but powerless to stop her voice.

"So you've got the spare key to Alonzo's apartment, right? Good. Now listen. *This* packet contains three copies of the will, stamped and notarized. You'll have to file in probate, but there shouldn't be any court proceedings. Alonzo lawyered everything. *This* folder lists all his leases and credit cards; you'll have to terminate those. Here's a bunch of contact info: Social Security, the post office, subscriptions, professional memberships. Don't forget to set up a bank account for the estate; Bank of America's probably the best since that's where Alonzo's money market fund is. He's also got two mortgages on the Mass. Ave. condo, so you'll have to keep up those payments for now. And, come spring, you'll have to file a personal tax return, but don't worry; I know an excellent accountant in Cleveland Park."

The only thing that stemmed the flow was the arrival of the waiter, who asked us if we'd looked over the menu.

"No, we have not," she snapped. "And I need another fifteen minutes before I can think about eating. *Fifteen* minutes. At which point I would love a Negroni. *Dry.* Splash of soda. Thanks much."

From the other side of the pile, a small white hand fanned him away as if he were an odor. Pure Alonzo, that gesture.

"Now, where was I? Oh! In *this* folder is a list of Alonzo's creditors. Ranked in order of how long he's been stiffing them. I recommend paying the Calvert-Woodley Wines and Spirits account *immediately*. Alonzo was also being sued by a drywall contractor whose name escapes me, but it's in *this* file, along with the case's disposition in Small Claims."

Below us lay Union Station's main hall, the marble tiles bouncing back the echoes of plates and silverware — and, beneath the clatter, the dull roar of human traffic. Commuters, shoppers, train passengers. All bound for somewhere.

"Henry, I can't tell. Are you paying attention?"

"I'm just wondering why Alonzo didn't make *you* his executor."

Her floury face craned around the pile. *"Me . . ."*

"You'd be so much better at it. You have all the records, you know where all the bodies — I mean, you're like the world's leading Alonzo expert."

"Henry," she said. "Look at me. Do I resemble someone who has the time to be an executor?"

And it was true, her date book was full for

the next six weeks. I know this because she rattled off every entry. Auction at Maggs. The Beijing book fair. Appointments with dealers in London, San Francisco. A conference at the Rare Book School in Charlottesville. Some promising leads in Milan. On and on it went, and each new item carried with it the same overtone: *Henry's got nothing in his date book.*

"Anyway," she went on, in a milder tone, "you shouldn't underrate yourself. You know Alonzo never did. He was always wondering what you'd think of some quarto or letter whenever it dropped in his lap. *Oh, Henry'd love this. I can't wait to show it to Henry.* He respected you; he did."

I paused then to consider: Was it respectful to phone someone just a few hours before killing yourself? Was that, in fact, a larger honor than it appeared?

I remembered that morning quite well. The twelfth of May: fitfully wet, smoky with pollen. I was sitting on the patio of Peregrine Espresso, just south of Eastern Market, with a $2.20 cup of Finca Nueva Armenia and a laptop and a stack of ruled paper. Children's compositions. I was being paid three hundred dollars to judge a creative-writing contest for a country day school in Herndon, Virginia. The theme of the competition was "Wow." All in all, I considered myself lucky to have the gig, but I hadn't read a single entry — the prospect of all that earnestness was chilling — and I spent most of that morning composing an ad for craigslist. My third of the year.

DWM, 44, hwp, clean and professional, looking for fun/companionship, with possibility of long-term . . .

From there, things always got trickier. *Big into reading . . . midnight phone conversations a must . . . have not ruled out kids.* Every line grew clammy with embarrassment, until at last I found myself veering toward pure non*fiction. Academic pariah . . . sketchily employed . . . faint odor of shame . . . haunted by the memory of two dead marriages, maybe not haunted enough . . .*
It was still a marvel to me then how gently failure could steal over you. One minute, you're a young man, loose in limb and high in sperm count, striding down the avenue, inhaling pollen. The next minute, you're one of those guys walking home from the Tunnicliff's bar. Walking very *slowly,* the better to conceal your condition and never realizing until you're home that no one was really monitoring you. Whatever holes you

thought you were punching into the world's exoskeleton have long since been absorbed.

It was in the midst of these thoughts that my cell phone began to vibrate. Actually crawled toward me across the tabletop, as if it were answering my ad.

I scanned the caller ID: UNKNOWN. That was how Alonzo always registered on my Nokia. I think it pleased him. I watched the phone go still before kicking back into life with a message. And even then I waited a good five or ten minutes to play it back.

From the depths of my voice mail came Alonzo's clenched drawl.

"Henry. Call me. The School of Night is back in session."

How to re-create the effect that old name had on me? I sat there amid the espresso steam and the coffee beans and the iPod tunes, and those words — *the School of Night* — refused to coalesce with anything else. Until finally there was no way to make them *fit* except to delete the message altogether.

And in that moment, a voice inside me said: *I've graduated.*

Which wasn't true, but give me this much credit; I was able to flush the call from my mind. And that very evening, a little after nine, Alonzo called a cab (because, of course, he was as averse as any Manhattan-

50

ite to owning a car) and asked to be taken to the end of MacArthur Boulevard — an area of Maryland he'd almost certainly never visited before. The driver remembered him because, as usual, Alonzo overtipped and because no fare had ever asked to be dropped off in the C&O National Historical Park so far past sunset. The cab pulled away, and Alonzo undertook perhaps the first hike of his life, which ended a fifth of a mile later when he climbed up the Washington Aqueduct Observation Deck and threw himself into the Potomac River.

He chose well: the exact point at which the river, carrying its freight of mountain water, narrows into the Mather Gorge and then cascades into Great Falls, dropping seventy-six feet in less than a mile.

Here's what Alonzo left behind: (1) A Baume & Mercier watch. (2) A pair of cordovan A. Testoni shoes, ready-made. (3) A note, in his own diffuse hand.

To thy black shades and desolation
I consecrate my life.

A Chapman lover to the end. And don't think I forgot the title of that particular poem — "The Shadow of Night" — or the group of men who may have inspired it.

And, above all, don't think I forgot Alonzo's final message: *The School of Night is back in session.*

Two days after he jumped, his black belted Joseph Abboud raincoat washed up on Bear Island, stained with his blood. To those of us who knew him, that raincoat was the closest we would ever get to an actual body. For, of course, he wore it in all kinds of weather, never even went to the bathroom without it. A few weeks later, Judge Wax prevailed on old colleagues in the District's probate court to grant a petition for presumption of death. An official certificate followed in short order, and now the world was free to grieve Alonzo Wax.

And I was free to ask myself the same questions, again and again: Who could have reconvened the School of Night? Who were its members? And was *this* part of its curriculum — Alonzo's own extinction?

There was one question, in particular, that wouldn't go away. How might things have been different if I'd just returned his damned phone call? What would that simple act have cost me?

All this had been quietly corroding inside me . . . and then an elderly British gentleman named Bernard Styles pulled me aside at Alonzo's memorial service and, in a few words, dragged everything from the shadows.

The School of Night was back in session, and I was still very much in the dark.

"Henry."

Lily's voice coiled around me like a garrote.

"The reverie thing," she said. "Maybe you could do that on your own time."

Her folders had been pushed to one side, and she sat there with her forearms wedged together like hocks.

"Tell me about Bernard Styles," I said.

She looked at me for a long moment. She said:

"What do you want to know?"

"I'm not sure. Is he legitimate?"

She waved her napkin. "He's listed with the Grolier Club. He's richer than a hundred sultans. He'd lay down his life for a Shakespeare quarto. Does that make him legitimate?"

She told me then that, far from being an obscure figure, Styles was one of Great Britain's preeminent bibliophiles. His earliest forays had been into Johnson and Boswell but, finding that stock increasingly depleted, he had switched in later life to Elizabethiana. No one was quite clear on the source of his wealth, but he was sufficiently liquid that he had never had to sell off inventory to make new acquisitions. Tens of millions of pounds' worth of books and illuminated manuscripts supposedly lay sequestered in his Georgian manse, but no one could be sure because the collection was off limits to the public. The queen had once or twice been granted a private tour, and rumor had it that Styles was in line for the Order of the British Empire.

"The queen is one thing," I said. "What did the *king* think of him?"

"You mean Alonzo."

"Yeah. What kind of relationship did he have with Styles?"

Lily gave the table a few taps. "Complicated," she said. "Like his relationship with everybody, only more so."

At bottom, she said, the conflict was philosophical. Alonzo hunted books to learn from them; Styles hunted for the pleasure of hunting.

"They had a few petty squabbles," said Lily. "And of course, Alonzo never forgave Styles for the Snowden business."

"Explain."

"Oh, God, this was two or three years ago. Cornelius Snowden. Old friend of Alonzo's, kept a bookstall near St. Paul's. Went for a walk in Postman's Park one evening and never came out again. Alive, anyway."

"Robbed?"

"But not for cash. The only thing they took was his first edition of Stow's *Annales*."

"And why did Alonzo blame Styles?"

"Because he knew Styles coveted that particular volume. But then everyone did, you know. And there was no evidence against Styles. The police never even questioned him, it was just — Alonzo and his melodrama."

"But it gave Alonzo a motive," I said, half to myself.

"Motive for what?"

And it was then I realized I'd never told her of my encounter with Styles. I pulled the digitized copy of Ralegh's letter from my shirt pocket. Unfolded it, laid it out on the table, and told her how I'd gotten it — and what had happened to the original.

"I've never seen this before," she said in a hushed voice. "Are you sure Alonzo took it?"

"That's what Styles said."

"But that doesn't — that's not Alonzo. It's not." She drew back from the table. "I don't get this, Henry."

"I don't either. I mean, even if this document is authentic, it's going to fetch, in

55

today's marketplace, what? Fifty thousand? Sixty?"

"I suppose," she said faintly. "More or less."

"So why would Bernard Styles offer twice that much to have it back?"

"I don't . . ."

Her white cheeks began to sag. Something swirled in her eyes.

"I wish . . ."

And now the grief she'd been at such pains to hold back came flooding through. Was it a comfort, I wonder, to have me there? One of those men who grow helpless before a woman's tears? All I could do was shove my napkin toward her and murmur:

"I know. I know."

"No," she answered. "You don't."

She pressed the napkin over her face and gave her skin a cauterizing rub. I remembered then that, many years ago, Alonzo had proposed marriage to her. For the first and probably last time in her life, she had told him no. It was a great relief to both of them.

The mood passed as quickly as it had come, and when her Negroni came, she drained it in short order and ordered another with her Maine lobster roll, and by lunch's end she was edging dangerously close to mirth. Caressing her strawlike hair, she glanced over the rail and, with a twist of her mouth, said:

"Friend of yours, Henry?"

I followed her gaze down to the main hall. To a Doric column, against which a tall man in a black vicuña coat stood staring back at us. Only one thing had changed about Halldor's appearance since last I'd seen him: his T-shirt. The lettering was visible from thirty yards off: FREEDOM ROCKS.

He showed no concern at being spotted. Silent as ever, he wheeled around, turned up the flaps of his coat and, in no apparent hurry, merged with the stream of traffic heading toward the Amtrak depot.

"Styles's man?" asked Lily.

"Yep."

We watched him go.

"Henry," said Lily at last. "Can I give you some friendly advice?"

By now, her second Negroni was beginning to tell. Vermouth dragged at each syllable.

"Don't fuck with gentleman collectors."

5

A ten-second google search was all it took. Up came the *Daily Telegraph* obituary:

Cornelius Snowden, who died on December 3 aged 66, was an antiquarian bookseller and collector best known for his eccentric business practices and latterly for his dedication to the works of Elizabethan historian John Stow.

A scant two-line reference to the circumstances of Snowden's death (*Police are still making enquiries*), but I was rewarded in the second-to-last graf with a testimonial from none other than Bernard Styles.

Cornelius's passion for the codex was so terribly infectious and such an inspiration to so many of us. He shall be missed beyond all measure.

"And I shall cherish his first edition until

I die," I said out loud.

At which point my land-line phone began to declaim at some volume, and as I raised the receiver to my ear Bernard Styles's gingery baritone came pouring out.

"Mr. Cavendish! How are we faring?"

He loomed so near me in that moment I could have sworn he was actually standing over me. Peering over my shoulder.

"Coming along," I said. "Coming . . . sorry, did I give you my home number?"

"No, indeed."

"It's unlisted, that's the only reason I ask."

"And for very good reasons, I'm sure. Now tell me. Have you seen any sign of my sad little document?"

"Oh!" I whirled away from the computer. "Sorry. I've been so busy with Alonzo's estate and all. Fiduciary duties —"

"Naturally."

"But I'm bound to come across it sooner or later. I'm really very confident."

"Well." A dry chuckle. "That's lovely to hear, Mr. Cavendish. Unfortunately, my time here is rather limited."

"Yes, I understand."

"Charming as your city is."

"Sure."

There was a silence then of some three or four seconds — I'd begun to wonder if we'd been cut off — and then Styles glided back in.

"I'll ring again tomorrow, shall I?"

"Or I can call *you,* if you'd —"

"I must be off, I'm afraid. I've promised Halldor he could go to Mount Vernon. Onward, Mr. Cavendish!"

Onward.

As I set the phone down, that word pricked me like a bodkin of guilt. I had taken Bernard Styles's money — spent a small chunk of it — and done so little to earn it. I wasn't keeping my eyes open. I wasn't tracking down leads. I was just waiting for that document to drop from a cloud.

Well, I could do this much. I could search the one place where a document was likeliest to be: Alonzo's apartment.

I had the key, after all. What I lacked was the will. The strength, I mean, to sift through Alonzo's belongings, to smell his traces in old piles of clothing, to feel his spirit badgering me from room to room. It was too much for one executor to bear. I would need company.

So I rang up Lily, but my call went straight into her voice mail. The best I could do was leave a message, asking her to meet me at the apartment the next day.

"One P.M., if that works. Let me know."

A day's reprieve. And, God knows, plenty to do in the meantime. Whole edifices of paper to scale: threatening letters and foreshortened projects and quarrelsome e-mail chains and all the other clotted detritus of a human life.

Debt, most of all. Oceans of debt. At least three mortgages that I could see. Credit cards. Home-equity loans. Unpaid wages (poor Lily). Unpaid dermatologists and travel agents and prosecco importers and, trailing directly behind, a small battery of collection agencies, baring their knuckles to no avail. It was hard to find a single economic sector that didn't own some small piece of Alonzo Wax.

As for the assets . . . well, those were harder to puzzle out. From his grandmother, he had inherited a modest living that would have sufficed for, say, a rent-controlled bachelor apartment on Connecticut Avenue. He had chosen to spring for a double suite in Cathedral Heights, which he had fitted out with his own vault. Virtually all his capital — his life — was tied up in books, and the only idea he'd ever had for bringing in money was to fling more money after it.

More than once I wondered if being named his executor was some kind of karmic debt for past sins. Especially when, late that night, I found a manila envelope bearing my name in black Magic Marker.

HENRY

Inside, a single sheet, with two other names.

The first, AMORY SWALE, and next to it a number with a 252 phone exchange. No longer in service, as I learned when I dialed it a few minutes later.

Which left the second name, forming a strange rhyme to the first: CLARISSA DALE.

From the realm of 904, wherever that was.

I called the next morning, and the reply was immediate — "Hello" — succinct and incisive, as though she'd been keeping vigil. And maybe she had been, for when I told her who I was, she said:

"I've been expecting you."

I told her I was trying to reconstruct Alonzo's affairs on behalf of his estate. I told her I'd found her name in one of his files, and I was curious to know if she'd had any dealings with him in the days before his death.

"We should talk, Henry."

"Aren't we — I mean, we're talking

now. . . ."

"In person might be best."

"See, the problem is I'm in D.C. —"

"So am I."

I raised myself to a seated position. "I wasn't aware of that."

"Are you home, Henry?"

"Um . . ." I dragged a hand down my face. "Sort of."

"Where would that be?"

"It's — do you know Capitol Hill?"

"Of course. I'm happy to stop by if that's convenient."

Pausing, I surveyed the carnage about me. Alonzo's papers: I could at least put those back into piles. The funerary heap of flies by the window: I could sweep them up, couldn't I? (Though I hadn't touched them in two weeks.) But there was nothing to do about the refrigerator's death rattle or the green bruises of plaster on the living-room wall.

"You know what?" I said. "The cleaning lady's here, and the vacuum gets kinda loud. Once she gets going. Why don't we meet somewhere? Tomorrow or —"

"Maybe you know Bullfeathers," she said.

"Yeah."

"Let's meet there. Today at noon. I'll make reservations."

She clicked off before I could say anything.

I squinted at my clock radio. Forty minutes to become human.

The shower helped. Shaving, too. But I still smelled of Evan Williams, so I gobbled down a handful of breath mints and dabbed my wrists with Scope and then, for good measure, sprayed Febreze on one of my two good Oxfords.

I got to Bullfeathers five minutes after noon. It was an odd meeting place to suggest: a midscale burger joint with Bull Moose trappings. Frequented mainly by Capitol Hill staffers and their lobbyists, plus the occasional family of tourists dragging their heat-wracked bodies off the Mall.

In that context, Clarissa was easy to pick out. She was wearing a yellow sundress, she had positioned herself against the wall, and she was looking at me as intently as she had answered the phone.

"Henry," she said.

My hand stopped in the act of meeting hers.

It was the woman from Alonzo's funeral.

My earlier take had been necessarily incomplete. She was a little older than I'd thought — thirty-one, thirty-two. And seen in direct light, her fair skin was more freckled than I remembered, her black hair a good deal more tangled — a swarm of warring ends. And the eyes, they were the color not of toffee but of something left much longer in the pan. . . .

Or ebony, I thought, suddenly recalling the King of Navarre's words. *Black as ebony . . . the hue of dungeons . . .*

And with that, I was back in the Annex with Alonzo, and the theme of our conversation was coming back at me in a slow arc.

"The School of Night," I murmured.

"Exactly," said Clarissa Dale.

6

Here's how it was. Alonzo Wax used to go broke on the order of once or twice a year. A certain pattern would then ensue. Alonzo would sell off some of his inventory (at modest profit but at great emotional cost). He would switch from Grey Goose to Svedka, he would give up his table at Chef Geoff's in favor of Korean takeout, and, more to the point, he would become better disposed to lecture invitations that otherwise would have been sent to the flames.

This was not lost on the public libraries and writer's centers and genealogical societies and independent-living facilities that all craved a moment with him. Word soon got around that Alonzo Wax, nationally recognized collector and scholar, could be had. If you paid his travel. And threw in an honorarium and a free meal. And didn't stint on the wine.

Somebody was always up for that bargain.

And so it came that, on a Thursday night in February of 2009, Alonzo held forth to the Civitan Club of St. Augustine, Florida.

To hear Clarissa tell it, the only thing more remarkable than his being there was *her* being there. She'd seen a notice strictly by chance in a local shopper, and she'd nearly missed the lecture altogether because, at some critical moment, she took a wrong turn on San Marco Avenue. Arriving fifteen minutes late, she tried to shrink into the back row, but Alonzo's voice seemed to find her there. Seemed actually to tap her on the arm.

"The suppressed unconscious of the Elizabethan age," he was saying.

Being new to Alonzo's world, she couldn't have known he'd been rehearsing the same theme since undergraduate days. The School of Night, in his mind, was Tudor England's psychic shadow. Looking out from the leaded casements of Sherborne Castle, Ralegh's Dorset home, the School's savants saw terror walking in broad daylight. They saw murderous intrigue, state-sponsored torture. Catholic citizens executed. Intellectual dissent violently suppressed. And surrounding all this terror, a vast and troubled silence. Only at Sherborne could the silence be lifted. Only in the blackest hours of night could the dayspring of truth emerge.

"From the night came the light," Alonzo told the Civitan Club.

And there was in Clarissa, too, a kind of dawning. As she remembered it, the people on either side of her appeared to melt away. The world itself dissolved. All that was left was her and Alonzo and this invisible cord, weaving around them.

And so Clarissa Dale did something she had never done before, not in grade school or high school or even college. She stayed after class.

"I wanted him to know how I felt," she said.

"And when you explained it, how did he respond?"

"You mean, did he run out the door?"

The slightest trace of Spanish moss on her vowels. *Doh-er.*

"Actually, he was very polite," she said. "God knows why, I was just blathering at him. He had this — funny little pickled smile that never went away. I figured he must be pretty happy, but then I realized it's just the way his mouth curves."

"Accident of birth," I agreed.

And then I made the mistake of looking down at my cheeseburger. God knows why

I even ordered it, I was in no state to eat, and after one look, I had to shroud it with my napkin.

"So after that," said Clarissa, "we exchanged a few friendly e-mails, he sent me some interesting articles, and then last May — May the twelfth — he sent me this strange voice mail. *The School of Night . . .*"

". . . *is back in session,*" I echoed faintly.

"You got the same message."

"Yeah."

"Well," she said, "here we are."

Her lips trembled then — the beginnings of a smile, quickly quashed. But enough to emphasize the natural redness of her lips.

"Okay," I said, willing myself back into focus, "here's what I still don't get. Why did you go listen to Alonzo in the first place? Are you . . ."

And even as I posed the question, I recoiled before the possible answer.

"Are you in the field?"

She scowled softly. "What field?"

"English lit. Or history. Academic something or other."

"Oh!" she cried. "God, no! Please!"

And now she really did smile. I'm not sure I can convey the change this produced in her. A kind of translucency, let me start there, calling the planes of her face into unexpected relief. No, it was more than that. From that smile, somebody entirely new emerged. Only she'd been there the whole time.

"I was never much of a reader," she said. "I mean, I was a business major at Central Florida. I think I've been to one Shakespeare play my whole life. It's embarrassing how little I know about that stuff."

"Then why were you there?"

"Well, see, that's hard to explain." She twirled her fork through a tangle of salad greens and blue cheese. "I guess I have a personal stake in Alonzo's subject."

"You do?"

"Well, yeah," she said. "The thing is, I've *seen* it. In person."

"Seen what?"

And here the skin around her cheekbones began to pink.

"I've seen the School of Night," she said.

"Like . . . in a picture?"

"Like in my head. Like a dream, except I'm not dreaming."

"Does it happen a lot?"

"You have no idea, Henry."

Shrugging, she picked up her fork and scooped up a little pile of blue cheese. The very sight of it made my stomach lurch.

"So how long has this been going on?" I

70

asked. "The visions and all."

"I don't know, almost a year? Maybe more."

"Every *night?*"

"Once or twice a week. Although sometimes I'll get them three or four nights in a row." She lowered her head a fraction, gave me a sheepish smile, and said, "I mean, I don't want to sound like I'm bragging or anything, Henry, but the School of Night? It's my very own personal curse."

Her eyes were dry and alert as she studied me.

"You're skeptical," she said.

"Um . . . yeah. Well . . . yeah."

"I would be, too." She nodded to herself. "I would. The point is, whether you believe me or not, something happened to Alonzo. And now, whether we like it or not, *we're* bound up in it, too."

She set her fork down and laced her hands together.

"Something *larger* is at work. You must have felt that, too, Henry. From the moment Alonzo died."

But the only thing I was conscious of right now was the swirling within my own body, the epinephrine surge that was kicking my heart into second life and dilating my pupils.

With a long and labored breath, I shoved

71

my plate away. "You know what, Clarissa? I *haven't* felt something larger at work. Apologies and whatever, but the time-travel visions? I think it's very clear —"

"I'm crazy."

"And know what else? I'm *not* bound up with you, I'm not bound up with anyone. For which I have a — a certain amount of gratitude. Especially now. And okay, Alonzo? Something didn't *happen* to him, he *made* it happen. That's what suicides do. They're not — speaking in the passive voice, okay?"

And now she was pushing her own plate away. "The man I met in St. Augustine would never have killed himself," she said. "Not in a million years."

Lines of sweat had sprung up behind my ears. My eyes were rocking inside their sockets.

"You know I'm right, don't you, Henry?"

I stared at my watch — 12:50. Lily might even now be waiting for me. "Very sorry," I murmured, staggering to my feet.

"What's wrong?"

"I've got to go to Alonzo's place."

And suddenly Clarissa was standing, too. Fronting me.

"I'm coming, too," she said.

"Oh." I put up a shaky hand. "You know what? It would be very boring for you."

But she was already hailing our waiter. And when the check arrived, she plucked it free of its glossy leatherette container and said, in a jaunty voice:

"You don't mind if I treat, right?"

She gave me a sidelong glance as she added:

"You don't look like the sort of guy who'd mind."

Alonzo's place had once been two apartments, but he had bribed the building management into tearing down the dividing wall and creating a master suite, penthousey in its aspirations. To the west lay the bedroom, with its armoire and canopied four-poster and acanthus-leaf scrolls. To the east was the kitchen, pristine with neglect. (The refrigerator, if memory served, contained only a bottle of champagne and a jar of mustard.)

And to the south? A balcony, almost as wide as the apartment. That's where I went now. Below me, in the early afternoon heat, slumbered a courtyard, with a gamely gurgling fountain and a playground, empty as usual, and a row of sycamores that seemed to stand at attention whenever the National Cathedral bells rang.

"Have you noticed it's freezing here?"

Clarissa was standing in the doorway, rubbing her bare white arms.

"Sixty-eight degrees Fahrenheit," I explained. "And fifty-two percent relative humidity. Optimal environment for book storage."

"And for driving up electric bills. Power company must have loved ol' Alonzo."

"Maybe not so much," I said, remembering the stack of overdue Pepco notices on my apartment floor.

"You know, Henry, it might be helpful if you told me what we're looking for."

"It's a paper."

"A paper?"

"A document."

"Old? New?"

"Old."

"Well, in that case . . ."

No need for her to point. It was the elephant in Alonzo's apartment. His book vault. A climate-controlled concrete-and-steel bunker, roughly three hundred cubic feet, so massive it seemed to have crash-landed in Alonzo's living room.

"Do you know the combo?" Clarissa asked.

"Unless he changed it."

I squared myself against the steel-plated door . . . but something kept snagging at the edge of my vision. A black faux-alligator handbag, resting on the floor under a marble-top end table. Instantly familiar, as was the BlackBerry Pearl smartphone inside.

Lily's.

The phone she took with her everywhere she went. The phone she'd once likened to a second womb. Taking custody of it now, I stared at the voice-mail icon on the screen. Three messages (one of them mine, presumably). And Lily not here to retrieve any of them.

A curious numbness stole into my fingertips as I tucked her phone into my pocket.

Don't overreact, I told myself. *She's somewhere.*

It wasn't like I needed her to open the vault for us. All I had to do was recall the date of George Chapman's death — a date I'd once known as well as my birthday — and then enter the numbers on the keypad.

But even this simple act was harder than it seemed. December, wasn't it?

Twelve . . .

And the date was . . . what the hell was the date?

Sixteen . . .

All I needed now was the year. But my hand wasn't able to punch the keys anymore, so I had to lay my other hand on top and press down.

One . . . six . . . three . . . four.

I thought at first I'd misremembered. But then, breaking into the midafternoon gloom, came a green light, followed by a high singing frequency.

"Wow," said Clarissa.

The vault door gave off a dyspeptic rumble. Clarissa and I each grabbed the handle — a faint crackle as our hands brushed — and together we pulled.

A sound like lips pulling away from skin, a swirl of cool, heavy air, and with a long amorous sigh the door swung open and Lily Pentzler rolled out.

Unfurled, like a Persian rug, she lay there, entirely still. Powder-blue throat and periwinkle lips. And the face — that staring face, with its swollen eyelids — the face had a shade all its own.

Alice blue, I thought, with a strange jolt of triumph.

Desperately, I crammed down the laugh that was starting to bubble inside me. It was Clarissa who had the presence of mind to step *over* the dead woman's body — as though it really were a rug — and peer into the vault's interior and deliver the news.

"The books," she said. "Alonzo's books are gone."

7

I had never met anyone named August until my first week at college, when I met *two*. I didn't meet any others until twenty-seven years later, that day in Alonzo's apartment. His name was August Acree — *Detective* August Acree — of the Violent Crimes Branch. A point guard's build, just melting into fat, and a dandyish mustache, whose promise of fun was undermined by ball-bearing eyes, severe, unpersuadable. Once or twice I caught him smiling. I'm not sure I saw him blink.

By now a forensic photographer was circling Lily's body, technicians from the Mobile Crime Lab were crawling in and out of Alonzo's vault, and two uniformed cops were standing outside the apartment door, looking vague and bored.

Outside, a phalanx of cop cars, a pair of local news crews, and a knot of worried widows: Alonzo's fellow tenants, wondering how bad things could happen in Northwest D.C., where residents were practically guaranteed a natural death.

Detective Acree knew different. No deference, no silver tongue. He treated the crime scene as if it were on the other side of the Anacostia. He stared down that vault as if it were a meth lab.

"It's got vents," he said. "Blowers."

"True," I said.

"In working order?"

"As far as I know."

He gave his tie a delicate twist. "Then there's no reason for that woman to suffocate. She should be alive right now."

"Detective?" said Clarissa, taking a step forward. "If I may?"

A crease lined August Acree's brow as he squared himself toward her.

"Your name, ma'am?"

"Clarissa Dale. I think I could be of help here."

"Ah."

You can say *ah* in many different ways, but you can't make it sound much less encouraging than that.

"Best I can tell," she said, "Mr. Wax's vault is built along the same lines as a bank vault. Which means it needs some way of suppressing fires. Your classic sprinkler system,

79

that's not going to work because it's going to soak the books. Might as well just let them burn, right?"

The crease in the detective's forehead got deeper.

"Now most banks," Clarissa said, "use a gas called halon. Pretty safe, not too toxic. But if you're not a regulated entity, you can get away with using carbon dioxide."

"Carbon dioxide."

"Now don't worry, Detective, I won't touch a thing. I'll just direct your attention to the vault's roof. Assume for a second that a fire's broken out. In that event, what happens is the carbon dioxide gets released from the ceiling, see? It floods the vault, it *squeezes* out the oxygen so the fire won't have anything to react with. Imagine a *hand,* okay? Pressing all the oxygen to the floor."

"So . . ." Acree took a step toward the vault. "If someone's actually inside when this is happening . . ."

"They'd have a few minutes is all. And if they know how the system works, they're gonna keep *low,* because that's where all the oxygen is. If there's any left. Now when we found Miss Pentzler, she was all the way down to the ground." Clarissa knelt in an attitude of prayer. "Her face was pressed against the door crack. My guess? She was fighting for air."

The detective gave his tie another twist.

"So how'd the smoke alarm get triggered?"

The question was answered by one of his own techs, emerging from the vault with a plastic bag raised like a war trophy. Inside was a soggy cigarette butt, no more than an inch long. Far too small, you'd have thought, to merit all the scrutiny it now received.

"Was Miss Pentzler a smoker?" asked Detective Acree.

"Not that I ever saw," I said. "She might have been."

"Geez, you're not a smoker, but you bring a lit cigarette into a vault, then get yourself locked inside. I don't know. In my world, that's . . ." He made a whistling sound.

"Maybe it was someone else's cigarette," I said.

"Then where's the someone else? If that cigarette was still burning, whoever it was couldn't have been far off. And forget the cigarette for a second. If Miss Pentzler knew what a fix she was in, why didn't she call someone? Building management, nine-one-one?"

With some regret, I drew Lily's Black-Berry from my pocket.

"We found it by the sofa," I said, fighting to keep my voice level.

Detective Acree watched as the phone was sealed in a bag. Then he turned his eyes back to the vault.

"No air," he said, half to himself. "No phone. No one to hear her scream."

"No *books*," added Clarissa.

Acree arched his eyebrows. "Sorry?"

"Detective, I don't mean to minimize Miss Pentzler's death, but there's another pretty serious crime that's taken place here. Mr. Wax's whole collection has gone missing."

"That so?"

In unison, Clarissa and Acree swiveled toward me. Awaiting confirmation.

"I'm afraid she's right, Detective. Alonzo had one of the most esteemed collections of Elizabethiana in the world. Shakespearean quartos and folios. First editions of Tudor poets. One of Queen Elizabeth's Bibles. We're talking a value of — I'd say three or four or five million dollars, and that's conservative."

"He wouldn't have sold it off?" asked Acree.

"Maybe a title or two, he's done that before. But not the whole inventory, he just wouldn't have."

"Why not?"

"The collection was his life."

Except Alonzo took his life, didn't he? After first taking the precaution of wiping out his computer's hard drive. With great care and deliberateness, he'd gone about erasing himself from this earth, and he'd done an uncommonly thorough job.

By five o'clock, the last forensic obeisances had been paid, and Lily Pentzler was ready for her plastic shroud. And when they lifted that plump, short-waisted figure onto the gurney, I felt something inside me go slack. Grief, I suddenly realized. Lily Pentzler had consecrated her life to one man, and this was how she'd been rewarded.

The balcony door was still open, and the air from outside had formed a high-pressure front with the apartment's climate-control system. From inside the vault, I could hear the arrhythmic skitter of Alonzo's hydrothermograph, protesting every fluctuation in humidity and temperature.

"Mr. Cavendish."

Detective Acree beckoned me toward him.

"I think you said you were Mr. Wax's executor."

"That's right."

"Then I hope you'll satisfy my curiosity.

Was his book collection insured?"

I blinked.

"Well, yes, it was."

"So who's the beneficiary?"

Two days earlier, I couldn't have told him. But having trawled for hours in the sea of Alonzo's paper, I knew. "Me," I said. "I'm the beneficiary."

I fully expected his mouth to turn up the way it did. What I didn't expect was the delicate climb of his voice as he said:

"Tough for you."

8

I woke the next morning, matted in sweat, my cell phone clamoring from the depths of my pants pocket.

"Mr. Cavendish!" said Bernard Styles. "We just saw the news coverage of Miss Pentzler's death. Tragic business!"

Whatever fog was left in my brain burned right off. For I was picturing not Styles but his silent emissary, Halldor. Standing in the main hall of Union Station, staring up at me and Lily.

"Yes," I said. "Very tragic."

"I knew her quite well, you know. Damned fine head on her shoulders. I always thought Alonzo was lucky to have her."

"It's funny," I said. "You know where *I* was yesterday, but maybe you could tell me where *you* were."

I'd meant it to sound tossed-off, that little query, but my voice betrayed me, for Styles held off a moment.

"Well, as I mentioned, we were planning to descend on Mount Vernon, but it seemed much too hot to be gadding about. So we went instead to the Museum of Crime and Punishment."

"I see."

"Fearfully interesting place. Oh, but hold on, we also saw something about Alonzo's books being stolen. *Beyond* scandalous! Never mind, these things always come to earth somewhere."

"Cornelius Snowden might disagree," I said.

"Who?"

"Old friend of yours. He was carrying Stow's *Annales* when he died. As far as I know, that book never came to earth anywhere."

I gave it a couple of seconds before adding:

"Snowden was kind of like Alonzo. He had something you wanted."

"Well, you'll pardon me, but I fail to see what Cornelius Snowden has to do with anything. As for Alonzo, the item in his possession was not his to possess, as I thought I made clear to you. I've engaged you, Mr. Cavendish, to recover a document that is legally mine."

"What if I can't?"

"If you really don't think you're up to the job, you need only return my check and we may take our leave of each other. You . . ." His voice dwindled down to a drawl. "You haven't *cashed* the check, have you, Mr. Cavendish?"

I pressed my eyelids down. "Of course I have."

"Oh," he said. "Oh, dear."

"Look, I just need us to be in the open, okay? If there's something funny going on — between you and Alonzo, you and *anyone* — I need to know it."

"I can assure you, Mr. Cavendish, I've nothing to hide. What about you?"

Clarissa called ten minutes later.

"Where are you?" I asked.

"Outside your door."

I went to the window. A tangle of black hair, strangely purposeful in the light of noon. I looked at her for longer than was strictly necessary. Then, with no warning, she tipped her head back and caught my eye. And waved.

"Oh, yeah, hi," I said into the phone. "How did you know where I live?"

"I dropped you off. In a taxi. Last night."

"Right."

"Can I come up?"

87

"It's kind of messy, honestly."

"You better fire her."

"Who?"

"Your cleaning lady. If she was over there yesterday, she's not doing much of a job."

"Oh. Yeah. Listen, give me ten minutes, I'll be right down."

She smelled of sunblock that morning. One of those non greasy sports solutions that remind you of your dad's aftershave. And, to tell the truth, her madras shorts could easily have been lifted from my father's wardrobe. They did have the advantage of revealing her legs, which were slender and lightly muscled and of Euclidean proportions. I did my best not to stare. I'm not sure I succeeded.

"Let's go to Stanton Park," Clarissa said. "It's shadier there."

She walked so quickly at first I had to struggle to keep up. And then, a couple of blocks on, her energy gave out altogether. So that, by the time we reached the park, she looked like she was crossing the Sun's Anvil.

"Hot," she gasped.

We found a bench under a cherry tree. I offered her a handkerchief — and saw too late the latticework of holes in the cotton. We fell silent.

"You seem to know the area," I said at last.

"I rent a place over on Fourth Street."

So Clarissa Dale was, of all ridiculous things, my neighbor. How long had this been going on?

"An apartment," I said. "That sounds kind of quasi-permanent."

"Not to me."

On the benches across from us sat a line of nannies. Their arms folded in an unbroken line, they regarded us with deep foreboding, and their young charges would stop in the midst of chalk drawing or climbing up a slide to stare at us, like animals sniffing a storm.

"Where'd you learn all that shit about bank vaults?" I asked.

I'd forgotten how gratifying it could be to make a woman laugh. A grunt of surprise . . . a sudden flash of gum, startlingly red . . . a white hand clapped over her mouth.

"I used to work for a bank," she explained. "Back in the day."

She wiped the sweat from her face. Spread the damp handkerchief across her lap.

"Listen, Henry, I've got Alonzo's hard drive."

I stared at her.

"How?"

"Well," she chirped, "first I took it out of Mr. Computer."

"No, I mean *when?*"

"Before the police got there."

Three, four minutes. No longer.

"I always keep a screwdriver in my bag," she said. As though that explained anything.

"The hard drive is evidence," I said.

"Not if it's been erased."

"But if it's erased . . . ?"

"Well, there's erased and then there's *erased.* You'd know that, Henry, if you'd ever been in the IT field."

As patiently as she could, she explained to me that hard drives don't really delete information, they just mark it as having been deleted. If it isn't copied over with other data, then, in many cases, it's recoverable.

So, having removed Alonzo's hard drive, Clarissa Dale, in the privacy of her own lodgings, transferred it to her computer, scanned the file structures with Windows Explorer, and was able finally to retrieve a few Word files and, more critically, the remains of a personal-appointment database.

She went straight to the entry for May 12 — Alonzo's last day on earth — and found three names on his to-call list.

"Me," she said. "You. *And* —"

"Amory Swale."

A flush of good humor stole into her cheeks as I told her how I'd come across Swale's name, just above hers, in Alonzo's folder.

"Okay," she said. "So you called his number, and then what?"

"It was out of service."

"And you didn't Google him? Never mind, I did. He's got a Web site. Swale's Antiquarian something something. So I dropped him an e-mail last night, just before bed, and what do you know, this very morning I hear back."

"What'd he say?"

"Very cagey. Didn't want to talk by computer or phone, asked me if I'd come see him in person."

"Where is he?"

"Nags Head, North Carolina."

Two-five-two, I remembered. Swale's area code.

"It's a five-hour drive, Henry. Not too much traffic this time of year. If we leave tomorrow — say, seven A.M. — we could be there for lunch."

"Seven A.M."

"Well, yeah, beat the traffic. You got

anything else on your plate?"

If nothing else, I had the sprawl of Alonzo's papers. Accounts to be opened, bills to be paid, appointments to be kept. God help me, a memorial service for Lily. And on top of that, a District of Columbia police detective who would look with ill favor on my skipping town with an investigation under way.

A mountain of obligation reared up before me . . . and opposing it, what? A woman who wanted to take a joy ride to a resort town?

"Seven it is," I said.

9

"Who's Kit?" Clarissa asked.

We were half an hour south of Richmond, and she had colonized the passenger seat of my '95 Toyota Corolla. Her head was bowed over Bernard Styles's digitized document, and her hair had fallen down on either side, screening her as comprehensively as a voting booth.

"Kit," I said.

"The very first line," she said. *"He would not be the first — lover, I guess — so to be served by Kit. Who would burn hot and cold in the space of but one breath . . ."*

"Oh, yeah. That's Marlowe."

"Marlowe?"

"Well, possibly."

"As in *Christopher* Marlowe?"

"Yeah."

"Like the playwright."

"Very much like the playwright."

"So he was pals with Ralegh."

"There's evidence, yeah. Ralegh wrote a jesting reply to one of Marlowe's poems. And some guy once accused Marlowe of reading 'the atheistic lecture to Sir Walter Ralegh and others.' "

"Others? Did he mean the School?"

"Not clear. The accuser was in cahoots with Ralegh's rival, the Earl of Essex. So Essex may have been trying to tar both men with the same brush. It may have been pure invention."

"Or else they really did know each other. And they really were atheists."

"Maybe."

Alonzo had never had much use for that word *maybe.* And neither did Clarissa, for she folded her lips down like a scolded toddler.

"Okay," she said, "one other thing. If Ralegh really wrote this letter, how come he can't spell his name? I mean, *R-a-w-l-e-y.* Where's the *i?*"

I pressed my hand to my temple. "You're kidding, right?"

"No."

"You really don't know about Elizabethan spellings."

"Hello. I was a business major."

"Okay," I said. "The English language back then wasn't standardized. There were

94

no official dictionaries. There was no — no cultural *belief* that words should always be spelled the same way. So people spelled things however they heard them or however made sense. I mean, the name *Shakespeare* had something like sixteen different spellings, and the way *he* spelled it isn't the way *we* spell it."

"And Ralegh?"

"Spelled it one way, his father spelled it another, his half-brother another. And the spellings changed from document to document. You wouldn't believe how many versions are out there. The only thing we're pretty sure of is how the name is pronounced."

"Okay, but I always thought Ralegh had an *i* in it. *R-a-l-e-i-g-h.*"

"You can blame that on his widow. She survived him, so she got to spell his name how she wanted to spell it. It's only recently that scholars have decided to take the *i* out again. And I could tell you why, but it might take hours, and in the meantime I have a question for you."

"Sure."

"If you're a business major, why aren't you in *business* somewhere?"

A delta of wrinkles appeared just above the bridge of her nose.

"Your tone, Henry."

"Sorry, you just — you appear to have vast, frankly unlimited amounts of time. And a certain amount of discretionary income, too. In which case I'd like to know the secret. Maybe the whole world should know."

"The world would be bored," she answered. "If you want to know, I took a buyout. From a company called StrategoStats, which specializes in automated content compliance. A staff of twenty-three, headquartered in Manchester, New Hampshire. Combined 2006 sales of $83.1 million. You could Google the whole operation, Henry, if that's not too straightforward for you."

"And you came to Washington why?"

Her dark lashes lowered a fraction.

"To pay my respects to Alonzo."

"He'd be touched."

"And to educate myself."

"About what?"

"Everything."

She put the paper back in the glove compartment. Then she stretched out her legs and let herself sag against the headrest.

"It's all right, Henry. I don't expect you to trust me."

And why, I wanted to ask, should I trust a

woman who couldn't even dress properly for a funeral?

Then again, how trustworthy was I? My Toyota, speaking strictly, belonged not to me but to an ex-girlfriend, currently domiciled in Hoboken. Who, speaking strictly, didn't know I had it. The legality of this never bothered me too much because, until Bernard Styles came along, I didn't have enough money to get the car out of its Pennsylvania Avenue garage-home. It had languished there through entire seasonal cycles, and by the time Clarissa and I came for it, it was so encased in dirt that someone had been able to scrawl a message on the back window.

For Christ's sake.

"Well, that's interesting," Clarissa had said. "For Christ's sake what? Oh, never mind, it says right here. *Clean me.*"

We stopped at Splash Car Wash on South Capitol Street, and then we got breakfast sandwiches from the adjoining McDonald's, and from there it was straight down 95 South. The radio didn't work, but the car persisted in a humming rattle, and my brain kept up a steady hum of its own: the image of Lily, rolling out of that vault, alternating with Halldor's tourist T-shirt and Alonzo's bloodstained raincoat.

97

And twining through all this: Clarissa. Her disciplined frame and her tiny wrists and that mighty collarbone, hinting at hidden powers. And the scent of sweat from where her thighs met the vinyl seats.

"I would trust you to drive," I said at last.

"Good," she said. "You drive like my dead granny."

We pulled into a rest stop off Route 64. Disarmingly new and clean, with fan windows and TVs that were set to CNN and a strapping, intergalactic Pepsi machine, from which Clarissa obtained two cans of diet soda. The first she drained on the spot, tipping her head back and pouring it in an even stream down her gullet.

The other can she placed in the car's cup rest. This was the first in an almost comical series of preparatory steps. Side mirror? Check. Rearview mirror? Check. Seat positioned at the exact 12.5-degree angle? Check. All we needed was clearance from Houston.

"Been thinking it over," she said. "We probably don't need to trust each other. I mean, *you* don't trust that Styles guy, and you're still working for him."

"Working." I slapped down the passenger-side visor. "Unless there's some 401(k) plan I haven't been apprised of, I'm not his

employee. I'm merely providing a deliverable."

"Like a consultant."

"If you will."

"You still don't trust him."

I stared at the oaks and crape myrtles along the roadside, parched with late-summer heat.

"I don't know," I said. "People just get very fragile whenever he's around. Actuarial tables stop working."

"You think he might have had something to do with Lily."

"Yeah. Well, yeah. And not just Lily."

She looked at me.

"Alonzo?"

"You said yourself, remember? Alonzo was the last guy in the world who'd kill himself. Think about the message he left us. It wasn't *So long,* it was *Hey, know what? The School of Night is back.* He was ready to move. He was all-systems-go."

Unless, I thought, he'd gone so far there was no coming back.

"That message he left us," Clarissa said. "It must have been about the Ralegh letter."

"I suppose so."

"Which means he thought it was genuine."

"I'm sure he did. And I'm sure Bernard

99

Styles does, too. Why else would he go to such trouble to get it back?"

She stopped a minute to consider.

"So you think he wanted it bad enough to kill Alonzo."

"I don't know," I shrugged. "You have to admit it's conceivable."

"But Styles is a *book* guy, right? I mean, book guys — they drink tea, they wear *cardigans*."

I told her then about Cornelius Snowden, a fully representative book guy, killed in the heart of London for a single volume. And the more I described the circumstances, the more I found myself gravitating toward Alonzo's construction of them. And hadn't I tasted something of Bernard Styles myself? Did I really think he would stop short of slaughter once he had fastened his mind around something?

We were silent a good while. Even the car's rattling seemed to subside beneath the weight of our thoughts.

"Here's what I want to know," Clarissa said.

"What?"

"Do *you* think the letter's real?"

I tipped my head against the window. And in that instant, the glass seemed to me no more than a profoundly unstable membrane between the heat outside and the car's arctic front. My head was resting not on substance but on an idea.

"You know what?" I said. "I'm not in that game anymore. I'm the last guy in the world to ask about a Walter Ralegh document. Believe it."

My eyes were still closed, but I could feel her, all right. The heat of her gaze.

"But you were a college professor, right? You must have been on a tenure track somewhere."

"I was."

A particularly heavy pause.

"Okay," she said. "I totally get if you don't want to talk about it. Just tell me to shut up."

And I could have, I suppose. But in this moment, for reasons I can't define, disclosing the truth seemed easier than concealing it.

So I told her about a young assistant professor at an eastern Pennsylvania university who, one day, received a rare gift. A previously unknown poem by Walter Ralegh.

Not just any poem but a love poem written to Ralegh's young wife, Elizabeth Throckmorton. She had been a hand-maiden to the queen, but when her secret marriage to Ralegh was exposed (by the birth of their first son), the queen, in a rage, tossed Ralegh into the Tower. He was able to buy his release, but he never regained his place in the queen's heart or in her court.

In this freshly discovered poem, Ralegh contemplated the cost of loving the woman who had been his undoing — the woman whose first name happened to be the same as the queen's. The effect, on first reading, was charming and complex: Ralegh vibrating between the two poles of Elizabeth.

Two appraisers verified the document as genuine, but the seller — a Peruvian bibliophile-adventurer domiciled in the Caymans — demanded a steep price. Some of the money came from research accounts, some from the dean, some from a competitive grant. And the rest? Borrowed from Alonzo Wax.

The document was unveiled at the annual meeting of the Renaissance Studies Association. Not the usual eight-page twenty-minute spiel in a subdivided hotel banquet room but the full ballroom: hundreds of academics . . . journalists and photographers . . . a major article set to appear the following week in the field's preeminent journal . . . a book contract in the works with a major university press . . . an air of suspended enchantment.

Ten minutes into the Q and A, an elderly Berkeley professor with a polka-dotted Frank Sinatra bow tie stood up and, in a mild voice that managed to carry from the very back of the ballroom, said.

"I'm afraid you've been led astray, Professor."

He'd been offered the same poem by the same Peruvian adventurer. Only he'd been told it was by Marlowe.

"Eventually," I said, "we found out who the real author was: William Henry Ireland."

"Never heard of him."

"A renowned scoundrel of the late eighteenth century. He once forged an entire Shakespeare play. Plus a letter from Shakespeare to his wife, complete with a lock of the Bard's hair. To hide his tracks, he wrote on the blank leaves of Elizabethan-era books. That's how he was able to fool a lot of appraisers.

"Well," I continued, "the end was swift. My article was junked. The book contract was scuttled. Not a journal in the world would print anything I wrote. The dean's wife looked sad for me at a faculty reception. I was done."

"So that was your crime," Clarissa said.

"Getting hoodwinked."

"Maybe, with a little more fortitude, I could've gone all postmodern with it. You know, 'Here's my deconstructive reading of the duality between the authentic and the fraudulent. I mean, dude, what's authenticity, anyway?' "Wincing, I shook my head. "I couldn't carry it off, not with any conviction. And I couldn't stand being the departmental fuckup."

"You wouldn't have been the first."

"In the world of Henry, I was the first. You know how people talk to you when there's *one* thing they're not supposed to talk about? Something very *compressed* happens to their voices. It's not a loud thing, but it feels loud."

"So you went where it was quiet."

"I went where I had friends. And by then I had only one: Alonzo. So that's how I ended up in Washington." I forced my eyes open. "Alonzo knew people, and I needed work. It seemed like a good idea at the time. Seven years ago. And, by the way, you should be very grateful. I've spared you many dark months of the soul."

Worse, I thought: gray years of the mind. An adjunct-professor gig at a local community college, teaching freshman composition for $2,000 a semester. Foundation proposals for 501(c)(3)s. Restaurant reviews for an alternative weekly. Proofreading, résumé editing, paralegal gigs. A stretch of advocacy writing, in which, depending on the client, I might be petitioning for fossil-fuel taxes or warning against climate-change hysteria. Brochures for a Jewish summer camp. Teaching night classes at community arts centers. Seasonal employment with Eddie Bauer.

Yes, I was sparing Clarissa quite a lot. Myself even more.

"So now you know," I said.

"No, wait. There's a sequel. Years go by. In walks a man named Bernard Styles. He says, *Excuse me, I've got a Walter Ralegh letter.* And there you are thinking —"

"*Kill me now.*" She laughed. "You could have turned him down."

"Yeah, see, he put this little check in my hands. I'm very respectful of liquidity."

She gave that some thought. Then, in a voice jarringly bright, she said:

"Want to know what bugs me? We don't have the first part of Ralegh's letter. I'd love to know who it's written *to.* Who's this 'tutelary genius'?"

"Yeah. Him."

"Oh, my God."

"What?"

"You know who it is, Henry. You do, you *know.*"

But I didn't. Not until that exact moment, when everything that had been building up inside — the events of the past week, the fragments of that letter — merged with old conversations and half-forgotten images and the prospect of those white wind-stropped North Carolina beaches, and everything cohered into one being. And this being had a name.

"Harriot," I said. "The letter was written to Thomas Harriot."

■ ■ ■ ■

Part Two

■ ■ ■ ■

All you possessed with indepressed
   spirits,
Indu'd with nimble and aspiring wits,
Come consecrate with me, to sacred
   Night
Your whole endeauors, and detest the
   light. . . .
No pen can any thing eternal write,
That is not steept in humour of the night.
              — George Chapman,
              "The Shadow of Night"

10

ISLEWORTH, ENGLAND *1603*

He still dreams of Virginia.

It's always high summer there. The air is piled in damp drifts, and everywhere there's a smoke of rotting persimmons. The clouds are sun-dizzy.

He was a young man when he went. Twenty-five: stuffed with books, cringing from the light. In no way prepared — how could he have been? — for the plenitude that met him. Tapestries of silken grass. Cedars and firs and maples and oaks. Gourds and pumpkins. Oysters, mussels. Thick-shelled walnuts and strawberries of supernal sweetness. A river as wide in places as the Thames. It was all more than he could bear in some moments, and yet, after a time, the thought of leaving it was harder to bear.

Now and then his throat would catch in wonder. Somewhere in this salt-stung wilderness lay (by his own estimate) twenty-eight types of beast never seen by Western man. And who was the man charged with finding them, knowing them, naming them? Tom Harriot of Oxfordshire. Charter of a new world.

For whole weeks he wandered. Every day a new day: mapping the flight of a marlin hawk, gauging the length of the native herring, comparing the different ways of cooking the *okindgier* bean (flatter than the English bean and altogether as good in taste as English peaze), studying the dyeing properties of the *Tangomóckonomindge* bark. By now the Algonquins left him largely to himself, so he passed hours and days unmolested, never so much as glimpsing another human being. In his quietest intervals, he could imagine himself the lord of his own vast green unpopulated island.

Here I will be, he remembers thinking. *Always.*

But outside his peaceable kingdom, things were falling apart. From the start, the colonists had been at odds with the Indians. Skirmishes had broken out, villages were raided and burned, a chieftain assassinated. When Sir Francis Drake came unexpectedly calling, the colony's leaders leaped at his generosity. To go back to England! To be free of these savages! It never occurred to them that one of their party might wish to stay.

They left in the middle of a hurricane. The sky was black, the breakers high as mastheads, and the pinnace carrying Harriot to sea kept grounding on sandbars. Desperate to be gone, the sailors began jettisoning everything on board. In silence, Harriot watched his chests and books, his writings and instruments — his astrolabe and cross-staff and lodestone — sinking in the teeming water. By the time the sailors were done, the only possessions left him were the clothes on his back and the pages he had tucked into his boots and a handful of roots in his pockets.

From the stern of Drake's bark, he watched the shoreline blur into mist and hail.

Wilderness is a distant memory now, for he lives in the shadow of one of England's grandest homes. Nature here has been plucked out, pushed back, domesticated. Which makes it a special pleasure for Harriot to watch the Thames oxbow, three or four times a year, overflow its banks, rising up from its gorge and rolling in a fat brown pool toward Syon House's gallery.

Where it is met in ceremonial fashion by

the house's master. No man may turn back the tide — it has been tried — but if anyone could, it would be Henry Percy, Earl of Northumberland, that paradigm of the modern peer: skeptical but loyal, impetuous but temperate, slow of speech but swift to answer. Abstracted, gregarious, a man of brilliance, a patron to poets and scientists. His ancestry is noble and ancient. Eight earls have preceded him; the queen has dined four times at his table. From the towers of Syon House, he may look north to Ealing, west to Isleworth, east to London, and south to the royal palace at Richmond. Turning in any direction, he may survey some part of the four thousand acres of forest and farm and pastureland over which he holds sovereignty.

It is a sign of his temperament that even his estate, the undisputed evidence of his greatness, can be a fund of mortification and humor. He stares, therefore, at the exact spot where the Thames's turbid stinking water meets the toe of his hunting boot.

— We have become the New Atlantis!

He is addressing no one in particular, but surely he intends the remark for Thomas Harriot, who is standing close by and who has read Plato's account of Atlantis in its original Greek and who is considered by some, the earl included, to be England's greatest natural philosopher — even as he is considered by others a figure of surpassing evil.

The irony is this: No more than two dozen of Harriot's countrymen would even know him by sight. He has passed forty-three years on God's earth, more than either his father or mother, and he has done it far from the common view, and in bleaker moments he thinks he might just as well have stayed in Virginia.

And yet how can he, in good conscience, complain? He has his own house on the grounds and a small retinue of servants, not to mention a hundred pounds a year, and nothing is required of him but to scythe a path through Nature's mysteries.

And yet, as the years pile on his head, the mysteries inside him take up more and more of his time and care. Sadness has become his second skin. It coats him like ash. He passes at least half the night without sleep, and day is worse than night. At any hour, without the slightest warning, he can burst into tears — womanly, corrosive, not always concealable. Two weeks ago he was speaking with the rat man about infestations in the pewter pots, when he felt his eyes suddenly prickle and dissolve.

— Are you quite yourself, Master Harriot?

He forced himself to smile, a note of reassurance that only caused the rat man to take a step backward and stare at his own boots.

— Very sorry to have troubled you.

To judge by the philosophers, his affliction is a gift. Melancholy, wrote Aristotle, lifts man to the level of the divine. "This *humor melancholicus*," wrote Agrippa, "has such power that they say it attracts certain demons into our bodies, through whose presence and activity men fall into ecstasies and pronounce many wonderful things." The principle can be seen in Dürer's great engraving: dark-faced Melancholy in the full voluptuousness of her dejection, the ladder of creation rising from her funk. Worlds beyond worlds.

But for Harriot, melancholy is not a stratagem but a birthright. A cirrus cloud, he imagines it, entering him with his first breath. Once, when he was eight or nine, his mother sent him to the butcher for drippings. No different from any other errand, except that the butcher fell apart laughing at the sight of him: a boy so young wearing a look of such primordial woe.

Even Ralegh used to tease him about it.

— Perhaps, Thomas, if you did not wear black at all hours, your spirits might improve. Recall, please, you are no longer at Oxford. You need not go about like a monk.

But during those long-ago evenings at Sherborne Castle, the sight of those white faces swimming in and out of candlelight roused the Anabaptist in him.

— For God's sake, he remembers saying. — We can't even see to write our figures. Is all this stagecraft necessary? Must we turn our work into a *play?*

Marlowe, predictably, was the most amused.

— Surely you do not conceive we are the only ones to be arraigned on that charge. What is a holy mass, Tom, if not a play? A wedding? A lecture? What is a *coronation?* Do you wish to know why I am a playmaker? Because I know that, at every moment, we are in the midst of some play. Only in an arena that calls itself theater may we stand outside the *real* theater — our lives — and see them in all their truth, Tom. By which, of course, I mean their tragedy.

Some years later, on an evilly cold December evening, Ralegh invited him to a play. Dragged him, better to say, for Marlowe by then was dead, and the theater had lost whatever savor it once had. Harriot disliked the forced intimacy . . . the stew of noise and odor . . . the courtiers, curried and buffed, perched at the edge of the stage, and the ruffians in the pits, clamoring . . . the jumble of *idiom,* so un-Aristotelian, comedy and tragedy tossed like stew meat into the same pot.

Tonight, at least, Ralegh was taking him not to the Swan or the Globe but to the Hall of the Middle Temple, where a regiment of law students had gathered under the great double hammer-beam roof to forget whatever it was they were studying.

—You shall relish this one, said Ralegh.

Relish. A predicate so thickly veiled in meaning that Harriot felt only dread when the four actors, arrayed as richly as any Westminster courtier, gathered before the High Table.

They were essaying the roles of young men of Spain, high-minded fools who had sworn off women for study. *Navarre,* declared their king,

shall be the wonder of the world;
Our court shall be a little Academe,
Still and contemplative in living art.

The shock came slowly — a gathering of unreality. Before the king had even finished talking, Harriot had come to doubt his existence. The existence of the play. Of himself, watching it.

No denying, though, the smile of grim satisfaction on Ralegh's lips. Harriot understood now: He was meant to hear that name one more time. The name they had given themselves all those years ago in Sherborne.

Our little Academe.

They had grasped from the start the presumption of likening themselves to Plato, so they had always made a point of stressing the adjective over the noun. Our *little* Academe. *Large matters for such a little Academe . . . Might I propose a theme for our wee little Academe?*

And now, in an act of rank impudence, the glover's son (as Marlowe, the shoemaker's son, had always called him) had puffed their name into a balloon of pretension. *Academe indeed,* Shakespeare was telling his audience. *Wait till a pretty girl swims past, we shall see how deep their thoughts run.*

And here, in the real-world academe of the Middle Temple, the message could not have been any better received. For two hours, Harriot sat on that cushioned bench, stunned by the laughter around him. All those young barristers, feeding off his corpse.

Later that night, as he was picking his way along the Strand, he turned back and saw that even Ralegh's manservant was grinning from the memory.

— Well now, said Ralegh.

The great man's dress was subdued to-night, which was to say his pearls had been sewn into his black velvet. One might almost have said he was traveling incognito, were it not for the fact that, at six feet, he stood a head taller than anyone else on the street.

— Never mind, Tom. What do we care if the world has swung against us? It will swing back.

Ralegh was limping that evening — a vestige of the raid on Cádiz, when explod-ing splinters had been driven into his leg like so many arrowheads. For some time they walked, and then, in the broad vowels of his Devonshire home, Ralegh spoke.

— Curious phrase.

— Which?

— The School of Night.

11

And in that breath they adopted it, just the two of them.

For the name fit, did it not? Hadn't they always made a point of meeting late in the evening? And in the ruins of the old castle, far from the servants' quarters . . . the eight of them talking until rosy-fingered dawn . . . every word in strictest confidence.

And if someone cared to discuss a forbidden volume — Machiavelli, Montaigne, Agrippa's *De occulta philosophia,* Hayward's *History of Henry IIII* — the book would have to be smuggled out in a cloth sack. There were no minutes, no abstracts. Each man was allotted but a single beeswax candle to guide him there, which meant that the room at first was even darker than night.

Then, as their eyes adapted, the darkness began to bristle with shapes: blurs of gray, whispering at the edge of sight. Invisible auditors, Harriot sometimes thought, urging the men on as they dashed up against hard questions.

It was Marlowe who dashed the hardest.

— Moses was a charlatan! Prove or disprove.

They might have been back at university, the way they went at it. There was Marlowe, arguing that Moses had used Egyptian magic to cow and gull Hebrew slaves. There was Chapman, warning that the sullying of Moses's revelations would bring the whole temple of Judeo-Christian belief crashing down. And there was everyone else, throwing in tinder. And if, in the end, they reached no conclusion — well, they had never desired one.

At the first glimmer of dawn, Ralegh would reach for his bottle of Canary sack and pour them each a glass.

— To our little Academe.

They would repeat it in unison and with glad hearts, because no matter how hard they had gone at it, they knew it was something of a miracle, finding — not like minds, exactly — like *hungers.* Whatever their differences in station or stature, they wished to know what could be known or couldn't.

And together they made one another brave. So it was that Northumberland, the reformed papist, could do something he

120

would never have dared in public: criticize the Act of Supremacy for turning Catholics into fugitives. Matthew Roydon proposed that the earth, far from being six thousand years old, as the Church fathers said, was closer to *sixteen* thousand. William Warner, in his cups, questioned the resurrection of the body, and Ralegh was moved one night to pose the same question about the soul.

Night after night was spent in this fashion. And every morning, as they fell into their beds, they felt only the aching glow of exertion. Whatever they had spoken of was already half forgotten.

And yet not forgotten at all. Despite all their vows of secrecy, word of their proceedings managed to leak out.

A year later, Marlowe stood accused of blasphemy and heresy, of "affirming that Moses was but a Juggler." A Jesuit priest had warned readers of Ralegh's "School of Atheism" and "the Conjurer" (Harriot) who taught young gentlemen to jest at the Old and New Testaments and spell God backward.

And before too much time had passed, a glover's son from Warwickshire was writing a comedy about foolish intellectuals who tempt fate and their own natures by sealing themselves in "a little Academe."

All their old stagecraft, the stuff of their arguments, coming back to them in fragments, warped, scarcely to be recognized. Like boys egging one another out to sea, they had wandered far out of their natural depth. And they would pay the price.

Marlowe was, for no good reason, murdered. Chapman was reduced to near-penury. Ralegh was hauled before an ecclesiastical commission, accused of denying the resurrection of the body and the existence of the soul.

And none of them bore a greater stain than Harriot. Men who had never met him were fully persuaded that he was a devil, a magus, the seducer of young men.

Socrates was called no worse than this. And if Harriot has yet to be proffered his cup of hemlock — well, surely that is because, unlike Socrates, he has taken himself from the world's view.

Yes, in these uncertain times, it is the height of wisdom to be *this* Thomas Harriot. Living on patronage, in quiet and seclusion, with Welsh mountain ewes for company.

Spring is late this year. The cart wheels still get lodged in the road ruts — he can hear the teamsters' curses, like jangling church bells — and the wind still blows in, sharp and damp, from the river, and the milk still crusts over in the pail. But the robins are here, mad with purpose in the water meadows, and the chiffchaffs are in the osiers, and he can smell, for the first time in months, the *earth,* yielding up its scents, one by one.

And even this gives him pause. Aren't secrets yielded up in the same way? Wasn't Marlowe murdered at the height of spring's glory?

And Ralegh — doesn't he have particular cause to dread the end of winter? For the queen has done something no one was quite sure she would: She has died. And from the north, her successor even now sweeps down, and great men who once bestrode the land now hang in the balance. Men like Walter Ralegh.

Ralegh is a bad match for the new king; everyone knows it. James favors peace, Ralegh lives for war. James loathes tobacco, Ralegh trades in it. James is pious, a theologian. And Ralegh . . . well, everyone *knows* he hails from the School of Atheism. Of which Thomas Harriot is the master.

One way or another, those long-ago nights at Sherborne Castle still have the capacity to harm. What a surprise, then, to read Ralegh's letter, arriving just two weeks after the queen's death. A recitation of doom spiced with the following:

Thou wilt excuse me, I trust, for laboring in this vein. I could find no better plaster for my wounds than memory. In parlous times, it is great joy to think upon that homely School, where we were glad to gather.

Harriot stares at those words: *great joy.*

The paper rests in his hands: weak, perishable. He should tear it up. He should burn it. No telling, in these times, where an intelligencer might be sequestered. King James, Robert Cecil, Northumberland himself — each sits at the center of a near-infinite web, drawing in secrets and allies and enemies.

Harriot raises the letter toward the candle. He watches the upper left corner shrink into flame.

He pulls the letter back.

To his right, a small commotion. Jerking his head, he finds a young woman in a gown of gray russet, bending over his working table, studying one of his papers, her face a mask of engrossment as her lips shape each syllable.

She looks up, catches his glance. The

fright in her eyes is as great as his and yet of such a different order that, in the next instant, his brain is reconfiguring the scene.

And already she is leaving — her leather shoes scraping against the wood — and with an urgency every bit as great, he hears himself calling after her.

— Can you read?

12

OUTER BANKS, NORTH CAROLINA *SEPTEMBER 2009*

True to Clarissa's prediction, it was a few minutes past noon when we drove across the Route 158 bridge into the Outer Banks. Had it been a summer weekend, the bridge alone might have sucked an hour from our lives, but this was the second Thursday in September, and the kids were back in school, the parents had followed, and a vacancy lay now across the strip malls and RV parks of South Croatan Highway.

In Nags Head, we found an oceanside motel called the Pelican Arms, a thin-walled entropic place with broken icemakers and empty vending machines and a film of twigs and candy wrappers on the outdoor swimming pool (now closed). The only other occupants we could detect were dogs — all of them, by motel statute, under fifty pounds — Pekingeses and toy poodles and long-haired dachshunds and, strangest of all, a miniature schnauzer who came strolling out of an elevator, entirely unaccompanied, stiff with entitlement.

I booked adjoining singles while Clarissa sat in the lobby, scanning her e-mail. No messages yet from Amory Swale, our elusive book dealer, and so, hungry beyond all measure, we walked to the local Five Guys franchise. The sight of meat and cheese this time was cheering in a strange way, and I dove right in. So did Clarissa. And then we sat back, faintly embarrassed, and wiped the grease from our hands.

"Tell me about this Harriot guy," she said.

So I just started talking, and one by one the things I'd once known about him — things I'd forgotten I ever knew — came percolating to the surface. And were still coming up fifteen minutes later, when Clarissa put out a hand to stop me.

"Okay, wait," she said. "Let me see if I've got this straight. Thomas Harriot is one of the great scientists of his age. He corresponds with Kepler, he influences Descartes, he sees Halley's comet seventy-five years before Halley does. He discovers some law of refraction — what is it again, Smell's Law?"

"*Snell's* Law."

"Discovers it before Snell did. Sees Jupiter's satellites before anyone else. Notices *sunspots* before anyone else. Becomes a pioneer in — I can't even keep track — ballistics and ciphers — spherical geometry —"

"And algebra," I said. "Harriot's the one who gave us these . . ."

I drew the two symbols across the last clean napkin.

$$< \quad >$$

"Crocodile swallows the bigger number," she whispered. "That's how Mrs. Clabault used to explain it in second grade."

She slowly traced the symbols, then looked back up at me.

"So what ties Harriot to the School of Night?"

"Well," I said, "he was on Ralegh's payroll for starters."

"Doing what?"

"Hanging out, mostly. No, that's not fair. He taught Ralegh navigation, he managed Ralegh's business affairs. Surveyed his estates. Stayed loyal to the end, even after Northumberland came calling."

"And Northumberland was — ?"

"Henry Percy, the Wizard Earl. Another friend of Ralegh's, another reputed School member. Richer than sin. Percy gave Harriot a hundred pounds a year just to live on his estate at Syon Park."

"Live and what else?"

"Think."

"Mm," she said. "No tenure track, no dissertation defense. Nice gig."

Tipping her chair back, she began to rock herself with her toes.

"That line from the letter," she said. "Something about *tutelary genius*."

"Outsunning every star, yeah. If there *was* a School of Night, Harriot would have been its master."

"Then why don't we know about him? I mean, he was the first English scientist to explore America, right? He was here before the Lost Colony was here."

"Blame Harriot," I said. "He published next to nothing while he was alive. His notebooks were lost for, like, a century and a half. We're still figuring out what he knew and when he knew it."

In just the last year, I told her, scholars had uncovered a dated document, proving that Harriot was the first man ever to make a telescopic drawing of the moon. Six months *before* Galileo. Mare Crisium, Mare Tranquillitatis, Mare Fecunditatis . . . they're all there. The lunar maps Harriot would go on to make over the next four or five years would remain unsurpassed for decades.

"Staring at the moon." Clarissa cupped her chin with her palm. "All those years. He must have been a dreamer."

With her draggy eyelids, she looked like something of a dreamer herself.

"Are you ever afraid, Henry?"

"Sure."

"I mean for no reason."

"Well, I don't know." I scratched my cheek. "There's probably always a reason. You just have to figure out what it is."

She looked at me.

"What if that's what you're afraid of?" she asked.

Outside the restaurant, the weather fronts were already at cross-purposes. A wall of smoky-wet air . . . the sun shooting looks from behind a cloud . . . and there, moving doggedly through, was Clarissa, studying each of her sandaled feet as it met the pavement.

"So what did he look like?" she asked.

"Harriot, you mean?"

"Yeah."

"Why do you want to know?"

She said nothing. Just watched her feet.

"You've seen him," I suggested. "Is that it?"

An irritable twitch. An answering crackle from the tangle of her hair.

"Look," I said, "I know I wasn't very receptive before. About your — whatever you — I mean, they're *visions,* right?"

"Alonzo called them *crossings,*" she said quietly.

"Well, see? You told *him* about it, you might as well tell me."

"His mind was a little less closed than yours."

"Okay. At this very moment, I am making a heroic — frankly a *manful* and courageous effort — to crack my mind open, okay? A millimeter."

She regarded me with coin-slot eyes.

"Go on," I gasped. "I can't keep holding it."

And so, right there, on the sidewalk of the Virginia Dare Trail, three blocks from the Pelican Arms and not two blocks from the local Hooters, Clarissa Dale told me about the man who, on any given night, might come calling.

It was night where he was, too. Late evening in September, though how she knew it was September she couldn't say. He more a black woolen cloak and a stiff square black hat, with rounded ridges like a biretta. Head to toe in black, which had the effect of calling out his face, was pale as a fish, grim and masklike.

"A priest?" I asked.

"I don't think so," she said. "No crosses, no crucifixes. No genuflecting."

"Then what's he doing, exactly? In this dream of yours?"

"He's got a handful of stones. Lapis stones, they look like. He's tossing them into a copper pan. And beneath the pan, there's a fire. And the whole time he's speaking. The same four words, again and again."

"What words?"

"Ex nihilo nihil fit."

She paused then — struck, maybe, by how the words sounded in her own voice.

"It was Alonzo who figured out what he was saying."

"From nothing comes nothing."

"That's right."

"And that's all the man says?"

"No. No, when he's done, he throws back his head and — *hollers,* really hollers. In English this time. At least I think it's English."

"Hollers what?"

"Long live the School of Night!"

132

To my great relief, she didn't scream it herself. But there was something unspeakable in the way she mimicked the motion — the way her neck snapped back as though someone had slipped a garrote around it.

"And you'd never heard that name before?" I asked.

"Never. And now it's all I hear."

We were walking again, without quite being aware of it. Walking close enough to brush elbows.

"So when you say you've *seen* the School of Night," I said, "this is what you mean."

She nodded.

"You haven't seen anyone else?"

"I wish I would," she answered, with an upturn of her mouth.

"Okay, one more question. Would you recognize his face? If you saw it again?"

"Henry. A man comes into your bedroom every week for upward of a year? You're going to remember what he looks like."

Clarissa's laptop was newer and faster than mine, so we set it on the tartan quilt of the motel-room bed, I dropped a few words into the Google grinder — and up came a picture.

"Was *this* the guy?" I asked, angling the screen toward her.

133

The man pictured there was small, simian, wary-looking, with a disproportionately large head. He wore the usual white ruff, and he had a pen in his hand and a Latin inscription ringing him around. *Si malum, meum peccatum; si bonum, Dei donum.*

At the sight of him, Clarissa burst out laughing. "Are you for real?"

"Yep."

"He looks like someone's pet."

"Just tell me if it's your guy."

"Absolutely not."

She looked at me.

"So I guess that's Thomas Harriot," she said.

"Nope," I said, turning the screen back toward me. "Although they *thought* it was for the longest time. Never mind. How 'bout this fella?"

A more presentable candidate this time: cerebral brow on angular face; pointed beard, thin lips, large all-seeing eyes; a deep but modest gravity.

"Huh. Wow."

She circled the image with her finger. Lowered her face closer and closer to the screen. Tilted her head from side to side.

"Well, the beard," she said, "that's kind of the same. The *forehead,* though, it's kinda slopy. I don't think it's . . ."

She drew back, squinted the image into focus one last time.

"No," she said. "Not him."

Her eyes met mine then. She took a long breath, and a welt of pink bled from her cheekbones.

"Good," I said at last. " 'Cause that's probably not Harriot either. Turns out we don't really have a definitive portrait of him. No one knows what he looked like."

With a soft grunt, she heaved herself off the bed and stood for a long while, looking out the window. Unaware, probably, of the way her hair burned darker against the sun. The bloom of light on her arms.

"So tell me," she said. "Did I pass?"

"The *second* test, yeah."

"What was the first?"

I flipped the screen down and slid the laptop away.

"The *School of Night* test," I said. "Thomas Harriot would never have used those words. They were Shakespeare's coinage, not his."

"Harriot couldn't have taken the name for himself?"

"Why would he? By the time Shakespeare wrote his play, the School — if it ever existed — was almost certainly finished. They wouldn't have called themselves anything."

She turned around. Stared at me.

"So you've been indulging me, Henry."

"No. I've been contextualizing you."

She leaned back against the window frame. "Fuck your context," she said.

It was the first time I'd heard her swear. But what struck me most was her tiredness. Her body was shutting down, just as it had yesterday in Stanton Park.

"If you'll excuse me," she said. "I'd like to take a nap."

I might have pointed out that she was in *my* room. Instead, I strolled down to what the motel called, with a certain wistfulness, its ocean veranda. The air was choked with salt, and just to the north of me, in an Adirondack chair, sat a blanketed Maltese dog, gazing out to sea like the doyenne of a sanatorium. We sat there, the two of us, for a good hour, I'd guess, watching the sea oats. And every time my attention flagged, there was Lily Pentzler to snap me back. Lily, with her Alice-blue face.

When I got back, Clarissa was still awake, looking up at the ceiling fan. *"Washington Post,"* I said, tossing the paper onto the square of bed by her head. "It's got Lily's obit."

"What does it say?"

"I don't know, I haven't read it."

Clarissa snatched up the paper and riffled to the back of the Metro section.

"Hey, wait a minute," she said. "You said she didn't have any family."

"She didn't, as far as I know."

"Well, according to this, there's a cousin. Joanna Frobisher. Of Hyattsville, Maryland."

Hyattsville was a twenty-minute drive from Lily's apartment. But it wasn't the proximity that was butting up against my brain.

"Read me that name again," I said.

"Joanna Frobisher. You know it?"

"I know it."

13

More than once, in the days since Alonzo's death, I'd asked myself the same question: *What if nobody had seen him jump?*

His suicide note could have blown away. The watch and shoes would have been easy prey for thieves. The coat that washed up a few days later on Bear Island? Just another piece of flotsam, not worth mentioning to anybody.

Yes, Alonzo Wax could have gone to his end entirely unnoticed if fate hadn't granted him a witness.

A forty-six-year-old Hyattsville woman who had gotten lost while taking a late-afternoon hike on the Gold Mine Loop and who, unable to get a cell signal, had decided to tack toward the river in hopes of finding help.

As she later told the police, all she saw when she approached the Washington Aqueduct Observation Deck was a khaki raincoat, flaring out of the darkness. The human form that stood inside that coat . . . this came to her only as she got nearer. And then, before she knew it, she was running toward the silent figure on top of the platform. Who was already jumping.

Stunned, she peered into the torrent of water where he had disappeared. But the night was cloudy, and she had no flashlight. Whoever the man was, whatever his sorrow had been, he was gone.

Testifying weeks later at Alonzo's inquest, she told the court how the whole experience had taught her to value life and never take anyone or anything for granted. You couldn't, I remember thinking, have scripted a more empathetic witness.

"And her name was Joanna Frobisher?" Clarissa asked me.

I nodded.

"So what are the chances there could be *two* Joanna Frobishers in Hyattsville?"

"Both tied to the same dead man? Not great. Not even particularly good."

Clarissa rocked herself to her feet.

"And nobody asked this woman if she knew Alonzo? Or knew *of* him?"

"Why would they?" I said. "It was an inquest, not a trial. Whatever happened was already a matter of record. Alonzo's family just wanted to put the whole thing to rest."

"So if Lily's cousin was out by the river that night . . ."

I pressed my knuckles into my temple. "Lily must have sent her there."

"But why?"

"Because a witness was needed."

"Why?"

I had to sound the answer in my head before I trusted myself to speak it.

"Because it was the only way people would believe Alonzo killed himself."

Because there were too many reasons he *wouldn't* have. Wouldn't have traveled miles from home to do a job he could have accomplished a few blocks from his apartment.

Whoever chose that bridge had had very specific criteria in mind. The place had to be dark, it had to be remote, and it had to be a place where nobody could ever know for sure what had happened.

"Whew," said Clarissa, blowing out two cheekfuls of air. "If you're right —"

"If I'm right, Lily Pentzler was part of a conspiracy to commit murder."

In the silence that ensued, that final word seemed actually to revolve in the air between us. Slowly, so we could study all its aspects.

I know. That's what I'd said to Lily, the last time I saw her alive. *I know.*

No. You don't.

Clarissa and I looked at each other.

"Police?" she suggested at last.

From my wallet I unearthed the card. Punched in the number.

"This is Detective August Acree. I am not available to take your call at this time. . . ."

I left a vague message and then a number and then, after great thought, the following afterword:

"Um, thanks."

And then, for several minutes, we sat there, listening to the hum of the air-conditioning window unit.

"Still no word?" I asked. "From who?"

"Mr. Swale the book dealer."

Absently, Clarissa reached for her Trio, scanned the roster of new messages.

"Nothing."

"Then what do you say we get out of here?"

"And go where?"

I briefly thought of saying, *Anywhere.* But in fact, I had a specific place in mind: the Fort Ralegh Historic Site.

Located not by the ocean but several miles inland and corresponding roughly to the site where Thomas Harriot and his fellow colonists hunkered down more than four centuries ago. The original settlements, of course, were long gone, and the only thing that still bore Harriot's name was a nature path, which, for reasons inscrutable, was listed as the Thomas *Harlot* trail.

"Ooh," said Clarissa. "I like the sound of that."

A remark just saucy enough to make me fall back a pace. For which I was rewarded by the sight of her gypsum-alabaster legs, striding down the path. It took me a hundred yards to catch up with her again.

"I'm guessing you've been married, Henry."

"Once or twice. Or so."

"What went wrong?"

"Um, *me,* I guess. Is this something we need to talk about?"

"No."

The only things we could hear now were the sounds of our feet, muffled by a carpet of loblolly pine needles.

"So what exactly is wrong with you, Henry? That you can't keep a woman?"

"Um . . ."

"You can be nice enough."

"Well — anyone can. Serial killers . . ."

"You're nice to look at."

God help me, I blushed.

"You mean for my age," I said.

"Any age," she answered, meeting my eyes. "One might even call you a catch, Henry."

"Well, every time I was caught, I was released. Shortly after."

"So what was the deal?"

"We're really going to talk about this."

"Only if you want."

I picked up a stick, swung it lightly at a red mulberry.

"The problem wasn't who I was, it was who I *wasn't*."

"Who were you *not?*"

Something quite impudent about her tone. But when I looked into the bitter-chocolate layers of her eyes, I found . . . no, better to say I was lost. For a second or two.

"Oh, you know. I wasn't the guy with the brilliant — you know, blazing, unassailable *future.* I used to think I was, but I wasn't. And unfortunately, I wasn't an artist, either."

"Not even with the love of a good woman?"

I paused to consider the implications of that question.

"Truthfully, no. That was the lesson of my second marriage."

"Well, never mind. I'm guessing you're a

good teacher."

"It would depend on your definition."

"Give me one."

"Um . . . I've never missed a class?"

"Good."

"I've never slept with any of my students?"

"Not *yet* you haven't."

And with that, I found myself suddenly paralyzed by the vision of Clarissa Dale, wild-haired, raspberry-lipped, in a pleated tartan skirt, craning her head around my office door.

Professor Cavendish?

The effect was so erotic and so unlikely that the only possible response was to laugh. A minute later, I was still laughing.

"So," she said. "You *do* know."

"What?"

"The way to happy."

"Well, yeah," I said. "In sprints I get there."

I thought then of asking Clarissa for her own history, but I wasn't sure I wanted to know. Or, rather, it wasn't clear to me that knowing would be better than not knowing.

We walked on. And as we went, the path began to decant, and the air between the cedars and oaks whitened and deepened, and suddenly there were no trees, and we were standing on a margin of sand, staring

144

out across a gray seethe of water.

Roanoke Sound.

I'd first seen it as a child, but I couldn't remember it being so turbulent. Scalloped and dimpled and threshed by wind. No more than a few feet at its deepest point, but only a local would know that. An out-sider . . . well, hadn't Thomas Harriot run aground in this very channel?

"Harriot never married," I said.

"Well," said Clarissa, "just because he didn't marry doesn't mean he didn't love someone."

"No historical record of it."

"You said there's no record of his birthday, either. But he was born."

We stood there for some time, a couple of yards separating us. The wind blew in hard from the south, and a pair of seagulls blew in just as hard toward the east, flinging their cries over their shoulders.

"Look," said Clarissa, "I never told you this."

"Okay."

"This guy . . . whoever he is."

"The one in your head."

"In my *visions,* not my head. Okay, I'm trying to find some way of saying this that doesn't make me sound crazier than you already think I am."

"Go on," I said.

"He's in some truly — some unimaginable, unholy kind of *pain.* It's there in his face, it's in his body. It's . . . it's *entire.*"

"So." I was taking special care not to look at her. "He's trying to heal himself, is that it? All that stuff with the stones?"

"I don't know."

She picked up a pinecone. Tossed it into the sound.

"How did Thomas Harriot die?" she asked.

"Cancer. Believe me, you would have noticed. It started in his nose, spread to his mouth. He was pretty disfigured by the time he was done."

Retribution, I used to think (back when I believed in retribution). Not so much for using tobacco as for pushing it on his fellow countrymen. Between them, Harriot and Ralegh helped make England a nation of smokers.

"How old was he?" asked Clarissa.

"Sixty. Or sixty-one."

"And what year would that have been?"

"Sixteen twenty-one."

"What month?"

"July, I think."

"Oh," she said. "In my visions, it's September. Or maybe October. *Fall,* anyway."

She was quiet for a while. And then, out of the pure blue, she said:

"It's nice out here."

"Mm."

It was very possibly an accident: the grazing of her bare forearm against mine; the carbonation in our respective skins. I turned toward her, and I was all set to speak when from behind us came the sound of something *other,* a crackling in the rhododendrons and mulberries.

Wheeling about, I caught a shiver of white, or off-white. A sleeve, maybe . . . a pant leg . . . or maybe nothing. Whatever it was passed like a dream, but me — I could have been one of those first colonists from England, soldiering through the alien growth, every sense sprung wide open.

And then, from below, came a sound of today. Clarissa's Trio, chiming from her back pocket.

"Showtime," she said.

"Amory Swale?"

"And he wants to see us now. Or sooner. Actually," she said, lifting her eyes to mine, "the word he uses is *emergency.*"

14

Amory swale lived right off the ocean in a development called Tarheel Estates. The name did nothing to convey the condition of those wooden A-frames. Peeling whitewash and collapsed sashes, sagging clotheslines, heaps and heaps of dead sea rushes — every lot in the full bloom of decay, and none quite so blooming as Number 7, which looked to be atoning for being closest to the ocean. Three-foot chunks of tar paper had been ripped from its flanks, the original steps had been replaced with cinder blocks, and the front yard was a play box of cigarette butts, pulverized seashells, and charred cypress seedlings.

To look at the place, you'd have figured it long abandoned, were it not for the freshly painted sign that someone had attached to a pediment. Aqua letters on a white background: SWALE'S ANTIQUARIAN BOOKS AND PRINTS.

We stepped with some care onto the skeleton porch. Clarissa knocked gently, and the door, pockmarked with rot, swung right open, like the entrance to a dream.

"Mr. Swale?"

It was past seven now, and the sun was sinking to the other side of the sound, so the interior of the house was inky and humid. From somewhere in the back we heard a soft, tenacious sound, and then a man stepped from shadow into half shadow. The first thing we saw was his bare white feet, and then the rest of him swam into focus.

"Why, hello," he said, tendrils of Locust Valley still clinging to his vowels.

He was wearing a dove-gray suit, only just past its prime, and a tie full of swans, and his mouth had opened into a shy and inviting smile. But the total effect of him — the narrow shoulders and wide womanly hips — the filmy, oversized eyeglasses — the crest of gray hair, shrinking back from his skull in an arc of terror — was so strange I couldn't return the greeting.

"You must be Mr. Swale," said Clarissa.

"Some tea," he answered.

And back he went into the shadows, reemerging a few minutes later with a cracked ceramic pot, smothered in a rooster cozy, and a tray of china teacups, grimy around the rims but angel-white inside.

"Please," he said. "Sit down."

He gestured toward an antique chintz couch, upholstered in hunting scenes and stained in places with what looked like old cat vomit. (One of the back cushions had tipped forward, as though it were dozing.) There was no coffee table, so he had to place the cups and saucers in our laps and pour the tea straight in.

"I hope you had a nice trip. I've always thought this is the best time of year to come down, when all those wretched tourists have gone. Oh, I suppose you're tourists, too, but not really. No, I consider you friends, I hope that's not presumptuous. Sugar, Miss Dale? Be careful, last week, I gave a friend of mine kosher salt instead. She will never drink lapsang souchong again."

A bitter, tarry smell rose from our laps. I took one fast sip, then set the cup on the floor.

"Mr. Swale, sorry, but you mentioned an emergency."

"Yes, I should say there was."

"Maybe you could explain? Since you don't seem to be in any peril?"

He sucked in his lips. His eyes fluttered behind his glasses.

"I'm not sure it would be . . . just yet . . ."

"Mr. Swale." Clarissa craned toward him. "I can assure you, all right? We are people to be trusted. The three of us, we have something in common. We were the last people Alonzo Wax talked to before he died."

"I suppose so," he said, sounding half bored.

"*The School of Night is back in session.* Isn't that what he told you?"

"I suppose he did."

"We believe Alonzo's message may have had something to do with a document he acquired," said Clarissa. "A letter from Walter Ralegh to Thomas Harriot. We think he may have been killed over this letter."

"And unless we find it," I added, "we believe other people might be in danger, too."

"Funny thing," said Swale, blowing softly on his tea. "About danger, I mean. You don't always know it when you see it." A comb of gray teeth budded forth. "Do you remember, Mr. Cavendish, what happened when that first party of English explorers visited the Indian villages? You'll find it in Harriot's book. Within days of receiving their visitors, the villagers began dying. In droves. Nobody could explain it. These strange pale men in their iron carapaces. So helpless — so *hopeless* at the basic acts of survival — and capable of such slaughter. Without even lifting . . ."

He held his own finger to the light.

"They were carriers," I said.

"Of the empire virus, yes. But who would have guessed? And who can imagine what *we* might be carrying right now?"

Clarissa rose from the couch. "Mr. Swale, with all due respect, I would be happy on most any other occasion to talk history and viruses with you, but, two people being dead, this would be a good time, if I might suggest, to work with us here. And maybe start with what the hell's going on. Why did you want us down here?"

He gulped a cup or two of air. Gazed with wild eyes at his watch.

"Oh, Jiminy Cricket! I'll be right back."

We watched him labor up the steps, push open a door, and then close it behind him.

"Phew," said Clarissa, slumping back on the couch. "And you thought *I* was crazy."

"No, what's crazy are the books."

Which, because they were so very visible, were somehow the most invisible part of the house. But there they were, stack upon stack, rimed with dust, sprawling across the linoleum floor, straining toward the cracked-stucco ceiling, overwhelming whatever wood-veneer shelf had been tasked with confining them.

Hardbacks, most of them. Elderly thrillers, ancient how-to manuals, Reader's Digest condensed volumes, tips from long-dead golfers . . . at least five separate copies of *The Shoes of the Fisherman.* The more towering the book, the more obscure it was likely to be: *Modeling with Balsa, Taped Exercises for Basic and Intermediate Italian, Annual of the Rose Society of Ontario 1918.* Now and then a jewel might shine forth — a *Jane Eyre,* for example, with Gothic woodcuts — but nothing like an organizing principle. Only sticky-fingered compulsion.

But if Amory Swale had skimped on his stewardship, he hadn't quite abandoned it. The humidity, I noticed, was low, and the air was in the vicinity of sixty-seven degrees. Ideal conditions for the storing of books. Should there be any worth storing.

At the sound of footsteps, Clarissa and I folded our hands in our laps and composed our faces. My composure held even when it became clear that the man walking down the steps wasn't Amory Swale. Or anyone I had ever seen before.

He was big, like a frost-free freezer. A lumberjack's shirt and a shawl of beard, with paintlike splotches of gray. His waist was an indeterminate swell, and his tread was gentle inside ungentle, steel-capped workman's boots. It was when he stopped, though, on the bottommost step, and turned out the prow of his chin . . . it was then I knew him. That attitude of hieratic defiance, never to be snuffed out, no matter how deeply it was buried.

"I knew you'd come," said Alonzo Wax.

15

"Jesus," Clarissa whispered.

I watched Alonzo totter toward us. I saw the pickled line of his lip gleaming through the thatch of beard.

"Henry," he said.

The distance between us melted away, and before I understood what I was doing I had placed my hand in the center of his chest — I could feel his heartbeat pulsing between my fingers — and pushed him to the floor.

He fell comprehensively, limbs splayed like rubble across the dirty linoleum floor, tongue pushed out like a clapper.

I stared at him for a long moment. And then I walked out.

Not far, as it turned out. To Amory Swale's backyard, a tiny mesa of compacted sand, pocked with beer bottles and cigarette butts and an empty container of fuel additive and the remains of a basketball net. An old NO

PARKING sign flapped on a haggard stretch of chain-link fence. It was evening now, just beginning to shade into night. And through the shivering frame of pampas grass came a fragment of ocean, scaly-silver.

Even muffled in sand, his tread was unmistakable.

"Henry."

"Go away."

"I *did.*"

And when I turned around, his arms were raised to either side.

"No," I said. "That's not adequate, Alonzo. That's not sufficient. You could explain your way into next Tuesday, and it would come not even remotely *close* to atoning for what you've done."

"So I was mourned?" He wedged his boots in the sand. "Gee, I *hoped,* but —"

And then he looked up to see me advancing on him once more, swatting away his hand and leaning into him and breathing out the two words that were burning in my brain.

"Fuck . . . you."

Tottering backward, Alonzo steadied himself against an overturned garbage can.

"Henry," he said. "Knowing me as you do, please tell me. Would I have gone to all this trouble just to mess with you?"

"Oh. Oh, the *least* of it is me. If I may jog your memory, there's your family. You have, I believe, parents; you have a sister, remember? Not to *mention* Lily —"

"I know," he said. "I know about Lily."

"Then you know what reward she got. For all her years of service."

"Henry, you can't legitimately think —"

"No, *tell* me what to think. An hour ago, you were dead. Two days ago, Lily was alive. So tell me what to think."

"That I'd sooner have cut off my right arm than harm Lily. Or allow her to be harmed. You *know* that."

"You still ran off," I said, jerking away from him. "And you left her with your mess."

When I turned around again, he was sitting on that damned trash can, his head lolling slightly to one side, his strangely small feet weaving parabolas in the sand.

"Lily knew the consequences," he said.

"Oh, sure."

"Henry, she was in my confidence. Right from the start."

"So she lied for you."

"Of course."

"And her cousin. She lied for you, too."

"Joanna? Well, first of all, the paper got it wrong, she's a *step*-cousin. She'd been

157

estranged from Lily for, I don't know, millennia. Joanna needed money for plastic surgery — all her other sources were dried up, her ex-husband included — *so* . . . she called Lily."

"And Lily told her she could have the money if she pretended to see something that never happened."

"Something like that."

"And where is she now, this step-cousin?"

"In Cinque Terre. With her new neck. I hope she enjoys it; it cost me an original of Lyly's *Endimion*."

I thought then of Alonzo's vault, stripped bare of John Lyly and John Donne and John Stow and everybody else.

"Your books," I said, faintly.

"I know about them, too."

There were no chairs, so I dropped straight to the ground. Rested my elbows on my knees and raked my fingers across my skull.

"Why in hell would you want to fake your own death?" I asked.

"Henry," he said. "If I hadn't taken my own life, it would have been taken for me."

He stood up and beckoned me toward the house.

"Come. You'll hear all."

But I just sat there in the sand, feeling the

cold inch up my legs. And thinking, with a kind of aching wonder, that I could leave. Leave everything. Climb the dune . . . trundle down the beach . . . make straight for the sea.

I should say I had no intention of killing myself. (I'd abandoned those thoughts a long time ago.) No, it was escape I was after. I could very clearly imagine the cradle of the waves, the track of the moon, my skin flashing like a dolphin's. And yet here I was, ten minutes later, no closer to making it happen. What was keeping me?

The answer was already fastening me around. I'd never even seen it coming.

"Henry!" Alonzo's voice, like a cornet summons. "We don't have all night!"

Two bare forty-watt bulbs were burning now in Amory Swale's house, and moving through the pools of light was Clarissa, sweeping her broom like a censer.

"Here's what I don't get," I said. "What the hell made you think Bernard Styles was going to kill you?"

"What makes me think the sun will rise in the morning? It's done the same thing before, that's all."

"So Styles is some kind of serial killer? Just 'cause one poor guy in London got his book taken?"

"*One* poor guy? Oh, Jesus, Amory, tell him already."

And there was Amory. In an apron that read BBQ NAKED, carrying a plate of Milano cookies freshly sprung from a Pepperidge Farm bag.

"Alonzo's quite right, you know. It wasn't just Cornelius Snowden. There was that poor librarian in Philadelphia —"

"Maisie Hartzbrinck."

"Tossed under a bus. And where was the Ben Jonson's *Works* that was Maisie's pride and joy? Nowhere, that's where it was. And just last fall, that specialist in metaphysical poetry — University of Southampton — what was his name, Alonzo?"

"MacGrath."

"Wrote a paper on George Herbert that made grown men weep. Fell from the School of Humanities roof. Didn't jump . . . *fell*. And where was John Donne's letter to Sir George More of March the seventh, 1602? The one he kept locked in his credenza?"

With an emphatic smack, Swale set the plate on the floor.

"Gone. That's what it was."

"And in each case," said Alonzo, prying a cookie free, "Bernard Styles had offered to buy the book or manuscript in question. In each case, he'd been turned down. In *each* case, he was somewhere in the vicinity when the person died. Along with that mongrel goon of his."

With those words, the image of Halldor came wafting back once more. Standing at attention in the Union Station gallery. I strode to the window, thrust the sash up as far as it would go.

"Sorry," I said. "I just don't buy it. This is the stuff of dreams, this is — biblio-myth."

"Myth," said Alonzo, stiffly, "is not the same as a lie."

"Thank you, but if you really, truly feared for your life, why didn't you call the police?"

"The police?" he repeated, incredulous. "And tell them what? That a kindly, elderly British gentleman sent oblique threats in my direction? I wouldn't have gotten past the receptionist."

He swallowed the last fragment of cookie, methodically sucked each finger clean.

"Henry. I know you've talked to Styles."

"And how would you know that?"

"Lily told me, how else? No, don't explain, there's no need. I can't blame you in the least for taking his money — I'd have done the same in your shoes. But you have to understand who you're dealing with. Bernard Styles is a rotten scholar, he's a hack and a fraud, but he's a genius at leaving no traces. If he'd gotten around to killing me, no one would have been a jot the wiser. Kindly consider what happened to Lily. Do you honestly think she dropped a *lit* cigarette in a book vault? With her ungodly command of detail?" He gave his head two mighty shakes. "Never in a thousand lifetimes."

"Allegations aside," said Clarissa, propping her broom against the staircase. "From a strictly legal standpoint, Styles has a beef against you, Alonzo. You swiped his document."

"Easily half the books in his collection have been *swiped.* Now that he's got his mitts on mine, we can raise that estimate to two-thirds."

"But not the Ralegh letter," I said. "*That* he came by —"

"Don't." Alonzo put up a hand. "I forbid you to say 'fair and square.' You mean he didn't regale you with how he outwitted that poor backward law firm? Paid them probably a hundredth, a *thousandth,* of what the thing's worth? Gloating the whole time like a miser with his golden hoard. If you don't think that's thievery, Henry, if you don't think that's against every ethic of book collecting, then I resign my place in humanity's rolls."

"So that makes it okay for you to steal from him?"

"More than that, it lifts the whole enterprise into the category of sport."

I pictured Halldor. Lily. *Some sport.*

"So where is it?" asked Clarissa. "This precious document."

"It's right by Henry's elbow."

As if by sleight of hand, a hall table had materialized. Crescent-shaped, with a rose granite top that bore the pot prints of long-dead plants. A single article rested there: a FedEx envelope, svelte and reticent.

The World on Time.

I had to smile. The purloined letter . . . hiding in plain sight.

Less than a quarter-inch thick, that package, but it seemed to acquire dimension the longer I watched it.

"Go ahead," Alonzo said. "I'm sure you washed your hands at some point today."

"Doesn't he need gloves?" Clarissa whispered.

"Shush! Gloves tear. Go on, Henry."

I pulled the tab. I wormed my index finger into the opening, swiveling it softly in the darkness until it settled on something hard and ridgelike. An *edge,* recoiling ever so slightly at my touch.

Taking it now between my fingers, I gave it the barest breath of a tug.

It moved, grudgingly at first and then obligingly. A second later, it was free: a cerement of bubble wrap.

"Keep going," murmured Alonzo.

Moving more ruthlessly now, my fingers tore at the Scotch tape. The wrap parted to reveal two sheets of archival-quality mat board. These in turn fell away, and now there was nothing against my skin but the thing itself.

Other men give their hearts to vellum or parchment. Me, I'm a rag-paper man. Paper in its most brutish and plebeian form, fashioned from linen pulp. I love everything about it: its translucency, its frangibility, its ragged edges, its bruises and discolorations.

This particular paper had a hairlike fringe protruding to one side and a nick in its upper left corner and, just beneath, a pinwheel stain, umber and henna. And all its original creases! No more than an inch apart, for Elizabethans folded their letters into tight little bundles, like the notes you slip to a friend in eleventh-grade American history.

Hearing Alonzo's reproving cough, I carried the letter to the sofa and set it on the one cushion that seemed to be free of cat puke. And then we all gathered around it, kneeling like Druids before a hazel tree, and for the first time I was able to see beyond the paper itself to the words printed there.

In parlous Times, it is grete joye to
thincke vppon that homelie Schoole,
where wee were glad to gathere.

The School of Night, I thought. *Back in session.*

"So that's it?" asked Clarissa. "This is why Styles stole all your books? And killed Lily?"

"It's why he'll kill us all before he's done."

"But it's just a piece of paper."

"Just a . . . ," stuttered Amory Swale, "piece of —"

"I mean, how high can the market value be? The only people in the world who'd pay *top* dollar — well, they're practically all in this room, aren't they?"

"She's got a point," I said.

Throwing himself on the couch, Alonzo drew in a gallon of air.

"For the love of all that's holy. It's not the *front* of the document, it's the back."

"The . . ." Clarissa cocked her head. "You mean Ralegh wrote a P.S. or something?"

"A *pee . . . ess?* Yes, that's right. *Love you lots, write when you get a chance, hi to the folks.* Don't be absurd, what's on the back

165

is not a postscript. It's not even in Ralegh's handwriting. It's something infinitely more valuable."

"Like what?"

"Thomas Harriot's scratch paper."

Which was perhaps the last thing that either Clarissa or I was expecting to hear.

"Hold up," she said. "You're telling me Thomas Harriot used a letter from Sir Walter Ralegh to *scribble* on? Like it was some circular he got in the mail?"

"It makes sense," I allowed. "Paper was hard to come by in those days. Expensive, too. Any time Elizabethans found a stretch of white space — it could be the flip side of a tradesman's bill, it could be the blank leaves of a book — they filled it with words."

"But this isn't just any old white space," Clarissa protested. "This is a letter from one of the great men of the age."

"To Harriot, Ralegh's just another friend. Who's probably sent him dozens of letters over the years, so what's one more? Harriot was a practical guy, remember. If he needed paper, he'd just grab the nearest piece."

Clarissa uncrossed her arms, squared her shoulders.

"Well, in that case," she said, "let's turn it over."

Only no one would. Not at first. Even

Alonzo — who had long ago claimed owner-ship of that piece of paper — even he remained frozen in place. It was finally my own compulsion that drove me to put my fingers to the letter once more. To raise it in the air and invert it and let it float back to earth.

And there it lay. And nothing about it made sense anymore.

"What the hell is this?" I asked.

"You might consider it a puzzle," said Amory Swale in his perspiring voice. "Left behind by Master Harriot."

Taking care not to touch the paper, Cla-rissa leaned over my arm and drew an invis-ible circle around that strange cross on the left.

50'N

Maab's
Beastiary

Bridgett's
Stone

Marteo's
Lodge

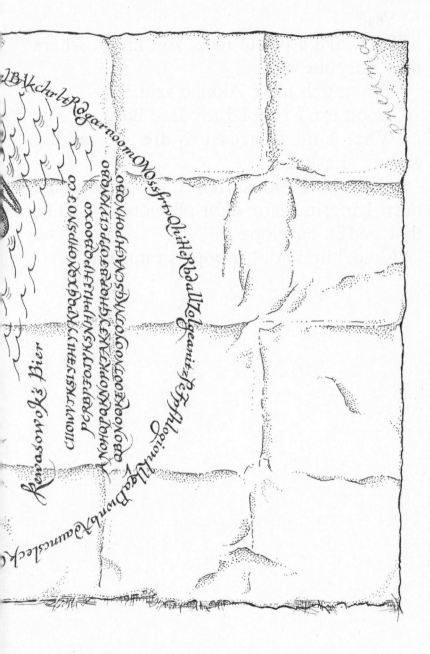

"Not to sound dumb or anything, but it looks —"

"Yes?"

"Well, like a pirate map. You know, where they bury the chest."

"Very much like," Alonzo said.

I stood up. I rubbed my face hard.

"What kind of treasure are we talking about?" I asked.

And to hear Alonzo tell it, the answer had been lying in plain sight all along, just like that FedEx envelope.

"Gold," he said. "A pope's ransom."

16

And the next words out of Alonzo's mouth were:

"Anyone up for dinner?"

So we left Amory Swale's shack and traveled a hundred yards inland to a strip mall, home to a Thai restaurant and a Fraternal Order of Eagles and, pressed inhospitably between them, a pub-and-billiards room, a darkly perspiring sort of place that seemed to swallow us the moment we walked in. We were shown at once to a banquette, and before another minute had passed, a young woman with proud and unsubjugated hair was asking us what we'd like to drink.

"A Pimm's Cup, if you please," said Alonzo.

"Um, I don't think we have those? But we've got more than fifty kinds of beer? And tonight? We have a special on PBR tallboys?"

His head lurched back.

"*Tall . . . boys?* Just get me a Ketel One on ice as soon as you can. And Amory, check the table; it looks viscous."

Alonzo had chosen strategically. Being a neighborhood dive, the place was thronged with locals, sun-seared and jocular and truculent, bent over nine-foot billiard tables and ranged around dartboards and foosball tables and pinball machines. The TVs were blaring ESPN, the music was strictly Nickelback, and the hum from the electronic smoke-eaters ensured that no one could hear our conversation.

"I don't think I mentioned," said Alonzo, "but my good friend Amory, among his other notable talents, is quite the authority on local Algonquin legends."

"Dear me, I don't know about that authority business, but I do follow them quite avidly. Now I'm not sure if Mattamuskeet is a name you're familiar with. They were the Indians who originally populated Hyde County, just south of here. I suppose we might begin our story in the year 1654, when a young English fur trader and his three companions ventured south from Virginia in a small rowboat, precious little in the way of defense."

Swale had added a violet foulard to his ensemble, and something violet had crept into his delivery, too. He lingered with such relish on the Tuscarora War and the decline of the Cacores that I was hunkering down for something Iliadic in length when he abruptly hurried to his point.

"You see, with the collapse of the Indian chiefdom, the Mattamuskeet people were gradually dispersed. Which is not to say *extinguished*, for many of them lingered on, intermarrying or self-segregating as needed. Thus, the oldest tribal legends were carried forward, often in undiluted form, across multiple generations. Maker's Mark? Thank you so much.

"Now, being orally transmitted, these legends often vary in their details. But one of them struck me with especial force. It concerned a white man, one of the first cohort of English settlers. This fellow apparently made quite an impression, for several reasons. First, he spoke the Algonquin language. *Most* unusual. Second, he came in peace and almost always came alone. And third . . . he was awash in gold."

Gasping, Swale took a swallow of whiskey.

"So much so," he continued, "that the white man was known as Weroance Wassador. Which translates roughly to King of the Bright Shining Metal. Many a chieftain's earrings came from this fellow. Gold ingots the size of rounceval peas, they say. Oh, and there's another curious aspect to the legend. This man asked for nothing in exchange but" — he began to rub the sides of his glass — "I suppose you'd call it information."

"What kind?" asked Clarissa.

"He wanted to know the names of things. What words they had for birds and trees. Where they hunted and fished. He wanted to hear about their gods, he wanted to know their *stories*. The Indians had never met a white man like this. Nor would they again for a very long time."

"This white man," said Alonzo. "His name has been passed down, too, hasn't it?"

"Oh, my, yes. *Ha-yot*."

Those two bare syllables seemed actually to reverberate before subsiding into silence. Swale grasped an onion ring, gave it a jeweler's squint.

"Well, now," he said, chewing around its periphery. "I'd been hearing this tale in one form or another for — oh, forever, I think, never imagining it to be based in actual history. And then one afternoon, I was attending an estate sale down in Ocracoke. Rather impoverished old gentleman, hard on his luck, but with deep roots in the area. Well, in the usual course of things, I bid a rather token sum on a box of —"

"Junk," suggested Alonzo.

Not entirely, Swale protested. For at the bottom of the box lay something completely unexpected. Not a set of chipped teacups or *Look* magazines, but a single pectoral cross. Four inches by two. Time-tarnished, closer now to amber than gold, but unmistakable in its provenance. The moment it touched Swale's hands, he knew what he had.

"And that's when I called Alonzo."

"Amory and I had it appraised, of course. Easily four hundred years old, as I suspected. Oh, but don't take *my* word for it."

From his jacket pocket came a small bundle in a white handkerchief. He placed it at the center of the table and peeled away each frond of silk.

"Please," he said, taking out a pocket magnifier and handing it to us. "Look."

My head lightly touched Clarissa's as we peered through the lens. I saw first three crudely carved letters at the cross's tip.

TEH

And, on the crossbar, another string of letters, half eroded but still legible:

MDLXXXVI

"Fifteen eighty-six," I murmured.

"The very year Thomas Harriot was on these shores," said Swale.

Clarissa sat back in the booth and stretched her pale arms behind her head.

"Okay, boys. Tell us how much this cross would fetch today."

"Given its provenance," Alonzo said, "up to ten thousand dollars at auction. Now please imagine that sum multiplied by a hundred. Five hundred, a *thousand.* This is the magnitude with which we're reckoning."

"Says who?" I said. "Come on now, it's a big leap from a gold cross to a stinkin' treasure chest. The etchings — I mean, who's to say when they were done? And the local legends — pardon me, they're so much noise. I hate to piss on your parade, Alonzo, but it's all kind of *thin.*"

"That's all right," he answered equably. "We can fatten it up."

"Except you've forgotten one little thing. There's not a word about gold in Harriot's *Report.* Or any of the other accounts of that expedition. I mean, if gold had come back to England from the New World? There'd have been another expedition on the next tide. The Lost Colony would never have been lost, you'd have had ten more colonies bringing up the rear."

"The gold didn't get back to England," said Alonzo. "It stayed right here."

17

"Amory," he declared. "Move the onion rings, would you?"

Reaching under the table, Alonzo pulled up a roll of newsprint, which he unfurled to reveal an enlarged second-generation copy of Harriot's map, daubed with yellow highlighter.

"Now if you all would oblige me by looking *here,*" he said. "Where somebody — Harriot, we presume — has drawn charming little curlicue waves. On what we may presume to be the easternmost edge of the map, since we lack a compass heading to tell us otherwise. We also find a drawing of a whale. Now wheeeere would Thomas Harriot have seen such a creature?"

With a wry smile, Clarissa raised her hand. "The Atlantic."

"An interesting idea. Now let's travel westward — *land*ward — to see if it can be borne out. We find these bizarre coordinates.

Places like . . ." His finger waltzed from point to point. "Manteo's Lodge . . . Bridgett's Stone . . . Kewasowok's Bier . . . These names simply didn't exist in England or anywhere else in Europe. Believe me, I've checked. Harriot can only have been talking about one particular corner of the world." He looked up and smiled. "The place he called Virginia."

"For all we know," I said, "the body of water could be the Irish Sea. Harriot did spend three years in Ireland, you know. The bier, the lodge — they could be anything, they could be nothing at all. It could all be some semielaborate joke."

"Your nearly metronomic predictability, Henry, is something I have missed. As you can *see*," he added, flipping the newsprint over, "I've taken the liberty of reprinting Harriot's own jottings. This is what he wrote just beneath the map."

CIIOWVTKSIYFHIYYKPQGXQNOHPSNOFCO
PCRBPFOJYKSNHPHLLHPQBOOXO
ANOHQPQKNOPKTAKFYGHQRBFOPPCIVKNQBO
QBONOQKEOOTNOOYOTNKGSCNACHPOHNQBO

"What is it?" asked Clarissa. "Some kind of code?"

"I admit I was expecting something rather

179

more sophisticated. What we have on our hands is a basic substitution cipher. Of a nearly *embarrassing* simplicity."

"Okay," she said. "Could you please embarrass me by explaining it?"

"Very well." He pulled out a sketch pad and a steel-tipped pen. "It boils down to this. Working from our regular alphabet, we create a substitution alphabet — simply by inserting a special key word. By way of example, let's choose *Henry*. Observe."

Regular alphabet	Substitution alphabet
A	H
B	E
C	N
D	R
E	Y

"As you can see, *A* becomes *H, B* becomes *E,* and so on. The rest of the alphabet changes accordingly."

Regular alphabet	Substitution alphabet
F	A
G	B
H	C
I/J	D
K . . .	F . . .

"How come you've doubled up I and J?" asked Clarissa.

"Because in the Elizabethan alphabet they were the same letter. Same with *U* and *V.* Very well, now, we've done our job, each letter in the original message now has a *substitute* letter, and the code flows very easily from there. Wherever you would normally write *A,* you write *H.* Wherever you'd write *F,* you write *A.* And so on. The task for the *decoder* is to figure out what that initial key word is.

"Now, the simplest thing to do is to use your own name. The trouble with Harriot's name — at least the way we spell it — is that it has a pair of repeated letters. Two *r's* won't work as well because you have to assign each *r* a different letter, which sows confusion. So I started looking at the *other* ways Harriot's name was spelled. And after some trial and error, I came up with this.

Regular alphabet	Substitution alphabet
A	H
B	E
C	R
D	Y
E	O
F	T

"From there, I just had to switch out the rest of the letters — making allowances, of course, for the fact that the Elizabethan alphabet had two fewer letters. By the way, Henry, you're welcome to try it, if you —"

"Go on."

"Well, once I'd done all *that,* the code was cracked. I had only to divide the letters into syntactical units and voilà!"

He turned the page over and pushed the pad toward us.

In New Found Land dost my treasure lie
Sich splendour as appalls the eye
Great stores of gold, matchlesse in
    worthe,
There to bee freede from Virginia's
    Earthe.

"New Found Land," said Alonzo. "That's straight from the title of Harriot's book. *Virginia's Earth.* We know where we are now, don't we? But what's *in* this blessed earth? *My treasure. Great stores of gold, matchlesse in worthe.*"

"Metaphor," I suggested.

"Don't be absurd. What was Harriot's whole purpose in coming here? To find natural wealth, minerals, tangible *things* that would give England a reason to take over

182

the neighborhood, yes? So I ask you: What's more tangible than gold? I grant you, if you look at the map or the cross or the old tales individually, they're thin gruel. But throw them all in the same pot and then toss in the *caramelizing* ingredient of Harriot's own words — well, I call that a meal. For kings."

I reached for my beer mug. Only to realize I'd drunk the whole thing.

"So Harriot the incorruptible," I said, "the guy Ralegh trusted with all his money. Stumbles on some massive trove of treasure and decides to keep it all for himself?"

"Let's just say he was laying in a store. For the future."

"Well, that's all very well," said Clarissa, taking a sip of her Heineken. "But it doesn't explain why he leaves the gold behind. What good would it do him buried *here?*"

"None at all," answered Alonzo. "Unless he intends to come back."

"And why would he?"

"Why would he *not?* Think about it. No one was a more valuable asset to the Crown than Harriot. He knew the local language, he knew the lay of the land, he'd charmed every chieftain in the region. They'd have been mad not to send him back."

"They didn't," I interjected.

"Oh, that's true," said Amory Swale, smiling fearfully. "But for reasons beyond anyone's control. England went to war with Spain, and the queen needed Ralegh, and Ralegh needed Harriot. The window of opportunity slammed shut."

"But where would Harriot have found gold in the first place?" Clarissa asked. "Carolina's very nice and all, but it ain't California."

"The gold didn't come by land," Alonzo explained. "It came by sea."

"Refills?" sang our waitress, hoving into view.

Alonzo turned his whole being toward her.

"How thoughtful of you. I *would* like a refill. And yet ranged against my own thirst is a touchingly archaic need for privacy. What an impasse! Here's what I suggest. Come back in exactly twelve minutes. And stamp very loudly when you come. I'm sure you can manage that, you strike me as highly adaptable. Bye-bye now."

He waved her away, then rolled up the newsprint and returned it to its home beneath the table.

"So tell me, kids," he said. "Other than *les frères Wright,* what are the Outer Banks best known for?"

"Wind," I said.

"Keep going."

"Storms."

"And . . ."

"Shipwrecks," answered Clarissa.

"Exactly. The Graveyard of the Atlantic. And if there's one thing the Atlantic had in those days, it was ships. Waiting to be buried."

It was the age of sail. Oceans swelled with square-masted cogs and carracks from Spain and France and Portugal, from Denmark and Sweden and the Dutch Republic, from Naples and Venice and Genoa, from Turkey and the Barbary Coast. A new boat on every tide, packed with settlers and traders and warriors and pirates and all the plundered wealth of the New World: spices, tobacco, gems, silver . . .

And gold.

"So your theory is what?" I asked. "Some Spanish galleon comes out of nowhere and hits a reef or a rock or a sandbar? Washes up at Harriot's feet? Isn't that a little improbable?"

"Not in the least," sniffed Alonzo. "Plenty of ships had already sunk here. Hundreds have done it since. Remember, they had no lighthouses, no accurate maps. This place was death to boats."

Clarissa leaned across the table. "But if some massive kind of shipwreck happened right off the Carolina coast, how come nobody but Harriot saw it?"

"Who was there to *see?* The whole colony had maybe a hundred men in it, and most of them were inland, defending their silly fort. Harriot was the only one with the freedom, the *job* description to roam. Miles and miles. Norfolk, Elizabeth City . . . he was there before any other white man. And for long stretches of time, we can assume he was functionally alone. Maybe he even preferred it that way."

"But we'd *know,*" said Clarissa. "A ship going down with all that treasure — there'd be some kind of record, right?"

Alonzo laid his hand over hers. "I'm going to excuse you on the grounds that you must be high. What kind of records do you think they kept in those days?"

"I don't know."

"And neither did they. In Bermuda, six hundred and some miles away, they're still peeling old wrecks off the reefs. None of them came with missing-ship reports. Whatever witnesses there were, Lord help them, went down with their ships. If Thomas Harriot had come across one of those wrecks, he'd have known it was finders keepers.

"To summarize," he said. "We have *geography* — a part of the world well-known for taking down grand ships. We have *opportunity* — a young Englishman roaming that same part of the world unescorted. And we have *testimony* — native accounts, a map, an encoded message in Harriot's own handwriting. *Great stores of gold, matchlesse in worthe.*"

He folded his hands together, leaned his elbows on the table.

"Ladies and gentlemen, I won't call it a slam dunk, but if you'll pardon me for torturing a metaphor, it's an easy layup."

This was the part where we were supposed to applaud, but my hands stayed right where they were.

"Oh, come on, Henry," he said. "Is there anyone in the world today who knows more about Harriot than you do? Is there anyone who can better unscramble his logic? You're the chosen one."

"Chosen for what?" I asked. And now I was looking at him straight on. "What exactly do you want from us, Alonzo?"

"What do I want? I want you all to help me find Harriot's treasure. And I want us to start now."

18

"And what if there's no treasure to be found?" I said.

"Then we won't find it."

"And what if we *do?*" Clarissa asked.

"You mean how do we split it up? Well, given that the venture is my brainchild, I might reasonably claim a slightly disproportionate share of the proceeds. Overcome as I am, however, by the spirit of the occasion, I am willing to waive my proprietary rights."

"Which means what?"

"We split it four ways."

"And when all this is over," said Clarissa, frowning, "you promise to shave that awful beard?"

"First thing. And head straight back to civilization. With the most persuasive amnesia story you've ever heard."

"And Bernard Styles gets his document back?"

"With my blessings."

Alonzo stopped and waited. Then, in a low and carefully uninflected voice, he asked:

"Are we all in?"

And as the seconds ticked away, I realized that everyone's eyes were fixed squarely on mine.

"So you're telling us you're going to find gold," I said. "Where no one else has ever found it."

"I mean to try. I mean to make history. How about you?"

I could hear the thump of pool balls against baize . . . the calliope sound of a pinball machine . . . Kid Rock singing . . . and, coursing beneath it all, the *basso continuo* of Alonzo Wax.

"Henry," he said. "For once in your life, avoid mediocrity."

It took me a second to absorb the blow. With great care, I slid out of the booth.

"Suck my dick."

I assumed I'd have the night to myself, but sharing the curb outside was a young redhead, taking angry hits off an unfiltered cigarette. Small but well-knit, with a wraparound jeans skirt I could very clearly imagine unpeeling. We stood there in silence, ten feet apart, rocking slightly in the wind.

"They stink, don't they?" she said.

"Sometimes," I allowed.

I would have said more, but my phone went off. I toyed with not answering, but then I saw the old familiar UNKNOWN, and the thought that Alonzo couldn't get off his fat ass and follow me was so deeply enraging that I didn't bother with a greeting.

"What?"

"You're a naughty puss," said Bernard Styles.

"I'm sorry?"

"Leaving town without telling us."

"Oh, yeah. Sorry. Family emergency . . ."

"And I've been so very curious to know how you're getting on."

"Significant progress is being made."

"I'll assume *you're* the person making the progress."

"Yes."

"One never knows with these passive-voice constructions. Well, then, it's beddy-bye for me. Halldor and I are off to see the Wright brothers' plane tomorrow."

"Their *plane?*" My brain lurched to a halt. "Where is the plane, exactly?"

"Why, the National Air and Space Museum, of course. On the National Mall." A long pause. "Where did you think I meant, Mr. Cavendish?"

"I got confused."

"But you're better now. And that's all that matters."

The redhead had gone inside, but I was still standing on the curb when the next call came. A Washington, D.C., exchange, unfamiliar to me, and a grainy, grudging voice, only slightly more familiar.

"This is Detective Acree, returning your call."

A call I'd placed six hours earlier. Before I knew that the guy everyone thought was dead was alive. And that people could be murdered for a book. And that a scientist born four hundred years ago could inspire people to plunder the wastes of North Carolina for a treasure chest that may never have existed.

"Mr. Cavendish?"

"Yeah, I just wanted you to know I'm in the Outer Banks on business. In case you thought I skipped town or something."

"So you haven't skipped town?"

"Well, no."

"Then I appreciate you telling me. Is there anything else?"

The cell phone was pulling away from my ear, inch by inch.

"Nothing," I said.

"Sorry, I didn't catch that."

"Nothing."

Alonzo was draining the last dregs of his vodka, and Amory Swale was twirling an onion ring around his finger like a tiny hula hoop, and Clarissa was rubbing the kinks out of her eyebrow muscles.

"I'm in," I said.

"Very well," said Alonzo. And then he glanced at his watch. "Ten twenty-three. The School of Night has begun."

19

On February 20, Margaret Crookenshanks, twenty-two, a scullery maid at Syon House, is summoned to the steward's quarters.

—You wished to see me, sir?

The steward is nobody too important in social terms — a poor and distant relation of the Earl of Northumberland — but he has a proud bearing and the snowy ruff of an officer of horse and a monarch's habit of speaking in first person plural.

— On the morrow, we desire that you apply yourself to a new position.

— Sir?

— Master Harriot requires an assistant housekeeper.

— Master Harriot, sir?

—Yes.

— At what time am I expected, sir?

— Cock's crow. Do not be late or unkempt.

—Yes, sir.

— You are to lodge there as well. Kindly bring your clothes and possessions. Any further questions may be addressed to Mr. Golliver, Master Harriot's butler, or to Mrs. Golliver, the housekeeper.

— Yes, sir.

Margaret is sketching out the beginning of a curtsy when a thought stops her.

— If I might, sir. Who is Master Harriot?

— We are happy to say he is a gentleman of excellence and quality. He undertakes experiments and is ever learning.

And at once, she knows who it is.

On her second day at Syon House — a December afternoon — she was carrying a tub of lather and grit down to the river when she looked up to see a gentleman of no certain years in a black cloak. Standing on the roof of his cottage, just above the eave, and holding what looked to be two musket balls, of differing sizes.

At some inaudible signal, his fingers sprang apart, and the balls dropped in unison. And here was the most remarkable thing: Someone was waiting for them below. A boy (one of the trebles from the chapel choir, she later learned) was lying on his side, his left eye flush to the ground, watching each pair of balls land.

— The same time, sir!

— Are you quite sure?

— Yes, sir.

They repeated the exercise at least three times, with identical results.

— The same, sir!

It was a source of great wonder to see labor like this. So divorced from the workings of a manor. So close to pastime. So near to joy.

The steward is rumored to be omniscient, and he does seem to divine the tenor of Margaret's thoughts.

— To speak in the vernacular, Master Harriot is a queer badger. But no danger to a young girl, you may depend on that. Even if our own daughter were to work there, we should sleep well at night.

The steward has no children, but his tone carries conviction.

— My duties, sir?

— You shall be duly advised. You are obliged, however, by entreaty of Her Ladyship, to heed one stricture above any other. Master Harriot requires silence. He will put up with a great many things, but he must have his quiet, mustn't he?

This is so impressed into Margaret's brain that, before knocking on the back door of

Harriot's house, she removes her leather shoes. Only to be reproved for it by Mrs. Golliver.

— What sort of girl walks about in her stocking feet? Why, Mr. Golliver, they've sent us a blue jay.

— Bit of a sloven, too.

— Small wonder! Coming from the scullery . . .

Like many long-married couples, the Gollivers have formed a joint edifice against the world, which threatens at any moment to fissure under private stresses. The husband is bald and ginger-bearded, with a bent, obdurate bulk, like something coaxed away from pasture. Mrs. Golliver is sweaty and blanched, with a bargelike shelf of stomach and an underbite and the appraising air of a hog butcher.

— You're pretty enough, I suppose. Not that *he* shall notice.

The Gollivers take great care to tell her all the things she may not do. These include speaking unless spoken to, retiring before anyone else, awakening after anyone else. Entertaining visitors, male or female. Missing chapel. Whining, protesting, answering back. Asking questions.

— And mark me well, my girl. (Mrs. Golliver's goiterish eyes become strangely radiant.) You are *not* to go near the master.

If he enters a room in which she is working, she is to leave at once. If he requests something within her hearing, she is to convey the request at once to Mr. or Mrs. Golliver. At no time is she to meet the master's eye or engage him in talk or touch a single of his belongings. Failure to obey any of these strictures will be cause for instant dismissal.

Mrs. Golliver reveals the places where her teeth used to be.

— You don't want to end up like Jane, do you?

Only later will Margaret learn who Jane was: the *previous* assistant housekeeper. Who, having concealed her condition for seven months, was obliged in January to confess she was with child.

The father was swiftly located: a stool maker from Richmond who had met the young woman once, at a bonfire. A marriage bond was drafted, the obligatory banns were reduced from three to one, and a week later, staggering with child, Jane Jasper became Jane Fitzwilliam.

— She started going astray in a small way, says Mrs. Golliver. — A missed stitch here. A dropped pail there. A voice raised beyond what was pleasing. Before we could stop it, she was spreading her legs for the first man what asked. *Don't you be like Jane.*

Each morning, Margaret is up at five, with the milkmaids. The cold wraps her around from the moment she rises and follows her through the house, lapping at her petticoat as she scoops out last night's ashes and lights the coal fires and then cleans and blacks the master's boots and fetches water.

After breakfast, she makes the beds and cleans the chamber pots and sweeps the floor and beats the rugs and stuffs the pallets with new hay. She works through the afternoon and the early evening, baking bread, churning butter, washing and pressing clothes, scrubbing floors, scouring plates and silver and Mrs. Golliver's cooking pots with hartshorn paste.

She takes her dinner alone in the attic: barley bread, with a piece of bacon or pork; ox cheeks every Sunday. She sleeps up there, too, on a truckle bed, her bones smoldering from weariness. There is but one window, so the darkness is utter (except for a single candle stub in a sconce). She doesn't mind. It frees her from having to look at her hands, which were once lovely.

Her glimpses of the master are few: a flash

of black on the stairs, a low voice in the next room. She comes to know him only at second hand. His unmade bed, for instance, with its man-prints, its man-smell. His boots, waiting for her by the hearth every morning. His clothes, nearly shocking in their sameness. Black cloaks, black shirts, black doublets, black hose . . . and white ruffs, which are always limp because he dislikes the scratch of starch against his neck.

Once a week, in warmer weather, she hangs the clothes on a line and beats them with a badler, and out come the scents of pomander and cloves, of anise seed and sulfur . . . and something beyond her power to name, bitter and smoky and mellow.

She smells it again while she's changing the bed linens and, after some searching, traces it to a trail of brown leaves, drying on a windowsill. They look like the shavings you'd find inside a doll. She takes up one of the leaves, rests it on her tongue, and is astonished to feel the tingle pass all the way to the back of her head.

The very next evening, lying abed, still too sore for sleep, she smells it again, spilling like a dream through her half-open window. Rising, she wraps her coverlet around her and looks out.

He is in the courtyard directly below her, sitting on an overturned cheese bucket with a clay pipe hanging off his lip. From this pipe a watery column of smoke pushes toward the night sky. She reaches out her hand and feels it wreathing around her, curing her skin.

The next thing she knows, the pipe is on the ground, and the master's head has toppled into his hands, and his whole frame is shaking and smoking, in the premonitory way of a volcano. No eruption, though. Just a slowly gathering stillness.

The next morning she can still smell the tobacco on her arm.

The steward comes twice a week, at unscheduled times, to inspect her work. He speaks in deep and sorrowing cadences.

— There is a large quantity of ash in the parlor hearth. Crumbs as well on the pantry floor. The napkins are dingy, the ewer spotted. We regret to say we saw a distinct bootprint on the hall floor. . . .

The Gollivers take up wherever he leaves off. In Margaret, they have found the common cause that allows them to forget, for minutes altogether, their grievances against each other.

— She calls that a seam, does she?

200

— Clumsy! You'd think she had two left hands.

— I wonder when she'll fill the master's water pitcher. Michaelmas, do you think?

And when they can't find anything particular to catch her out on, they fall back on prophesy.

— She'll turn out just like Jane, I expect.

How wide the gibe misses its mark, for Margaret has long ceased to think of Jane as an example to avoid. Jane has jumped the wall. She has a husband, a child . . . a future. A young woman could do worse than Jane.

One Thursday in April, Mrs. Golliver takes ill with one of her stomach pains. She writhes on her bed, biting her pillow to stifle the cries. Having applied a henbane poultice to no effect, Mr. Golliver despairs of her and, with a wild straggling eye, calls out to Margaret.

— Here! Go and dust the laboratorium. Quick about it! And come straight back!

Laboratorium. Such a rich strange word and such a small mean room. Two joint stools. Three chests for papers. One plain, rough working table. No rug or cushion or wall hanging. And no clear place to begin cleaning.

Vaguely she waves her duster among the pewter vessels and pots, the rods and bronze disks and magnifying lenses, the used-up goose quills, the dried inkwells. A sea of objects, islanded with paper.

And here is the question she will never be able to answer: Why does she pause over *this* particular paper?

There is nothing remarkable in its appearance: its blots of ink, its scabs of grease and wax. It is a table, no more. Names and figures.

Cyprium	*2.43*
Adamas	*2.42*
Sapphir	*1.76*
Krystallos	*2.00*
Rubeus	*1.76*
Achates	*1.54*
Mel	*1.49*

What stops her, finally, are the words scratched across the top of the paper.

Problema: Datis fractionibus ab aere ad aqua et ab aere ad vitrum: fractionem ab aqua ad vitrum invenire.

Her eyes sift out the words, and her lips form around them.

Aere . . . aqua . . . vitrum.

And from some dark well, the meanings drop onto her mind's slate.

Air . . . water . . . glass.

And with that, the old music rushes back. A sound so thrilling and sad she stands there in a daze, outside time. Only to be called back by a rustle of black at the edge of her vision.

The master.

Sitting on one of his hard oaken chairs, a paper spread across his lap.

How did she fail to see him? Was it the spell of the words themselves?

She knows the rules. *Do not speak. Leave at once. Report directly.* Something about him, though, won't let her.

She tries to speak, to explain herself. *Mrs. Golliver . . . she's ill. . . .* The words won't come, nor will the curtsy. It is fear at last that sends her rushing blindly from the room.

She is nearly out of the house when he calls after her. And the words are the more dreadful because they are the first he's ever addressed to her. They seem to thunder in her ears.

— *Can you read?*

20

Margaret Crookenshanks *can* read.

She owes this to two quirks of fate. Her father loved books, and her father lacked sons.

When Margaret's older sister proved unsuited to word magic, Margaret happily took up the hornbook. Lifted its transparent sheet and gazed at those strange, pregnant symbols.

Aa . . . Bb . . . Cc . . .

The Lord's Prayer was the first thing she learned to read. *Sang* it, to hear her father tell it, as if the words were dancing straight off her tongue.

After that, her days were peopled with Tom Thumb and Dick Whittington and Robin Hood and King Arthur. And when the time came for more serious reading, her father guided her through the Geneva Bible and Foxe's *Book of Martyrs*. And when he saw her passion rise to each new challenge, he guided her through the maze of Latin.

Nominative and genitive and dative and accusative. Tenses and moods and persons and voices and aspects. She read Lily's grammar and then crawled, line by line, through Cicero and Terence, through the *Eclogues* and the *Metamorphoses* and the *Commentaries* of Caesar, through Horace and Tully and Lucretius.

Sometimes, in the midst of reading, she would become aware of her own breath steaming the pages, and it would seem to her then that she'd wandered (of her own will) into a greenhouse, warmed by word-light, and cooled by her father's firm cadences.

— Try again, Margaret.

On the way home from his shop, Mr. Crookenshanks sometimes veered over to the west door of St. Paul's and bought her a volume of love sonnets. *With how sad steps, O moon! . . . Come sleep, O sleep! . . . Leave me, O Love! . . . One day I write her name upon the sand. . . . Since there's no help, come, let us kiss and part. . . .*

Mrs. Crookenshanks couldn't read, but she understood the radiance that took hold of her daughter in these moments, the way her lips parted to receive each offering.

205

— Put them away! At once!

Margaret was old enough now to grasp that she was both cause and captive in her parents' war and that the only way to safety was through the very books her mother hated.

When Margaret turned twelve, her father took the unprecedented step of teaching her how to write. Mrs. Crookenshanks, who could do no more than make her mark, received this as a direct blow.

— She shall be unfit for work or marriage!

One afternoon, Margaret found her frowning down at a sheet of her daughter's scribblings.

— Mother?

Mrs. Crookenshanks swung her face away, but not quickly enough, for her daughter could see the film that lay across her eyes.

Two weeks after Margaret's fourteenth birthday, Mr. Crookenshanks's hosiery shop burned to the ground. There was no capital to rebuild, so he tried selling his apparel on the streets, but he had no stomach for the work or for the city air. He took to bed earlier and earlier — there was no longer time to read — and shortly after Advent he took ill with indecent haste. He died in his bed two days later, an ivory crucifix lolling from his wasted neck.

The next morning, Mrs. Crookenshanks took all of Margaret's volumes — her Ovid, her Tully, her Montaigne, her Astrophel and Stella — and tossed them into a sack and sold them to a book dealer.

— No need for these any longer, said Mrs. Crookenshanks.

She was merely being practical. Her husband's debts had blighted any hope of dowries or advancement for her daughters. The family's task now was to survive.

At the age of fifteen, Margaret Crookenshanks went into service. A cousin got her a job making hay in the Lambeth fields. She wore a red stammel petticoat and a vast straw hat, and sneezed a dozen times a day. In the autumn, she hired on as a milkmaid, but her shoulders weren't stout enough for the pails, and after her third tumble she was discharged.

She made malt; she cleaned chapels; she picked oakum. On good weeks, she made sixpence; other weeks, none. Most days, she got by on a single meal. In still moments, she could actually feel the weight dropping from her, ounce by ounce — except for her bones, which became impossibly dense.

In the summer, she took ill with goat fever. Lay in her bed, sweating out whatever was left in her. Her mother nursed her, and when Margaret was ready to stand, it was Mrs. Crookenshanks who was ready with the tidings. An old friend of her father's had arranged for her to journey to the Isleworth fair to meet the comptroller of Syon House.

— Imagine it, Margaret! The Earl of Northumberland!

Her hands were still pretty then, and to make her color richer, she walked for an hour before her interview. She kept her voice low and her eyes lower. She was engaged on the spot.

Five years have passed, and Margaret Crookenshanks is still an apprentice, but come next spring, she hopes to earn a wage. Thirty shillings per annum, if she's lucky.

She keeps no books. She would not read them if she did.

This is the kindling into which Master Harriot, without meaning to, tossed his spark. Margaret Crookenshanks *can* read, and from the start it has been her undoing.

Will it be so once more? Surely, Master Harriot, outraged by her intrusion, will convey his feelings to the Gollivers. Tomorrow morning, Mrs. Golliver, pleased to have her dire predictions confirmed, will take away her livery and send her on her way, not a penny in her purse.

She rises at five the next morning, goes about her appointed rounds with a doomful tread. Stooping to scrub the soot from the hearth, she hears from behind her the loping step of Mrs. Golliver, roused from her sickbed. Closing her eyes, Margaret steels herself for what is to come.

And is startled to feel not a slap or a box but a tickle. In the vicinity of her left ankle.

— Beastly girl! You left it behind you.

She stares down at the top of an old cotton stocking. Her cleaning rag.

— The master had to bring it himself.

She cannot at first credit her own reprieve. But the morning wears on, and her bones ache in all the old ways, and the Gollivers snarl at each other just as they have always done. By noon, she is sufficiently lulled that when the door of the north parlor opens behind her she doesn't even turn her head.

Then she hears the clearing of throat. A sound far too discreet to be made by a Golliver.

It is the master. Dressed as usual in a plain black gown, a skullcap pressed over his short-cropped hair.

— I pray your pardon, he says. — I appear to have frightened you.

He smiles then. Or, rather, he gives it his very best effort, but his teeth, fine and even and only slightly gray, scurry back into the safety of his mouth.

— I do have a way of going unnoticed, he tells her. — Or else *too* noticed. I can't seem to find the golden mean.

She does not hear the apology in his voice, she is too busy making her own amends.

— Oh, sir. I am so very sorry. I meant nothing. I was putting things tidy. Please don't speak to Mrs. Golliver.

— But I *have* spoken. That is to say, I have returned your rag.

And still she cannot bring herself to look him in the eye.

— I feared I might have offended, sir.

— But why?

— I am not to touch your things, sir. It is strictly forbidden; it is a rule.

— I am not at all sure I know these rules myself. It seems to me someone might do me the favor of elucidating them. Hold a bit. Is that why it's so deathly quiet in this house?

— Yes, sir. That's the first rule of all.

— Ahh.

He takes a single step into the parlor.

Briefly considers whether or not to step back.

— May I ask. Have you been working here long?

— Three weeks, sir.

— There was another girl, wasn't there?

— Yes, sir. Jane. She has gone and married.

— Has she?

He considers this news. Then:

— And *your* name . . .

— Margaret.

— From London, by the sound of you.

— Yes, sir.

He nods, three or four times. He attempts to smile.

— Well, then, my name is Harriot.

— Yes, sir, I know.

— Oh, of course. They must have said as much.

The faintest streaks of color along his cheekbones.

— It is a pleasure to make your acquaintance, Margaret.

— I thank you, sir.

— There we are.

Raising his hand in a gesture of farewell, he stares, as if for the first time, at the paper tweezed between his fingers. Clearing his throat once more, he drops the paper on the trestle table.

She doesn't recognize it at first. Then the Latin flashes on her eye.

—You, you may take it if you wish.

—Take it, sir?

— I am occupied with other business at present. It occurred to me you might wish to peruse it. At your leisure, I mean.

At her leisure.

— I thank you, sir.

— It's in Latin, of course.

—Yes.

— I did not know if you could —

— I can, sir. A bit.

He doesn't smile, exactly. His lips enact a kind of wincing motion, which, under the circumstances, is not altogether unpleasant.

—Very well. Bring it back tomorrow, then. If that be satisfactory.

—Yes, sir.

The only trick is concealing the page from the Gollivers. She tucks it inside her stomacher, and only late at night, an hour after everyone else has retired, does she dare to withdraw it. She lays it out across her pallet and studies it by candlelight, taking the greatest care not to drip wax. She reads like a fugitive.

The next day, she makes sure to station

herself in the parlor by noon. She is ready for him this time.

— I beg you to forgive me, sir. I was not much for following. Not the whole way.

His lips are thin but not cold.

— Tell me where you faltered.

— Oh.

Stiff as whalebone, she sets the paper on the table.

— *From air to water . . .* that line is quite simple. *From air to glass, from water to glass.* All well, but then comes the *fractio*—

— *Fractionibis.*

— That is the one. I take it to be some sort of fraction. . . .

— Yes, I am guilty of shorthand. The fraction in question is the refractive index.

— And please, sir, what is that?

— Oh. Well, now. When light — when it is met by some other substance — a transparent medium, let us say, on the order of glass or, or water — well, then it will be *bent* at a particular angle. The refractive index is simply a way of measuring the degree to which a particular substance bends, or refracts, light. Forgive me. I fear I have been obscure.

— Oh, no, sir, I was merely thinking how strange it is.

— Strange.

— Why, that light should bend at all.

— Nothing strange about it. You have seen a rainbow, have you not? That is merely the effect of light being *bent,* as it were, into its constituent lights. Similarly, if one were to poke a stick into a pond, why, the stick would — it would appear to *bend* suddenly at the point where it breaks the pond's surface. This, of course, is no more than an optical illusion brought about by the agency of, of *refraction.*

She nods. She tells herself it is time to go. And then, to her own great shock, she hears herself speak again.

— And how could one even measure such a thing?

— Well, yes, that strikes at a most interesting question. Through experimentation, I have ascertained a rather persuasive correlation between the, the angle of *incidence* — that is, the angle at which the light converges with the other object — and the angle of *refraction* — that is, the emerging ray. Divide the sine of the first angle by the sine of the second, why, then, the quotient is the refractive index. At least so far as I have been able to calculate.

Her fingers lightly stroke the paper.

— So all these figures, sir. They are the refractive indices?

— For different media, yes. You can surely translate the Latin. There is glass and crystal and marble. Rubies. Copper ore. Even brimstone! The devil, it seems, has a devilishly dark time of it down there.

He chuckles. Then, fearing he has overstepped, falls silent. She, too, is quiet for a long while before gathering up her nerve.

— Please, sir. Why do you care to know all this?

The question catches him squarely in his middle and pumps out a gasp of air.

— Why do I . . . well, now, I would not confess this to just anybody, but I subscribe to the, the school of *Democritus,* which holds matter to be composed of entities called *atoms.* These entities are believed to be both, erm, indivisible and indestructible. And, by their very nature, far too minute to be observed by the naked eye. That is where light proves itself such an unsurpassable gift to the human mind, for it can disclose to us the structure that lies beneath the surface of all things. The more light we shine into these manifold substances, the more they reveal their innermost natures and the closer we come to the nature of . . .

His own words jar him to a stop. He laces his hands together and, in a low judicial tone, concludes.

— Well, the nature of life itself. If that coheres into any sort of sense . . .

— Yes, sir, it does. I consider it to be most grand and noble.

At once she regrets the words. *Grand . . . noble . . .* how paltry do they sound alongside the world he has just revealed to her. Light. Atoms. *Life.*

— My object, Margaret — and I do delude myself into believing I have one — is to devise a mathematical relationship between the three variables. By which I mean density and molecular structure and refractive index. And in so doing to — oh, dear, I fear I've grown confoundedly tedious. I must apologize, I was so enjoying our little interview.

— No, sir, the pleasure has been mine. The *honor.* Truly.

— Oh.

He draws away. Scratches a patch along his jaw.

— I don't know about honor.

She understands then. Flattery is a kind of grief to him.

— Margaret.

— Yes, sir?

— Would you care to *observe* some of the work in question? At closer quarters?

— Observe, sir?

— It so falls that tomorrow afternoon I shall be taking the measure of *amber.* If you should choose to be a fly on the wall, I should not at all be put out. Oh, God's wounds, such a look. Am I breaking another rule?

— I fear so, sir.

His lips coil into a knot. And then, *ex nihilo,* a thought flies up.

— Perhaps I might speak to Mrs. Golliver about it! I cannot see how she could protest overmuch. A ten-minute respite from your diurnal rounds, no great harm, is there?

Margaret scarcely knows what to say. Mrs. Golliver *will* protest. She will protest very loudly. And yet it is the master proposing it. Who can gainsay him?

— Sir, I should be . . . whatsoever you see fit to . . .

— Then let us propose three in the afternoon. In my laboratory.

And now that there are coordinates attached to it — a time, a place — his plan grows the more fearsome in her eyes. And she the more powerless before it. The words spill from her like a sentence of doom.

— As you wish, sir.

21

And what of that earlier school? The one Alonzo Wax and I had formed in college all those years ago?

We never did declare a formal halt to it, but as the spring of our freshman year wore down, we saw less and less of each other. We both put a brave face on things, but we knew the real truant was me, and I was no less puzzled than Alonzo. Did I have any place better to be? A more generous or loyal friend? A better curriculum than reading poetry, arguing philosophy, and getting high?

Alonzo never demanded all my time or cordoned me off from my other friends. His interest in men was widely assumed, but he never did anything so crass as make a pass at me. And still I could feel the itch of something unconsummated in our time together. I began to invent reasons for not showing up, and sometimes I didn't bother with reasons. And Alonzo, whose vision of himself had once seemed so impregnable, grew more and more fretful and querulous, like a teacher whose class has slipped out behind his back.

By fall, I'd managed to acquire a girlfriend, a poli-sci major from Austin with a gorgeous sulk, and Alonzo had discovered Kenneth Martineau, heir to a cardboard-box fortune. Their relationship began as platonic and, even at its most passionate, would never have qualified as torrid, but Kenneth had a weakness for shock effects and, on the anniversary of his mother's death, announced he was dedicating his life to Alonzo. The rest of Kenneth's family issued threats and recriminations, and when all the debris was cleared off, Kenneth had cleared off, too. To La Jolla, where he became muse and patron to a found-object constructivist.

As for Alonzo, he quit before the semester was done. But he made a point of keeping in touch, and out of guilt and, yes, residual affection, I answered in kind. Our school may have ceased, but it never really shut its doors.

And now we were once more matriculants, gathering each morning in Amory Swale's shack. (Amory himself was sent on errands.)

That first morning, I brought a plastic thermos of coffee and a pint of orange juice and some harvest muffins and a dozen and a half bagels, which Alonzo dove into like a refugee. "I've been — sorry — I've been thinking over how the work should be divided. For now . . ." He licked the last residue of crumbs from his lip. "I'm thinking Amory and I will handle the fieldwork. Combing through old sources, consulting authorities, doing site inspections . . . whatever it takes to reconstruct Harriot's tracks. You and Clarissa —"

"Yes?"

And then he showed me the wheel.

I'd missed it in my first perusal. A ring of letters, minuscule in size, circling the map like a globe. Alonzo, working with a magnifier, had come up with a clockwise sequence.

PsjAYStrooxeidDVegaLOkuxTmLikcy
CUsSxGAzyrnrmuOrrLBAkchrltRdga
rnoomONOssfrtvQhiHeRbdallZolgean
itzPeFpfhlogionLlLqaBwnbAdauncsle
ckQooTiatGlgKIkiWfleatHEstRqiabaOt
zKCdMCpnfeffkuv

"This is the map's legend," said Alonzo. "I'm convinced of it. If we crack the wheel, we crack the map."

By now my coffee was cold enough to stir with my finger.

"Just so you know," I said. "I'm not a cryptologist."

"Never fear, Clarissa's a whiz with computers. What I want *you* to do is provide the frame of reference. Look for phrases, names, words. Anything you can tie to the man or the period, jump on it like a loose penny."

He gave his belly a Falstaffian pat and, with just the driest particle of mischief in his voice, said:

"By the way, Henry, I enjoyed your eulogy."

I put down my muffin. I looked right into his irises.

"Oh, God."

For what, after all, was my most indelible memory of Alonzo's memorial service? Lily Pentzler muttering into her sleeve like a madwoman.

"My God, you had Lily wired," I said. "She was *livecasting* your fucking funeral."

"And it was all very touching, Henry. You weren't sentimental, which you know I abhor. Oh, but tell me what you think of Clarissa."

"Um . . ." I made a gesture to the ceiling. "She's game."

Alonzo roared. "Why don't you just go ahead and say she's *yar?*"

"Well, I don't know. Do *you* believe Thomas Harriot comes to visit her every night?"

"I believe that's what she's seeing, yes. I believe these visions are coming from someplace that's not her."

"Because she coughed up some Latin."

"Because she doesn't *want* them to come. Because she wishes like hell they'd go away."

"Schizophrenics wish the same thing."

And even as I said that, I was recalling how I'd left Clarissa that morning. In the hotel's common room, sitting on a cane-bottom chair, bowed over a single croissant, her eyes almost glaucomic when she lifted them to mine.

"And another thing," I said. "Why is she here in the first place? An attractive young woman like that, she must have surer bets elsewhere."

"People go where they need to be," said Alonzo, draining the last drop of orange juice straight from the carton. "Don't you think, Henry?"

A good question. Was *I* where I needed to be?

I was the last person in the world who

expected us to find gold. But the fact remained that twice in the last twenty-four hours I'd had the chance to leave, and it wasn't Thomas Harriot who'd kept me here. And knowing this, the pink masonry of the Pelican Arms filled me with a certain alarm as I approached. Clarissa was on the ocean-side veranda, her eyes closed, her hair breeze-fraught, wearing her canary-yellow sundress, which looked preposterous against the sad gray cushions. Her toenails had been painted — beefsteak red — and I admit I was briefly seized by the prospect of chewing on them.

"We've got a job," I said.

And so she seated herself in the room's lone armchair, fired up her Mac Notebook and set to work with a vengeance. Oh she took an occasional bathroom break, an occasional stretch, a swig of iced tea, but no diversion lasted longer than a minute, and then she went straight back to her decryption programs.

Me, I took out a legal pad on my lap and scribbled down every name I could associate with Harriot. Ralegh and Percy and Marlowe and Chapman and all the reputed members of the School. Richard Hakluyt, Harriot's geography instructor. Thomas Allen, Harriot's mathematics instructor.

Kepler, Harriot's correspondent. Galileo, Harriot's rival. And Bruno and Brahe and Roger Bacon. And John Dee and George Ripley and Avicenna.

All of Harriot's friends and all his equally numerous foes. The Earl of Essex, Percy's brother-in-law. Robert Cecil, chief adviser to both Queen Elizabeth and King James. Anthony à Wood, who accused Harriot of having "strange thoughts of the Scriptures" and casting off the Old Testament. Father Robert Parsons, the Jesuit priest who said Harriot taught young gentlemen to jeer at Moses and Jesus. Nicholas Jefferys, who said Harriot had denied "the resurrection of the body." Chief Justice Popham, who, in sentencing Ralegh to death, urged him to wrest himself free of "that devil Harriot."

Then I started compiling place-names. Clifton, where Harriot's father may once have worked as a blacksmith. Oxford and St. Mary Hall, where Harriot matriculated at the age of seventeen. Sherborne Castle, where the School of Night would probably have met. Durham House, Ralegh's London estate. Molanna Abbey, Ralegh's Irish estate. Various stations on the way to America: Plymouth and Puerto Rico and Hispaniola and Wococon.

Name after name, each one canceling the

one before, none more promising than any other. It was, in fact, a perverse comfort that Clarissa was making no better progress than I was. By now, she'd established that the letter string wasn't a substitution cipher or an algorithm. But no matter what terms she fed into her decryption engines, the result was only more abstraction.

We worked through lunch and the rest of the afternoon, and at seven-thirty, we ordered a Three Meat Treat pizza from the local Little Caesar's, which we supplemented with a six-pack of Sierra Nevada. Clarissa sat cross-legged on the damp white shag carpet, shoveling in one slice after another, glancing from time to time at her napkin as if she were trying to place its name.

"*So,*" she said. "Tell me something. Do you hate him?"

"Who?"

"Walter Ralegh."

I took a swallow of beer, squinted back at her.

"Why should I?"

"He killed your career."

"Ralegh had nothing to do with it. I've never — I mean, if you must know — more than ever, I just want to do right by him."

"But who's doing *wrong* by him?"

"Well . . ." I kneaded the back of my neck. "*History,* in a way. It masks him. Before anything else, he was a *poet.* Who, in his spare time, you know, was storming Cádiz and fighting the Armada and sailing down the Arapahoe River and —"

"Throwing his cloak over that puddle! For Queen Elizabeth."

"Which may never have happened. You look at all the stuff he actually *did,* all the people he *was* — courtier and soldier — explorer, patron — everything was just an extension of his true calling. And that was poetry. It's the only way his life makes sense, as this kind of epic verse, never resolving."

Which was more than I'd spoken on the subject in ages.

"Well, now," said Clarissa, framing me over the rim of her bottle. "What kind of poem is *your* life, Henry Cavendish?"

"Prose. All prose."

A slow, seraphic smile. She pushed herself off the bed. Gave her eyes a rub and, in a flat voice, said:

"Remind me whose room this is."

"Mine."

"Okay, good night."

"It's still early, isn't it?"

"Not for me. I'll see you in the morning."

I watched her go. Wondering the whole

226

time what would happen if I had asked her to stay.

The beer by now was gone, so I drove to a local Brew Thru for a one-liter bottle of Purple Moon Shiraz, which I managed to spill on my bathroom floor not ten minutes later.

I had enough left over for a prodigious buzz. I turned on Turner Classic Movies and, through the husks of my eyes, watched Jeanette MacDonald fight for Clark Gable's soul. She was still at it when I dropped off to sleep.

I awoke hours later to the pounding of my own head. Which quickly relocated itself to the door, ten feet away.

It was Clarissa, in a T-shirt of her own, gymnasium gray. She took a step into the room. Her eyes were hot and white.

"It *is* Harriot," she said.

"Okay."

"It *is*."

"All right."

"And someone's *with* him. Her name is Margaret."

22

ISLEWORTH, ENGLAND *1603*

Here is the first surprise: The laboratory in which Master Thomas Harriot seeks enlightenment is . . . almost entirely dark.

Someone, it seems, has thrown horse blankets over the windows. Pausing at the room's entrance, Margaret peers into the murk, spies a shifting shape, hears a voice burred with impatience.

— Come in. Come in.

She takes two strides into the room and waits for her eyes to adapt.

— You may be seated.

At last objects merge. A worktable, roughly two yards long, covered in butcher's paper. On the table, a burnished triangle of amber. And directly above, a single lamp, hanging from a chain.

There is no preamble or explanation from the master. Only a flurry of last-minute calculations as he measures off each distance and angle.

At last he sets down his compass and ruler. He pauses. Then he slides a length of slotted black wood into the lamp's base.

The effect is instant. The cloud of lamplight is winnowed into a single lancing beam, which strikes the amber triangle along its exposed flank. At once, a sister ray surges off on its own tangent, carving the amber in two and yet leaving it magically whole.

No time to admire the effect. The master grabs his protractor and sets to work, murmuring the name of each angle (*ABH . . . GBI . . . FBM . . .*) and then scribbling down each figure. The work is slow, for he insists on taking each measure twice, and over the next ten minutes she recedes so far from his thoughts that she must repeat herself before he hears her.

— Pardon, sir. My duties . . .

— Ohh. Yes.

At a loss for protocol, she takes a step back, curtsies, and makes a straight line for the doorway. *Quick and smart,* she tells herself. *Heels off the ground . . .*

And just as he did in their first meeting, he calls after her.

— Come back tomorrow, then.

She goes back tomorrow. The day after and

the day after. Always pausing just outside the door until she hears the three chimes. Then presenting herself with a bowed head.

— I have come, sir. As you asked.

And why has he asked? What does he want of her? As best she can tell, he requires nothing more of her than an audience. And yet he has none of the actor's vanity. He fidgets, he grumbles, he scratches, loses his place, remonstrates with his quill . . . behaves like a man enslaved to himself. All the more surprising that, one afternoon, the fog around him should part long enough for him to say:

— Margaret, might I trouble you to take down the figures?

She balks at first. She has had precious little practice penning numbers, and her only recourse at first is to ape his hand: the jagged underloops of his 3s and 5s, the squint of his 2s, the dangling edges of his 4s. So thoroughly does she absorb it all that the style becomes her own, and soon the quill is sliding across the paper with a sweet ease. Degree by degree, minute by minute, the master's columns fill up, and playing even this small part in the production gives her an uncommon excitement. Or is it just the relief that comes of doing?

Without her knowing it, her intervals in

the laboratory stretch from ten minutes to fifteen to twenty. And when at last she excuses herself, he gives her the same mask of puzzlement each time, as if she were a variable he has yet to sew into an equation.

One afternoon, he sets a large crystal sphere on the table. *A seer's sphere,* she thinks. And there is something of the necromancer in the ponderousness of his motions, in the theatricality of his pauses. The way his hand actually trembles when he slides the black board into the lamp.

Once again, the ray of light comes surging forth, but with this difference. It doesn't so much strike the sphere as detonate it.

The crystal explodes into a diadem of color. Indigo and violet and red and orange. Searing yellow. A green she can almost smell. Every sense is inflamed, and yet no single sense, no combination of senses, can contain it all.

Dazed, she rises from her stool, dimly aware of some violence to her right. The inkhorn . . . tipped on its side . . . a river of gall ink crawling toward the sheet of figures.

The master reacts before she does, snatching the paper clear. But in his haste he strikes the lamp with his shoulder, and down it comes in a gale of glass. A second later, the table is ablaze.

Gasping, Margaret grabs the quill and the horn, feeling the lick of flame against her fingers. She watches as the master seizes the blanket from the window and hurls it across the table. But the flames come right back, redoubled in force, swallowing the wool like air.

From without comes the sound of running feet. Margaret turns to see Mrs. Golliver lurching into the room with a bucket of water. The sight is enough to make her laugh, but already the water is cascading over the table. There comes a great hiss . . . a dying sigh . . . the fire is transformed into a cordon of smoke.

Panting, triumphant, Mrs. Golliver sets the bucket down. Her voice is as grave as a sibyl.

— Master Harriot, you cannot say you went unwarned.

— It was my fault entirely.

— Permitting a mere girl to serve in such a capacity goes against Nature and common sense. It perverts the natural order of things.

Watching Mrs. Golliver bear down, Margaret suddenly realizes: This is the moment she's been waiting for.

— You must be made to see, Master. The girl was engaged to *work* for us. Not *make*

232

work for us.

— Is that so?

He means, possibly, to challenge the idea. But there is no challenge in his voice, only an agitation that slowly communicates itself to other parts: eyebrows, fingers, feet.

How he wavers in the face of true fixity! Margaret could almost despise him if she did not feel instead a pang of fellowship. Master Thomas Harriot has no more say in the running of his life than she does in hers.

— Enough of *this,* says Mrs. Golliver. — Come, Margaret.

She cuffs her under the chin. A light cuff only. It is the words that sting. *Enough of this.* As if the old housekeeper had somehow joined league with her mother.

No need for these any longer.

That night, Margaret lies in her cold bed, the tips of her fingers still stinging, the memory of the fire scalding in every pore. She cannot imagine she will ever sleep, but in fact she has just slipped free of consciousness when she hears a light tapping. A voice follows hard on.

— Margaret? Are you about?

Rising quickly, she wraps her coverlet around her shift and unlatches the door.

He stands there. Bareheaded in his black

gown. Holding a candle. His voice straining toward cheer.

— So! Your natural habitation . . .

More than once, in her fancy, a man has come to her bedchamber. He looked nothing like the master.

— I wonder, Margaret, if you would oblige me.

— Sir?

— There is something I should like to show you.

He pauses.

— Out-of-doors, if that is not disagreeable.

He waits on the step while she climbs back into her petticoat and skirt and waistcoat. Then he signals her to follow him down. Pausing on the bottommost stair, he taps a finger to his ear: *Listen.*

From the darkness of the inner rooms comes a sound like converging oceans. The Gollivers' snoring.

— Mister G has the quavering treble, says Master Harriot. — The *basso continuo* would be his fair paramour.

It is ten minutes till midnight, everyone in Syon House is abed, and the earth itself is snoring into the gray poplars and the silver birches.

She looks down. In the master's hands

234

rests a cylinder, one foot and a half in length, encased in mildewed leather.

— My perspective trunk, Margaret. Of some ancient vintage. I brought it to Virginia ages ago. The local Algonkin were most taken with it. Please . . .

With some awkwardness, she grasps it. Puts the glass to her eye, tilts her head toward the sky . . .

And falls back before the onslaught. Stars where there was only night.

It must be a trick, she thinks, but then the moon itself swarms into view. So massive she cannot bring herself to believe in it. Or take her eyes from it.

— It magnifies only to the third power, and the field of view is rather narrow, as you may see. I cannot help but posit that one day, with the, the right configuration of convex and concave lenses, one might — well, it's difficult to foretell . . .

— One might see the moon for true, she says, lowering the glass to her side.

— Why, yes, the moon. In all its — all its particularity. We may prove with some degree of confidence that it is not composed of green cheese.

Or tired stars, she thinks. That's what her father used to tell her when she was a girl. Every night, the sleepiest stars would swim down to the moon and lie there a short while — until they felt ready to climb back up.

— Sir.

—Yes?

— May I look one last time?

— Of course.

Once again the moon shivers into view: not quite full, or real, but giddy with itself. Why is it she can never find a word equal to the experience?

And why should she bother? The world is conversing quite enough. Frogs, whippoorwills, barn owls, nightjars, bobwhites . . . churring and jangling and now and then rhyming in some perverse way. Off to the south, the midnight bells, dividing the sound into pulses. And the moon somehow riding atop it all.

She hears the master's voice, low and firm.

—Yes. I should say so.

She looks up at him.

— Sir?

— I should say the nighttime would do rather well.

She gives her head a shake.

— Pardon, he says. — I was merely considering the, the maximal conditions for inquiries of an optical nature. It seems to me that the nighttime, with its more intense contrasts of light and dark, might permit us more detailed measurements. Of refraction and, and the like.

The *us* is not lost on her. Or him. He slaps the heels of his boots together.

— As we have already determined, the Gollivers are quite insensible this time of evening. We should be left to ourselves, I should think. Barring any more bonfires.

He is seeking her consent, she understands this now. She understands, too, that sleep is the one luxury left to her. For what seems to her an eternity, she stands there, in the very pitch of night.

— As you wish, sir.

23

The next evening, just past the stroke of nine, she is there.

At first blush, there is nothing so different in meeting at this hour. The work is largely the same: laborious measurements, recorded row after row. The room is no darker than before, except that the shadows run deeper and the light carves harder.

And there is this difference, too: The act of transcription, which had a certain enchantment by daylight, becomes at night a form of penance. Her hand drags along the paper, the figures swim in and out of focus. Even the master's voice subsides, for seconds altogether, into an undifferentiated buzzing.

Does he notice her inattention? Does he even know she's in the room? It's true there are times when he will cease muttering to himself and address her directly. Now and then, he will even make an effort to explain something to her — the computation of sines and cosines, say — but even this carries a professorial tone. And though her Latin is good, she has had only the rudiments of geometry. She knows what a right angle is but not a hypotenuse. Trigonometry is as explicable to her as Aramaic.

— Of course, what makes the sine and cosine functions so especially telling, Margaret, is that they are not dependent upon the *size* of the triangle. They are merely expressions of the relations between angles. . . .

— Yes, sir.

The words cascade over her, and she seems to evaporate beneath them. And then he calls out another measurement, and her hand scrawls it down, and the work goes on.

Angulus refractus . . . hdb per calculum . . . in aqua incidentia . . .

And when the work is done for the night, he takes his rest with a common man's relish. Pulls out his pipe, fills it with tobacco, lights it by the nearest candle, and drinks it in. The smoke billows across the room in shivering spirals: a new layer of sting to Margaret's already smarting eyes.

At some point, she finds voice enough to excuse herself. His head angles toward her.

— Good night, then. My thanks.

Leaving, she always steals a look back, but he is always exactly as she left him. Still seated. No sign of retiring himself.

Then again, he may sleep as late as he likes. Margaret, on most nights, is abed by one and up again four hours later. For a week or so, the terror of being found out is enough to keep her in motion, but as the short nights bleed into the long days, she finds it harder and harder to hear the cock's crow. One morning she has to be wakened by Mrs. Golliver.

— Lazy girl!

She snatches sleep where she can; more often, it snatches her. In the midst of sweeping the study, she must lean against a wall or risk giving way altogether. Bending over a bucket of wash, she wakes to find her head resting on the bucket's rim. In the midst of dressing a bed, she actually tumbles into it, as though it were a pond.

Her undoing comes on a Friday morning in April. She is carrying a skirtful of eggs from the henyard when some combination of sun and wind throws a dazzle into her eye. She weaves for a few seconds — a Southwark cock on its last legs — then falls chest-first to the ground.

It is the wetness that rouses her. The eggs, crushed by her weight, seep through her

240

skirt, throw a chill into her skin. She rolls over . . . waits for the blood to return to her head . . . and then opens her eyes to the livid specter of Mr. Golliver.

— Have you taken ill, my girl?

She could pretend she had, but they might call in a physician. Or even the steward.

— I am sorry, sir. I appear to have lost my balance.

— That is not the picture that presents itself to me. The picture that presents itself to me is of a girl deficient in duty.

Slowly, in stages, she rises to her feet. Surveys that strangely shaming puddle on her skirt.

— It shall not happen again, sir.

— No. It shall *not*.

Seizing Margaret by the sleeve, he marches her through the back door. And as they pass the kitchen, Mrs. Golliver, answering to some silent alarum, falls into line behind them.

To the Tower, thinks Margaret, in her befogged state. *We're off to the Tower.*

The master is doing what he always does this time of day. Composing his correspondence.

—Yes?

— Master, we have dire news.

There follows the arraignment. She can-

241

not help but be awed by the litany of her offenses. Oversleeping, inadequate dusting, overhaste, underhaste, effrontery, sluttishness. The excess of it is very nearly amusing, and in fact she must smother her laugh when Mrs. Golliver, warming to her subject, shouts:

— Does she think eggs grow on trees?

Through the whole recitation, the temple of the master's hands holds firm. The only unstable part of him is his eyes, which range from Golliver to Golliver, from floor to ceiling, and then rest with a peculiar intangible discomfort on Margaret's skirt, stinking with sulfur.

The room falls silent. In a voice barely audible, the master says:

— I believe you have apprehended the wrong malefactor.

— Sir?

— If Margaret is indeed unequipped to carry out her duties, it is because I have been most selfishly claiming her time for my own uses.

Mr. Golliver's mouth folds over the word as if it were a piece of gristle.

— *Uses?*

— Experiments, yes, of a highly sensitive nature. And of sufficient importance to both Crown and Church that they must be conducted after hours. Lest they be compromised.

And now it is Mrs. Golliver's turn to work through the implications.

— At *night?*

Margaret sinks onto the nearest stool. Closes her eyes. She would float away altogether if the master's voice weren't pulling her back to earth.

— My apologies, Mrs. Golliver. I neglected to inform you of my decision.

— Decision, sir?

— Upon deliberation, I believe the time is ripe for engaging a laboratory assistant.

Margaret fingers her lids apart — and is astonished to find every pair of eyes in the room resting on hers. And still she cannot grasp what has happened until she hears the master continue.

— I trust you will be able to start at once, Margaret. No, not at once. Take until week's end to recover yourself. A good night's sleep or two should be all the cure needed. We cannot be having any more accidents for Mrs. Golliver to clean up.

A dreadful silence then, broken by the old woman's cry.

— It will not do!

— It cannot! cries the old man.

— I fear it must, says Harriot.

243

— But who will perform Margaret's duties?

— The steward was good enough to send her our way. I hold great confidence in his ability to discover a new girl every bit as competent.

Only now do the Gollivers fully understand: They have a new master. Who will require new tacks.

In a voice teeming with subtlety, Mr. Golliver says:

— I am not at all sure what the earl will say about this.

— I thank you for recalling it to me, Golliver. If memory serves, I am engaged with His Grace tomorrow afternoon, from the hours of one until three. I shall take it up with him then. I have no fear he can be persuaded on the matter. We ask him for so little, do we not, Golliver?

For several seconds longer, the master holds their gaze. Then, with a smile of apology, he gestures toward his correspondence.

— I pray now you will leave me to my labors. As I shall leave you to yours. Oh, Golliver?

— Sir.

— I thank you for calling the matter to my notice. Good day.

24

The earl of Northumberland is the possessor of one of England's great libraries: scores upon scores of moldering volumes, tattooed with his marginalia. It says something, then, of his character that he so freely forsakes their company for Nature's library.

On this particular afternoon in April, he is seated beneath a willow tree, overlooking the Isleworth Mill Stream. He holds an angling rod in his right hand, his boots are smeared in spring mud, his breathing is slow and even. One could almost imagine him young again.

In marked contrast is his companion, whose black garments give him the look of a rain cloud invading the willow's sanctuary. Thomas Harriot brings to angling the same zeal for the definite that seizes him in his laboratory. Indeed, the only way he can justify these outings to himself is by supposing that he and the earl are inching toward inviolable scientific principles that will light the way for all future generations of fishers.

Today, those principles are elusive: The two men have not caught a single trout in two hours. This despite the fact that Harriot has personally designed their flies from black wool and drake's feathers. Should he have painted the feathers' undersides yellow? Should he first have immersed them in fennel? Should he have given them another fortnight's weathering?

In this manner, Harriot becomes wholly lost to the present: the singing of willow branches, the light and motion embracing on the stream's surface. The only thing that can halt his mind's revolutions is the sound of the earl clearing his throat.

— My dear Tom. As regards this laboratory assistant of yours . . .

There is no conclusion to the sentence. The earl merely leaves a space of silence into which Harriot must now dash.

— The truth is, Your Grace, I have long required an assistant and have been too proud to ask. As matters now stand, I am obliged to waylay others of your retinue, which lays an unacceptable strain upon your estate and your hospitality.

How dry his mouth is.

— More to the present point, I have embarked on a particularly sensitive stage of my optics work, and I find the contributions of Miss Crookenshanks to be invaluable in forwarding these inquiries to their, their hoped-for end.

And still the earl is silent.

— Naturally, Your Grace, I have no intention of placing any additional burden upon the Gollivers, who have been ever loyal to me. If new housemaids are wanting, I am perfectly content to bear all consequences. Disorder, dust, slovenliness — I should be the last to complain. Or even notice.

The earl switches the angling rod to his left hand, gives a pair of soft tugs on the line, then resettles himself against the willow's trunk.

— You are quite resolved on this point, Tom?

— I should never have broached it if I were not.

— And you are bound and determined to engage this particular person?

— I am.

Another tug on the line.

— How shall I make my meaning felt, Tom? If it's companionship you require — no, pray hear me out — if it's a *companion* you're after, I should be the last man in

Christendom to begrudge you one. You needn't create a *want* merely to . . . justify some other want.

The very delicacy of his language drives Harriot in the opposite direction.

— Miss Crookenshanks is not my lover.

— I impute no dishonor to you, Tom, I am merely puzzled. If memory serves aright, you have never taken a direct interest in the affairs of any servant. What, then, is so extraordinary about this one?

— I don't know that I can say.

— Pretty, is she?

— Perhaps. Not so very. I don't know.

The earl laughs.

— I fear you will never be a sonneteer.

— My respect for her, Your Grace, has nothing to do with her person. She has a *quality,* which I confess I am sore pressed to define.

— Do your best.

Harriot stares across the stream, where a sycamore is futilely waving at him.

— I think it is this, Your Grace. She has not yet *resigned* herself to the world's ways as other girls might in her situation. She is fighting toward the light. Only she no longer perceives that she is.

— How then do you perceive it?

— Because I was the same way at her age.

When I look at her, I see myself.

The earl smiles absently. Shakes his head.

— The two of you could hardly be more opposed, Tom. You are a *man,* with a man's capacities. You cannot expect Nature to equip a woman in the same fashion.

— Your Grace, I do not pretend to know what Nature intends for the sexes. I only know that if I were Margaret's age and someone had told me that I might not — might not *learn* . . . might not *hurl* myself at the world and all its mysteries, its *possibilities* . . . If it's a question of money, Your Grace, I will happily remunerate her from my own account.

— Oh, money. I hemorrhage it by the hour. No physician could have bled me more conscientiously than has my own estate.

The earl stretches out his legs and lets his fishing rod dangle for a moment in the water.

— Very well, Tom, you may consider your petition granted.

— Your Grace —

— And in return, you will be so good as to grant *my* petition.

The earl lowers his voice by no more than a degree.

— On Sunday, the eighth of June, Syon

House is to be given the unspeakable and exalted honor of hosting His Majesty the King of England. I have told no one but you. And having paid you that signal compliment, I must balance out the scales with an insult.

— Your Grace?

— I must kindly entreat you to stay away.

Their eyes lock. The earl is the first to look away.

— You are a casualty, Tom, of our uncertain age. Being still green in office, the king vacillates daily as to who is with him and who against. There is one man, lamentably, about whom he has never vacillated.

— Sir Walter.

— His Majesty regards our friend as a gangrenous limb. Once he begins cutting off one appendage, what is to save all the limbs connected thereto?

— So you mean to stem the tide of infection.

— I mean to protect you, Tom. And all of us. You are better known in court circles than you know. Once the king's eyes fall on you, he will be put in mind of Sir Walter. This will then recall to him that so-called School of Atheism. Before another second has passed, the king will be put out of humor altogether. I cannot afford for him to be put out of humor.

He does not use the word *afford* lightly. The earl holds this land on lease only. If he can ingratiate himself enough with the king, he may one day have Syon Park as a free-hold.

— I am glad at least that Your Grace has escaped the same taint as Sir Walter and I.

— I have been at great pains, as you know, to scour myself. We shall see if my efforts are crowned.

A touch of rue now comes to Master Harriot's smile.

— What more can I say, Your Grace? Show me to the nearest monastery. There I shall repair.

— Do not forget we live on the grounds of an abbey. Your own house should be cloister enough.

The earl exhales. Puts his hand on the smaller man's shoulder.

— As I remember, court life has never much agreed with you.

— That is so.

— Live, then, in this hope. That once I have persuaded the king of my intentions, I may woo him toward clemency. For you *and* Sir Walter.

The earl's head has drooped slightly to one side, and his eyes are half closed. An onlooker might suspect him of dozing were his voice not so lean and hard.

— There is no sign of it, I suppose.

— Sign of what, Your Grace?

— Our dark treasure.

That was Marlowe's name for it. And how better to describe that product of a night's labor: five men working until dawn, urging one another through their terrors . . . and all the more terrified to see what they had made.

— The treasure, Your Grace, is as lost to me now as it was ten years ago.

— Then we will pray it remains so. Of late, so many things seem intent on being found.

He gazes into the Isleworth Mill Stream.

— Excepting trout.

25

"A woman?"

With great effort, Alonzo managed to keep the Morning Glory muffin in his mouth. He took a swig of cranberry juice and, in the flintiest voice he could muster, declared:

"There is no record of Thomas Harriot being with *a woman.*"

"Well, that's not quite true," I said. "He had a sister; she's mentioned in his will. He left bequests for a housekeeper, an assistant housekeeper. He socialized with Lady Ralegh, Lady Northumberland. . . ."

"Henry, since you're willfully and wildly choosing to ignore my drift, let me qualify my original statement. There is no record in the Harriot papers of anybody named *Margaret.*"

At which point Clarissa's words came spooling back to me.

There's no record of his birthday, either. But he was born.

253

Very deliberately, Alonzo emptied three packets of Sweet 'n Low into his coffee. "Aren't you the in-house skeptic, Henry?"

"Isn't it you who thinks Clarissa's visions — wait, how did you put it? — they come from someplace that's *not her*. I just figured you'd want the latest dispatches. From said place."

"As it happens, we have better things to do than chase after Margarets. Or Bettys. This very afternoon, I'm driving down to Ocracoke to meet an expert in Algonquin history. An old friend of — Christ, where the hell is Amory?"

But the house's nominal owner was nowhere to be seen. Taking my leave ten minutes later, I found him loitering in the gravel driveway. A new costume: seersucker pants and a tuxedo shirt. A new face, too. Every muscle in it was surrendering.

"I can't get him to listen," he said.

"Alonzo?"

"I keep telling him. Everything's shifted, hasn't it?"

"Everything's —"

"That's what barrier islands do. They *shift,* they *reconfigure.*"

For thousands and thousands of years, he wanted me to know, the Outer Banks had been in motion: sand washing in from offshore bars or washing away on the next tide. In the 420-plus years since Harriot's party had come to Roanoke Island, the northern shore had fallen back a quarter mile, all but one of the island's inlets were gone, and most of the islands to the southwest had vanished.

"I keep telling Alonzo, but he won't listen. Wherever Harriot thought he was leaving his treasure, it's not there anymore."

I found myself in the strange position of wanting to comfort Amory Swale.

"Harriot might have left it inland," I suggested.

Amory inspected the whorls of dead sand on his undersoles.

"I do sometimes wonder," he murmured, "if we should be doing this at all. Digging up things. Perhaps it would be a greater kindness not to."

And then, abruptly, he cast off his gloom. Showed me his teeth in all their valor.

"Have a lovely day," he said.

That afternoon, Clarissa and I took a different tack. Instead of feeding names into the decryption engines, we fed them number upon number. Harriot's birth year: 1560. His death year: 1621. The year he came to London: 1580. The year he sailed for

Roanoke: 1585. The date of Elizabeth's birth and death, the dates of James's coronation. Hell, we threw in the Battle of Hastings and the signing of the Magna Carta and every commemorative occasion we could think of.

Next we spent a couple of hours combining key names and numbers. And then we tried equations. We tried Latin and Greek characters and Roman numerals and Gaelic and Sanskrit. . . .

On and on, an essay in futility, and once again the day slipped away from us. I had just enough strength to collect meatball subs from Quizno's and a liter bottle of Svedka, which Clarissa, after some hesitation, declined to drink from.

We ate quickly. I downed a couple of shots, and then we cleared our throats, and Clarissa was just reaching for her laptop when I said:

"Let's go for a walk."

I didn't have any destination in mind, so we made for the beach. And as we paused at the top of the dune and kicked off our shoes and felt the uprush of wind, the scent was instantly tonic: salt and decayed kelp and a lingering summer char.

The moon had laid a track straight across the water. A tethered kite was flapping; in the distance, the remains of a campfire smoldered. We had the place to ourselves.

Clarissa grabbed a stick and carved a horseshoe shape in the sand.

"Are there other Cavendishes in the world?" she asked.

"I've got a brother, five years younger. He's a doctor."

"Like you."

"The kind that helps people. My parents are highly competent old people, very happily retired. My mother is Mary Queen of Scottsdale."

"You came up with that."

"Which is why she hates it."

"What about kids?"

"Me? God, no. I mean, for the *kids*' sake, thank God."

I stared out to sea. The moon's track was fading from gold to a clotted cream.

"What about you?" I asked. "Any family in the mix?"

"All gone."

"Boyfriends, naturally."

"Oh, I guess. They used up a lot of time. You remind me of one of them."

"That can't be good."

"Have you ever —" She stopped, gave herself a preemptive pat on the head. "Never mind."

257

"What?"

"I don't want you to be mad."

"For Christ's sake."

"I was only going to say . . . you seem to . . . drink a lot." She made a close study of the sand. "I think I know why you do it, and I just wish you wouldn't. Because all those bad things you think about yourself, they're not true. And that's all I'm going to say, I promise."

To my own surprise, I began to laugh.

"What?" she said.

"I don't know. I never expected to have — *interventions.* I never expected to be *this.*"

"What did you expect to be?"

"I don't know, something. I mean, I know this sounds completely stupid, but back in the day, I was . . ."

"Go on."

"Okay, at the risk of sounding like a totally egomaniacal asshole, I was the kind of guy — of whom things were . . ."

"Expected."

"Well, yeah. I mean, maybe, yeah. I was summa cum laude. I had my Ph.D. by twenty-six. Oriel freakin' College invited me to read a paper. An American! Talking about Ralegh! I know it sounds ridiculous, this English-lit prof thinking he's — well, not God — all I can say is, at the beginning it felt like the world was sort of bending my way, and then suddenly the world was bending *me*. And before I knew it, I was . . ."

"Bent."

"Yeah. Okay."

"Henry, I don't know if it's any comfort, but life bends everyone, doesn't it? A little bit?"

"Oh, sure."

"You were just unlucky. All things considered, you're doing okay."

"That's kind of you. That's a very generous standard of — of *okay*ness."

We were walking again, more slowly now, our clothes billowing behind us. We came at last to a shock of pampas grass, which had curled over the sand to form a tiny arbor.

"Anybody home?" Clarissa called, poking her head inside.

But the arbor was as empty as the rest of the beach. The kind of place, frankly, I would have brought a crush to in middle school. Only there was no starter-bra awkwardness in Clarissa. Lips parted, eyes shining, she leaned toward me and, just as I was aligning myself for a response, she said.

"That poem."

"Which one?"

"The one that got you in trouble. The Ralegh poem."

Frowning, I took a step back.

"It wasn't Ralegh."

"Just tell me the title."

"You're killing me."

"Please."

"You're fucking killing me."

"I'm not, I really want to know."

" 'One Name.' Happy?"

"That's an odd title. 'One Name.' "

"Well, there you are."

Without warning, she dropped into the sand. Pulled my jacket more tightly around her. "Could you recite some of it?" she asked.

"Jesus."

"Please. I'll be your best friend. I'll make you brownies."

I laughed.

"Just two lines," she cooed.

I canvassed my mind for further objections.

"It'll have to be four," I said. "It was written in quatrains."

"Okay, four," she answered, patting the square of sand next to her.

I was already reciting as I sat down. Hoping to get through it as fast as I could, honestly, but the wind was drowning out my voice, so I had to lift it into a new register. I thought of Demosthenes, roaring over the waves.

> One name hath been my joy and curse
> My borning cry, my sable hearse
> My life's redoubt, my soul's sweet death
> Two fates — one name — Elizabeth.

I expected it to resound with its own hollowness. But tonight it had an angle of defiance.

"I can see why you liked it," said Clarissa.

"I liked it because it was Ralegh."

"No, it's pretty. It doesn't become *lesser* because someone else wrote it."

"Um, yes. Yes, it does." I whisked the sand from my calves. "I'm not sure it was worth a career."

"What would *he* say?"

I stared at her.

"Ralegh, I mean. Oh, wait!" She clapped her hand on top of her head. "I just realized Ralegh rhymes with *folly!* Oh my God, did you ever notice that?"

I never had. Never once.

All that time I'd spent in carrels and library stacks and seminar rooms, filling out grant applications, sweet-talking archive gatekeepers, burying my nose in boxes full of dust and insect shit — and all time the notes of my doom were sounding in my ear.

Ralegh . . . folly.

"There was no one to warn me," I said now, with a strangled laugh. "You weren't around."

And because the full import of those words was slow to reach me, I had to say them again.

"You weren't around."

She pulled her legs closer to her chest as if to protect herself and then, in a gesture of contrary purpose, let her head topple onto my shoulder. I slipped my fingers under her chin. I raised her mouth to mine.

"Mm," she whispered. "Salt."

Her finger ran the length of my lower lip, then drew away. And then, with redoubled force, she brought our mouths together.

Oh, there were the usual encumbrances: the friction of sand against skin, the inability to find a single resting point, the trancelike fear of being discovered, which had lost whatever frisson it had in my youth.

I suppose the only difference with Clarissa was that the awkwardness of the setting didn't carry into the act. We fell into each other, with a shock of recognition.

And afterward, she curled up against my bare chest and closed her eyes and . . . slept. A covenant of trust. Obscurely but powerfully stirring, for in all my life — and the rolls of my partners are not superhumanly long — I had never once fallen asleep *after* the woman.

I didn't pause to consider what this said about me, I was too entranced with this feeling, this *sensation* of being free from scrutiny. My own, worst of all.

I watched her sleep, that's all. And marveled at how congruent she was with her surroundings. In the ocean light, her tangle of hair was like a bed of kelp, and her skin was the color of conch shells, and her eyes were dark as sea urchins. She was to this particular manor born, but it wasn't Hamlet I was thinking of, it was baby Perdita, stranded on the Bohemian coast, growing up in Nature's bosom.

And with that, a snatch of *Winter's Tale* sang in my ears.

When you do dance, I wish you
A wave o' the sea, that you might ever do
Nothing but that.

Well, you see, when I quote Shakespeare to myself, that's usually a sign of — let me just say this: I was glad enough to be Clarissa's sentry.

Not that I had much to guard against. An

old man in clam diggers, swinging a metal detector like Merlin's wand. Another pair of lovers, younger, still vertical, with a widening nimbus of pot around their heads.

And at last, just before midnight, when the arm supporting Clarissa's weight had lost its last trace of feeling, a bichon frise wandered by.

"Shoo," I hissed. "Scram."

And in that same instant, I heard Clarissa whispering:

"Go away."

It made me smile, that little echo of hers. Until I realized she was still sleeping.

And then her eyelids broke open and her torso surged straight toward the sky. And for a minute, I heard nothing but the sound of her lungs, reclaiming the air they had lost.

"It's Margaret," she whispered. "Something's wrong."

"It's okay."

"No. It's not. We're all dead."

26

We spoke not a word the whole way back to the motel. A curious reticence: not embarrassment, not shyness. We just wanted to be alone with our thoughts. Our bodies, too, for we didn't bother with a good-night kiss, although Clarissa did give my cheek a light stroke with her index finger just before she closed her door.

It was ten minutes shy of midnight when I opened the door to my room. My brain must have been half slumbering already because I didn't notice the lamp blazing by the window, and I'd never even have known I had a visitor if I hadn't heard him speak from the corner.

"About bloody time!"

Alonzo. In a rattan throne. Wearing a massive silk kimono, robin's-egg blue, and waving a half-empty bottle of Grey Goose like a Salvation Army bell.

"You might have left a clean cup," he

growled.

"You might have cleaned one. We have running water, you know."

"Running from where?"

I watched him pour a thimbleful of vodka into the bottle's cap and swallow it down.

"What are you doing here, Alonzo?"

He poured another capful. But his aim was off this time, and a tiny cataract of vodka fell to the floor.

"Case of nerves," I suggested.

"Everyone gets them."

"Certainly."

"No disgrace. I mean, it'd be one thing if *Amory* were home."

"Where is he?"

"How should I know? He's a night crawler. Naps by day, putters through the evening. Impossible to find. Unless, of course, you don't need him, at which point he sticks to you like nettles."

Alonzo stared at the bottle for a while, then set it gingerly on the floor.

"What can I say, Henry? I was lying in that purgatorial shack of his, I was — I was *trying* to sleep, and I couldn't. Even with help. Also, there were noises. . . ."

He paused, as if expecting me to hear them, too.

"Nothing out of the way," he hurried on.

"I just thought I might benefit from a little human propinquity. And you were the best I could find."

"I'm honored," I said. "You won't mind if I go to sleep."

"Do as you like," he said airily.

I didn't bother to undress, just fell headlong into the first double bed I saw.

"Feel free to take the other one," I mumbled.

"Oh, yes."

But when I awoke the next morning, a little before eight, he was still in that chair, groggy but awake. I couldn't tell you if he'd even closed his eyes. The only detectable change was the amount of air inside that bottle.

"Morning," I mumbled.

Alonzo said nothing. I heaved myself up and went in the bathroom and threw on a pair of shorts I had worn two days earlier and, without another word to my roommate, went down to the veranda.

The day was heating up already, and the beach was just as empty as it had been last night. Except for a barefoot figure passing south in slow procession. Tall and built. He wore a fishing hat and a white T-shirt with SURF'S UP! in hot-pink letters and knee-length shorts that, on anyone else, would

267

have qualified as trousers. His tread was rhythmic, pacific. He never once looked my way.

Ten seconds later, I was back in my room. Alonzo's eyes widened at the sight of me.

"What is it?" he asked.

"Trouble."

And even as I spoke, I was remembering what Clarissa had said on the beach, just a few hours earlier.

We're all dead.

Amory Swale's shack looked even more porous than usual. The front door was unlocked. When we called upstairs, we heard no answer, and when we inspected Amory's room, we found a fully made bed.

"I don't like this," said Clarissa.

Scowling, Alonzo led us back down to the living room, then executed a slow 360-degree scan.

"Tell me something, Henry. When you saw Halldor this morning, did he see *you?*"

"I don't know."

"You don't *know?*"

"Well, it doesn't matter, does it? If Halldor's here, your buddy Bernard Styles knows where we are."

Alonzo lowered himself onto the chintz

couch. Tied another knot in his kimono sash.

"It doesn't matter so much if Styles knows where *you* are, Henry. You can always make a plausible case that you're here on his business. As for *me* . . . well, to the best of his knowledge, I'm still part of the Chesapeake Bay watershed. Why would he think otherwise? *You* two wouldn't tell him. *Amory* wouldn't —"

And then something snagged in Alonzo's brain.

"Where. The. Hell. Is. Amory."

"Aren't those *his?*" asked Clarissa.

She was pointing to an area just to the left of the couch, where a pair of eyeglasses lay strewn like an old magazine. Oversized aviator frames, thickly ground, speckled with dust and pollen. One of the temples had been half wrenched from its frame.

"He must have stepped on them," said Alonzo. "Clumsy soul."

"Can he see without them?" asked Clarissa.

"Not a lick."

I picked up the frames. Weighed them in my hand. It was as easy to imagine Amory without skin as without glasses.

"Alonzo," I said. "When did you last see him?"

"I don't know, seven P.M.-ish? We had cocktails, we ate French-bread pizza . . . I had some reading to do. Amory just — *left.* Said he had errands."

"He didn't say where?"

"No."

"Maybe he left a note," Clarissa suggested.

But a quick canvass of the house's first floor found only take-out Korean menus and Food Lion coupons and a raft of credit card solicitations, doodled almost beyond recognition, and an old book jacket for *Shakespearean Negotiations* (minus the book), and, the one surprise, a brochure for Anguilla: two beach umbrellas on empty white sand.

"The document," I said. "The Ralegh letter. Where is it?"

Alonzo's eyes went absolutely still for a few seconds. Then, kneeling on the floor, he rapped on a piece of moldy wainscoting, until it puffed away from the wall. He drew out the FedEx envelope, pressed his eye against the opening.

"Thank God," he breathed.

"Yeah, except Amory's still missing," I said. "What about his friends? Is there anyone he might have paid a visit to?"

"There's Mrs. Poole. Older than God.

Lives in Whalebone, a few miles down the road. Raises chinchillas. Amory's been spooling her along for years with May Sarton first editions, waiting for her to . . ." He paused. "He's been cultivating her."

"Maybe Amory went to see her?"

"No, no, she always sends a car."

"Any other friends?"

"God, I don't know. How can I think when it's this cold?"

I was the one who moved to close the oceanside window. But it was Clarissa who glanced past my arm and saw what was lying just outside.

"Jesus."

I was the second to see it, and what struck me most was its surreal normality. Amory Swale's backyard was already a graveyard of butts and bottles and cans and string. To discover a hand protruding from the sand . . . well, that was just another found object, wasn't it?

From behind me, I heard the sludgy low-fi sound of Alonzo's voice.

"Henry. There are a couple of shovels in the back."

271

27

The sand, freshly loosened, flew off in spadefuls. The hand gave way to an arm, spindly and larval. The arm gave way to a shoulder. A neck. And at last came the face, shellacked with grit, weirdly young without its eyeglasses.

We were the only witnesses. For we were standing in a great bowl of sand, screened on every side by dunes and shrubs and sea oats — and by that sad, sad house, which would be even more vacant now than I ever thought possible. Even now, in broad daylight, a hundred people could walk by us — more than a dozen already had, I guessed, in the last twenty minutes — no wiser as to what had gone on here.

I stood up slowly. I slapped the sand from my hands.

"What are you doing?" snapped Alonzo.

"I'm calling nine-one-one."

"And just what are you planning to

tell them?"

"I hadn't, you know, rehearsed it. Something like there's this guy. Who was alive and now is not."

"And hence is beyond our help."

The hair on my skin actually shrank.

"Guess you're mourning in your own way, huh, Alonzo?"

"I'm very sorry, but right now, mourning is an indulgence."

"*I'll* make the call," said Clarissa. "Alonzo won't need to be a part of this."

"Oh, and how could I not be?" he snapped, rounding on her. "Amory was *my* friend, wasn't he? And you came here on *my* account, did you not?"

"We can't *leave* him here," I said.

To which Alonzo said nothing — or, rather, his silence said as much as speech. In that instant, two things became abundantly clear. Leaving Amory was something that could be done. Leaving Amory was exactly what he intended to do.

The same conclusions must have dawned on Clarissa, for I saw her blanch, even as her irises blackened.

"We can *not*. Leave this man here."

"Did I say anything about forever?"

"Oh, my God."

"Did you hear me say forever?"

"He was your friend."

"A couple of lousy days!" shouted Alonzo.

His own vehemence stunned him briefly into silence. He cast his eyes down and, in a more appeasing tone, added:

"Forty-eight hours. That's all I'm asking. Just to crack things open."

Clarissa opened her mouth, but he had already put out a hand to stop her.

"By my reckoning, we have exactly two choices. We finish what we started, or it will be finished for us. Just ask Amory."

An agitation in Alonzo's throat . . . a nod in the direction of the body.

"If it's all the same to you, *I'm* going to choose my final resting place, not Bernard Styles."

"Alonzo," I said. "If you're right about who did this —"

"*If* I'm right?"

"Then, among other things, we're letting a murderer walk these beaches."

"Don't be penny dreadful. The field of potential victims is quite shockingly small. In fact, you're looking at all of them. Shall we examine the facts? Amory Swale was murdered. Why? For Harriot's map, of course. If Amory had actually *known* where it was, they would have it in their hands right now. Believe me, he'd have given it up in a heartbeat. He'd have given *me* up if I'd been here."

Only Alonzo *wasn't* here, I thought. He was bivouacked in my motel room, drinking himself half blind. An attack of nerves, that's how we'd diagnosed it. Today, it looked like a fit of prescience.

"Okay," I said. "If Amory didn't know anything, why would they kill him?"

"Because they wanted to send a message."

"And what exactly is this message? Please translate."

Alonzo waited a few seconds.

"Bernard Styles wants us to know that *he* knows."

"Knows what?"

"Everything we're up to. Styles knows about Harriot's treasure and he wants it every bit as much as we do. And, as we've now seen, he's willing to go to any length to find it. Believe me, Amory wouldn't have lasted five minutes without spilling."

As if in confirmation, my phone began to ring.

UNKNOWN.

I flipped open the lid.

"Mr. Cavendish!" came the familiar reedy voice. "I fear I have become the proverbial squeaky wheel, but I'm most curious to hear about your progress."

I stared at that pale torso, granulating before my eyes.

"May we first talk about Amory Swale?"

"*Swale,*" said Bernard Styles. "I don't believe I've had the pleasure."

"See, I believe you have."

"Well, then, you must refresh my memory. Who exactly is he?"

I waited for the surge of heat in my skull to pass. But it wouldn't.

"I saw Halldor this morning," I said.

"What a lovely surprise that must have been. He's been pining for salt air, and we were told the beaches in North Carolina were rather nicer than the ones in Delaware."

"So his turning up here would be on the order of coincidence."

"Well, yes, it would. Because, of course, you never told us where you were, Mr. Cavendish. Or with whom."

"I know what you're doing," I said.

"That makes two of us, Mr. Cavendish. Nevertheless, I continue to repose the greatest confidence in your abilities, and I remain hopeful that we may conclude our business on the happiest of terms."

And then he delivered his postscript.

"The best of luck to you and your com-

panions. And please send my regards to
Alonzo."

28

"Now," said Alonzo. *"Now* do you believe me?"

We were sitting, the three of us, legs akimbo, in Amory's great ashtray of a yard. The wind had picked up, and a fine layer of sand-silt was stinging our eyes, and a squadron of no-see-ums was sucking the sweat from our necks.

"He didn't confess," said Clarissa. "Exactly."

"Why would he confess?" said Alonzo. "Would *you?*"

She drove a twig into the sand.

"So to save ourselves from Styles, we need to find Styles's treasure."

"Excuse me. The treasure does not belong to Styles, it never has. It's Harriot's."

"Styles doesn't seem to think so," I pointed out.

"Which is why I prefer to regard the whole affair as an Elizabethan comedy. The happy outcome being just one or two acts away."

A comedy, I thought, staring at the Ozymandias head of Amory Swale, disappearing under the blowing sand.

"We should call the police," I said.

"May I once more ask why?"

"So we can be *safe,*" said Clarissa.

He regarded us singly first, then in tandem.

"And what do you want to be safe from? I can assure you — given the fact that I'm not even approximately dead — once you call the police, *I* will be arrested in short order for fraud. *You* — and I am using the plural pronoun — will be arrested as my accomplices. And, by the way, does the phrase 'suspicion of murder' carry any resonance for you?"

As theatrical effects go, it was more Victorian than Elizabethan. Which is to say, greasily effective.

"That's ridiculous," said Clarissa. "Henry saw Halldor. He *saw* him —"

"*Strolling.* Along a beach. Half a mile from here. Not exactly a smoking gun, is it? That's Styles's one true gift, he doesn't leave fingerprints. Or footprints. If the local constables act in the way they usually do, they're going to round up the life forms that are closest to hand. And God help us when they do."

"*We* had no motive to kill Amory," I said.

"Oh, motive." His head described a circle of mockery. "You really think that's going to stop them? Give me half a minute, I'll come up with a motive. Falling out among thieves . . . lover's quarrel . . . too many Twizzlers . . . all they're going to fasten on, *believe* me, is the three people who've been in Amory Swale's immediate neighborhood the past few days and nights. The rest goes to hell.

"And once we're in their gun sights, how *safe* do you think you'll be? Any misdemeanors in your back history, Clarissa? That car of yours, Henry. The police might want to see the registration. The title, too. If you really think your lives will stand up to that kind of scrutiny — if you think you can pull yourself off any cross they want to nail you to — well, then, by all means, take out your cell phones. Do it now."

I confess. My mind was already fastening around Detective August Acree. As for what was going on in Clarissa's head, I couldn't tell you, but I think it's fair to say that in that moment she and I understood our impotence. Between Bernard Styles and Alonzo Wax, we were no longer masters of ourselves.

"I'll give you twenty-four hours," I said, keeping my eyes on her. "That's all I'll agree to. And then we call the police."

"I believe we have a deal," said Alonzo.

And now he was looking at Clarissa, too. Waiting for a sign. But her final redoubt of dignity was to walk into the house.

Less than a minute later, she returned with a pillow: one of the hunting tableaux from Amory Swale's couch. She knelt down and placed it under the dead man's head. She looked at him for another minute. And then she said:

"He must have family somewhere."

"None."

Even Alonzo was struck, I think, by the baldness of his reply, for he bowed his head an inch.

"Tell me when this ends," said Clarissa, turning her gaze toward him.

"What do you mean?"

"I mean there was Lily. And now there's Amory."

"It ends when *we* say it ends," answered Alonzo. "No one else."

And then he seized the nearest shovel and said:

"Shall we get on with it?"

I did what I was told; I made that body vanish into its hangar of sand. Went about my work so blindly that Alonzo at last had to tap me on the shoulder and say:

"Enough."

By now, not even a finger was protruding from the surface.

I started walking — up the side of the bowl, down the path — pausing at the first sight of ocean, where I hoisted myself onto a bench, the base of which had been laid bare by years of erosion. For some time I sat there, not thinking about anything in particular. The water was emerald in its valleys, brown in its peaks, royal purple at the horizon. The whitecaps looked like porpoises.

Alonzo was exactly where I'd left him. Gummed with sweat and grit. Still wearing his blue kimono.

We trudged back inside . . . just as Clarissa came barreling through the front door, a grocery bag cradled in each of her lean white arms.

"You must be hungry," she said.

It was, in many respects, the most inhuman breakfast I've ever taken part in. And the most human. Especially when Clarissa turned to Alonzo and asked:

"When did you first meet Amory?"

"If you must know, I insulted him."

The two men met on a Shakespeare Society panel titled "*Who* Wrote the Plays?" Alonzo took the radical position that it was Shakespeare; Amory, sitting just to his left, was in the Earl of Oxford's camp. This in itself could scarcely be borne, but when Amory announced he wanted to disinter the earl's coffin to see which plays had been buried with him, Alonzo's patience crumbled like chalk.

"I said, 'Pardon me, Mr. Swale, but you are the most eye-popping fool I've ever had the misfortune to meet. In just a few years,' I said, 'the Earl of Oxford theory will go right in the ashcan with the Earl of Rutland theory. *And* the Earl of Derby theory. *And* the Christopher Marlowe theory, not to *mention* the Francis Bacon theory.'

"But here was the thing with Amory: The more you insulted him, the better he liked you. Which made for an exhausting codependency, I don't mind saying. All the same, we found ourselves in accord on most points, and he had a *scoutmasterly* quality that, in the right light, was endearing. He was particularly helpful tracking down a Robert Cecil letter. It had gone to ground somewhere in Islamorada, but Amory knew a widow — he was *always* knowing widows — sorry, Henry, are you quite all right?"

I was staring directly out the window, with such conviction that both Alonzo and Clarissa turned their heads to see what was there.

"I know," I said.

Alonzo reared up on the couch.

"What do you know?"

"Harriot's code. I know which code he used."

29

"Get me to a computer," I said.

We made our way back to the Pelican Arms, where I took Clarissa's laptop into my arms and carried it with foundling care to my room.

"Leave the map here," I said. "And come back in an hour."

The hour winged past, and when I opened the door and ushered the other two into the room, the synapses in my brain were still carbonating.

"You say *I'm* a drama queen," said Alonzo, dropping negligently into the armchair. "By the way, your room smells of old ladies."

"It does now. Can everyone see the laptop screen? Yes?"

"Yes yes yes."

"Well, then, before we begin," I said, "may I tender a salaam to Alonzo? Truly, I have him to thank."

"For so many things."

"This in particular. You're the one who mentioned Francis Bacon."

"Who was . . . ?" asked Clarissa.

"Scientist. Statesman. Lawyer. Corrupt judge. And, as it happens, one of the great philosophers of the Middle Ages. And, more to our purposes, a premier cryptologist. Alonzo, when those silly people wanted to prove Bacon wrote Shakespeare's plays, what did they do? They combed through every line of verse, looking for —"

"Embedded ciphers," said Alonzo, nodding impatiently. "But here's the difference, Henry. They were fools; Harriot was not. And maybe you've forgotten, Bacon didn't publish his ciphers until 1623, two years after Harriot's death."

"Maybe *you've* forgotten. Bacon came up with his most famous cipher when he was in Paris, working for the English ambassador. Sometime between 1576 and 1579."

"And what are the chances he shared it with Harriot?" Clarissa asked.

"Well, that's where I stalled. See, I figured they *had* to know each other. That they knew *of* each other was incontestable. They were almost exact contemporaries. Bacon actually *mentions* Harriot in *Commentarius Solutus.* The problem was they were locked in rival camps. Bacon was on Essex's side,

Harriot was with Ralegh. It was only when Essex mounted his sorta-maybe coup against Elizabeth that Bacon took one sniff of the wind and jumped. I'd say there's a better than even chance that, at some point in their life spans, England's two famous intellectuals sat down for some shop talk. And what better subject than ciphers? Harriot was no mean codesmith himself."

"But what exactly *is* Bacon's cipher?" asked Clarissa.

"You remember me telling you to treat all those characters like computer language? I had no idea what a genius I was — I mean, seriously, I'm a genius because Bacon's code was one of civilization's first great binary systems. For every letter of plain text, he substituted some combination of A and B. A was AAAAA, B was AAAAB, C was AAABA, and so on. All the way up to Z: BABBB."

Clarissa's brows drew down over her eyes.

"I get it," she said. "It's tougher to break than a substitution cipher because you can't tweeze out the most commonly used letters. All those *e*'s and *t*'s and *a*'s, they're buried in binary code. That's why letter frequency analysis won't work. Any piece of text will have roughly the same number of A's and B's."

"Oh, come on," said Alonzo. "Bacon developed his cipher more than four centuries ago. You're telling me a modern decryption program couldn't crack it open?"

"Not necessarily," I said. "See, it's not a true cipher. Technically — okay, I'm sorry to do this — it's *steganography.* From the Greek *stegein,* to cover. It's a way of writing code without letting anyone know you're writing code. The cipher is embedded in what looks like normal text."

"Security through obscurity," said Clarissa. "Only the sender and the recipient know what's going on."

"Exactly."

"But wait. The legend on Harriot's map . . . that's not normal text. Call it up, Henry."

PsjAYStrooxeidDVegaLOkuxTmLikcy CUsSxGAzyrnrmuOrrLBAkchrltRdga rnoomONOssfrtvQhiHeRbdallZolgean itzPeFpfhlogionLlLqaBwnbAdauncsle ckQooTiatGlgKIkiWfleatHEstRqiabaOt zKCdMCpnfeffkuv

"No one's going to look at *that,*" said Clarissa, "and mistake it for a letter to Mom. I mean, it practically screams code."

"But not in the way we think it does," I

288

answered. "Harriot's a smart guy, right? He knows how people's brains work. We look at a string of letters, we start reading it as *text*. That's how we *want* to read it. We have to step away from the *content* and look only at how it's laid out on the page. And now, with that in mind, what do you see?"

Alonzo screwed up his eye.

"Letters," he growled.

"But what distinguishes some of them from others?"

"At the risk of sounding obvious," said Clarissa, "some are capital and some aren't."

"And that's exactly why we miss it. Because it's so damn obvious."

Alonzo took one long step back from the screen.

"Jesus," he gasped. "It's case-sensitive. Oh, I'm an imbecile, I assumed it was —"

"The usual Elizabethan randomness, I know. Me, too. But not this time. So let's just see what we've got on our hands, shall we? Assign B to all the upper-case letters . . . assign A to all the lower-case letters . . . presto chango switcheroony . . ."

I paged down to the next screen.

BAABBBAAAAAAAABBAAABBAAABABAA
AABBABABBAAAAAAABAABBBAAAAAABA
AAAAAAABBBAAAAAABAABABAAAAABA
AAAAAAAABABAAAAAAAABABAABAAA
BAAAAAAAAAABAABAAABAABBAABAAAA
ABBAABAAAAABAABBABBAAAAAAAAA

"Bacon's cipher," murmured Alonzo.

"In all its binary glory. And if you break it off after every fifth letter, you can figure out the exact letter equivalents. Build it up, piece by piece, and pretty soon you'll know just what Harriot was trying to tell us."

No parades for me. No statues. Alonzo just thrust out his hands and, in the highest dudgeon, cried:

"Well, Christ! Decode it."

"Already have," I said, paging down to the next screen.

U/V R B S S I/J O N A U/V R E A P A T R
I/J A L A C T E A C I/J U/V E D E C O R A

"Are you having fun with us?" Clarissa asked. "This doesn't make any more sense than the cipher."

"Because you never learned Latin," Alonzo snapped. "Out of my way."

Bending over the keyboard, he used the space bar to break the letters into chunks of text.

U/V R B S S I/J O N A U/V R E A P A T R
I/J A L A C T E A C I/J U/V E D E C O R A

"*Urbs Sion aurea,*" he chanted. "*Patria lactea, cive decora. . . .*" His face spilled open with wonder. "Bernard of Cluny," he murmured.

"Who *is* —" said Clarissa.

"A Benedictine monk," I told her. "English, probably, living in the first half of the early twelfth century. He was a poet and a fierce critic of the medieval church. He wrote a satire called *De Contemptu Mundi,* which attacked the whole Catholic hierarchy, starting with the priests and nuns and going all the way up to the Vatican. It was reprinted countless times. The early Protestant reformers made it one of their urtexts, and by the sixteenth and seventeenth centuries any literate Protestant would have known it, possibly by heart."

"And for the School of Night," added Alonzo, "it would have been an ideal textbook. A critique of Catholicism that was, by extension, a critique of all religion."

Clarissa's arm rose toward the ceiling.

"Excuse me. The business major who never took Latin wants to get back to Harriot's map. Can someone please translate these lines into English?"

"Roughly speaking," said Alonzo, "it's *Golden city of Zion, land of milk and* — well, there's no mention of honey — *land of milk, adorned with citizens.* I admit it sounds better in Latin."

"So Harriot's trying to tell us something about Jerusalem?"

"Not Jerusalem," I said pointedly. *"Sion."*

Even now, looking back on this moment, I can't tease apart all the emotions that played across Alonzo's face, in part because they negated one another. Pride fell before humility, which gave way to shock. The death of one theory had inaugurated the birth of another.

"Syon House," he breathed.

"If Harriot's gold exists, *that's* where he left it. In his own backyard. The estate where he spent the last quarter century of his life. *Golden Sion.*"

"But Harriot specifically mentioned Virginia," said Clarissa.

"His idea of a good joke, maybe. If you don't believe me, let's take another look at that map."

With due understanding of his holy office, Alonzo laid it across the Pelican Arms's mothbally bedspread.

"It turns out our Harriot was a funny guy," I said. "Who knew? These place-names — *Bridgett's Stone, Ahab's Beastiary, Manteo's Lodge.* Such an exotic sound to them. Your mind conjures up pirate coves, hidden inlets, Indian haunts. Poor Amory went to his grave thinking of the New World. In fact, we're very much in the *Old* World. Specifically, the part of it that Thomas Harriot inhabited."

"Nonsense," replied Alonzo. "Manteo is an Indian name. Travel a few miles south from this very spot, you'll find a town with the same name."

"You'll also find that Manteo was a historical figure. He may never have made it to Syon House, but I can guarantee he wasn't too far away. When did the very first English party land in Roanoke?"

"Fifteen eighty-four."

"Exactly. A year before Harriot got there. That same party came away with a human prize. A very helpful Croatan who served as their guide and translator. *And* — whether he liked it or not — their ambassador to the local natives. Which didn't make the guy too popular with his fellow Indians. But the English? They valued him so highly they brought him back to London and, in short order, baptized him — although, unlike Pocahontas, he got to keep his name."

"Manteo," murmured Alonzo.

"The very guy. He and his comrade Wanchese were Harriot's tutors in Algonquin. They're the reason he was fluent before he even reached the New World. And where did they stay during their year in England? At Walter Ralegh's estate, Durham House. Which, as the arrow indicates, is roughly east of Syon Park."

One of Alonzo's hands began to fan the air.

"Go on," he said.

And so I did. Name by name . . .

Bridgett's Stone.

Before it becomes a rich man's pleasure dome, Syon House is a holy sanctuary.

King Henry V, haunted by his father's complicity in the murder of Richard II, decides to expiate that original sin by creating one of England's richest monasteries. And to which saint is it dedicated? In whose name are stone after righteous stone piled?

Saint Bridget.

"Keep going," growled Alonzo.

Ahab's Beastiary.

Soon after King Henry VIII declares himself head of England's church, his chief minister produces a report "certefyinge the Incontynensye of the Nunnes of Syon with the Priores." The monastery is confiscated for the Crown, and the Order of Saint Bridget is cast to the winds. Furious over this desecration, a Franciscan friar warns Henry that God's judgments will fall on his head and that one day "the dogs would lick his blood as they had done Ahab's."

On February 15, 1547, King Henry, now a corpse, is set down for the night at Syon House. Sometime after dark his coffin bursts open. The next morning, horrified servants awake to find a dog licking up their late king's remains.

Ahab has met his beast. In the great hall of Syon House.

"Go a little further," said Alonzo.

Kewasowok's Bier

March 1603. Queen Elizabeth is dying. Most of her subjects cannot recall any other monarch; some have half suspected her of being immortal. Now her ministers and councilors must scramble to determine her successor.

The likeliest candidate seems to be Scotland's King James VI, son of Elizabeth's old antagonist Mary Queen of Scots. From Syon House, the Earl of Northumberland samples the prevailing winds and writes James, telling him that his time is at hand. The king writes back to assure the earl of "what high account you are with your most loving friend, JAMES R."

On the morning of March 24, the queen passes to her reward. Harriot records the event in a subversive fashion. *Kewasowok* is the Algonquin word for "images of gods in the form of men." As for Kewasowok's *bier,* where else would it be but in the place where Elizabeth drew her last breath?

Richmond Palace in Surrey. Due south of Syon House, on the other side of the Thames.

"Which not only confirms my theory," I added, "but narrows our historical window. We can say for certain now that this map was composed sometime after March 24, 1603."

Alonzo's face began to twitch. "But not too long after," he said. "Remember those phrases from Ralegh's letter? *Parlous times. My woundes.* With James on the throne, he knew what danger he was in."

"What danger *was* he in?" asked Clarissa.

"Well, put it this way. The queen died in March. In July, Ralegh was arrested for treason. In November, he was sentenced to death."

"And not just any death," I added. "Judge Popham decreed that Ralegh should first be hanged and then cut down while he was still alive, and then his heart and bowels were to be plucked out and his genitals cut off and thrown in the fire — right before his eyes — and then his head lopped off and his body divided in three quarters —"

"I get the picture," said Clarissa.

"Luckily for Ralegh," I added, "King James overturned the death sentence. But he was still locked away in the Tower for the next thirteen years."

"And don't forget," interjected Alonzo, "what *else* Popham said at Ralegh's trial."

"How could I? *'Let not any devil Harriot, nor any such doctor, persuade you there is no eternity in Heaven. If you think thus, you shall find eternity in Hell fire.'* "

" *'Devil Harriot,'* " echoed Clarissa.

She strolled to the window. Coiled the blinds cord around her wrist.

"Well, Henry. There's only one problem I can see with your theory. The *whale.*"

We all stared at the map in front of us.

"That's where I got stuck the longest," I conceded. "All I can say is thank God for Professor Google. A few years back, it

seems, a seven-ton whale swam up the Thames — past the Houses of Parliament — got as far upstream as Chelsea before it got stuck. Never made it back."

"God, I remember reading that," gasped Alonzo.

"So you'll also remember that the Thames is a tidal river. Every so often a whale gets disoriented and wanders in. It's been happening for centuries; you can look it up."

Once again, I waved my hand over Harriot's map.

"That body of water isn't an ocean at all, it's a river. The river *Thames.* And there," I said, planting my finger on Harriot's cross, "just where we'd expect to find it — Syon Park. Where his treasure is."

All was silent. Nothing was silent. The jaded rattle of the window units, the wire-taut hum of a mosquito, exploring our nether quarters . . . and from Alonzo Wax a hiss so soft it sounded like his dying breath.

"Perfidious Albion."

I understood his sadness. All his Saturday-afternoon-serial visions of buried chests and trails of blood and Spanish doubloons had been torched. As comprehensively as a captured galleon.

But there was a countervailing heat for which I had not reckoned. Gold fever. Not scourged at all, just reattaching itself to a new host.

"How soon," he asked, "may we catch a flight to London?"

"Well, I don't know," I said, folding my arms. "How soon can a dead man roust up a passport?"

This clouded him, but only briefly.

"I'll give Imahoro a call!"

Four syllables, and a new realm of mystery: *Imahoro.*

And still another mystery: Clarissa chose that moment to slide her hand into mine. Not a covert action at all but a manifesto, punctuated by a crackle of static. The School of Night had let in a bit of light.

Scowling, Alonzo stared at the exact point where our hands were interlocked.

"You know how I feel about *emotion,* Henry."

"I know."

"It complicates. It bifurcates."

"I know."

He stared into our grinning faces and, finding no leeway, heaved a groan of Job-like proportions.

"Oh, all *right*. But I forbid you to kiss in my presence."

■ ■ ■ ■

PART THREE

■ ■ ■ ■

Our soules, whose faculties can
   comprehend
The wondrous Architecture of the world:
And measure every wandring plannets
   course:
Still climing after knowledge infinite,
And alwaies mooving as the restles
   Spheares,
Will us to weare ourselves and never rest,
Until we reach the ripest fruit of all,
That perfect blisse and sole felicitie,
The sweet fruition of an earthly crowne.
              — CHRISTOPHER MARLOWE,
                Tamburlaine the Great

30

ISLEWORTH, ENGLAND *1603*

They are no longer obliged to meet in darkness, but neither of them thinks to change it. They pick up exactly where they left off: the master assuming his place by the worktable, Margaret smoothing the paper before her, taking up the ink-stiffened quill —

Only to find the quill being taken from her. By the master himself.

—You are no more my housemaid.

His import is slow in reaching her. Can he really mean her to take the measurements herself?

— My theories can bear no weight, Margaret, unless some other arrive at the same results.

She approaches the table like a new midwife, fearstruck by her own hands. She takes up the half-disk protractor. She positions it against the beams of light. She summons up each angle's name . . .

FCD . . . ECG . . .

She hears her own voice, dry and weight-less.

— *Angulus refractus.* Ten degrees. I pray your pardon, *eleven* degrees. Shall we say *forty-eight* minutes?

After an hour or so, the interrogative lilt leaves her voice. After a few nights more, the task of measuring angles is as simple as sewing a seam. Simpler, in a way, for if she measures true, there can be but the one result.

May passes into June, solids give way to liquids. Salt water, turpentine, spirits of alcohol — each solvent poured into a hollow glass prism and bombarded with light at angles of 5 and 10 and 20 and 30 and 40 and 50 degrees, each change in incidence producing a corresponding change in refraction, each measurement taken twice, then laid down in columns.

The computations are saved until the very end, and here, too, the master demands that she rise to her new position, even if it means rehearsing her in mathematical rudiments.

— As you may recall, Margaret, sine is the length of the opposite divided by the length of the hypotenuse.

— But which is the opposite side, sir?

— Why, the side *opposed* to whichever angle we are studying. In effect, sine tells us how quickly that angle *ascends,* whereas cosine tells us how far it moves *laterally.* An eternal tension between rise and run. Do you follow?

She doesn't. Not at first. And then, slowly, she does. No searing revelation, just a slow accretion of confidence. In her mind, it is something like plunging into a lowland mist. Vision fails you, all the other ways of coping drop away, only doggedness takes you to the other side. The *opposite* side.

— Extraordinary, isn't it, Margaret? Always the same proportion between incidence and refraction. If one were looking for — for a priori evidence of the divinity's existence, one might do far worse.

They are together from nine in the evening until four in the morning: gravely polite, eating but little, conversing less. The master is still so used to his solitude that he speaks largely to himself and dispenses with most civilities, and there comes a moment every night when, driven to some pitch of restlessness, he dashes from the room without a word, taking only the nearest candle.

Watching him go, she cannot help but fear for him, wandering alone in the dark. What if the guard dogs attack? What if the grange keeper mistakes him for a poacher? But he passes always in safety and returns always in a flush of rude health, bearing some offering: an old weather vane; the discarded skin of a grass snake; a bucket of rainwater, teeming with baby newts. One evening, smiling enigmatically, he presents her with a pig's bladder, inflated to its full capacity.

— I have found a near-perfect sphere. I would bid you now imagine *three* lines, radiating from the sphere's center and touching the surface at three different points. Now, if we were to connect these points, what figure would show forth?

— A triangle, sir?

—Yes, but of a most alarming kind. None of its sides would have any prayer of remaining straight, try as they might. They would look rather like this.

He sketches it on the paper.

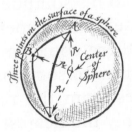

—The challenge lies in determining what the area of such a triangle should be.

Having voiced the problem, he then proceeds to ignore it. But it won't release him. Over the next few hours, it catches him in the act of pouring, in the middle of measuring; it stops his brain mid-motion; it teases the very life from his eyes.

Then, just as the first streaks of light are appearing over the river, the master rises from his chair, very deliberately, in the manner of a man who's stayed too long at a tavern.

With the quill, he delineates three points on the bladder. Then, with the measuring edge, he draws a near-perfect scalene triangle.

— We take the sum of all three angles.

His index finger jumps from corner to corner.

— From this sum we subtract 180 degrees. The remainder is then set as the numerator, with a denominator of 360.

He nods. Once. Twice.

— The resulting fraction tells us — yes — what portion of the hemisphere's surface is occupied by our — our most elusive triangle.

He looks up at her. His smile is oblique, but his eyes are not.

— Shall we test it, Margaret?

The cock is already crowing when she drops

onto her pallet. She is spent, yes, but she is more awake than anyone else in Syon Park.

Numbers. Figures. Angles. These are the last lovers she expected to follow her to bed. When she closes her eyes, they grow only more importunate. A ravishment of rises and runs. They follow her into her dreams, they sing to her, caress her neck, they lift her from her bed, they enter her, every last willing part of her.

Waking the next morning, she is startled to feel the dampness between her legs. Her phantom lovers, come and gone.

Later, coming down the steps, she sees Harriot staggering through the door, his hand pressed to his eyes.

— Master?

— I am not injured.

— But you are!

It is several minutes before he confesses how he has been celebrating last night's achievement.

— Measuring the *sun,* sir?

— Well, naturally, I waited until it had passed beyond a thin cloud, so that its diameter remained distinct. After some minutes of observation, I noticed the cloud darkening. I turned around to face Syon House . . . and the whole world was dark.

By now, he's sitting in a chair, and she's fussing over him like an old nursemaid, fetching him beer, wrapping linen around his eyes.

— You must take greater care, sir.

— Oh, I doubt not but that the damage is fleeting. I am most curious, I confess, to observe those *spots* on the sun's surface of which John of Worcester has written. I should like also to calculate the axial rotation. A measurement which I believe may be — may *best* be effected by —

He pries the bandage off his right eye, peers into the room's shadows.

— Crows.

— Sir?

— I see a company of crows. Flying all together. At a great distance.

Margaret glances toward the windows. The curtains are drawn.

— Never mind, sir.

The crows stay with him for two days. He lies in bed, a cool towel draped across his face. With his blessing, Margaret uses the time to go through his trunks — an Augean stable of bent, shuffled, creased, waxed, stained paper, at the heart of which lies a curiously orderly bundle of documents: deeds, bills of sale, inventories, invoices, all arranged by chronology and dotted with mysterious initials.

Must take up wt W.R. . . . W.R. approve? . . . Cf W.R. exptrs '01 . . .

— Pardon me, sir.

He glances up from his bed. The bandage is off, the crows are growing fainter.

— I wondered if you might tell me, who is W.R.?

— Why, that is Sir Walter.

How simply he speaks the name.

— *Ralegh,* do you mean?

— Yes, yes. He has asked me to oversee certain estate matters. Pertaining to Sherborne and Durham House.

She stands there for some time. At last, to cover her embarrassment, she says:

— Sir Walter writes poetry, does he not?

— Lives for it. Erato over Clio, that's always been his watchword.

He pries his eyelids apart.

— Do you care for verse, Margaret?

She is slow to answer, for the question has the flavor of a trap. But then, to her astonishment, he begins to recite.

Not at the first sight, nor with a dribbed
    shot,
Loue gaue the wound, which, while I
    breathe, will bleede;
But knowne worth did in tract of time

proceed,
Till by degrees, it had full conquest got.

And in that instant, her past comes rushing toward her.

— Have I spoken amiss, Margaret?

— No, sir. It is only the poem, *Astrophel and Stella.* That was —

She swallows.

— It was always a great favorite of mine.

— Then you must be amused to ponder the close quarters we share with Stella's sister.

— Sir?

— Has nobody apprised you of this? *Well,* then . . .

Sidney's sonnet sequence, he explains, was inspired by one of the age's great beauties: a gilded maid named Penelope Devereux. Her brother was the second Earl of Essex, but even in battle, they say, the earl never slew as many men as did Penelope's dark eyes. She went on to marry Robert Rich — against her will, rumor had it — and Sidney . . . well, he wed old Walsingham's daughter. The image of Penelope stayed bright within him, though, and her name was ever on his lips in the month it took him to die.

— That would have been in the aftermath

of the Battle of Zutphen, where he was pierced in the thigh and where, to his great honor, he gave water to a subordinate, saying, *Your necessity is greater than mine.*

Margaret has never heard Harriot talk at such length or with such sentiment.

— But if Penelope was Stella . . . who was Stella's sister, sir?

— *Dorothy* Devereux. Not so beautiful as Penelope but markedly more intelligent. A match for any man in wit. After running rather quickly through one husband, she then consented, after arduous negotiations, to marry Henry Percy. And brought him Syon House in the bargain. Where she now reigns as mistress.

In her time here, Margaret has seen Lady Percy perhaps half a dozen times. Always from a distance, no more connected to a servant than a Moorish prince. And yet connected all the same, through this skein of circumstance.

To think how many other wonders are to be unearthed and concatenated. Some afternoons she walks through the house in a bright daze, as though she were following Ptolemy's lantern.

It is the Gollivers who bring her back to earth. All it takes is the cricket-like chirring of the old man as he labors up the stair. Or

— more personally — the hiss Mrs. Golliver makes whenever they cross paths.

— Ssssow.

— Sssslattern.

— Sssslut.

One afternoon, more vexed than usual,
Mrs. Golliver makes the mistake of leading
with a hard consonant.

— *Bitch.*

Margaret spins around.

— I should not wish to convey that to the
master!

It is a bluff, no more. But when she sees
the spasm of fear cross Mrs. Golliver's face,
she grasps for the first time her new power.
No, the power she has had all along without
knowing it.

— Bless us, Margaret . . . you heard me
wrong . . . I should never . . .

From here on, the old woman speaks not
a word in her presence. She has been driven
underground.

— Ha!

Their pens are scratching, nearly in unison, across two parallel sheets of paper. A
ripe river air is pouring through the open
windows, and the quiet is so thickly banked
that the master's outburst affects her like a
box on the ears.

— Sir?

— The School of Night.

He does not look at her when he says it. Nor does he explain his meaning. But there is no mistaking the change in his eyes, from a glow of reverie to a hard deep chill.

— Margaret, would you kindly fetch my cloak?

31

The late queen's annual progresses were the ruin of many a noble. With her retinue of courtiers and attendants and riders and messengers and musicians, all clamoring to be housed and fed and provisioned and entertained, Elizabeth had but to descend on an estate to drive its owner into insolvency.

King James, in keeping with his own character and the straitened times, travels light and sober. He declares in advance he will not stay at Syon House for more than a night. He cares not if the clocks are stopped in his honor. He abjures the pageants, the fireworks, the cannons, the tumbling and juggling and tilts and plays and masques. His restraint extends even to leaving his queen at home (though this is no great hardship for him). He is paying a call, no more.

But when a king comes to call, there is

work to be done. A table to prepare, a menu to draw up, musicians to engage. New livery must be ordered, the Venetian glasses must be cleaned, every surface in every room scrubbed to a rare shine. Tapestries, carpets, linen, china must be made ready, and an entire quadrant of Syon House must be set aside for the royal party's pleasure.

And that doesn't account for the event itself, which will demand all the servants the earl can spare. Even Margaret is enlisted — for one night alone and with Master Harriot's consent — in her old capacity in the scullery. How fantastical the place seems to her now. *Surely,* she thinks, as she fires up the old stoves and scours the floor and worktables and cleans the dishes and silverware and swills the floors and carries out the rubbish, *surely it wasn't me who once toiled here. Surely it was some other girl.*

But her limbs take to the tasks as if she has never been away, and, knowing that her term is only a few hours, she can even take pleasure in this labor; she can lose herself in it until the blast of trumpets, coming at six minutes before eight, recalls her to tonight's occasion.

And then she hears the clatter of pots and the roars of cooks and the bellows of the footmen and housemaids. She will not see the king's procession. She will not see Lady Percy's elongated curtsy, she will not hear the ceremonial poem of welcome, nor will she feel the crackle of tension as the king and the earl walk side by side, with fixed smiles, into the great hall.

There can be no denying the two men's differences. His Majesty steeps himself in theology and poetry; the Earl, natural science and philosophy. The king is Scottish; the earl's family has been hunting Scots for generations. Worse still, the earl once contemplated marriage to Lady Arbella Stuart, an alliance that might have cost James the English Crown.

And yet was it not the earl who made the legitimizing gesture of meeting the new king at Enfield Chase? Was it not the earl who rode into London at the king's right hand? Let us consign the past to the past. For the present — on this balmy moth-speckled night — the earl and the king, with the help of Spanish Bastard wine and fat meat and jumbles and gingerbread, manage to elide their old differences and part something close to friends.

And in so doing, they make a kind of inner glow within the outer spectacle. A spectacle that Margaret wakens to only when her work is done. By then it is two in the morning, and there is enough light on every side of her to illuminate all of England. Every chamber in the house ablaze . . . two parallel rows of torches scorching out a path to the river . . . and out on the water, the royal barge and, encircling it, an armada of tilt boats, wherries and hoys, all at anchor, all singing with light. And each light finding its mirror image in the water and an answering light in the stars.

A great dazzlement and, behind it, a single word.

Refraction.

Light strikes an object, and this encounter forever changes the light and forever reveals the object. *The structure that lies beneath the surface of all things.* That's how the master put it, and even then it affected her like a promise. To have that promise so rewarded, as it is in this moment, to feel herself pressed against the world's skin, gazing through its pores . . . where are there words for such a thing?

A minute ago, she could barely stand, and now she is running as fast as her bruised feet will take her. She wants him to know. He must know that nothing she has done in his company has been idle.

The master's house, in contrast to its surroundings, is virtually dark, and it takes her some minutes to locate him, for he is not in the laboratory but in the study. Slouched in one of those hard oak chairs he favors. His book — the collection of Montaigne essays he no doubt intended to read all night — remains unopened in his lap.

He sees her. He stammers, he half rises, the book tumbles from his lap, he stoops for it, then jerks upright. All these actions betray him, but more than anything else, it is his eyes, the way they receive her image and bend it and absorb it and send it back.

So this is how love looks, she thinks. *Not at all what I would have guessed.*

32

I suppose it doesn't speak too well for America's national security that, on the evening of September 23, 2009, a dead man was able to catch a flight to London.

Let me say this much in TSA's defense. By the time Alonzo Wax made it to Dulles International Airport, he was Solomon Spiegel. Very much in the land of the living, with a Social Security number and passport to prove it.

Consider this, too. Alonzo looked even less like his living self now than he had in the Outer Banks. True, the moonshiner's beard was gone, but his hair now rose from his head in a pompadour cliff, dyed butterscotch, and he was wrapped in a Big and Tall glen plaid suit, with a stripy-warp Van Heusen tie. You'd have pegged him for agribusiness.

All this artifice had now been crammed into an aisle seat in the fifty-eighth row of a

Virgin Atlantic Airbus A340 bound for Heathrow. Alonzo hated flying economy, but Clarissa was footing the bill for the tickets, and even he didn't have the crust to demand business class. Particularly since it had been Clarissa who'd called the Dare County, North Carolina, police from an airport pay phone to tell them about a dead man buried in the sand.

Maybe that took more out of her than I guessed, because as soon as she got on the plane she swallowed two Ambiens, popped on her earphones, and watched a Sandra Bullock movie until her eyes went from tolerant to closed.

I draped a blanket over her and I was thinking about inserting one of the micropillows behind her head when, from the other side of me, Alonzo snarled:

"Do *not*."

"What?"

"If you are even *thinking* at this moment that she's purty when she sleeps, I will strike you."

I inched the top of my seat back by two inches.

"No one sleeps as purty as you, Alonzo."

"Solomon," he hissed. "And how would *you* know?"

He had a point there. I had never, to the

321

best of my recall, seen him asleep. I had dozed off on him, though, hadn't I? Most recently in that Nags Head motel room, but something similar had happened at the tail end of one of our collegiate bull sessions. I woke at noon to find him frowning at me as if I were a misdelivered package.

"Think strategically," I told him now. "We could give Clarissa slinky clothes and have her seduce You Know Who."

Alonzo slipped the Virgin Atlantic eyeshades over his face. "If you are referring to Mr. Bernard Styles, I believe he prefers the tall assassin type."

"What the hell is it with you and Styles?"

"Other than his stealing all my books. And the small matter of his wanting me dead."

"I just mean it's my impression that collectors get along a little better than you two. Generally."

"You persist in calling him a collector. This is maddening of you. Let me tell you how I first became aware of You Know *Whom*. I'd gone to London for one of Bloomsbury's auctions. As you know, I always make a habit of reviewing the merchandise the day before if possible. Only this time I wasn't alone. Trailing me across the floor was this young man — no, rat*fink* would be the mot juste. Wiry and smiley.

Springy feet. Possibly he had been a satellite TV salesman but not a good one. Even worse at espionage. Everywhere I went, he followed, scribbling away in his wide-ruled theme book.

"I thought nothing of him, and then the next day at auction, I noticed that every item I placed a bid on — mirabile dictu — had another bidder. The same bidder. Pockets as deep as his effrontery. Before the day had passed, the mole's employer, *Mister* Bernard Styles, had snapped up every single volume in my crosshairs. This, I don't need to tell you, was beyond the pale."

Alonzo waited until the next Bloomsbury auction. Sure enough, the same springy man showed up, and Alonzo led him on a merry chase, pausing before the most worthless items in the catalog. The next day, he had the satisfaction of watching Bernard Styles throw thousands of pounds at rubbish.

"Well, the day after that, I received a summons from His Nibs. Most anxious to make amends. Poured my tea for me, did everything but rub my corns. Was I swayed? I was not. 'The next time you want my opinions,' I said, 'you can pay for them like everybody else.' He said, 'Very well, how much?' 'To *you,*' I said, 'I am not for sale.' "

"Don't you ever wonder what would've

happened if, you know . . ."

"What?"

"You'd made a little nicer with him, that's all."

"That is not the recommended approach with reptiles. You keep them in full view and keep a sharp edge handy."

Within another minute, the lights around us began to go out, one by one. I leaned back toward Alonzo.

"So if you and Styles had such bad blood from the get-go, why did he let you into his collections? Why were you even in touch with him?"

"You should know this by now, Henry. Collectors never burn bridges. It is never in our interest to do so. Upon further reflection, I decided to throw Styles a few bones. He responded with a few more bones. An entirely specious cordiality ensued. And if it meant enduring his rather vulgar civility, then . . ." He stifled a yawn. "Well, in the end, it has all proved worth it."

Worth it, I thought. Lily suffocated in a vault. Amory buried in the Carolina sand. Alonzo a felon and an international refugee. Me, very possibly, a suspected murderer. *Worth it.*

"Here's what I still can't figure out," he said. "If Harriot didn't find his gold in

Virginia, where did he find it? He never left England again; he virtually never left his house."

"Maybe Ralegh gave it to him. Or Northumberland. I mean, both those guys were in trouble at some point. The Crown was confiscating their assets. Maybe they wanted to keep something around for posterity."

"But on the map, Harriot calls it '*my* treasure.' You're not suggesting he kept the money for himself?"

If he had, I thought, he would have earned himself some fierce enemies. And the record showed none of that. Ralegh, in his will, referred to Harriot as a "trustye & faithfull frinde" and, in a strangely sweet gesture, bequeathed him "all such blacke suites of apparell as I haue in the same house." As for Northumberland, one of his first acts on leaving the Tower was to purchase a monument to Harriot's memory. If they ever felt betrayed by their old teacher, they did a good job of hiding it.

"I suppose there's one other possibility," Alonzo drawled.

"Which is?"

"Perhaps you'll recall what Thomas Harriot was studying between 1599 and 1600."

■ ■ ■ ■

In fact, Harriot was harkening to the same siren call that had lured so many other great minds onto the rocks. Leibniz heard it, too. So did Robert Boyle and Tycho Brahe. Isaac Newton went to his death dreaming not of gravity or calculus but of the philosopher's stone.

For these men, alchemy was about more than turning lead into gold. It was about transformation. If they could alter the properties of inanimate matter, they might one day effect the same change in *human* matter. And then? Well, our last fleshly impurities would burn away like dross, and the whole earth would be left in a state of ecstatic perfection.

That kind of dream doesn't loosen its hold on the dreamer. No wonder, then, that Harriot fired up the burners and hurled himself at immortality. There was only one problem. . . .

"It can't be done," I reminded Alonzo.

"What?"

"You can't change lead to gold all by yourself. That's why Harriot gave up."

"Henry, listen. In optics, in astronomy, in

326

physics, Thomas Harriot was years — *decades* — ahead of other scientists, okay? What's to say, in this particular matter, he wasn't a few centuries ahead?"

"Oh, I get it. Harriot just — what — whips himself up this honking pot of gold. Then he buries it in the ground. Like a fucking leprechaun. Never tells another soul about it, just lets it rot there."

"He couldn't risk it. In King James's world, alchemy verged on heresy."

"God, where to begin, Alonzo?"

"Solomon."

"A gold atom, *Solomon,* has three fewer protons than a lead atom. You can't make up that difference in some rinky-dink Tudor laboratory. You need — Christ, something like a particle accelerator. And even then, whatever gold you make is going to be worth far less than the energy you put into it."

A light hum began to emerge from Alonzo's nostrils, declining gradually into text.

"There are more things —"

"God."

". . . in heaven and earth —"

"Stop."

". . . than are dreamt of in your philosophy."

"Yeah, and guess what? Shakespeare

327

didn't know squat about particle physics. And with all due respect, neither did Harriot."

Alonzo was silent after that, but I knew his silences. They generally held not an ounce of concession. As for me, my Benadryl was finally kicking in. I put on the eyeshade and pulled that thin acrylic blanket over me and eased the seat back another couple of inches.

"Jesus," I muttered. "Alchemy."

I didn't let a single crack show in my skeptic's face. What I failed to tell Alonzo was that, three days earlier, in a moment of passing distraction, I had glanced at Harriot's original map. There was no particular reason to look. There was nothing on that page I hadn't already seen a dozen times.

Only there was.

On the lower right-hand corner, rising up like a scar, lay a single word. Scratched in the thinnest of ink, visible only in this particular slant of late-afternoon light: *pneuma.*

Not Harriot's hand, as best I could tell. It wasn't even cursive: the letters sat isolated from each other, and the final *a* straggled nearly off the page.

For a long time, I stared at the page. I knew, at one level, I was simply looking at another word, the Greek word for *spirit.* Aristotle threw it around like candy.

But I knew I was looking at something else. The building block of medieval alchemy.

Pneuma was the active principle or vital force believed to dwell within all earthly matter. To transmute one thing into another, an alchemist like Thomas Harriot would have had to transform its *pneuma* — its portion of heavenly quintessence — becoming, in effect, a *re*-creator, sparking new forms from chaos.

Amazing to think now that, from this single string of letters, so many questions could swarm forth. Was Harriot still carrying out alchemical experiments after 1600? Did he stumble across something that never made it into the historical record? Could he actually have *made* the gold he was at such pains to hide? Or, at the very least, *believed* he had?

Somewhere over the Atlantic Ocean, Harriot entered my dreams. It wasn't a vision on the order of Clarissa's — just your basic dog-and-pony show from the subconscious. There was the great man himself, head to toe in black, standing before his Bath-brick cottage. I could feel a faint nip in the air . . .

329

I could hear a rustle of clouds overhead . . . and, oh, yes, the house was erupting with gold.

From the eaves, from the windows, through the doorways, out of the very earth. Bars and coins and scepters and diadems, piling higher and higher like wheat in a granary. And in the midst of that profusion, Harriot stood grimacing in apology.

"I can't seem to make it stop," he said.

33

They were waiting for us when we left customs.

And with such an air of expectation that I actually looked to see if they were holding welcome signs: HENRY CAVENDISH. CLARISSA DALE.

No welcome, though, in their attitude. Or in their clothes: black bespoke suits, tropical wool, and black loafers polished down to the aglets. The smaller of the two men was ruddy and pitted; he tapped his left toe like a filly in a paddock and eyed us from a slight angle as if he'd caught us stealing his cable signal. The other was closely shaven, frappuccino-colored, big as a Visigoth, with a stone-lidded countenance that parted suddenly to reveal a chorine's grin.

"Welcome!" he called. "How was your flight?"

Clarissa was the first to stop . . . then me . . . but the Visigoth was already making straight for Alonzo.

"Mr. *Spiegel.*" (The thinnest lacquer of irony over that bogus name.) "I'm Agent Mooney. And this is Agent Milberg. And we're — oh, wait, hold on!"

Fumbling through his pockets, he extracted a laminated badge.

"Very sorry. Interpol."

"Interpol," repeated Alonzo faintly.

"Now you're in safe hands, Mr. Spiegel, please know that. We've no desire to make a public display. No *perp* walks."

"No handcuffs," his comrade added.

"That's not how we roll, is it? All we're after is a bit of a chat, upon conclusion of which you may be on your merry way. Rejoicing in London's many sights and sounds."

Alonzo had rebounded enough now to give his chest a pouter-pigeon swell.

"I'm a very busy man."

"I knew you would be."

"Kindly tell me the theme of this chat."

"Can't go into it."

"Where is it to take place?"

"HQ, of course. Everything on the up and up, you'll see."

And then he clapped his hands together and, in the voice of a camp counselor, cried:

"*Shall* we?"

"My friends," remonstrated Alonzo.

"Oh!" The Visigoth wheeled around on us. "They can come, too!"

" 'Course they can," added Agent Milberg.

Only in England could we have been taken into custody so politely and neatly. Not a voice raised, no pleasantry overlooked. We gathered our bags from the carousel, rolled them to the curb, blinked in the light of early morning, and then climbed without protest into a state-of-the-art Lincoln Town Car, black clearcoat, with power lumbar and programmable memory seat and leather upholstery so pristine it recoiled from our touch.

Clarissa camped herself in the middle of the back seat. Of the three of us, she was the only one not taking things in a spirit of resignation.

"I've never been to England before," she said, "but given that we're just a few miles from London, and given that *you* gentlemen are Interpol, ten bucks says you're taking us to the Secretariat."

Her wager barely seemed to clear the headrest. It was left to Agent Milberg, slouching against the passenger-side door, to mutter:

" 'S right."

"Oh, no, no, wait," said Clarissa, waving a finger. "The Interpol Secretariat is in Lyon. Lyon, *France.* God knows what I was thinking."

She fell silent, but there something dangerously tensile about her now, like a balloon bending before the pin's first prick. I don't know why, but I chose that exact moment to look out the window. Expecting, naturally, to be heading eastward on the M4 toward London. When, in fact, we were northbound on the A312 Trunk Road. Making for parts unknown.

And that's when I realized Clarissa wasn't addressing her remarks to the two agents. She was speaking to me and Alonzo. She was raising the alarm.

"Well, anyway," she said, "this has been very educational for me. Now that I've had time to think about it, I seem to recall that Interpol agents aren't authorized to arrest people."

More silence from the front seat. At last, Agent Milberg, tipping his head a couple of inches our way, mumbled:

"Change of regs, isn't it?"

"You must be right. There must have been a recent change in the regulatory structure of Interpol. Which I was not aware of, apologies."

And just like that, the locks went down on either side of us.

My initial reaction, oddly, was relief. We *weren't* being arrested. I *wasn't* in immediate danger of prison. Because these guys had as much to do with law enforcement as I did.

And yet we were just as surely in their power, were we not?

No point in presuming they were unarmed — those black suit jackets could conceal any manner of pistol or revolver. No point, either, in trying to phone for help. We were in a foreign country, in a foreign car, bound for God knows where. Not to put too fine a point on it, we were fucked.

And at first, when I saw the fluttering of Clarissa's fingers against her thigh, I assumed she was drinking from the same well of distress. Only gradually did I see that those fingers were alive with intention.

Which is to say, she was texting.

And with the fluency of a girl in eleventh-grade American history, glancing down every now and then to track her progress. It took her no more than a minute to draft and send the message, and I didn't even have time to wonder who the hell was receiving it, because in the next moment Alonzo's phone vibrated into life.

He peered down at the screen, gave Clarissa a single questioning look, and deleted the message with two pulses of his finger. Then, with great ponderousness, he swept the back of his arm across his forehand.

"Sorry," he said. "Would you gentlemen mind? The air conditioner?"

Clarissa gave it twenty seconds.

"Alonzo," she said. "What's wrong?"

"Not good," he said, pressing his hands to his temples and softly swaying. "Not . . . mouth . . ."

"Mouth *what?*"

"Tingly."

A shorter beat this time.

"Jesus," whispered Clarissa.

The trembling began in Alonzo's head. Then it passed, inch by inch, down the column of his neck, radiating out to his arms and fingers, until the very air seemed to be vibrating.

Agent Milberg half turned his head. "Got the shakes, does he?"

"If by *shakes*" — Clarissa made a studied effort to calm herself — "if by shakes, you mean hypoglycemia, then yes, he does have the shakes. Alonzo, I need you to tell me. When did you last take your insulin?"

Insulin.

"Last night," he muttered between trem-
ors.

"Last *night?* Jesus —"

And with that I swung into action.

"It's my fault," I said.

Clarissa snapped her head toward me.

"What are you talking about?"

"I told him not to pack his insulin kit in
the carry-on."

"Why?"

"Come on, you know how weird airport
security can be about needles."

"Oh, that's great, Henry. Wow, your advice
was — thank you so much for that. Alonzo,
listen to me. *Where* are the syringes?"

He grunted. The shaking had spread now
to his torso.

"Where?" Clarissa asked. "Just tell me
where."

"Luggage . . ."

Clarissa sat back up. Heaved out a river of
air.

"Shit."

Impossible to say how much of our histri-
onic display had filtered to the front of the
car. Agent Milberg was moved enough to
say:

"Be there in no time."

"Um . . ."

Clarissa tweezed her fingers around the bridge of her nose. "See, here's the deal. That's not soon enough."

And, getting no response, she added, in a brittle voice:

"Would you please *look* at him?"

When at last Agent Milberg consented to turn around, this is what he beheld: a two-hundred-and-forty-pound man (conservatively estimated) with half-shut eyes and blanched face, quivering all over like an aspen in a thunderstorm.

"I don't want to be alarmist," said Clarissa. "And it's not like you asked, but I feel I should tell you he's on the verge of a diabetic coma. Which is kind of serious."

"Alonzo," I murmured, reaching for his shoulder. "It's all right. Hold on."

"He needs his insulin, okay? We need to stop the car."

The first stirrings of disquiet appeared in Agent Milberg's dour face. He cast a glance at Alonzo, then his partner, and slowly turned back around.

"Look," I said. "If you want this man to die right here, in the back of your car, that's fine. I doubt *Interpol* would be too happy about it."

And, getting no reply, I lifted my voice into a more strained register.

"He's worth a lot more alive than dead."

Still no answer. I was just getting around to my next tack when I heard Agent Mooney ask, in a low voice: "Where's his kit?"

"In his suitcase," Clarissa said. "I can get it."

"*I* can get it," I said.

"Henry, please. You're hopeless at finding things. It'll take me half a minute, tops."

Both of us stared at the back of Agent Mooney's head, waiting for a sign. But the only sign came from the car itself, which, without warning, swerved onto the left shoulder, coming to a full stop in a cloud of gravel alongside a culvert.

"You've got one minute," said Agent Mooney.

And as Clarissa began clambering over me to the door, he added, in an impish voice:

"My partner would be happy to assist you."

This was a surprise to his partner, whose face squeezed down into sharpei folds.

"Simon's really very good at this," the Visigoth went on, barely suppressing his glee. "Aren't you, Simon?"

A low rumble issued from Agent Milberg's chest as he shouldered his door open, stalked to the back of the car, and flipped open the lid of the trunk.

And now whatever fear I had kept at bay rushed back with a leering force. Clarissa could stall as long as she liked, but sooner or later, they would comb through the entire contents of Alonzo's bag, and they would find no syringes, no needles, no insulin.

And that would be an end to all our chances.

As if he were divining my thoughts, Agent Mooney called back from the driver's seat.

"I'd hate to think you were having us on now. When we've gone out of our way to be pleasant and agreeable."

Rather than reply, I unbuckled my seat belt, took off my jacket, and flung it over Alonzo's trembling bulk.

"Hold on," I crooned. "Just a few more seconds."

Only the seconds shaded into minutes, and the trunk remained steadfastly upright. And not a sound emerged.

"So tell me," I said, hearing the thinness of my own tone. "Have you worked for Bernard Styles a long time?"

"Never heard of him," said Agent Mooney.

"Oh, that's funny, 'cause — you know, I can't really think who else would want to talk to us."

"Not for me to say, is it? *Cripes!*" he

snapped, giving the horn three light taps.

I could see his eyes ranging across the rearview mirror, the whorls of discontent on his smooth round face. He hummed under his breath. He danced his hands on the steering wheel. At last, when he could bear it no longer, he thumbed down the power window and turned his head to one side and yelled:

"Simon! We ain't got all day!"

And in that instant, he came face-to-face with a gun.

A Desert Eagle semiautomatic pistol, to be specific. Looking even larger than usual in the small white hands of Clarissa Dale.

"If you would," she said, only slightly panting, "please step out of the car."

" 'Course I will. 'Course I will, sweet-heart."

Even as one of his hands moved to open the door, the other reached under his jacket.

"Disarmed him, did you, sweetheart? That was very clever."

The folds of his coat billowed as he talked. Some intricate Braille-like maneuver . . . followed by a brief pause . . . and then his hand began slowly to reemerge.

"Easy does it," I said.

Normally, I would have stood no chance against him — it took both my hands just

341

to encircle his wrist — but in this case, the numbers were in my favor. There was Clarissa, armed, unblinking. Directly behind was Alonzo, sitting up now, rude with health. It took the Visigoth no more than a couple of seconds to calculate his odds. Then, with a curiously bashful smile, he loosened his grip on the gun.

A second later, it was resting, warm and bulbous, in my palm.

"Okay," said Clarissa. "Let me explain how this works, Agent Mooney. You step out of the car. You stay on *this* side of the car, and you keep your head down. I don't want any passing motorists taking pity on you. Is that clear enough?"

"Clear as a bell, love."

Only it must not have been. The moment he stepped out of the Town Car, his head — by instinct, maybe — began to go vertical. For which presumption it received a clout from Clarissa's gun. Stunned, the Visigoth sank, wobbling, to his knees.

"God, these things are *heavy,* aren't they?" Clarissa said. "I'm not sure Interpol agents would be packing heat, either, but I could be wrong. What do you think, Henry?"

I couldn't answer because I had just found Agent Milberg. Sprawled on the gravel. Not completely still but the closest thing.

"How?" I whispered.

"Oh," said Clarissa. "I took a self-defense course once. Works best when least expected."

"So what next, Femme Nikita?"

"Well, we should probably have Agent Mooney lie down on his stomach."

Nothing but cheer irradiated the Visigoth's face as he palmed his way into a fully prone position. You might have thought he was glad for the rest.

"What do you have, Henry?" Clarissa's voice was low and hard. "A belt, maybe?"

"I've got a belt."

"Then —"

Half exasperated, she swept her hands in the direction of the prone man. I knelt by him and drew his hands behind his back. Heard his voice percolating up from the ground.

"Listen, mate."

I wrapped my belt around his wrist. One loop . . . two . . .

"You're not even in this," he murmured. "No one's got a beef against *you.*"

I cinched the belt tight. Tucked the end into the buckle.

"See, right now?" he said. "You are *aggravating* the situation. You *know* that, don't you?"

"Personally," said Clarissa, "I think the situation is getting better."

She knelt down, unknotted the red tie that dangled from Agent Mooney's neck, and used it to bind his ankles. So lost was she in her labor I'm not sure she even heard his monologue.

"Listen to me. The both of you, you've been *marked* now, see? I'm just saying you leave things like this, you walk away, I'm not responsible for what happens later, eh? You capeesh? No, really, are you —"

It took a kick in the flank from Clarissa to stop his flow.

"Sorry," she said. "I'm just trying to find your phone."

It was an iPhone 3GS, with cheetah wallpaper. I dug it out of his pocket and scrolled through the list of contacts, looking for Bernard Styles or Halldor. Nothing.

So I carried it back to the car and set it with great care in the direct path of the front tire.

"Okay then," said Clarissa.

With her left foot, she gave Agent Mooney a single push . . . and watched him roll into the culvert, accelerating as he went. I give him this: He was silent the whole way, although I've no doubt his mind was noisy with revenge.

Through all this activity, Alonzo never even left the car. (He was a man accustomed to outsourcing.) And when Clarissa and I climbed into the front seat, his only remark was:

"I am waiting."

"For what?" I asked.

"The praise due my thespian efforts. Garrick and Kean would have wept with envy. Shakespeare would have written whole historical cycles for me."

"You were great," said Clarissa negligently, inclining her seat toward the steering wheel. "Henry, they don't have a GPS. You think you can get us in the right direction?"

"I think so."

"Then off we go, kids."

She rolled the car just far enough forward to hear the crunch of Agent Mooney's iPhone. Then she leaned into me and kissed me hard and square. Her lips tasted of sweat and copper and airline chicken.

"Mm," I said.

"Mm," she said.

"Um, *hello?*" cried Alonzo from the back seat. "Bonnie? Clyde? We've got business to do."

34

Amazing that he ever thought her plain.

Was it the smallness of her mouth? He had yet to see it in all its moods: damp with curiosity, plumped by humor, folding down in moments of highest concentration. He had yet to see how her rounded chin chimed with her round fern-green eyes. The larger music of her: that Roman nose and the tracery of Delft-blue veins along her temple and the hint of power in her corded forearms. He recalls once more — how can he not? — those lines of Sidney's.

> Not at the first sight, nor with a dribbed
>   shot,
> Loue gaue the wound, which, while I
>   breathe, will bleede;
> But knowne worth did in tract of time
>   proceed,
> Till by degrees, it had full conquest got.

Known worth, yes. And now, being fully

conquered by it, what may he do?

They carry on as before; they must. But the wound has changed his manner toward her. He is sullen one minute, snappish the next. Most disagreeable when most distracted by the green-apple scent of her.

— Come! You take too long about it.

— Can you not write faster?

— My light is blocked!

She bears it all with great mildness.

— I am very sorry, Master.

This only incenses him further.

— Why must you call me Master? There is no call.

— As you wish, sir.

— Sir neither.

— What shall I call you then?

He has given it precious little thought himself.

— It seems to me my friends have called me always Tom.

But he can see at once this is too great a liberty for her. And now he is too late to correct it. Denied the old form of address, she will be forced to call him nothing at all.

The two of them still gravitate toward the dark, but hide though they might, the summer days come and find them: stretch further into the evening, visit a few minutes

347

earlier each morning. There is a wisdom in Nature, after all, that no mortal can resist. So, after some discussion, they agree to devote their afternoons to outings.

Nothing of a common cast, he is firm on this point. No theater or bear-baiting, no cockfighting. If they are to go out in the world, they must take something away for their pains. And so they study the dispersal patterns of the swans around Chiswick Eyot. They track tides at Brentford Ait, they use an astrolabe to take latitude readings from London Bridge, they track the refraction of sunlight at the fogbound Blackfriars Stairs.

In the second week of June, wild news comes from Greenwich. A monstrous fish, discovered in Rainham Creek, has been chased upriver with harping irons and fish spears, getting as far as the Isle of Dogs before beaching on an outlying shoal.

No one can explain why the fish should have wandered so far from sea or why the fishermen pursuing it should have forborne to kill it on the spot. But their charity has won its reward: a steady current of gawkers, lured by promise of a great sea beast and willing to pay a halfpenny each to glimpse it.

Seeing how much they stand to make, the

fishermen decide to charge an additional penny for the privilege of touching the beast. Margaret and Harriot are only too glad to pay. By the time they clamber down the embankment, the tide has gone out, and everything above the creature's tail lies starkly revealed. The white belly, the sickle-shaped fin, the escarpment of the head. Against such mass Harriot can only oppose numbers.

— One and twenty in length, by my guess. Sixteen in height. Girth I should reckon at a dozen, perhaps thirteen. . . .

But they have brought no paper or pen or inkwell, and Margaret is too busy anyway, circling the great fish. Abashed, he follows her, pausing each time she pauses, studying each gash in the creature's underbelly and head . . . compelled at every moment to *explain.*

— No doubt it has collided with boats during its journey. Or else it has been dragged along the riverbed. To judge from my own soundings, the Thames is no more than two fathoms in any of its oxbows. . . .

She just keeps walking.

— Extraordinary, is it not, Margaret? That it should be breathing, I mean, after all this time. I have never known a fish with such a capacity for —

And then the skin of the fish's head wrinkles open to reveal an eye.

Lashless, dry, veined . . . appallingly small. For a few long seconds, it shudders in its socket, then sinks out of sight. And with that, everything seems to change, though not in any way he can identify.

Margaret lifts her head. She murmurs:

— Upriver.

— Pardon?

— It was looking upriver. That is most curious, is it not? Why not down? To where it came from?

— Well, I suspect it had no choice in the matter. This is — this is simply the position in which it ran aground.

She shakes her head.

— It must have had business up here.

— Dear me, how should a fish have — more likely, it was *addled* by some magnetic shift in the sea tides. Perhaps connected to the motion of the stars. I myself have long noted the correlation between the orbital motions of Mars and . . . and . . .

Her lips fold down, just as they always do when she is concentrating. Only she is not concentrating on him.

— What if we pushed it? she asks.

— Pushed it?

— Back in the water.

— My dear Margaret . . .

— It might then find its way back.

— 'Tis against all reason. The beast weighs well above two tons. We would want five score men simply to move it, and even then, the creature would have no, no *strength* remaining for its journey. . . .

He is being rational. And when has rationality ever felt so inadequate?

Margaret lays one hand on the fish's sun-bleached flank. Rests it there. Then, in a voice of soft wonder, she says:

— How late it has grown. We must be getting back.

The great fish's life is prolonged briefly, by a late-evening shower. The next morning, at three minutes past seven, it breathes its last. Another day's worth of gawkers file past. Then the beast is hewn into pieces and boiled in cauldrons for oil.

In the days following, Harriot finds himself more and more persuaded that something has changed between him and Margaret. Lacking any means to verify his theory, he catches himself spying on her when she isn't looking, constructing theses for her silences. Only in brave moments will he hazard direct queries.

— Are you happy here, Margaret?

—Yes.

— I mean content.

—Yes, of course.

—You do not long for some other occupation?

— This suits quite well.

The words are meant to reassure, he knows that, but would Astrophel and Stella have spoken like this?

And how exactly did Sidney's lovers become Thomas Harriot's paradigms?

Something is softening in him, no doubt. More often than he would like, he tumbles back to his past — his childhood — a habit that becomes more pronounced with the approach of Midsummer's Eve. It was the one night of the year when his father danced. (The Bishop of Chester's jig, the only dance he knew.) It was the one night when Harriot felt safe in his father's company. And now, if he closes his eyes, he can actually feel the blast of the old bonfires. He can see himself, no more than six or seven, tossing in scraps of kindling and gathering birch boughs and pinning larkspur and Saint-John's-wort over the door lintel.

In due course, June 24 arrives, and Harriot seems to unravel before it. He blots figures, breaks vials, asks Margaret again and again to repeat herself. At last he wheels away from the worktable.

— I cannot!

To which she says what she always says.

— As you wish.

But there is an element of grace to those words now. Freed from his duties, he rounds on her and, in a giddy voice, cries:

— How shall it be if we take a holiday?

— Tonight, do you mean?

—Yes.

She is caught off guard, he can see that. It is even obscurely pleasing to him.

— As you wish.

From the pantry, they take a flagon of hard Devon cider, some walnuts, slabs of Dutch cheese. Harriot fills his pipe; Margaret lights it for him in the hearth coals. They step through the door, and the summer air that greets them stops them as surely as a great northern wind.

Margaret's voice is strangely faint.

—Where shall we go?

He beckons her to follow. They pass through a gate, around scarlet oaks and white poplars, past a sward of Michaelmas daisies, past a nightingale garden . . . right up to the Bath-stone façade of the great house itself. With a sly smile, Harriot raises his arm and points toward the very tip of the northwest turret.

— Up there?

— Naturally.

— All the way, do you mean?

— You may take my arm if the steps are too many.

A faint starchiness to her reply:

— I need no help, thank you.

Many of the estate's servants have been given their liberty tonight, so there is no one to stop them, no one to inquire where they are bound. As they climb the spiraling steps, the only sound that follows them is the scrape of their shoes.

They come to a stout wooden door, girded with black iron. From his cloak, Harriot removes a key, fits it into the lock and presses his full weight against the door. It groans open, and in the next moment he and Margaret are standing atop Syon House.

And what a difference is made by their elevation! From here, they can see bonfires to the south and west. Cattle browsing in the water meadows. The sun's pomegranate rays swimming through the willows.

Margaret leans into one of the tower's crenellations, bows her head.

— Are you weary? he asks.

— No, I am only recalling my youth. My mother warned us to take great *care* on Midsummer's Eve lest our souls be coaxed from our bodies.

— God's blood . . .

— The best way to keep safe was to stay awake all the night, with others about you. If you were so rash as to set yourself alongside a churchyard, you might see lost souls flying past, and one of them might snatch you up and bear you along.

— Then we shall put it to a test. This very night.

— Oh, no! I have done it. When I was fourteen years, my sister and I sneaked out to Saint Botolph's. Blankets we brought, and we lay down by the children's graves because we thought they were most in want of company. I must have fallen asleep, for I was wakened by my sister's scream. All white in the face she was. Pointing toward the lych-gate. *I saw it, Margaret! I saw it!*

— A soul?

— Yes, she took it first for a puff of smoke. But there was something so very *sad* about its passage, she said, that she knew it to be some wretch's spirit.

The smile fades slowly from her lips.

— My father died before another year was out. To this day, my sister believes it was *his* ghost she saw that night. Inspecting its future resting place.

Harriot draws down a draught of tobacco, stares out across the fields and forests.

— Is he abroad tonight, do you think? Your father?

She makes no answer, and he does not press her. Silence folds them around. The sun gives off its last rays, stars bleed from the dusk, and the day's scents — clover and hay and horse and sheep manure — form threads around them.

— Ah!

Margaret lightly slaps her cheek.

— I have quite forgot! Wait here!

She is gone ten minutes, and when she returns, it is well and truly night, and she is nearly out of breath from the climb, and whatever she has brought with her is dangling now by her side, like a vestigial limb. The moonlight is just strong enough to call out its shape: a cylinder, familiar in its ratios, wrapped in a green hide.

His perspective trunk.

— I wondered where it had gone.

— Yes, I have used it most grievous . . .

She presses her fist to her sternum, waiting for the air to come back.

— It looks no worse for the wear, Margaret.

— The better, I hope. Do you recall? You told me that a — a different configuration of — of convex and concave — might yield a larger power of magnification?

— My thoughts have tended that way. . . .

— In my free hours, I have subjected your theory to — to parlous trials. Drawing upon the sine law, I have altered the angles — the lens diameters, as well. It would be tedious to limn every detail, but after much error and confusion, I — I *conceive* I have raised its magnification by a power or two. But *you* must be the judge.

He takes the instrument from her. Raises it to his eye. Arcs it across the sky.

— Margaret, this is . . .

— Yes?

— It is quite extraordinary!

— Do you think?

— Oh, by my faith! Everything is most agreeably enlarged! The resolution and the — the *grain* . . .

A laugh escapes his throat as the stars swarm toward him.

— All my old friends! Shining like new again. There is Libra . . . there is Ursa Minor . . . there is —

The moon, he is about to say. Only it sits in a different quadrant of sky.

Back and forth he swings the glass, unable

to credit his senses. *Two* moons. One like the moon of old. One paler and smaller, ready at any moment to shrink back into darkness . . .

God have mercy.

— Venus.

He whispers the name. He whispers it again.

— *Venus . . .*

For many centuries, men have spoken of Venus's phases, but few have ever glimpsed them with the naked eye. So few indeed that Harriot has long since ceased to believe they exist.

And now, in a trice, legend has become truth. And there lies Venus. Stuck against the heavens' blotter, like the clipping of someone's thumbnail.

To his shock, he feels his eyes soften. Not with the old dampness, which tasted of pitch and gall, but something more lucid.

Already he is muttering his excuses.

— The smoke, I think . . . blowing cross-river . . .

She takes his hand and looks at him. And what a relief to see how free of pity her eyes are. All he can say is:

— Thank you, Margaret.

And then he kisses her. And those lips

that, in his blindness, he once believed too small . . . how they swell to his touch. How they taste of *her*.

35

Lover.

Nothing about it grows any clearer, any less strange with usage. How sensible, he thinks, were the old Romans. Knowing how elusive their quarry was, they came at it with a battalion of verbs. *Amare,* they called it. And *diligere* and *delectare* and *placere* and *observare.*

Where in that linguistic stew lie his feelings? *Amare,* yes, he has known some of that. When he first went to London as a young man, he frequented the Cardinal's Hat, where brisk and practiced women asked for their eighteenpence up front and arranged themselves on tear sheets and unbuttoned themselves just far enough to get the act done.

It never occurred to him that the same act could be carried out at leisure, that it could be ushered in and teased along, savored and recollected, distilled . . . more verbs! There are days, indeed, when he imagines himself entirely reconjugated. And other days when he feels . . .

— Too old.

He says it once without even thinking. It is an hour or two before dawn, and they are in his fourposter, pressed against each other like mortise and tenon. His hand circles that miraculous thatch of honey-colored hair, that part of the female anatomy never before vouchsafed to him.

— Too old for what? she asks.

— For this. For you.

— Oh . . .

She reaches around him, caresses the space between his shoulder blades.

— How soft your skin is. A baby's skin.

But there is nothing remotely maternal in the way her fingers scuttle down his ribs, hook around the blade of his pelvis. And this, too, is a revelation. That his body, which he has spent most of his life shrouding, might long for the light. That it might desire, might *be* desired.

He draws her closer. He feels her parting to admit him. Not in submission but in power, for when they have finished, he cannot help but gasp the same word.

— Stay.

And her reply is ever the same.

— It is late.

— An hour more . . .

She will not relent. And how he feels the lack of her when she is gone. This spartan bed, once barely large enough to contain him, yawns open. The linen holds her shape, the wool her scent.

One night, Harriot brings to bed an old bottle of *spiritus dulcis,* and the aroma of grapes and roses and candy so overcomes him he decants it, in slow dribs, across Margaret's body and licks each drop away. She performs the same unction on him, and before they can even rise to a consummation, they have fallen asleep in each other's arms.

Where they are found the next morning by Mrs. Golliver, sailing in like some raven spirit, eyes glittering, face frozen.

— Forgive me, Master. I — I thought . . .

The next afternoon, Harriot is summoned for an audience — unscheduled — with the Earl of Northumberland. They meet in the earl's library, which, in keeping with the primacy he attaches to it, runs the entire length of the house's northern front. The best river views may be found here, but the earl is always to be found facing the other way, toward those rows of books, with their sumptuous calf-leather covers, their calf-vellum pages, their gilt-ruled spines, their richly annotated pages.

— Reports have reached my ears, Tom.

Even in addressing him, the earl does not change his position so much as a hair. It is Harriot who must come to him.

— Do these reports concern my assistant?

— Yes.

— Do they emanate from my house-keeper?

The earl waits before answering.

— 'Tis a fractious household of which you are master, Tom.

— I have never pretended to be its master.

— Nor I yours. In the normal sway of things, my steward would never worry my peace with domestic alarums. In your case, he has made an exception.

— I am grieved to have troubled him.

— Understand me, Tom, I would not shame you for the world. How you live is your concern. It pains me, however, to see your good name sullied by rumor.

— My name is not so good, perhaps, as you believe.

The earl studies him. Then slowly draws out an oaken armchair. Lowers himself into it and motions to Harriot to do the same.

— So it is true.

— That my heart has a claimant? Yes.

— Your heart.

The earl's brows fork together. His hand passes before his lips.

— If Kit could see you now, Tom. . . .

— I hope he would not see as you do.

— And how am I in error?

— Your Grace believes I am casting myself away on a girl of low estate. You could not be more in the wrong. Margaret Crooken-shanks possesses one of the finest — finest *natural* minds I have ever had the privilege to encounter. If you would but suffer me, I might show you some of the marvels she has effected with —

— Doctor Dee has wrought great marvels. So, too, Herr Kepler, they say. I do not believe you entertain the same passion for them.

Harriot folds his hands together. Lowers his head as if for a schoolmaster's repri-mand. And is all the more surprised to hear the earl's gentle voice.

— Tell me, Tom.

— Yes?

— Is it a great wonder? This passion of yours.

— Much of the time it is terrible, Your Grace. Much of the time it is wondrous. And it is everything that lies between.

The earl nods, as if satisfied. Then rises

and turns away.

— In that event, I suggest you pursue your inquiries to their natural end.

Taking this for dismissal, Harriot tenders his bow and makes for the doorway. The earl's resonant drawl stops him two feet shy of freedom.

— You might, at some juncture, consider marrying the girl, Tom. I should be the last to raise an objection, having one less mouth to feed.

A moment's pause before he adds:

— There is *honor* in marriage.

A grand flare to his nostrils when he speaks, as if he were exhaling an entire code of conduct.

But this has never been Harriot's code. His work has always been the most jealous of mates. That a woman might come along who could embrace it and be embraced by it . . . this had never once crossed his mind. And now that he has found such a woman, the old assumptions can no longer hold. And so, as much as the Earl's words rankle him, they also harry him.

There is honor in marriage.

For a week, he broods on the question. He catches himself staring at her, as if her very presence might jar him in one direction or the other. In strange moments, he actually clears his throat, like a Saint Crispin's Day orator, ready to hold forth. Each time, she gives him the same expectant look; each time, his well runs dry.

On Sunday afternoon, she finds him in his study, half loafing through an old volume of Sallust. Sly with mischief, she curls her finger at him.

— Come.

They follow the same path they took on Midsummer's Eve: to the house's northwest tower, Margaret leading the way this time. No perspective trunk in her hands, but her stride is martial with purpose. She leads him up the steps; she draws the keys from her apron pocket; she shoves open the door, and then, striding onto the parapet, points westward.

There, on either side of the sinking sun, stand two shards of rainbow. Nothing but air between them.

Harriot blinks. His mouth hinges open.

Parhelion, that is what men of learning call it. But what rises up in his mind is the name he first heard as a child: *sun dog.* His mother used to tell him that, whenever God grew jealous of the rainbow's beauty, he would snatch it up in its very birthing and leave behind only those two stubborn roots of light, with just the tiniest halo to connect them.

He had believed her, of course. And the shock of seeing it once more, coupled with the sensation of being *here,* fifty feet above the earth, with Margaret's shoulder pressed against his . . . once more he is mute before the occasion.

It is up to Margaret to find the words.

— The light is red, as you see, on the sides nearest the sun. Blue on the sides opposite. In between . . . well, violet, to be sure, but mark how blurry and indistinct are these hues. When set alongside those of a fully formed rainbow —

He marks how the dropping sun makes a translucency of her fair skin. How it calls out that trembling blue vein on her left temple.

— I am disposed to wonder if some additional order of refraction is at work, she says. — A form of crystal, invisible to our eyes. Something there must be, do you not think? Driving the rays from their natural —

— Marry me.

He had meant it to sound self-evident — the most natural proposition in the world. But she jerks away, as if from a musket blast, and all the attention she had given those trunks of light bears down on him.

— You ask me to marry you?

— I do.

— And you ask this freely? Of your own heart?

— I do.

— Knowing I am *not* with child? That you bear no duty of any kind towards me?

— I know all this.

— Then let me answer you with another query: Why must we marry? He raises his hands in a gesture of supplication.

— What else shall we do?

— Carry on as before.

— I do not know that we can. I do not know that I wish it.

And by now all the translucency is gone from her skin. Her face is a brittle white mask.

— What in heaven's name has possessed you? The two of us . . .

— Yes?

— Begin with this! We scarcely know each other. We hail from altogether different spheres — different *worlds*. Not two months ago, I was your housemaid.

— And in the days since, have we not spent virtually every waking and sleeping moment together? Is there any part of my heart, of my — are we not known to each other in all aspects?

Flushing, she wheels away. Walks to the other side of the parapet, with the sun dog at her back. Her voice comes back low and nettled.

— I can just hear the gossips now. They will say I maneuvered you into it. What a schemer they will think me —

— Margaret . . .

— A *whore*. Far worse is being said already, I've no doubt, under the good offices of the Gollivers.

— What care you for the world's opinion? What care I?

They are both silent. Then, very slowly, she comes to him. She takes his long chalky fingers in her hand. She raises her eyes to his.

— I wish I had words to tell you.

— Tell what you can.

— For the first time in my life, I feel free. And that freedom is your gift to me. I beg you, do not take it away from me.

— But I never should —

— Not by design, I know that. You would marry with the very best of intentions — most men do — and the end would be the same. I would be your property.

— What do you take me for? *Property* . . .

— And that being the case, I should

sooner be your servant.

She puts her hand to his cheek. Not in anger, it seems, but in pity.

— I love you, Tom. But I must not be your wife.

He spends the next day apart from her. Not from wounded feeling, as she must think, but from a surfeit of feeling. She has refused him, yes, but for the first time, his Christian name has tumbled from her lips. And in this extraordinary context.

I . . . love . . . you . . . Tom.

How elusive that verb had once seemed to him. And now it has been unmistakably conjugated, with Harriot as its direct object. And this somehow trumps every other consideration: the Gollivers' ill will, the earl's proprieties, even Harriot's own sense of mission. There can *be* no mission without her inside it.

The next evening, he reports to the laboratory at the usual time. She is waiting for him. Neither says a word about what has passed. They carry on. And, indeed, it is in the act of carrying on that he resigns himself fully to Margaret's refusal — or, more truthfully, sees the lie in it.

For it becomes clearer with each second:

370

She has refused him nothing. She is well and truly his.

Look how instinctively she circles him in the cramped space, adjusting to his orbits. Listen to her quiet humming as she clears the worktable. Watch her slip away just before midnight to fetch him a stoup of beer.

And now watch him leave half the stoup for her. Listen to the unemphatic affection with which he says her name: *Thank you, Margaret. . . . Yes, Margaret, that should do nicely.* They have plighted no troth, but everything about them sings of a pact, quietly and gladly borne.

And later tonight, will they not adjourn to his feather mattress (his one extravagance)? Will he not explore her with a newlywed's vigor? And what if she slips away by morning? She will be here the following afternoon. Making herself useful, as she always does. Setting out the vials and prisms. Polishing the pewter pots and bronze disks. Chiding him for his slowness in measuring. Leaning over him as he performs his calculations, or else scratching out her own sheets of figures.

And always at some point, asking him:

— Why will you never publish?

To which he can only mumble:

— Someday . . . I do believe . . . perhaps next year . . .

Here and here alone does he keep his own counsel. As an atomist and an alleged atheist and a friend to the most hated man in the realm, he must let the world be if he wants it to let him be.

She knows none of this, and so she sets herself with a merry heart against all those papers, piling them in high stacks, wrapping them in pretty bows of twine — suggesting with each touch of finger that here lie the seeds of some magnum opus, germinating even now in his brain's loam.

One night, rummaging through one of his trunks, she finds the rotting remains of a secret compartment. Prying away the last fragments of damp wood, she comes up with a stack of yellow foolscap. A long chain of scraggly dust trails after it as she drags it to the light.

— What can this be, Tom?

— The annals of my failure.

She is only half listening. Already her finger is crawling toward that single word, boldly scrawled across the topmost page.

— *Aurum.*

She looks up at him.

— Alchemy?

He nods. And something in him grows

cold at the heat in her eye. For this is when she begins to be lost to him.

36

LONDON *SEPTEMBER 2009*

We ditched the Lincoln Town Car as soon as we could and grabbed the first tube at the Osterley station. And as the Piccadilly Line train bore us steadily northeast and then east toward London, we sat there, the three of us, grappling with a fundamental question.

What kind of fugitives *were* we?

We were able to agree on this much: No police dragnets were circling us. Our two captors, with their unorthodox procedures and their limited knowledge of international law, were too obviously working for a private party.

So then we paused to consider this party. Having missed one audience with us, would he not go to a similar trouble for a second? And if he was, as Alonzo fervently believed, Bernard Styles, would his capital not give him ample resources to pursue us?

That being the case, should we act under

the presumption that we were being followed at all times — travel to the opposite side of London, pretend we were doing everything *but* the thing we were doing? Or should we carry on as before, confident that our purposes could never be guessed?

In the end, we chose a variation of the latter path, but with hedges. Which is to say we hung our hats in Old Brentford, a West London suburb just a couple of bus stops from Syon Park. We took a pass on the Holiday Inn and the Travelodge — too public — and lugged our bags to the Dragon's Tongue, a Victorian bed-and-breakfast about twenty years past its last renovation and two years shy of its next. The key chains were weighty oaken slabs from the age of pillions, but the TV screens were flat, the rooms came with free Wi-Fi, and the gastropub downstairs served mushy peas that were a bright wasabi green.

The Disraeli room went to Alonzo because he liked its crepuscular gloom. (An ancient mulberry tree kept all the sun out.) "Give me an hour," he said, shutting the door behind him. "Or a day," he called out a second later. Clarissa and I hauled our luggage into the adjacent Pitt the Elder chamber, optimistic but spartan, with a single cane-bottom chair and a faux-mahogany dresser and a sleigh bed with a tea-rose coverlet.

"Are we going to Syon House today?" she asked.

"More like tomorrow. Alonzo won't want to even get dressed without a plan."

She nodded absently. Walked to the window, pulled the shutters apart, stared out at the low grave clouds that had settled over the river.

"You think we'll find it?"

"Sorry . . ."

"Harriot's treasure."

"No idea."

Two seconds later, I felt the concussion of her body next to mine, sending out tiny concentric waves across the mattress. The tickle of her hair against my cheek. A scent of bergamot.

"Are you still tired?" she asked.

"Um." I opened my eyes. "I could *not* be."

And by the time I said it, I wasn't.

This I believe: the second-best and maybe sometimes even the best thing about sharing a bed with someone is the indolent sprawl that follows. The pond formations of her breasts. Your own spent sex, lolling against your leg with a summer ease.

"Henry."

"Yes."

"Tell me something about yourself."

I angled my head toward her.

"You mean like height or weight?"

"I can *feel* how much you weigh. Something you wouldn't have told me two days ago."

I took her hand, pressed it to my forehead like a compress.

"Mm," I said. "Drawing a blank. I think you should go first."

So that's when she told me about her narcoleptic father. Who, being prideful, insisted on driving during family vacations. Which turned every trip into a pilgrimage of terror, punctuated at intervals by her mother's calm voice: "Lissie?" That was Clarissa's cue to swat her father on the right side of his head so he wouldn't drive them off the road.

"Why didn't your mother drive?" I asked.

"We never even thought of that as an option. I guess mothers didn't do that then."

"And the whole situation didn't strike you as odd?"

"I just figured all dads did that. You mean they didn't?"

I kissed her on her eyebrow. Then full on the eye.

"Okay," I said. "When I was fifteen, I

wrote a poem."

"Come *on.* I wrote ten thousand —"

"No, this wasn't about carousels or unicorns, okay? It was a Petrarchan sonnet."

"Oh."

"Inspired by Sally Markowitz, who was a grade below me and on the drill team, with only a kind of subliterate understanding that I was alive. So I wrote this poem, and then I showed it to my mother."

"God."

"Because she was an *English* teacher. And because if it passed muster with her, Sally Markowitz would have to, you know, fall in line."

"So your mom read it . . ."

"And started laughing from the very first line. I think it was maybe the best laugh she'd had in — maybe ever? And then she showed it to my dad, and he started laughing."

"And what'd *you* do?"

"Um . . . I went back to my room. And I pretty much *torched* that poem from my consciousness. I couldn't even begin to recite it for you now."

She placed her hand on my sternum.

"I'm sorry, Henry."

"No. I mean, you *asked* me, and that was the first thing I —"

"Okay."

"So don't be."

"I won't."

She lay still for a while.

"Was that when you became a writer?" she ventured.

"That's when I grasped the value of studying *other* writers."

With a peal of laughter, she rolled on top of me. Her hair was falling between my lips, and her black eyes were shining, and she was playing with my forelock, curling it around her index finger. Her breath smelled like cardamom.

"You know what, Henry? If you made that up, I will kill you."

"And you probably could, too," I said. "But it happens to be true."

"All right then. I won't even ask if you cried."

"I did not. It was a point of pride."

"Mm." Her eyes closed in slow stages. "You know what, Henry? We could have put *your* mom in the car with *my* dad and solved all our problems."

For the rest of the afternoon, we lay in bed, dozing in and out, softening and hardening. Never quite pulling away. I would wake at intervals and find myself at some different quadrant of her — tasting an earlobe or the braid of spine in her lower back, describing circles around her aureole — stunned by the variety of her. For something like ten minutes, I dedicated myself to the lunar landscape of her pubic bone, the way the angles bled into roundness and the whole structure flirted with verticality before giving way to declivity. . . .

"Henry?"

Her voice floated down as if through an arbor.

"Are you hearing me?"

"Yep."

"What if we left?"

"What if we —"

"What if we just gave up? Went home?"

I raised my head.

"Why would we do that?" I asked.

"Because we can."

I rolled myself on top of her. Rested my chin on her flat, immaculate abdomen.

"Okay," I said. "Where would home be, exactly?"

"I've given that some thought."

"Yeah?"

"I'm currently inclined toward Kiawah Island."

"Wow."

"It's lovely there."

"Of course it is, I'm just — what would

we do? There's caddying, I guess. Grounds-
keeping . . ."

"I see you as a park ranger. Somewhere
on the mainland."

"Steady work," I conceded.

"And you'd look great in the uniform.
And while you're busy, I'd be — you know,
making jewelry from recycled elements. And
learning golf, and we could go on *poker*
cruises, Henry."

"And with you around," I said, "we'd
never have to worry about muggers."

"There are no muggers on Kiawah. A
couple alligators, that's it. You could read
on the beach. Every sonnet Shakespeare
ever wrote. Toes in the sand, Henry. Mojito
thermos at your elbow. Imagine it."

I tried, I really did. But when I closed my
eyes and thought of beaches, I just dozed
off again — only to be jarred awake by the
dream-memory of Amory Swale's hand
poking through the sand. I blinked myself
back to consciousness and found myself
gazing up the smooth white plain of Clarissa's torso. Found her watching me back.

"Or, you know, maybe I was kidding," she
said.

"It's a fine idea."

"I know."

"It's just — practicalities . . ."

"Forget I mentioned it."

She didn't sound angry, but just to be sure I crawled toward her, until my face was directly over hers.

"So one more question," she said.

"Okay."

"If Alonzo weren't in the picture, would you leave now?"

"What do you mean if he weren't? He is."

She said nothing, and with a long-dying groan, I rolled off her. Stared up at the coffered ceiling.

"Alonzo took me in," I said. "When no one else would. I owe him."

"I get that, I do. I just wonder — I mean, how do you know when you've stopped owing someone?"

Her finger made a skiing motion from my ear down to my clavicle.

"Because if you need someone to take you *in*, Henry, I'll do it."

This was all the invitation I needed. At least, I took it for an invitation, and indeed, when I rolled back on top of her, her face blossomed with consent. It was only days later, when everything had come apart, that I wondered if I'd quite taken her meaning.

The sun went down, but I couldn't have told you when. In our room, it was a kind of permanent twilight, twinned with dawn, so that every time I thought I was waking up, I was really going back down. The outside world dimly interceded: a wheezing water pipe, fragments of a street argument, a siren (imagined, maybe). At some point, I heard the hall clock tolling the hours. One, two . . . I lost count after eight . . . and I would have sailed right back to sleep, but instinctively, I reached for the other side of the bed and, finding no one there, jerked straight up.

"Clarissa?"

Squinting into the shadows, I found her, naked, half gilded by the streetlights. Nothing more than an outline, adding weight as my eyes adapted.

She was standing near the window. Her hair was sleep-mashed, but her posture was erect and attentive.

"Clarissa?"

She turned toward me. With the most vacant eyes I have ever seen on a human being. And then she spoke.

"She's dying. We've got to help her. Margaret's dying."

37

"Lord help us," said Alonzo. "What do they *do* to the chickens over here?"

He pushed away his gunmetal-gray scrambled eggs, folded his massive arms against his chest.

"And why the hell does this Margaret woman keep intruding? Who is she, anyway? And why should we care if she's dying?"

"I'm just the messenger," I answered, putting up my hands in surrender.

"Very well, *Hermes,* should your little chippie ever decide to come down, please relay the following message. She needs to channel some new visions. On the order of *gold.* Spell the word if you must. *G-O-L-D.*"

I herded my baked beans and grilled mushrooms around my plate. Twelve hours of sleep, and I still wasn't hungry.

"She bailed us out of one hell of a fix, Alonzo. We wouldn't even be here without her."

"Agreed."

"More to the point, she can't *control* her visions, you said so yourself. That's why you believe in them."

"I have no doubt they're genuine. I'm just not persuaded they're helpful anymore." He popped the last link of sausage into his mouth. "And by the way, didn't you say she took Ambien on the plane?"

"So?"

"Well, on the rather long list of Ambien's side effects — right up there with sleepwalking and sleep eating — you will find *amnesia.* A cousin of mine took two of those pills, lost an entire night in Dubai. Came to just as she was plunging down a waterslide."

"Clarissa hasn't forgotten anything. If anything, she's —"

Remembering, is what I was going to say. But it was instantly replaced by another predicate.

Going mad.

Because, when she turned and looked at me in that room, all I could see was the shadow around her eyes. It seemed to me I was peering straight into the recesses of her mind. And there was no end.

"The point *is,* Henry, once we leave these walls, the Lady Macbeth routine needs to stop. If she can't contribute, she should just stay in her room and wash her hands."

But when Clarissa bounded down the stairs, a little after nine, she looked far fresher than Alonzo or me. She downed two coffees, a glass of grapefruit juice, and two stacks of wheat toast, lavishly buttered.

"Shall we?" she cried.

We approached the house not from the west, as the Earl of Northumberland's more esteemed visitors would have come, but from the north, in the manner of a trades-man or peddler. It was a long walk. We passed a large clearing that would, in short order, become a Hilton hotel . . . squat institutional buildings . . . an indoor adven-ture playground. And the final touch of modernity: jet planes, buzzing over our heads every few minutes, carrying new tour-ists into Heathrow.

We came at last to the Syon Park garden center, with a refectory and tearooms and an aquatics store where you could buy your very own three-step waterfall kit for 359 pounds. We limited ourselves to the nine-pound admission price, then passed onto a gravel pathway that curved around the building's northern perimeter. And as we went, the rasp of our soles took on both undertones and overtones, so that we seemed to be walking right on top of ourselves. The clouds began to squeeze out more and more of the sky, and a wind sparked up from the north, pressing my trousers against my legs.

And suddenly we weren't traveling forward or back but *through.* It was the same feeling I'd had at Fort Ralegh: that I'd slipped into one of time's crevices and, at any moment, I might be confronted by a man with a ruff and doublet or a woman in petticoats, and the farther I went, the farther I would wander from anything that was mine.

"Henry?"

I felt Clarissa's hand on my arm. We were standing under a porte cochere. And that was enough, finally, to break the spell, for this structure had never existed in Thomas Harriot's time, and the great hall into which we stepped was nothing Harriot would have recognized. Gone were the pitched roof, the mud and mortar, the leather and wood. In their place: marble, stucco, Greco-Roman statuary. The improving hand of Scottish architect Robert Adam had transformed a crumbling Tudor hall into a resplendent showcase of neoclassicism. By the time he was done, he had extinguished everything but the bones of Henry Percy's house.

Or at least he had tried. The one room that still smelled of olden times was the long gallery, where the Wizard Earl had once roamed from shelf to shelf, exulting in his luxuriously bound volumes. But the gallery gave way to a print room, festooned with eighteenth-century artists like Gainsborough and Van Dyck, which opened onto a sitting room, all mahogany and satinwood, which opened onto a green drawing room with a scagliola fireplace . . . and by degrees, the notion that anything of Thomas Harriot's might still be secreted here became too much to conceive.

With each new room, my spirits sank lower, and when a stout woman in an argyle cardigan came striding toward us, we gazed at her in a perfect stupor.

"Do you have any questions?" she asked.

"None you can answer," Alonzo muttered at last.

We were inside that house no more than ten minutes, but by the time we reeled out, it no longer mattered that the wind had died down or that we could see patches of sky simmering with sun or that there were cows lowing us back to old England. Old England had never seemed farther away.

I couldn't even muster a smile at Alonzo's disguise, which lay strangely exposed in the noon half-light. Custardy golf shirt, Sansa-belt referee pants, Conway Twitty hair — singly and in sum, they proclaimed our defeat.

"Well," said Alonzo. "Well then."

From the cramped confines of his slacks, he drew out a copy of Harriot's map. Gave it a magus stare.

"You know," he said. "There's no reason to think it's in the house."

An effortful brightening in his brow, which found its match in Clarissa's voice.

"If it *were,* they'd have found it by now. All those renovations, all those walls getting knocked down . . ."

"He'd have been a fool," I said.

And in this manner, we hoisted ourselves toward hope. Why, the house was the last place we should be looking! If Harriot had something to hide, he'd have found someplace on the grounds. Somewhere only *he* knew about. Somewhere he could go back to whenever he needed.

"All we need to do now," said Alonzo, pointing to Harriot's cross on the map, "is figure out the starting point."

"And from there," said Clarissa, "we just have to walk fifty feet north."

"In *that* case," I said, "why not start with Harriot's house?"

50'N

There was at least one good reason why not. There *was* no house. Only some foundations, roughly a hundred yards from Syon House, buried under at least three feet of solid earth.

We went there anyway. Entered a gate, passed an old ice house and stood at last on a hillock — in the exact spot where Harriot had once lived and worked.

From documents, we knew the house had been ninety-five feet long and eighteen feet high. Tiled. It had a chamber, long study, dining room, pantry, kitchen, library. The whole place was swimming in paper, in "bookes of all sorts of learning" (so reported the king's agent who searched the house and inventoried its contents). But all that was left now was a feeling. The queer, vertiginous sense of standing where something had once happened.

A minute more passed in silence. And then Alonzo said:

"Let's walk."

"Where?"

"Where *else?* North. Fifty feet."

From one of his Sansabelt pouches, he extracted a baseplate compass, and we set off, counting the distance as we went. And when we had finished counting, we were standing . . . in a grove of trees, all planted long after Harriot had died. No carved arrows, no coded messages, no crosses or markers, just trunks and roots and the season's first deposit of leaves, whispering beneath our shoes.

"What are we . . . ?" Alonzo began to sketch a slow circle among the poplars and birches and pines. "Where do we . . . ?"

I leaned against an old cedar tree. Massaged my temples.

"It doesn't look good."

Only Clarissa was bound and determined to keep her spirits bright. "Hey, wait a minute. Isn't there still an Earl of Northumberland?"

"There's a Duke."

"Well, why don't we pay him a call? Tell him we have this exciting project and would he like to be our partner in a — in an archaeological *dig.*"

"Oh, and by the way, there might be some gold at the end of it. But don't worry, we'll just take it with us when we go. Happy

Christmas!"

Rather than bridle at Alonzo's tone, Clarissa simply stood there a long while, scenting the air. Then she began walking.

Back to the site of Harriot's house. Back through the gate, where she paused briefly and then turned west, heading toward the long mall of Lime Avenue.

Only when she reached the pepper-pot lodges — those twin sentinels that Northumberland had begun building in 1603 — only then did she turn around.

And by now, Alonzo and I were standing on either side of her, and we were all gazing back at Syon House. A classic Renaissance-era quadrangle, three stories high, with an interior courtyard and a crenellated tower at each corner.

In my mind's eye, I rubbed out the central entrance gate, replaced it with two side ones. I scraped away the Bath-stone exterior to reveal the old bricks. I added a pitched roof and penciled in a million chimneys, all belching coal smoke, and sketched out two brick buildings, extending from each side. . . .

And then I saw Clarissa extend her arm.

"There," she said.

She was pointing toward the northwest tower. The very tower, brick with ashlar facing, that would have been closest to Harriot's house.

"There," she said once more.

"Alonzo," I said, quietly. "How high do you suppose that tower is?"

"How should I know?"

Before I could even run to find a docent, Clarissa was snapping a picture of it with her Trio.

"What are you doing?" I asked.

"Just an app I have. Measures buildings for you."

A killer app because, in less than a minute, she had an answer.

"Give or take? Fifty feet."

And that's when I started to laugh.

"Henry," said Alonzo. "Please don't be macabre."

"I can't help it," I said, wiping my eyes. "Harriot's fooled us again."

"And how is that?"

"Because we thought when he said north, he meant *latitude.*"

"What else could he have meant?"

"Altitude."

Alonzo's mask of bafflement cracked into a wondering grin. He gazed up at that turret and, in a voice of sacred awe, said:

"The bastard. He buried it aboveground."

"Fifty *feet* aboveground."

It was left to Clarissa to pose the question that followed as naturally as autumn to summer.

"How the hell are we going to get it?"

38

How indeed? The question was enough to flummox Alonzo into a silence that nothing could break. Only as he strode through the front door of the Dragon's Tongue and marched up the stairs to his room did he think to call back to us.

"Give me the rest of the day," he said, and disappeared.

"To do what?" Clarissa asked me.

"Well, knowing him, he's going to call people."

"People."

"A better word might be 'confederates.' "

She gave me the full heat of her gaze.

"You're talking about criminals."

"Nothing of the kind."

"But how would Alonzo know people like that? He comes from a nice family."

The very best, I agreed. In earlier times, Judge Wax had been one of the District of Columbia's most eminent criminal defense attorneys. Fraud, sex offenses, DUI, drug possession and distribution, assaults, armed robberies, murders . . . well, in the course of tilling all that rancid earth, a lawyer can turn up some interesting larvae. And if the lawyer has a smart *son,* well, that son will learn how to harvest the larvae without his father's even knowing.

Clarissa pressed her lips together.

"So Alonzo's got, what, a gangster Rolodex?"

"Nothing that subpoenable. More like a phone chain."

"Extending all the way to London?"

"It got him here, didn't it? How many dead guys do you know of who can come up with a passport in forty-eight hours?"

We were back in the Pitt the Elder room now, and I was sitting in the cane-bottom chair, and Clarissa was sitting right in my lap, and I was engaged in the deeply satisfying work of untangling her hair when she said:

"Henry."

"Yeah?"

"When I first told you I'd seen the School of Night, I know you thought I was starkers. No, you *did,* and I don't blame you. I mean, I've watched those psychic shows."

"So how is it different for you?"

"I'm not a psychic. I've never been able to predict a blessed thing. And no one's talking in my ear, no one's there at all, it's — it's *spasms. Flashes.*"

"And that tower was one of the flashes."

She blew out a cheekful of air.

"I have no idea if there's any treasure up there. I only know *he* was there. And *she* was there."

With an air of some regret, she hoisted herself from my lap (only that still-tender tumescence to show she had been there).

"Okay," I said. "So where does this Margaret Crookenshanks fit in with Harriot's treasure?"

"I don't know."

"And how exactly is she dying?"

"I don't *know.* She's in a room and — God, I can *feel* the life going from her." She paused a good long while. "There's someone in the room with her."

"Is it Harriot?"

"If he *is* Harriot, then yes. How's that for an answer?"

"So what's he doing?"

"I think he's killing her. . . ."

We'd previously thought it the wisest course to remain in our room, far from the murdering crowd. Now, though, the thought of staying *here,* walled about by ghosts, was more than we could bear. So we put aside any lingering fears of Agents Mooney and Milberg and strolled over to Kew Bridge.

Strolled implies more daring than I really felt at that moment. For the first few blocks, the world seemed to glow with my paranoia, and in fact, the manner in which every pedestrian ignored me struck me as the sincerest token of his enmity. It was Clarissa who — well, I was going to say she made me braver, but all she gave me, really, was an infusion of life force. Simply by brushing her shoulder against mine she had the effect of recalling me to my body and making me realize that I was, to my surprise, hungry. In an extremely domestic way. And was this not, under the circumstances, as good a reason as any to keep walking?

And so, by the time we reached the bridge, I'd completely forgotten about who might or might not be following us, and I was able to look down with no small pleasure on the Thames. That seethe of chop and tide, bearing leaves and twigs in a fury of purpose, and yet serene enough to grant passage to a single canoe, oared by two men in parka vests. Neither of whom gave us so much as a passing glance.

How different this picture would have

been in Harriot's time. A fleet of barges with square sails carrying produce from upriver. Wherries and tilt boats and dung boats and, from the landings, passengers calling "Oars! Oars!" to the sunburnt watermen. It was a wilder beast in those days, the Thames. It flooded its banks without a moment's notice, and it was so choked with mud — and rubbish and shit and dead dogs and hog intestines — that even the haddock couldn't see to swim.

I wrapped my coat around Clarissa and pulled her toward me.

"Let's say there was a Margaret," I said, "and let's say we're right about when this map was written."

"Sixteen ought three."

"In that case, it's worth remembering that sixteen ought three, in addition to being the year of James's succession, was a plague year."

"No," she said. "The London plague was sixteen *sixty-five*, right? A year before the big fire."

"That was the *Great* Plague," I explained. "Hygiene being what it was in those days, fleas and rats being what *they* were, plagues came along pretty much once a generation. And the one that came in sixteen ought *three*" — I clicked my tongue against my teeth — "that was one of the worst."

The scourge struck in Southwark first, then worked its way north and west into the city. By the end of July, it was claiming nearly fourteen hundred lives a week; in September, more than three thousand. At any moment, one in every six Londoners was either sick or dying. The town was so deserted that grass grew in Cheapside.

"They closed all the theaters," I said. "They canceled feasts and assemblies, they stopped calling juries. King James was supposed to take a triumphant passage through the city, but he had to hightail it to Hampton Court. He ended up in Salisbury. You couldn't even get into the royal palace unless you had a certificate saying you were from an uninfected district."

Clarissa stared at a flotilla of swans coming downriver.

"So you're saying Margaret could have been killed by the plague?"

"I'm saying if she was a resident of the greater London population, there's at least a decent chance."

"But how would we know for sure?"

"The bills of mortality. Once a week, the city leaders compiled a list of plague deaths. That's how they tracked the epidemic. They couldn't catch every single death, but those parish clerks were damn thorough. I think it's worth a search."

"The British Library?"

I shook my head. "Too much time. I've got a friend who teaches Tudor history at Columbia. I'll call her."

"A friend," she said, narrowing her eyes. "Old or new?"

"Old."

That wasn't quite correct. Sabina and I were new at being friends, but we were old hands at being divorced. Altogether, we'd been divorced three times as long as we'd been married and with somewhat more success.

Which is to explain why, when I called her, she sounded friendlier than she had on our wedding night. Then again, she hadn't just caught me flirting with the Filipina barmaid at the St. Regis. We had never really sorted through the detritus of our marriage, but the mere fact that so many of our mutual friends were happy — or at least settled — had forced us by default into a tiny support group. Which, of course, could only be sustained so long as we each remained single and unhappy.

And so it was with a tremor of disloyalty

that I glanced over now at Clarissa, standing at the northern end of Kew Bridge. Resplendently cold in her woolen car coat. Her red lips even redder in the wind.

"Sabina," I said into the phone, "I'm in kind of a hurry. I'm in London, or near there, and a colleague of mine has a question."

"A colleague." She exhaled long and hard. "Tell me what you need, Henry."

Clarissa's stomach was rattling as loudly as mine when we got back to the Dragon's Tongue. We considered heading straight for the gastro-pub, but Clarissa wanted to put on a sweater first, so we climbed the stairs to our room, and I pulled the heavy wooden key chain from my pocket — and just then Alonzo came bursting from his room. Clutching two shopping bags, grinning like a televangelist.

"I know *your* size, Henry, but I had to guess Clarissa's."

He shoved a bag in each of our arms and waited with ill-disguised impatience.

"Try them *on,* for Christ's sake."

"Try what?"

And then I saw Clarissa drawing out a corset and a pair of stockings and a farthingale and a kirtle skirt and a petticoat. And

402

then I looked in my bag and found a feathered hat and a short cloak and a small snowy ruff, limp from old sweat.

"Tell me you didn't pay good money for this," I said.

"Don't worry your pretty little head. Oh, and dinner's on me, too. But you have to promise to go right to bed afterward. No rutting, please, we need *all* our energy for tomorrow."

"Where are we going, a costume party?"

How he beamed at us then! With the fury of a thousand suns.

"We're going to a wedding, kids."

39

Meet the happy couple.

She: vice president for investment banking at the London office of Morgan Stanley Smith Barney. *He:* senior copywriter in the brand development division of Ralph Lauren. Together, they were clearing well over five hundred thousand pounds a year, and when the time came to merge their assets, they merged as well on a key detail. Having met at an Elizabethan costume ball, they wanted, more than anything, a Tudor wedding. And what better location than Syon House — which, on Saturdays, is closed to the public but open to private rites, the more private the better?

And so, on this Saturday evening in September, several hundred of London's wealthiest citizens were squeezing themselves into garters and petticoats and mockado stomachers and buckram waistcoats — for the purpose of attending an event that, from a certain distance, resembled a high-end Renaissance Faire.

This was the welter of mortified privilege into which Alonzo Wax proposed to plunge us. And if he had a plan for getting us out, he was doing a good job of hiding it. Every question we popped at him, he stirred away, like sugar in weak tea.

"Why would we go to a wedding reception?"

"Because it gets us on the grounds."

"Why a *night* reception?"

"Because we're the by-God School of *Night.*"

"How are we going to get by the security guards?"

"They follow tightly appointed rounds. Believe me, I've cased the joint. A sentence, by the way, I never thought I'd use."

"How are we going to keep from setting off the house alarms?"

"Oh, yes," said Alonzo, already sounding fatigued. "That's what Seamus is for."

He said nothing more on the subject until Seamus himself arrived two hours before the event, dressed as a Cistercian monk. A year or two short of thirty. Small, wire-taut, Groucho-browed, grim as coal. He carried a rucksack and sat perfectly still, spoke only when spoken to, expended just enough energy to survive.

"Don't let his demeanor fool you," Alonzo instructed us. "Seamus here is a climbing dynamo. He's summited Mount Rainier and Makalu, hasn't he? Not to mention Annapurna and K2. A perfect paragon with technical alpine rock *and* high-altitude glaciated volcanoes. Honestly, we couldn't find anyone better suited."

"Better suited for what?" I asked.

"Henry. The distance from the ground to the top of that tower at Syon House is what?"

"Fifty feet."

"How high is K2?"

"Higher."

"So which would be easier to climb?"

"Syon House."

"Exactly."

I looked at him. "You're proposing to *scale* the northwest turret?"

"Compared to Annapurna, it's a tiptoe up the tulips. We could be up and over in ten minutes, isn't that right, Seamus?"

"Hold on," I said. *"We?"*

A fleck of red flashed from Alonzo's cornea.

"Well, come on, Henry, you're in decent enough shape, aren't you?"

"I haven't climbed Annapurna! And just

where are *you* planning to be all this time?"

"On the ground, of course, with Miss Dale. We'll be keeping lookout."

"And catching *you*," added Clarissa, with a wink.

I gulped down the last dregs of my coffee and closed my eyes and pictured myself crashing through her outstretched arms.

"Okay," I said, "one more question. How exactly are we getting into this event? It sounds kind of exclusive."

"Can it be, Henry, that you have no experience crashing weddings?"

"Only my own."

"Then listen to me. It can be done. I've crashed inaugurations, coronations. Circumcisions. It takes a dash of ruthlessness, that's all."

Of ruthlessness, Alonzo had more than a dash, but even he was surprised, I think, by the level of security surrounding Syon Park that evening. You couldn't even go as far as the parking lot without having your Bentley or Jaguar or Lexus hybrid stopped by a ginger-bearded pirate, who used his one patch-free eye to inspect your driver's license down to its finest grain. So we took the bus and, rather than stroll right in, we traced out a route by the river that brought us over a ha-ha and left us, by some strange miracle, twenty feet from the reception tent. Such an easy passage that once again I felt as if natural laws were being bent back in the face of Alonzo's will.

Standing before the entrance, however, was something that would not bend: a Myrmidon in an executioner's suit. Arms fused to his chest, earphones sprouting from his square head. Animosity in every pore. Four hundred years earlier, he'd have been Topcliffe's chief assistant, driving screws under the fingers of Catholic recusants.

Rather than front him, we reconstituted ourselves around a Mercedes G-Class, pretending it was ours, and watched the legitimate guests, in their costume-shop regalia, process onto the conservatory grounds, feeling for the watches and cell phones and PDAs that could, in a pinch, take them back to modernity.

"They look scared," I said.

"Who can blame 'em?" Clarissa asked. "I'd sooner *leave* a Tudor wedding than attend one."

It was altogether half an hour before we spotted a potential ally. A lithe, rawboned woman, somewhere between forty and sixty, with a terrace of false orange curls and a pannier skirt that was no more Tudor than Robin Hood but had the advantage of sweeping everything from its path.

"Could we fit under that dress?" Alonzo wondered.

"Room enough for Henry," said Clarissa.

Physically speaking, Seamus the hardbody was a better candidate for the seducer's job, but he had already retreated into the purdah of his iPod, from which the urgent chords of Panic! at the Disco now came pouring forth, and Clarissa insisted that my Earl of Essex drag showed my legs to good advantage, and Alonzo didn't disagree, so, without any preamble, Alonzo and Clarissa gave me a shove, and out I went.

The woman was fumbling through her clutch purse when I approached. Her fine marsupial features were pinched with aggrievement as she swore to herself.

"Is this what you're looking for?" I asked, proffering a cigarette lighter.

She was too surprised to protest, but as soon as her Camel No. 9 was lit, she took her sweet time looking me over.

"Bloody nerve," she said at last.

Meaning me, I figured, but in the next breath, she added, "If it's to be a smoke-free wedding, tell us in advance. Spell it out in the wretched invitation. Don't leave us at the mercy of some little . . . air-quality Gestapo."

She took a long, defiant drag. Studied me awhile longer.

"American, are you? How do you fit in?"

"I'm Aurelia's cousin. From New York."

Her perfectly manicured left eyebrow rose half a centimeter.

"She's never mentioned Yankee relations."

"Why should she? We're an embarrassment. I was told on no uncertain terms to keep to myself and speak to nobody."

"You have failed at your charge."

"Under the circumstances, I can't regret it."

I smiled, and after some consideration she did, too.

"Tell me, Mister . . ."

"Daniell."

"Where are you staying?"

"Kew."

"They *do* want to hide you away."

"I can't complain, it's Aurelia's day."

She passed her hand over her mouth.

"Well then, I shall have to keep you to myself, Mr. Daniell."

"I'm happy to be kept. But what am I to call you?"

"Millicent."

"Is that your real name?"

"For now."

I took out a cigarette of my own, and we

410

puffed together in silence. Then she hooked her hand lightly around my arm.

"Back to the horror," she announced.

At the sight of me, the executioner's face tightened appreciably. His shoulders squared, his hand went to his earpiece . . . and then Millicent drawled:

"Mr. Daniell is with me."

Five words in a languid public-school accent, and the proletarian giant backed away.

No time to savor my triumph, for the moment we entered the tent, the sunlight fell away and we were swaddled in a crepuscular pall, relieved at intervals by tiki torches, which blazed away in defiance of any fire code, broiling the air into incense. Sweat sprang from me as I peered through the helices of smoke and listened to the jangled accents of harps and pennywhistles and hammered dulcimers.

"Can you believe the shit they serve?" Millicent said. "Smoked turkey legs. *Ale.* Who wouldn't I screw for some champagne right now?"

Gradually, as my retinas let in more light, the jumble of limbs around me began to cohere into guests . . . who were no less discordant for being fully formed. Queen Elizabeth chatted on happy terms with Mary Queen of Scots. Henry the Eighth

411

necked with the pope. A young bishop gavotted with an ancient milkmaid. And a madrigal choir of stout matrons sang:

Up and down he wandered
whilst she was missing;
When he found her,
O then they fell a-kissing.

Millicent's fingers were dancing on my wrist. She had been talking to me for at least two minutes.

". . . Well, never mind, what right have I to complain? *My* wedding was an agony of tulle. It pains me to think of it."

I stared at her ring finger.

"Is your husband here?" I asked.

"Possibly."

And now a hive of fire jugglers had surrounded us. The heat was flying off them in punishing waves — I was too scorched even to perspire — and when I closed my eyes, the tent ceiling came rushing toward me.

I gasped . . . blinked myself awake. Millicent, in my brain's absence, had somehow procured two goblets of champagne.

"Ain't I the cleverest thing?" she crowed.

"They're saving that for the toast, aren't they?"

"Our need is greater."

412

Her hand had stolen into mine, and the touch of her skin was strangely healing. I was close enough now to see the fineness of her bones, to smell the talc beneath her Elizabethan wig, and to imagine her driving me to a pied-à-terre in Notting Hill with a plumply cushioned daybed. . . .

And then, puncturing that image: a stab of scruple. For standing outside this tent, not fifty yards away, was Clarissa Dale. And the distance between me and her struck me now as an affliction. Even as my new companion wove lines of chatter around me, touched my hand, my arm, my waist, all I could think was: Where is Clarissa? How can I get her here?

Ironically, it was Millicent who came to my rescue. After we'd taken a rather awkward turn across the dance floor to "Now Is the Month of Maying," she drained another glass of champagne and then slid two crisp fifty-pound notes into my hand.

"Be a dear and ask the bouncer for some coke."

I stared at the bills.

"Come now," she said. "You've done this before."

"Only with men who won't kill me."

"Ohh." She caressed my jaw. "He's *in that line,* you know. We've done business before."

And still I hesitated, at which point she planted her hands on me as preemptively as Clarissa and Alonzo had done.

"Go."

From the back, the bouncer looked even larger. Some massive block of granite that the oceans had been washing over for centuries and had succeeded only in finishing to an onyx gleam.

"The lady," I blurted.

The muscles around his jaw began to gather.

"She wants to know," I said, "if she might have something more stimulating than tobacco."

For at least five seconds, he seemed to be picturing what my face would look like once it had been driven through my skull. Then he took a half step back and jerked his head to the right.

I followed, waving my hands behind me. The gesture felt futile, but when I turned around, I was pleased to see my co-conspirators passing like a breeze through the now-open doorway. I followed a minute later, with my pockets of dime bags.

"Clever boy," said Millicent in her throaty alto.

She had no intention of sharing. She clutched her booty to her corset and made straight for the handpainted sign that read PRIVEE.

"Never stand between a woman and her blow," said Alonzo.

With those disproportionately small feet of his, he had once again managed to sneak up behind me.

"Where's Seamus?" I asked.

"Napping."

"That's not possible."

"We found a quiet place between the virginals and the clavicytherium. Now listen. I'm talking to you as if we've just met. One minute, no more, and then we part. Please remember this principle. You don't know me any better than the other guests. And you are not to react in any way when I give you this."

Something sleek and cool slid into the sheath alongside my right hip.

"What's that?" I asked.

"A rapier, of course. No Elizabethan gentleman would have been without one."

"Doesn't seem long enough."

"Well, excuse me, a carving knife was the nearest thing to hand. I stole it from one of the caterers."

"And I need this because . . ."

"Because one never knows, do one?"

"Okay, just tell me where Clarissa is."

"*Some*where, that's where. Waiting to stumble into you. Kindly avoid any libidinal eruptions."

Territorial urges, though, were another matter. When I found her ten minutes later, she was locked in conversation with an amorous goatherd, who was doing everything but wrap his crook around her neck. I had the pleasure of seeing her mask of boredom crack open at sight of me.

"Oh, hey," she said, tapping the goatherd on the shoulder. "Could you refill my flagon of mead?"

He obliged, a bit sulkily. I swerved right into his abandoned space.

"We have one minute to speak," I said. "According to Alonzo."

"In that case . . . I love you."

To which my first response, I'm ashamed to say, was a guffaw. Loud enough to send at least three heads rippling our way. Then I looked more closely into her eyes, which had not a spark of humor in them.

"You don't believe me?" she asked.

"I don't believe or disbelieve. I don't . . . I'm just —"

I loved you from the moment you walked into Alonzo's funeral.

The words were queued up on my tongue, and maybe I would have said them, or maybe I would have been too stunned by the suddenness with which we had just vaulted past months and months of boundary-setting and indirection and mis-direction. A part of me, a large part of me, couldn't believe in this moment. For the simple reason that nothing could ever be as simple as saying *I love you* and meaning it and having someone else say it right back and mean it.

And so I ceased even to sputter, and I stared at her helplessly and watched the light behind her eyes fade, and I would have said something, anything, to bring it back, but then I felt a tap on my shoulder. Not the goatherd, as I first thought, but a heavy-faced, baggy-eyed man in his early sixties, wearing a Thomas More costume like Marley's chains.

"Would you tell my wife?" he said in a once-robust North Country accent.

"Your wife?"

He nodded toward the far end, where Millicent, shiny and transported, was wrapping one of her legs around the tent pole. Her wig had tipped to one side, her bodice was stained, and her shoes had gone missing.

"Tell her I'm fagged out," her husband was saying. "She can find me in the car."

He stood alongside me for another

minute, watching his wife shake her slender haunches and douse her wrists with champagne.

"She does love to dance," he allowed.

The party took its sweet time winding down, but the effects of humidity and wool and salted food, aggravated by the natural hysteria that wedding receptions keep only partly at bay, began to exact a toll. Feeling a little dehydrated myself, I went in search of Clarissa, who was slumped on a milking stool next to the ice station. Not the same tiredness that the other guests were experiencing, closer to the pall that had taken her in Stanton Park. She looked as if the lights were being turned off inside, cell by cell.

"Jesus," I said. "You all right?"

"Yeah."

"You sure?"

"Mm."

I turned half away, stared across the floor. And then I heard her say:

"Henry."

She tried briefly to stand, then sat back down at once.

"Sorry," she said. "What I said earlier."

"Oh. Whatever."

"The *mead*, I guess. It does something to a girl."

"No, it's fine."

And because once again I was powerless to say anything more, I just stood there, waiting for some color to come back to her cheeks.

And then I felt a throbbing against my hip. Not my rapier but my cell phone, chafing with alarm.

"Hello?"

"You fucking owe me," said Sabina.

"Wait," I said. "I can't hear you."

I turned away and, after some searching, found a rack of ermine robes that partially muffled the noise. I plugged a finger in one ear and said:

"Go ahead."

"Well, to begin with, the bills of mortality only tell you how many people died in any given parish. They don't give you any names."

"Uh-huh."

"So, because I'm a fucking saint, I combed through all the parish death records for 1603. Parish by parish, you *so* owe me."

"And what did you find?"

"Nothing exactly like Crookenshanks. The closest was — um, Croken-*shents*. In St. Helen's Bishopsgate. Mother and daughter. Deceased within a couple of weeks of each other."

"Do the records say how they died?"

"Nope. But given the time frame, you'd have to think plague."

"Christian names?"

"Okay, the mother's was Audrey."

"And the daughter's was Margaret."

"Uh, no, Miss Marple. That's why I held off calling you. But since it was such a rare sort of name — I mean for that day — I figured you'd want to hear it anyway."

But I *couldn't* hear it, not the first time she said it, so I asked her to repeat it.

"Henry, are you there?"

"Yeah," I said, feeling the strain in my eye sockets. "Sorry."

"It's *noisy* where you are."

"I'm at a party."

"I suppose your *colleague* is there, too?"

My colleague.

I spun around, parted the ermine robes . . . and found Clarissa exactly where I'd left her. On the stool by the ice station. Still and spent.

And whatever relief I felt was dispersed in the next moment. For, in the fifty feet of space that separated us, a new figure had interposed itself. And this same figure was walking toward Clarissa in a slow and meaningful cadence.

His size was outlandish, but there was

something genteel about Halldor, too, now that he had cast aside the tourist T-shirts of America for the cloak and ruff and feathered hat of an officer of horse. He was moving like a hyperelongated dancer, straight in the spine, liquid in the shoulders, and his torso, as it swiveled, provided passing glimpses of Clarissa's face.

Sabina's voice was jagged in my ear.

"Henry. Henry, what's wrong?"

But I was too busy running to answer.

Or at least I was *trying* to run, but the entire wedding party had joined league against me. A court jester in a papier-mâché crown blocked me on one side; Justice Shallow and Othello on the other. I turned my shoulder like a tailback and broke though their ranks but ran headlong into a group of Shoreditch whores, locked in gossip, and just when I had freed myself from them, a ring of Morris dancers circled me, kicking up their sturdy white thighs. I hurled myself at them, shouting, but no one could hear me over the ocarinas and the hang drums, no one even saw me stumbling toward the ice station, where the chair formerly occupied by Clarissa Dale now sat vacant.

She was gone.

40

If a chasm had opened up beneath her and sucked her into the earth's mantle, she could have not disappeared more effectually. I canvassed the surrounding area. I fanned out in concentric circles. I sussed out niches and recesses and corners, traced and retraced all possible escape routes, I did everything but whip the wedding guests into a dragnet. It was no use. Clarissa was gone.

Until then, I had imagined I knew what helplessness was, only because I'd watched most of my life pass without doing much in the way of stopping it. But I had never known anything like this agony of waiting.

And so the call, when it came ten minutes later, was nothing less than mercy. Even the courtly croon of Bernard Styles sounded very nearly sweet.

"Mr. Cavendish," he said.

"Where is she?"

"*Resting,* dear boy. She's quite done in."

My hand had begun to squeeze my phone.

"You fucking bastard."

"Now if anybody should be *cross,* Mr. Cavendish . . . You know full well if you had been forthcoming with me from the beginning, matters would never have reached this juncture."

"I don't think either of us has been perfectly forthcoming, do you?"

My voice was calm, but my eyes were scanning every last inch of that tent, looking for just one head with just one cell phone pressed to its ear.

"If you're looking for *me,*" said Bernard Styles, "I'm afraid you won't have much luck. I'm not even in Syon Park. Never mind, Mr. Cavendish, I take your point. Candor on *both* sides is warranted. Shall I begin? We each have something the other wants. All that's required now is a simple trade."

"You mean the letter," I said.

"Of course."

"Well, then, you've got the wrong man. I don't have it. Alonzo has it."

"Ah, yes, the *late* Alonzo. Well, that's very unfortunate, Mr. Cavendish. I had expected more entrepreneurial initiative from you. Given the stakes."

But the stakes, I knew, were different for Alonzo than they were for me. Given the choice between saving Clarissa and finding Harriot's treasure, Alonzo would err on the latter side. Of that, I had no doubt. I would have to find something else to feed Bernard Styles.

"Let's make the stakes higher," I heard myself say.

And if I thought I was being too oblique, the laughter that greeted me was perfectly knowing.

"Mr. Cavendish, you don't honestly think I credit all that rot about Harriot's treasure, do you?"

"Then why have you been stringing us along?"

"An old man needs amusement."

"It's real," I said. "The treasure's real."

This time, at least, he didn't laugh. I fastened onto his silence as if it were a vine.

"I was a doubter, too, Mr. Styles. *Believe* me, I doubted. But I can't overlook the evidence anymore. The treasure is there."

"And why should you wish to persuade *me?*"

"Because if you give me a few hours, it can be yours."

"How gracious," he said dryly. "And what would you demand in return? For these charitable labors?"

I pressed my thumb against my eye. Pressed hard.

"I believe you mentioned an exchange," I said. "That would be all I'm interested in."

"Oh, Mr. Cavendish, you are quite the gallant." You could almost *hear* his eyes twinkling.

"Never mind, just give me until three A.M. That's all I'm asking for."

Another pause, of longer duration.

"If you know where this golden hoard is," said Styles, "why don't you simply tell me? Save yourself all the bother."

"That I can't do. You have to believe me, I'm the only one who can retrieve it."

"And why should I trust you after all that has passed?"

"Because. Because when it comes to Clarissa, you can —" I had to wait several seconds to master myself. "You can trust me."

I closed my eyes and counted. *One* . . . *two* . . .

And then I heard Bernard Styles say:

"Very well."

He disappeared into a cloud of static before abruptly returning.

"I shall expect a call from you at the very stroke of three. If I do not hear from you, I shall consider our arrangement null and void. Is that clear?"

I thought then of those other figures from Bernard Styles's past. Cornelius Snowden, murdered in Postman's Park. Maisie Hartzbrinck, tossed under a bus. That Southampton professor thrown from a roof. Amory Swale. All of them rendered null and void.

"I understand," I said.

Alonzo found me just a few minutes later, wandering beneath a canopy of white silicone doves.

"Jesus," he said. "You look like someone sealed you in a crypt."

"I think I had some of Millicent's snow."

"You think?"

"It's blurry."

"I can't tell you how much this pleases me, Henry. *Every* hunting party requires a cokehead, don't you find? I hope Clarissa, at least, has kept it together."

"Clarissa left."

How thinly it sounded. What a tinny afterecho.

"She left," said Alonzo.

"She took ill. Scrammed back to the hotel. Between you and me, I think she was scared shitless. And honestly, who needs that kind of energy dragging us down? We have to stay linear."

He was *staring* at me now, as though my skin were falling away in long strips.

"Perhaps you're right," he said at last. "Perhaps Clarissa has served her function."

Just the slightest lash imparted to that last word. It was left to me to puzzle out whether an insult was intended and whether I was the intended mark.

"Let's see," he said. "Ceremonial dances are done. Toasts are done. Groom's mother is plastered beyond repair. Yes, I'd say things will be winding down very soon."

"What should I be doing?"

"Staying linear, of course."

By eleven-thirty the groom and bride had fled, and by midnight the guests were being, more or less forcefully, expelled from the grounds. Except for three guests who weren't rushing anywhere.

It was nearly as easy as Alonzo had promised. We slipped around the rear of the Great Conservatory. We crept into the Syon Park gardens. We found the rucksack Seamus had buried under a pile of leaves. All we had to do now was wait.

And even the rain, when it came, was more sound than anything else: a shirring against the scarlet oaks and chestnuts. The stars had slipped behind orange-gray clouds, and from somewhere in the distance, Millicent's alto spilled toward us like a ghostly river.

"Mr. Daniell? . . . Mr. Daniell, where *a-a-are* you?"

For a moment or two I was persuaded she would find us. But then her calls tapered away, and in my mind's eye I pictured her finding her way to the magnetic north of her car, where her slumbering, abiding husband was even now waiting for her.

All we could hear after a while were the musicians calling good night to one another and the catering vans loading up and the crackle of the security crew's walkie-talkies. And then nothing but nightingales.

Until my phone went off.

"Don't answer," Alonzo hissed.

But instinct overrode caution. I was already pressing the receiver to my ear.

"Mr. Cavendish?"

"Yes."

"This is Detective Acree with the MPD."

It was a sign of how far along I was that this name at first meant nothing to me. I had to come at it in sections. Metropolitan Police Department. Washington, D.C. My city of residence . . .

"Hello," I said faintly.

"Do you have a moment, Mr. Cavendish?"

Well, let's see, Detective, I'm about to scale a tower. For the purpose of finding buried treasure. Before the night is done, the woman I love might be dead, and I might be, too. And an officially dead man might be dead once more.

Or else we might all be billionaires.

We'll certainly be criminals.

"I have just a moment," I said.

"Did I get you in bed?"

"No."

"You sound quiet."

"It must be the connection. If you must know, I'm overseas."

"I wasn't aware of that, Mr. Cavendish."

"I didn't tell you."

If he was surprised by my insolence, he didn't let on.

"I thought you might want to know," he said. "We've been investigating Miss Pentzler's death, and there's something I'd like to show you."

"Yes?"

"But you being abroad . . ."

"Maybe you could tell me what it is."

There was a very long pause.

"I can promise you," I said. "I'm not a flight risk."

The habit of holding me under suspicion must have been a hard one to break, so I can't really explain why he decided ultimately to take me in his confidence. Or why, having heard what he had to tell me, my brain should have resisted the implications for as long as it did.

"Mr. Cavendish?"

"I'll be in touch as soon as I'm back in D.C. Is that all right?"

"When will that be?"

"I only have . . . there's a few more hours of business here, so . . . Monday or Tuesday? That all right?"

"I guess it'll have to be, Mr. Cavendish."

I drew the phone away from my ear, then put it straight back.

"Detective? Are you still there?"

A moment of weakness, I confess. And it took just one look from Alonzo to dispel it. For that look said what I already knew. The time to speak had been on that beach in the Outer Banks, when I first saw Amory Swale's arm protruding from the sand. We had come too far to go back.

Detective Acree's voice was buzzing in my ear. "Mr. Cavendish?"

"Sorry, I just wanted to say thanks. For the call."

"Doing my job, Mr. Cavendish."

"Sure."

"Good luck with your business."

"Thanks."

I held the phone in my hand. Then I put it back in my pocket.

The rain had stopped. A scythe of moon poked through the cloud.

"It's time," said Alonzo.

41

History does not record why Syon House's original owner, the Duke of Somerset, decided to build those fifty-foot towers at each corner of the quadrangle. Did he just want a nicer view of the river? His enemies preferred to see the towers as fortifications, aggressive in intent, and Somerset was eventually executed for his sedition.

Somehow or other, the towers remained standing. And it's safe to say that even the Duke couldn't have envisioned an assailant quite like Seamus, who came at the northwest tower not with arquebuses and longbows and siege engines but with a sack of gadgets: *étriers* and gear slings and angles and bat hooks, each item engineered to pack the greatest tensile strength into the smallest form.

Seamus himself was engineered along the same lines. According to Alonzo, he had a resting pulse of thirty-six beats a minute

("Like bears in winter, Henry"), and there was something nearly ursine in the way he pawed at his gear and something wild, too, in the sheer tautness of his small frame — he had long since stripped down to a quarter-zip microfleece and zoner shorts — the way his muscles corded and bristled beneath his skin. He was half a foot smaller than me, but I wouldn't have dreamed of intruding on him. Even Alonzo preferred to absent himself.

"I'll just be in the way," he said.

"But where are you going?" I asked.

Alonzo tipped his head toward the neighboring woods.

"Don't worry," he added. "I'm on the qui vive. No one will get by without my seeing them. Now listen, Henry, the moment you're up there, you *call* me, is that understood? I want to know the layout. Every crevice, every crack, do you understand? Between us, we are going to find this. Oh, and Henry . . ."

"Yeah?"

"Be great."

I couldn't help it; I smiled. "Just keep 'em out of our way," I said.

Thank God there was no question of us hugging. Still, some crackle of feeling must have been exchanged, because when he turned and walked toward the woods, the sight of his bargelike frame (and those discombobulatingly small feet) caught me smack in the chest. Was I seriously proposing to hand over Alonzo's treasure?

And then, superimposing itself over our shared history: the image of Clarissa, as I'd last seen her, framed on either side of Halldor's swiveling body.

I closed my eyes, but that last image wouldn't be blotted away, so I looked instead at Seamus, laying out his gear in small clean formations.

"Seamus," I said. "Could I ask you something?"

"Mm."

"Why are you doing this?"

The faintest of grunts as he drove the first grappling hook into the mortar.

"Gonna fund me next climb."

"Who is?" I asked. "Alonzo?"

His shoulders rose an inch. "It's the big 'un," he said. "Nanga Parbat. The Man Eater. Forty-six-hundred-meter drop."

He gave me a nod for emphasis, but I admit I was less in awe of Nanga Parbat than of Alonzo's bold-facedness. Whatever happened tonight, the chance of Seamus getting a shilling for his labor was even less than our finding treasure, and I felt something near tenderness watching him strap the Black Diamond Icon headlamp onto his skull and slip his Five Ten Moccasym rock shoes into the web ladder.

"When I'm up," he said, "I'll flash me light at you. Twice and off, no more. You tie the rope to your harness, give me two tugs. I start pullin'."

"You're pulling me up?"

"I've lifted bigger cows than you."

Which was both insulting and reassuring.

"Won't I need the lamp to climb?" I asked.

"A pair of feet is all."

Seamus made one last survey of his handiwork, fastened me into my harness, and then quickly genuflected before hoisting himself onto the first hook.

"Cheers, mate."

And up he went.

Except that plain sentence does nothing to convey the purity, the parsimony, the tongue-and-groove rhythm of it. He gouged into the mortar, he planted his boot, he hauled himself to the next level — all in a single unbroken rhythm. It was like watching a life form evolve before your eyes. Or, to be more accurate, *two* organisms evolving together: the tower and Seamus, twining their DNA pools into a golden strand.

So it was a shock to look up after just ten

minutes and find Seamus no longer attached to the tower's surface. Would the tower itself come crumbling down? But the only thing that fell, finally, was a length of rope, amazingly thin: polyester sheath around a nylon core. I waited and then, from above, came the signal: two tiny flashes of light, directly over my head.

I threaded the rope through the belaying loop and knotted it and gave it a pair of tugs. Before I knew it, it had tautened into life and my legs had left the ground. A bubble of panic sprang from my chest as I swung myself toward the wall. My feet, encased in their sticky slippers, scrabbled against the still-damp bricks and then, with the next pulse of rope, took their first coltish step toward the heavens.

I wasn't moving as quickly as Seamus had, but there was no getting around what I was doing. I was rappelling up Syon House. And the only way to skate over that reality was to stare up into that velvety orange night sky and tell myself I was *descending,* not rising. *Lowering* myself into a warm clementine sea.

That illusion lapsed the moment my topmost foot slipped, so I replaced it with another image: Clarissa. Waiting at the top, her arms in long pale columns. *She* was what I fastened onto, finally, as I came within sight of the tower's crenellations and merlons. And she would have held me in good stead, I do believe that, had a voice not rung through the darkness.

"Who's there?"

An eerily ancient sound: It might have been a laird's sentinel calling down to a stranger on a dusty nag. Perched forty feet above God's earth, I found myself suddenly arraigned — *obliged* to answer — but then I heard Alonzo's voice booming from the woods below.

"I'm so sorry! Can you help me?"

The rope was no longer pulling, and I was no longer climbing. I was hanging there in the dark, an imperfect suspension, my feet brushing against the tower.

Another minute passed. All breathing stopped. Then from below came fragments of Alonzo's voice, brimming over with apology.

"So very sorry! . . . Must have fallen asleep . . . can't seem to find the . . . sorry to be so troublesome . . . lovely wedding, wasn't it?"

He was using his own scale — his size, his volume — to blind them. With each protestation, he drew them farther and farther from the house, and his voice grew fainter and less distinct.

I waited: one minute, two. Then I braced my feet once more against the tower's skin and tugged on the rope.

Seamus was waiting at the top — as I expected, as I didn't at all expect — and in the instant he pulled me in, the relief squeezed out of me in a long pipe-organ blast.

I slipped out of my harness. Dragged myself to my feet and stared up into the sky.

The moon was bright as fever. And as I stood there, Clarissa's absence affected me like a weather front. I drew in my shoulders and turned around, and there was Seamus, tautly still, waiting for me to . . . act.

"Alonzo," I said, reaching for my cell phone.

"I wouldn't," said Seamus.

He was right. If Alonzo was in custody, the last thing I should do was phone him.

"Okay then," I said. "Can I borrow your lamp?"

"If you don't go splashin' light every-bloody-where."

I dropped to my knees and gently guided the light around the base of the platform, watching the stones spark to life and then melt back into obscurity. No magically opening door. No arrow scratched in old blood. Just blankness. And behind it more blankness. I was standing atop one of England's greatest old homes and no closer to what I was seeking than I'd been on the other side of the ocean.

"Over there," said Seamus.

Seasoned climber that he was, he'd spotted a rectangular line of mortar — large enough in area for a box, or a human, to fit through — and darker by just a few degrees than the mortar on either side of it.

Darker from *use,* I thought at once. Darker because someone had once tampered with it.

"Bit crumbly," said Seamus, tucking his finger into the crevice. He reached into his sack and drew out an achingly thin, double-tapered blade. "Let's see what the ol' pecker will do."

If I'd had the strength, I would have laughed. But he was already jabbing the blade into the mortar. And then from the sack he drew larger and larger wedges — knife blades and angles — and he used a wall hammer to pound them still deeper, and the mortar fell away divot by divot, casting up tiny clouds of protest, until finally there was nothing visible but the stone itself, nakedly projecting.

Seamus wiped his brow, set his wedge down, and took a long breath. He never looked at me, but as soon as I said, "Try it," he took up his hammer and gave the stone a few exploratory taps. Then he started in hammering for real, muscle against rock. And yet because each stroke was so perfectly struck, the sound died away at our feet.

Until this point, his gains had been so incremental that I think both of us expected the stone to yield in the same way, square inch by square inch. But the silent work of centuries — of water and cold and heat and time — erupted into sudden fruition at the tenth blow. The stone exploded in a gust of fragments — and then just as suddenly vanished. We were staring into a canvas of pure blackness.

"Christ," I murmured.

I dropped to my knees, ranged my hand through the cavity . . . and felt only air. Pressing my chest to the ground, I plunged my arm still farther. More air.

For a long time I stared into that hole, waiting for the darkness to resolve into something. But the only thing that came back at me was a current of smoky cold, like something stealing from a well.

"You've got to lower me down there," I said.

One of Seamus's burly brows rose.

"It's a straight drop," he said.

"I know."

"There won't be any seeing you. The light goes only so far."

"I know. I wish I could see another way."

The only protest he raised now was his silence. To which I had just one last thing to oppose.

"Between us," I said, "I think I'm the one who knows what to look for."

Of course, I didn't know anything, not really. But Seamus was persuaded enough to help me into my harness and fit the lamp onto my head. Then he took his station by the pulley and, after giving me another few seconds to reconsider, he called out:

"Ready?"

Ready.

Except I couldn't say the word. All I could do was nod, and even that was more taxing than I could have guessed.

Although not as taxing as the complex act of getting in. The cavity Seamus had made was wide enough to admit but not to welcome. Previously unseen barriers came from nowhere: tangents and outcroppings that raked my ribs and kidneys and breastbone.

The stone scraped my knees and snagged my hips and, just when I thought I was clear, it closed around me so quickly that I felt as if I'd been lodged in the house's throat.

Gravity released me in the end, and as I worked my way down into the darkness the channel broadened like an esophagus. My back was no longer scraping against the stone, my knees were swinging free. . . .

And then I landed, with unpardonable rudeness, on something hard and brittle and outraged. No way to touch it — there wasn't room to bend — so I lifted my right foot and set it down again and listened to the echo. And then I did it again, just to be sure.

Wood.

I was standing on a wooden box.

I can't tell you how much time passed between that moment and the arrival of Seamus's voice. It took me a good minute just to understand what he was saying.

"Okay?"

I was about to answer, but I was distracted by a rich, dark pounding. The sound of my heart, I soon realized. So magnified by this small space that it seemed to be hammering against the house's foundations.

"Okay," I called back.

And then I remembered: I had a lamp strapped to my skull.

I tilted my head down, and the light splashed around my feet, pushing away the darkness to reveal . . . nothing.

Until, from the darkness, there welled up a length of wood, knotted and oaken, softly splintered beneath my weight. And secreted deep inside, a canvas bag, bunched around something I could neither reach nor see.

In retrospect, I can see I should have gone back up. Told Seamus what I'd found and worked out a plan for dragging the box to light. But the combination of wanting to know what was in it and not being able to was so bitter and intoxicating I couldn't leave my post. And so I bent and wriggled and did everything I could to see just what I was standing on.

It never occurred to me that the same rot and decay that had plied themselves against the building's exterior might have been at work on the inside. That the ledge supporting this box might have been waiting all these centuries to give way before the shock of one man's weight.

But that's exactly what happened. Before I could utter a prayer or a protest, I was falling in a free straight terrible line.

And then, even more shocking, I was no

longer falling. The rope, still anchored to Seamus's pulley, tautened around me and snatched me back up. The impact sent a shock wave straight up my spine, and my stomach lurched against my chest, and my legs dangled now in the void, and from below I could hear the crash of wood on stone . . . but here I was. Alive.

As to what happened *next* — well, in less kind moments, I blame my father.

When I was eight years old, I informed him that my friends Isaac Shapiro and Hans Bjornen had both become Boy Scouts, which clearly indicated I was meant to be one, too. My father reminded me that I was already playing baseball and soccer and that the task of driving me to a third activity every week was more than he or any parent should have to bear.

"You want to be a scout?" he said. "Give up one of your other sports. And if you expect me to be a scout*master,* forget it."

So I never joined the local pack. And for this reason, I never became truly competent at tying knots. Which meant that, on this particular night, I fastened my harness to the rope with what I thought was a sturdy bowline but was, in fact, an incorrectly tied half-hitch. Closer to a quarter-hitch. Closer to nothing at all because it was now *unraveling* itself.

Dull-eyed, I watched as my fingers scrambled to coil the loop back, but the rest of me, the *mass* of me, was working against them, and from my cold-numbed hands, the fibers of rope began slipping away like grains. And by the time my brain had grasped what was happening, it was too late, and I was once again falling. Only with this difference: Nothing was tethering me to the world above.

I fell without sound, without impediment. And indeed, beneath my terror, some quiet part of me imagined falling straight through the earth and out into morning.

It took less than a second for me to be disabused, for the earth embraced me with a lover's ardor. Pain spangled through every extremity. A new darkness flowered up from inside and joined with the darkness around me.

"Margaret," I whispered.

And then the night swallowed me whole.

42
ISLEWORTH, ENGLAND *AUGUST 1603*

He gives her a table of her own. He arranges all the instruments: the scale; the pans and pots; the twenty-six glass vessels, alphabetically organized, their bases luted with fire clay. Page by page, he lays out his notes, shows her the degree of pressure or heat or cold he applied to each substance. More reluctantly, he shows her where each experiment broke off, the mysteries that yielded themselves up and the ones that stayed out of reach.

— The challenge, Margaret, at least as I see it, is to destroy all the impurities in the base element while, in the same breath, reconstituting the balance of elements that adheres in Nature. The resulting metal would perforce share in the, the *quintessence* which may be found in the planets and stars and heavens.

He would carry on, but he has come to dislike this teacher's voice of his. And would it not indeed tempt fate to speak of the alchemist's true object? That philosopher's stone whose very perfection would have the power to transmute creation itself?

Men as great as Aquinas and Roger Bacon have broken themselves against that rock, and it is with no small qualm that he enlists Margaret in their ranks. He can have no great expectations of her success — or anyone's — but he cannot bear to bar this door against her any more than he could have closed it on himself. And so, on that first day, he can do no more than smile and take two steps back.

— Call out if you have need of anything.

And here is his final touch: the damask curtain, which he's attached to the ceiling by iron rods, dividing the laboratory in half. With a courtly nod, he closes the curtain after him. She is alone.

A full minute passes before she is able to move. And even then she trusts herself to perform only the simplest acts.

Pick up lead bar.
Drop bar in glass flask.
Place flask in rack above brazier.
Light coals.
Wait.

The transformation is slow at first, nearly invisible. First a skin of sweat appears on

447

the bar. Then a bubble of silver wells up. The lead shimmers, bubbles — then, with shocking abruptness, throws off a coruscation of red flame, which dies in the next instant, leaving behind a coat of brittle ash. Having expressed itself in this fashion, the lead withdraws into itself, and no amount of heat will coax it back.

With her cotton gloves, Margaret lifts the flask off the coals and peers inside. Black. The color of failure, she knows that much. A sign that the dross, after its brief flirtation with "other," has gone back to being dross.

And yet it is not the black that stays in her mind. It is that flash of red. This is what draws her back the next evening: the possibility of seeing it once more and persuading it to stay just a fraction longer, and then a fraction longer still, until it is bound in a transformative spiral, spinning through every last color of the rainbow.

She experiments with temperature: low and infrequent doses versus higher initial heat with longer periods of cooling. She adjusts the positions of flask and flame. She uses a vise to exert varying degrees of pressure on the lead. She tries different kinds of coal: anthracite, bituminous. The red refuses to come back.

Harriot had assumed at the start that she

would devote only an hour a night to alchemical studies and spend the rest of her time assisting him with his optics. But it becomes harder and harder for her to break away. One night, he calls her name three times without her hearing. He must thrust his face finally around the curtain and declare, with mock gravity:

— My dear Miss Crookenshanks, I have the distinct honor of informing you I shall be taking the refractive measure of brown mortar. . . .

Normally, she would smile. Tonight, she is like a sleeper roused before her time.

— Of course.

He can hear the hesitation. His brows draw together. He says:

— Why should you not carry on as you are?

— Are you quite sure?

— I would not stay the tide of progress.

Each day, without intending it, without even noticing, she steals more and more time for herself. He never complains. Indeed, he becomes almost unbearably solicitous on her behalf, tiptoeing from corner to corner.

— So sorry, my dear. I dropped the shoeing horn. . . .

And when he is not apologizing, he is

making excuses to absent himself.

— A little stroll should clear the head. . . .

He is gone for upward of an hour at a time. And though he returns always in high spirits, she can see how carefully that cheer has been constructed. She imagines him stacking it, brick by brick, in the hallway outside.

— Good fortune, Margaret? No? Well, stay at it.

But no amount of effort will reverse her fortunes. Every day is a roster of burnt fingers, scalded wrists, seared eyebrows. Flasks explode. Boiling pitch scorches the walls, eats through the floorboards. Mysterious gases sting her nostrils, scald her throat.

And what does she have to show for it? Cloddish residues that are neither earthly nor transcendent. Lumps of nothing.

One evening Harriot comes back to find her at the furthest extremity of despair, staring at a cracked vessel and a deposit of black lava crusting over on the worktable.

He says nothing, only makes a show of reaching into the flask's remains.

— Take care! she calls. — You shall be burned.

— Ah, but what is this?

With a sly smile, he draws forth a fully

formed gold ring.

— You have wrought wonders, Margaret!

She cannot help herself, she laughs. But when he extends the ring toward her, she understands it is more than a joke.

— Have no fear, he assures her. — It is not a betrothal ring. You may wear it wherever you like. Or keep it under your pillow, I shall take no offense.

She chooses, in the end, to place it on the fifth finger of her left hand, reasoning that it will be less in the way there. They say no more on the subject, but the next morning, by the light of her window, she finds a message on the ring's inner surface.

Ex nihilo nihil fit.

Nothing comes from nothing.

Being still unversed in the atomists, she cannot know these are Parmenides' words. Or that Parmenides was squaring himself against the doctrine of *creatio ex nihilo,* creation from nothing. According to the Greeks, the world could never have been fashioned from a void for the world has always in some form existed and will always exist. Man is mortal, matter eternal.

Margaret knows nothing of this. All she can feel at first is the negation of these words. *Nothing comes from nothing.*

It is, finally, her own faith in Harriot — in

his faith in her — that drives her toward an opposite construction. Nothing can be accomplished if nothing is expended. Which means that everything smolders with possibility.

Some day, she thinks, I will give him a ring of his own. From my very own gold.

She slides the ring back onto her finger and sets to work.

After lead comes zinc. Then tin. No elements have ever been subjected to greater trials. Blaze after blaze, they go up like Christian martyrs. And there stands Margaret, minutely observing their agonies, charting every torment of color and form. And the greatest torment of all: to come away with nothing but charred and oozing lumps.

She is not too proud to confide her bafflement to Harriot.

— Is the *pneuma* not composed utterly of atoms? Like all living matter? How can those atoms not be *reconfigured* under duress? Water, after all, becomes ice. Fire becomes ash. How can lead resist its own transformation?

Harriot shakes his head.

— There is no earthly reason.

Only later, thinking over his words, does she hear the passing stress he has placed on *earthly.* She has rushed into this labor without a backward look, but in quiet moments she can understand why a man as pious as King James should have a special horror of alchemy, blurring as it does the distinction between creator and created, making man the author of his universe.

And then, one afternoon, in the midst of heating copper, something extraordinary happens. After contracting into the usual sullen black lump, it springs forth with color.

And *such* color! Silver . . . violet . . . blue . . . green . . .

She can feel her own breath curling back on her. *The peacock's tail.*

The very effect she has been striving toward all these weeks. Prima facie evidence, or so it is believed, that an element is being transformed and perfected.

And it is happening here. Now. Before her half-disbelieving eyes, the green is giving way to an electric yellow, a resplendent orange. And as she watches, the orange at last explodes into red.

No mere flash this time but a stately procession through red's full spectrum, from rose to ruby to crimson and, finally, to a scarlet of extraordinary vibrancy, a scarlet that any Roman priest would have been proud to robe himself in.

She does not realize how loudly her gasp has resounded, but in the next instant, Harriot is tearing open the curtain and gazing at the last dying echo of red. The color of perfection, and *she* has called it into being.

And how apart from him she feels in that moment. No matter what he says, no matter how he strives to tune himself to her, that red belongs to her. It always will.

They have grown awkward in each other's presence. No longer anticipating each other's movements, they bump and jar, or else they stop just shy of collision and stare at each other in confoundment.

The only time they are at ease is in bed, and even here she is not entirely his. Not as she was before, when his skin and his body commanded her full attention. Now her responses are the product of reflex, and though she endeavors to hide her feelings, he *feels* them. One night, with more than a trace of bitterness, he asks:

— What can be infecting your mind, I wonder? Visions of *aurum?*

Not gold at all, she wants to tell him. A dinner table.

And at this table sit Aristotle and Aquinas

and Kepler and Copernicus and Bruno and Tycho Brahe — and Thomas Harriot — all gathered for supper. And there lies the place that has been cleared for her, and how can she bring herself to sit there? What has *she,* Margaret Crookenshanks of St. Helen's Bishopsgate, done to merit it?

It is the bitterest of all ironies that, in seeking to be worthy of him, she should drive him further and further away.

He no longer apologizes for making noise.

He no longer stays awake for her.

He is always up and about by the time she wakes.

She no longer notices when he pokes his head around the curtain.

The more she fails, the more she presses on, and the more the rest of the world falls away. When she is not working in the laboratory, she is immersing herself in hermetic texts, for it is an article of faith that today's alchemists are merely rediscovering the lost art of the ancients, which lies hidden behind nearly infinite veils of allusion, symbol, allegory.

And so she leafs through the Old Testament and the Apocrypha. Ovid's *Metamorphoses.* The old myths of King Midas, of Jason and the Argonauts, of Hercules and his seven labors. But no matter how hard she plies herself, the words simply stare back at her.

In early July, she switches her attentions to quicksilver. The effects on her are slow to build, but they are dire. Two of her back teeth fall out. Her hands fall into fits of palsy. Each morning she finds a deposit of hair on her pillow.

It is the fumes that affect her most. One afternoon, she is observing the final stage of devolution when a cloud of gas spews from the flask and envelops her whole. Every last nerve in her is stopped like a clock.

— Margaret!

Harriot kneels over her. She has just enough presence of mind to forestall him.

— I am quite well.

She rises to her feet. Gives her apron a brush and, after one last sway, heads straight back to the table.

He watches her for some minutes. Then disappears on the other side of the curtain.

The next afternoon, she is coming down the stairs when she finds Harriot in his traveling clothes. It is a sign of how far things have gone that the sight of him venturing out by himself neither surprises nor alarms her. It is for politeness' sake that she asks:

— Where are you bound?

— To see a friend.

43

There is this much comfort: Walter Ralegh has seen worse lodgings.

His current cell, after all, is larger than a ship's cabin. More comfortable, to be sure, than the Guianan forests, where he spent so many insect-haunted nights. Safer than Cádiz. Closer to the heart of things than Munster or the Isle of Jersey. The ventilation is good, the chest and table functional, and if the straw pallet isn't quite to scale, what bed has ever been large enough for Sir Walter?

Yes, thinks Harriot, if one didn't care about imminent death, one could do far worse than the Bloody Tower.

Sir Walter pokes at his teeth with a sweetwood pick.

— I hope the meal agrees with you, Tom.

Fried rabbit. Shoulder of mutton. Hen boiled with leeks and mushrooms. Two glasses of Italian white *vernage.*

— It does.

— You brought your pipe, I trust.

They seat themselves by the fire — even in the height of summer, the Tower is bone-cold — and Ralegh's servant lights their tobacco for them, and they puff in silence and with no small contentment. For a minute or two, they might actually be back in Sherborne Castle.

Except for one troubling detail: Ralegh's beard.

Always so neatly combed before. Always tapering to the same exquisite point, with no aid from the curling irons that other gentlemen favor. Hanging now loose and shapeless, like a beaten rug swinging from a kitchen window.

— They have forbade me razors, you see.

Leave it to Ralegh to divine the tenor of his thoughts.

— I had wondered, yes.

— I assured them that, should I ever again attempt to destroy myself, I would find more effectual means than a razor. As you know, I have a tolerable familiarity with poisons.

And yet it was not some exotic toxin that Ralegh chose three weeks earlier but a humble carving knife, driven straight toward the heart — arrested only by the intervention of Ralegh's rib. His secretary, Edward Hancock, was far more successful in taking his own life, and this is perhaps the largest humiliation that has yet been heaped upon the great man's head. Or is it rather a perverse testament to his life force that he cannot, no matter how he tries, erase himself.

The wound now is hidden away behind layers of black velvet, and the great man's gaze is veiled with torpor as he turns toward the window.

— Bess and Wat? They are well?

— They are Raleghs.

— Raleghs without a roof before long.

— You have many friends who will take them in.

— I have more enemies, I fear.

He knocks the ash from his pipe against the hearthstone.

— They blame me for Essex's death, of course. They say I intrigued for it.

— That is not so.

— You say that because you know me, Tom. The common man knows me only by repute.

He sets his pipe down. Labors to his feet.

— I should be grateful for a spot of exercise.

It is another gesture to Ralegh's status that

he is allowed his own walking place on the walls. In fine weather, he can see all the way to Greenwich. Today, a steady rain falls on London, merging with the river and mist to enrobe the Tower in a mock curtain, disappearing the moment it is touched.

— I'm afraid I have made quite a mess of things, Tom.

— Not through any sin of yours.

— Then I need not defend myself?

— Oh, my friend! How could I suppose you capable of such infamy? In league with Spain? Conspiring against the king's life? It is an insult to all reason.

— And yet they are bound on proving it. Lacking any proof, they will only make their own. Already, Cobham has accused me. Under torture, the other conspirators will follow.

— You have walked out of Lion Gate a free man before. You will do so again.

The great man smiles softly.

— Never mind, Tom. — I wish only to be assured that Bess and Wat will not starve.

— Of that you have my word.

Ralegh looks down toward the river. Even now, ships with square sails come driving through the rain. From Holland, from Sweden. From Genoa, Venice, France. Places he will never see again.

— You came here by water, Tom?

— It was the only way. The city has shut down.

Ralegh nods. — They say the plague is even making its way up the Tower. Three yeomen warders have been carried off in as many days. Perhaps I will be saved the dance of empty air after all. *And* the butcher's block.

— I beseech you, my friend. Do not speak in this way. Recall — *please* — your family, your friends, holding you fast in their prayers. . . .

— And to whom are they all praying, Tom?

Sir Walter's eyes are no longer sleepy but cold and bright. Speaking very deliberately, Harriot answers.

— To that God Who created the universe. Who even now steers our ship's course by virtue of His loving and eternal wisdom.

— Naturally.

Sir Walter's voice is dry as kindling.

— All the same, Tom, you have recalled me to something I have been meaning to ask you.

—Yes?

—What has happened to our dark treasure?

It is the same question the Earl of Northumberland posed all those weeks ago. And here is the natural result. As the waterman ferries him upriver to Syon House, Harriot's mind washes back to that summer night at Sherborne.

Only the five of them in attendance: Harriot, Ralegh, Northumberland, Marlowe . . . and a stranger to their midst. Marlowe's latest acolyte, granted (at Kit's request) a rare berth in the Academe's sanctum.

Being green and easily cowed, the young man sat off to the side for most of the night, refraining from comment. It was Harriot who, out of character, took the lead. For he wished to speak of Virginia.

— Sir Walter here may tell you what my charge was. To take stock of such natural and human riches as might be useful for commercial exploitation. Do I misspeak, Sir Walter?

— No.

— Toward that end, I traveled at great length, and with great delight, amongst the Algonkins. From village to village I passed, taking great care to develop a special familiarity with the priests. Who were in the whole most welcoming to me and most fascinated by all I had to show them. Guns and mathematical instruments. Compasses and spyglasses, astrolabes. The simplest things would occasion the greatest awe. The spring clock! Mark how it goes of itself, with no hand to set it in motion. Hail the spring clock!

— They would take these magical talismans in their rough hands and, one after another, they would ask, Are these the works of gods or men?

— Of *men,* I said. But I hastened to add that these men were in turn created and inspired by a great and all-knowing God. I made a point of showing them our Bible. They could not read it, of course, so they did what was to them second nature. They rubbed it on their chests, and they pressed it against their heads, and they kissed it, again and again, so infatuated were they.

— Good Christian that I was, I strove to correct their idolatry. I informed them that God's healing force derives not from the book *materially and of itself* but rather from the contents therein. Which was, need I say, the true doctrine of salvation through Christ.

— This distinction meant nothing to them. The Bible was miraculous, certainly — it had words written in it, after all, and they had never seen such things — but it was no more miraculous than the spring clock. The Gospel was — how shall I put it?

464

— one more weapon in our English arsenal. It occupied the same rank as a musket or buckler.

— And so, by degrees, I brought these savage priests to the side of Christ. Did I accomplish this through the power of divine revelation? No. I dazzled them with tricks. (Moses the juggler, do you recall, Kit?) I played on their credulity. I pretended our inventions were divinely sent. I led them to believe that, without our God, their villages and crops would be destroyed. And even as they lay dying, I persuaded them it was God's will. Machiavelli could have asked no better of me.

— Oh, you may look with scorn upon these savages, so like unto sheep. But now I ask you, my friends. Were you and I any different in how we came to God? Were we not, as children, seduced by tricks — by music and incense and signs and omens? Were we not dazzled by power? Our parents, our priests, our kings and queens, all claiming a divine sanction for their sovereignty over us? Were we any less credulous than the natives of Virginia? Any less quick to obey?

— From the very moment of our birth, we were played upon. And we were *conquered*, gentlemen, just as surely as the Algonkins. Why? Because without our consent, without the consent of *all* men, a society — a church — a monarchy — cannot hope to endure. It follows, then, that said consent must be secured by the quickest and surest means to hand. Which is to say . . . *God.*

— Tonight, then, I ask you. Has God ever spoken to you? His mouth to your ear? Or was God just the birch rod that brought you to your knees?

They were silent a good while. Not, as he well knew, from outrage — the little Academe had tiptoed to the end of many a branch before this — but from the desire to find the pithiest reply.

It was Marlowe at last who seized a candle, a pen, and paper and began to write.

— We will follow this out, he said. — To its *end,* natural or unnatural. And we will do it *together.*

And so that night they wrote a poem.

It was composed in rhymed iambic pentameter. Marlowe, the show-off, had petitioned for a Petrarchan sonnet sequence, but the others ignored him and tossed line after line into the mix — even Marlowe's acolyte offered a phrase or two — and the poem grew beyond the bounds set for it. And as each new page was blackened over with blottings, Marlowe simply took out another sheet and kept writing.

It was half an hour past dawn when he scribbled out the final line. Eyes febrile, hands trembling, he rose and held the sheets out to them.

— Behold! Our dark treasure!

And then, in a firm and measured voice, he began to read. It was only then that they grasped how far they had trespassed.

Then some sage man, above the vulgar
    wise,
Knowing that laws could not in quiet
    dwell,
Unless they were observed, did first
    devise
The names of God, religion, Heaven, and
    Hell
Whereas indeed they were mere fictions.

Far from chastened, Marlowe sounded giddier and giddier as he went along, and his voice surged still higher as he recited the two lines that were his particular invention.

Only bug-bears to keep the world in fear
And make them quietly the yoke to bear.

The day's first light was just creeping

around the curtains, and the candles had contracted into tiny stubs when Marlowe came at last to the final stanza.

> In death's void kingdom reigns eternal
>   night,
> Secure of evil, secure of foes,
> Where nothing doth the wicked man
>   affright
> No more than him who dies in doing right.
> Then since in death nothing shall to us
>   fall,
> Here while I live I will have a snatch at
>   all.

They had done just as Marlowe had suggested. They had followed things out — and found no end at all.

It was Ralegh who, after a long silence, said:

— Perhaps the best tribute to our labor might be to burn it.

With an almost shy smile, he added:

— Lest we ourselves end in fire.

And here was the final surprise. It was Marlowe's acolyte, so silent through much of the night, who was the first to act, snatching the paper from the table and flinging it into the fire.

A single tear coursed down Christopher

Marlowe's cheek as he watched the work of an evening vanish.

They might have been excused for thinking that was the last of it. But three years later, an anonymous tragedy began making the rounds of London. An appalling piece of dramaturgy titled *The First Part of the Tragicall Raigne of Selimus*. It concerned a tyrannical Turk who, as rationale for murdering his father, offers the very poem the Academe's members had written that long-ago night at Sherborne.

How had the dark treasure survived its own incineration? And who had shepherded it to publication? Marlowe by now was dead. Neither Ralegh nor Northumberland would have dared drag it to the light, any more than Harriot. The only possible suspect was that mild young man whom Marlowe had brought to Sherborne.

And suddenly this nearly silent figure bloomed with unguessed possibilities. Had he, in fact, been committing their lines to memory the whole time? Or had he engaged in some last-minute sleight of hand, sliding the dark treasure under his cloak as he tossed some other sheet onto the flames? Was he even now borrowing Marlowe's preferred form — the tragedy — to flaunt his power over the School's remaining members?

The only saving grace was that the text made no mention of the Academe or its members. But behind the scenes, a connection had already been forged. Marlowe, before his murder, had been charged with heresy and blasphemy. And within weeks of the publication of *Selimus,* Ralegh and Harriot were called before an ecclesiastical commission to answer charges of atheism and apostasy. The evidence was scant and the charges were dismissed, but the taint lingered.

And now, with Sir Walter Ralegh soon to stand trial for treason, those lines of old verse might just bear him to his grave.

Small wonder, then, that standing with Harriot atop the Bloody Tower, he should think to ask:

— What has happened to our dark treasure?

With a sorrowing heart Harriot answers:

— Quite as lost to us now as it was then.

— By that, you mean it is still in one gentleman's possession?

— As best I can determine.

Ralegh watches a pair of gulls wheeling and diving among the idled ships' masts. Then, to Harriot's surprise, he begins to roar with laughter.

— Kit should have taken greater care with his lovers, would you not say?

44

August 1603: London is dying.

Dying by the thousands. Soul by soul, hour by hour. Dying in taverns, in shuttered-up homes. In brakes and ditches and alleys. On the doorsteps of churches.

Sometimes the plague gives a day's warning, sometimes only a few minutes. The streets that were thronged weeks earlier for King James's coronation have now a spectral stillness. Those who must travel on errands hew to the center of the road, the better to avoid contagion, but there is no escaping the *sounds.* A threnody of groans, and every so often a brief cry of astonishment, as though death were a kind of pinch.

King James is far away, and the richest Londoners have long since abandoned the city. The poor, lacking any better choice, straggle into the countryside with nothing to guide them. Not a house or village will admit them, and many perish by the road, in fields, in barns. One man, dragging a barrow after him, makes it as far as Syon Reach, a seven-mile distance, before the plague catches him. He dies in the muck of the riverbank, at 8:31 in the evening, to the sound of larks.

At nearby Syon House, the Earl of Northumberland has announced his intention to move his household to Tynemouth Castle. Every member of the earl's retinue, high and low, is set to work. Even the three wise men who live on the earl's patronage, even *they* must set aside their customary duties. Robert Hues oversees the packaging of plate and crystal, William Warner is given charge of key artworks, and Thomas Harriot is made master of the books.

After all, such a library as the earl's cannot be entrusted to a common knave. Imagine what might happen on the road. The drayman nods off, the wheel rolls into a ditch . . . the massed sum of Western wisdom swims in mud and sheep shit.

— It must be you, Tom, says the earl. — Nobody else would feel the wound so.

And so Harriot culls a representative sampling of two hundred volumes, sets them in a cushion of straw, watches over them as they're loaded, covers them with three tarpaulins . . . and then travels with them all the way to Northumbria.

A three days' journey on either side. And, during that time, an unquiet silence settles over Harriot's house. By day, the rooms belong to the Gollivers, who alternate between packing and sniping. By night, Margaret treads the laboratory boards, setting her blazes ever higher.

She never sees the Gollivers, and they make a point of avoiding her. She is all the more astonished, then, to find Mrs. Golliver waiting for her with a silver tray, on which lies a single sheet of rag paper, folded in quarters and sealed with a stamp of red wax.

— For you, I suppose.

A note from Harriot, surely. Last-minute instructions for the arrangement of his instruments. Or else a little burst of feeling, transcribed somewhere on the Old London Road.

But it is not Harriot. It is the last correspondent in the world she would have expected. Her mother.

My dearest Margret,
  I am most dredfully ill. I long for you by my side. Might you come? If not, then pray for mee, my girl.

A foreign hand. For, of course, Mrs.

Crookenshanks can only make her mark and must have enlisted a neighbor or clergyman.

Still more foreign: the language. *My girl — I long for you — dearest Margret.* So plaintive and awkward. So unlike her mother, who has shunned the giving and receiving of endearments for as long as Margaret has known her.

And what better sign of her mother's extremity, that in her final hours she should become what she was meant to be all along? Before life worked its hardness on her?

Again and again, Margaret reads the note. Conscious all the while of the absence on the other side of the curtain. Although she can well imagine what Harriot would say if he were here.

The letter is as much as a week old, Margaret. Your mother, God rest her soul, is very likely dead. Perhaps even buried. Beyond the power of you or anyone else to comfort her.

This, too, Harriot would say: *The moment you enter your mother's house, the door will be barred against you. A deputy of the city government will be placed outside to ensure you never leave. Your only hope of egress, Margaret —* your only hope *— will be to die yourself. As you almost certainly will.*

And should this argument fail to move

her, Harriot would recall her to the urgency of her experiments.

Already, for the sake of transmutation, you have let everything else fall away: your health, your peace of mind — our love —

No, he would be too decorous to bring up that last part. But his point would be taken. By leaving now, she would be abandoning not just her work but her newly smithed identity. To succor the woman who fought so hard to suppress it.

For hours, Margaret sits staring at her mother's words until they cease to be readable.

Nothing is any clearer when she goes to bed, though one memory does seep through: the afternoon she found her mother staring at her writing. Unable to make sense of the markings, Mrs. Crookenshanks's eyes leaked with shame. And with rage, too, was that it? For the chances that had been denied her.

A fugitive weakness, quickly suppressed, but cracking open a whole history of loss. And this is the moment to which Margaret cannot help but return. For it is the moment in which, strangely enough, she and her mother were most united.

Harriot returns the next evening: aching in

every corner of his body, cross with boredom. Crosser still to find no one but the Gollivers waiting for him and his papers still not packed away. And the earl's entire house hold due to leave tomorrow!

—Where in God's name is Margaret?

They make no reply. They just hand him the paper.

Tom —

My mother has asked me to come to her. She is not well.

I did not stay for your return because you would have bid me stay. And I might have listened.

My debt to you is greater than I can say. Pray do not consider your faith in me squandered.

I have not acted rashly.

Words are nothing. Know my heart.

Margaret

So slowly does he drop that he is not even aware of what's happening until the floor catches him and the wall comes at him from behind. In every other respect, his mind is lucid.

She has gone to London.

With rare tact, the Gollivers quit the parlor. He scarcely notices. He is utterly still, and all the same he is tumbling through space and time, and nothing is as he left it.

— Margaret . . .

He covers his face. Ten minutes pass. Twenty. At last he draws his hands away, and his eyes, freed from darkness, fasten on something in the near distance. A small white object in the back of the hearth.

Slowly he rises and walks toward the remains of yesterday's fire. There lies a fragment of paper, spared from destruction by the wood's dampness.

His first thought is that it is *another* note from her. A revision of the first. She has changed her mind. Even now, she is winging back to him, begging forgiveness for her foolishness.

But this is not Margaret's hand. This letter comes from someone he has never met.

To Miss Crookenshanks,
Your sister wished to apprise you that your mother went to her Maker this Wednesday past. Her suffering was considerable but brief in duration. She was reconciled to her God.
You have my profou
The Rever

The lower corner has been burnt away,

but the rest of the document is shocking in its clarity.

Pressing the sheet between his hands, he walks down the hall to the kitchen, where the Gollivers are bowed over cups of muddy ale. He sets the paper in front of them. He watches their eyes widen. And in a tremulous voice, he says:

— You have been clumsy, it appears.

How stupid they grow in this moment of revealing: their heads ducking to one side, their gazes shifting away. *Like cornered dogs,* he thinks.

— Unless I mistake, this was the letter that Margaret *should* have received.

Still they won't look at him.

— You gave her *another* letter, did you not? A forged letter. You led her to believe her mother was still alive. And was expecting her.

He can't bear to look at their faces now, so he circles around behind and stares down at their blockish heads.

— I'm sure you know what you have done. You have *murdered* her, the both of you. As surely as if you had taken a dagger and plunged it into her heart.

It is characteristic of them that, at the first sign of pressure, they should break ranks.

— *He's* the one that wrote it.

—'Twasn't my notion, 'twas *hers.*

— Ooh, he was quick to go along, wasn't he?

— Never thought the girl'd rise to it.

— You let her walk out that door, didn't you?

— Same as *you,* woman.

Harriot's hand slams down on the section of table between them.

— You are vile. The both of you.

He turns away and gazes out the kitchen window and waits until he is master of himself again.

— Did you hate Margaret so very much?

He has no expectation of an answer. He certainly does not expect this: the surge of bile rising straight up from Mrs. Golliver's throat.

— *I* might have been of use, too! Once! *It isn't fair!*

45

Clarissa's flesh was pressed against mine. Her legs were twined around my hips, her breath was warm on my neck, her hand was cupping my cheek, she was stroking me back to life . . . she was . . .

Cold as death.

I woke. To find someone else's hand pressed against my cheek. A dead hand.

With a roar, I jerked myself free, watched the bone fingers sail into the darkness. I sat there, half expecting them to crawl back, but the only thing moving now was me. My lungs, my heart, my skull . . . every last part vibrating from cold and pain and shock.

Where am I?

As best I could tell, I had tumbled not so much down as *back.* Through something like six centuries. For this cold, dank, recoiling space could only have belonged to the abbey from whose ruins Syon House rose.

And it was with a gulp of sorrowing

laughter that I recognized how fitting a place I'd found within which to be buried for all time.

By now I'd forgotten all about Seamus, still waiting atop the tower. I'd forgotten about Alonzo, last heard trying to extricate himself from Syon Park security. I'd even forgotten about Clarissa and what would happen if I didn't give Bernard Styles what he wanted by three o'clock in the morning.

No, my memory could stretch back only so far and no more. So I returned to that moment — five minutes ago? fifty? — just before my fall. And I remembered, with a flush of second discovery, just what I'd been standing on when everything gave way.

A box.

A wooden box, its contents not quite visible. Falling just in advance of me, crashing on the same stone floor. *Waiting* for me in this impenetrable darkness.

And now I was *crawling* across that floor, windmilling my arms in every direction — and discovering, with each sweep, new wellsprings of pain in my ribs, my knees, my shoulders. The cold soaked through my skin, and before long I was swinging my arms simply to keep my blood flowing . . . until my left hand landed on something hard and unyielding.

Slowly, I traced its outlines. A corner. Another corner.

And then a lid, splintered into nothingness.

I bent over the opening. Something stirred from the blackness. A metal object, bright enough to peel away some of the shadows.

I closed my hand around it, raised it to my eye, but the darkness was still too thick. My brain, though, was slowly filling with light because it was in this moment that I remembered my climber's lamp.

Somehow, through all my collisions, it had remained fastened to my head. Somehow, God knows how, it was still shining its fine straight beam into the empty air.

They make these things tough, I thought. *Like Seamus.*

Unstrapping the lamp now, I directed its beam at the object lying in my palm.

A ring.

Simple and elegant. Gold. With four words inscribed inside, barely legible but immediately resonant: *Ex nihilo nihil fit.*

The very words from Clarissa's vision.

With the lamp's help, I inventoried the rest of the box's contents. And then at last I turned away. Propped myself against the box and stared straight ahead, deaf to the world — until a strange scratching sound met my ears.

I took it at first for rats. But the sound died abruptly away and then, after another ten or fifteen seconds, mounted a hundredfold. Without warning, the wall in front of me burst open, and a shower of dust and stone rained down as two figures staggered into the room, brandishing LED flashlights that seemed to fill that black space with cones of fire.

The first figure, instantly familiar, was Halldor, still in the Elizabethan officer's costume he'd sported at the wedding reception. Following close behind: Bernard Styles, in a pink-striped white suit, pointing his umbrella like a saber.

"Mr. Cavendish," he said.

He looked like one of those gentleman eccentrics of the nineteenth century, stepping from the balloon that has just landed him in the Pyrenees. He seemed genuinely surprised when I started laughing.

"Well, now," he said, brushing the masonry powder from his sleeve. "I am glad to find you in good spirits, Mr. Cavendish. By my watch, it's just a hair past three in the morning. You are a man of your word, I congratulate you."

"And I congratulate you," I said. "That was some fucking entrance."

"Halldor, I am happy to say, has absorbed many useful skills in his career, demolition being just one of them."

"You didn't think you might demolish *me?*"

"Do you know it never occurred to us? Were you badly injured?"

"Not by you," I said, rubbing my ribs. "I took the long way here."

"Well, never mind, you shall have acres of time for convalescence. Now if you would kindly step away from the box . . . ."

I rose to my feet.

"Correct me if I'm wrong," I said, "but I believe we spoke of an exchange."

"Indeed we did."

He nodded to Halldor, who leaned through the opening in the wall. A second later, Clarissa was walking toward me. Pale and small and nearly illusory.

"Are you . . . ?"

I didn't finish my question. Or rather I answered it for myself by wrapping my arms around her — with a force that surprised me. And her. Pore to pore we stood, and my relief was so great that I might have stayed many hours like that . . . had she not pulled away so abruptly and with an air of such blushing regret.

"Well, there we are," said Bernard Styles,

sounding only slightly embarrassed. "All's well that ends well, wouldn't you say, Mr. Cavendish? And now at the risk of being rude, I shall have to repeat myself. Kindly step away from the box."

"On second thought," came a thundering voice. *"Stay right where you are, Henry!"*

Silly me, thinking there was no way to top Bernard Styles's coup de théâtre. But what Alonzo's entrance lacked in pyrotechnics, it made up for in sheer effrontery. Very nearly comedic, the way he strode through that crater in the wall, belly leading, chest following close behind, declaiming like Sir Donald Wolfit as the LED torches converged on him like spotlights.

"Good evening, everyone. Or perhaps I should say good morning."

Morning, I thought. *Is that what it is?*

And that was the final blow to my sense of reality. The idea, I mean, that, a dozen or so feet over our heads, the world was carrying on as before. While, down here, two of the world's preeminent book collectors were circling each other like Bowery brawlers.

"Alonzo."

"Bernard."

The enameled overtones of clubmen. Oddly poignant under the circumstances, for there was Styles, still baptized in pulverized stone and mortar dust, and there was Alonzo, dragging his absurd Tudor raiment after him. Neither of them conscious of any loss in station.

"Henry," said Alonzo. "May I ask you something?"

"Mm."

"Why would you cut a deal with such a putz?"

"Because he was going to kill Clarissa."

"No. He wasn't."

"You don't *know* —"

"I *do* know. Clarissa is one of *his.*"

And, in the very moment he said it, I happened to be looking straight at her. Wondering why she wouldn't bridge the six feet of space that she'd put between us. Such a short distance, after all, and nothing to fill it but Alonzo's voice.

"Didn't you ever wonder, Henry? How Styles was able to keep on top of us from the start? How he was able to follow you to D.C. and North Carolina and now *here?* It's really astonishing when you think about it. He knew exactly where you were at every moment of every day. Either he had to have the most spectacularly well-engineered crystal ball or — well, I concluded a *mole* was the likelier prospect.

"At first, I admit, I figured it for being

Amory. A dear fellow, yes, but he could be had for the price of French toast. Unfortunately, just as I was preparing to confront him on the subject, he took the rather surprising step of dying. Which means he could never have told Styles we were bound for England. Let alone which wedding we were attending on which evening. That particular intelligence would have had to come from some other source. Would it *not,* Miss Dale?"

Her face — for I was watching very closely — was utterly bare of expression. It was Alonzo's that broke into lines of sorrow.

"Oh, my apologies, it's not Dale at all, is it? *Gordon.* Clarissa Gordon. Security consultant to Mr. Bernard Styles.

"And what a splendid job you did covering your tracks. Not a single item on Google to link you with your employer, and believe me, I looked. But you couldn't quite escape being photographed last spring at the Grolier Club banquet. An event I could hardly attend, being already dead, but one I've been able to catch up on in my spare time. I only wish I'd seen the picture earlier, as it might have spared my good friend Henry some collateral damage."

In the next second, his hand had buried itself in the wilted white ruff that, to my great fascination, still encircled my neck. It took him no more than ten seconds to emerge with a square inch of hinged metal, glacier blue in the artificial light.

"GPS, by the looks of it," he said, cradling it in his palm. "I believe they use the same device to track children."

Tell him. Every last one of my neurons was sending Clarissa the same message. *Tell him he's wrong.*

But her eyes were too dead even to avoid my gaze. With no one to contravene him, Alonzo carried on.

"She probably planted it on you this very afternoon, Henry. How else could she and Styles have traced you, after all? They didn't want to give you the chance to back out. And really, Henry, you should consider it a *compliment* that they had such faith in your abilities."

He was trying to be kind, possibly. But if you'd given me a choice of whom to strangle in that room, I might have chosen him.

"Oh, now, don't look like that, Henry, I'd have told you earlier but I didn't have any hard evidence. It wasn't until we got to England that I was able to make more *pointed* inquiries. And to see the value of playing out this particular game as far as it could go.

489

"But you're quite right, Henry, to feel betrayed. I'd feel the same in your shoes. Nevertheless, you must see the upside in all this. Clarissa is no longer yours to protect. She never was. And therefore, these savages have no hold over you now. We are *our own theme,* Henry. We may do as we will."

Styles cleared his throat.

"There is the small matter of the law, Alonzo. Please consider that you are a fraud and a thief."

"And you, Bernard, are a burglar and a terrorist who has just blown a hole through one of England's great homes. For politeness' sake, I've omitted that you are also a murderer."

"He didn't kill anyone," said Clarissa, her eyes tucking downward.

"Ohhh!" Smiling, Alonzo turned on her. "Is that the illusion you've been clutching to your little bosom? That your employer is a good and honorable man? Lily and Amory might take issue on that point."

"Dear *me.*" Styles clapped his hands around his jaw. "You can't truly think me capable of such cold-bloodedness, can you, Alonzo? You certainly can't *prove* it. To anybody's satisfaction but yours."

"I don't need to," Alonzo answered levelly. "The only thing I'm obliged to do is savor the look in your eyes when Henry and I take what is ours."

A slight edge had appeared in Bernard Styles's croon.

"Take what is *yours?* The document belongs to me, it always has."

"And all the intellectual property pertaining thereto? If I may say so, that is to laugh. Until I came along, you had no clue what you held in your hands."

Styles smiled thinly. "And you have no clue what you hold in yours."

"Enough!"

The two collectors turned on me with frankly astonished expressions.

"I wish you could see how ridiculous you both look," I said. "Arguing over your precious loot. May I suggest, before you say another word, you *inspect* your spoils?"

Interestingly, neither of them was in a hurry. Styles may simply have sniffed a trick. Alonzo's case was more complex. I think he had been picturing this moment so long it had become for him immutable, and reality was the only thing now that could disturb its perfection. And so, at the very brink of fruition, he flinched. And, like his rival, stood mute and frozen on the abbey floor.

It was left to Clarissa to snatch the flashlight from Halldor and snap:

"God's *sake.*"

She trained the light on the box, lowered her face to it. Peered inside. Then rose and slowly turned around.

And now, one by one, they came forward: Alonzo, Styles, even Halldor. The same sequence: bending, rising, groping for language.

"I don't . . ."

"It's . . ."

And for the first and last time in my life, I heard Halldor speak.

"No."

I couldn't blame him. He was looking down not at gold but at the remains of a human being. The skull pried open in mocking laughter, the right arm half raised in a salute, which was marred only by the absence of a hand. The hand that had, ten minutes earlier, been caressing my cheek.

"Say hello to Harriot's treasure," I declared.

46

"Sit down," I said. "Let me tell you a story."

Only there was nowhere for the others to sit, really. So they stood, and the only one who sat was me. On the cold hard floor, propped up on that old groaning splintered box.

"Thomas Harriot never married," I said. "But he did *love*. A woman named Margaret Crookenshanks."

Clarissa turned her head toward mine.

"Records indicate she died in September of 1603," I said. "In St. Helen's Bishopsgate. Two weeks after her mother. Given the time and locale, we can probably conclude she died from the plague. Somehow, Harriot was able to spirit her body back here. He buried her in a part of Syon House where no one else would find her. A place that had special significance for him — and her, too, possibly. The northwest tower."

No storyteller could have asked for a more

gratifying silence from his audience.

"Well, time passed. Harriot's grief did not. My guess is that, more than anything else, he found comfort in one idea. That the woman he loved might one day be *known*. Not to his contemporaries, they wouldn't have understood. No, he was pinning his hopes on the future.

"Of course, he could have just declared his grief straight out. But it pleased him to do what he did best, and maybe he even thought she would have preferred it that way. To be encoded, *refracted* through numbers and letters. So that some like-minded souls would know something of what he felt. *All* he felt."

A scowl carved itself across Alonzo Wax's face.

"Oh, for the love of — Harriot didn't leave us a Book of the *Dead*, Henry, he left us a map. He couldn't have been more explicit. *Great stores of gold, matchlesse in worthe, / There to bee freede from Virginia's Earthe.*"

"Yeah, funny thing. A good friend of mine just went through the parish registers for 1603. Margaret Crookenshanks is listed, all right. Only her Christian name wasn't Margaret. The name she was given at baptism was something far less common, some-thing a young girl might have been embarrassed to own up to, given its connotations."

Clarissa's lips parted, and the name passed out of her like breath.

"Virginia."

"What better way," I asked, "for patriotic parents to honor Elizabeth, the Virgin Queen, than by calling their baby daughter Virginia?"

I stood now. Gazed at each pair of eyes in turn.

"Thomas Harriot didn't bury gold in Syon House. He buried his *heart's* treasure. And *here* . . ." I nodded down to that half-shattered container. "*Here* his treasure lies."

In slow, aching steps, Clarissa advanced. Peered into the box's cavity and studied those old bones one last time.

And then something sparked in her eye. She reached in and drew out a long cylinder, encased in ancient leather, oxidized to a hunter green.

"Let me see that!" cried Alonzo.

But she wrapped her arms around it as if it had come straight from her womb.

"Don't worry," I said. "It's not treasure. At least not the kind you're looking for. It's a perspective trunk. That's how Harriot was able to see the stars. And the moon."

"And *Venus*," murmured Clarissa, to no one in particular. "The phases of Venus."

A deep silence fell over us now. Broken at last by Alonzo's great, sorrowing bark of laughter.

"The old bastard!"

He sank, by inches, to the floor, and another laugh tore from him as he buried his face in his hands.

"So that's our reward," he said. "After all this. A goddamned spyglass and a bag of bones."

He clapped his hands together like gongs.

"*Well* now," he said. "There's no cause to lose faith. We just took a wrong turn, that's all. We misread the damned thing."

"Alonzo . . ."

"Personally, I always thought it was a mistake coming here. Amory and I were making serious headway with the Indian lore. Really, if we hadn't been diverted, we'd have — no, believe me, it would have just been a matter of *time* before —"

"Alonzo!"

I positioned myself about an inch from his nose and waited for him to blink me into view.

"It's over," he said.

"Well, yes," declared Bernard Styles. "And then again, no."

He inscribed a tiny ellipse around us with

his flashlight before settling the beam on Alonzo.

"Your little *King Solomon's Mines* nonsense," he said. "*That's* quite finished. And a good thing, too, I've always felt there's nothing more vulgar than a treasure hunt. However, there remains the small matter of my letter."

He put out his hand like a tray.

"I suggest you return it now, Alonzo, while I'm still in a clement frame of mind. After all, it won't do you a bit of good now."

Alonzo said nothing. And, in reply, Bernard Styles's voice grew only milder.

"Now see here, *mon vieux.* I'm quite prepared to overlook everything that's happened. I know we've had our differences in the past, but there's no reason we can't patch things up once more. You need only give me what is mine."

"I don't have it," said Alonzo.

"Of course you do."

"I don't."

"Alonzo," said Styles, with a long-suffering air. "You've made many questionable errors in judgment, but not even *you* could be so criminally stupid as to lose the thing. My patience is vast and deep, as you know; it is also finite. Perhaps I should count to ten?"

"You can count to ten million."

There they stood, the two of them, one in light, one in shadow. And if, in the future, a pair of men hate each other as much as *they* did in that instant, I hope I'm not alive to see it.

"I can't tell you how unfortunate this is," said Bernard Styles.

He made a barely perceptible nod, and everything changed. Like a panther sprung from a briar thicket, Halldor threw himself at Alonzo. Wrapped his long arm around Alonzo's thick neck and, with the other arm, pulled out a long and cold and pristine blade.

A bare bodkin, I thought, but my gulp of laughter died the moment I saw the pearl of blood well up from Alonzo's neck.

"Bernard," said Clarissa in a tight voice. "Please."

"I believe it was Alonzo who said I had no hold over him. I am merely endeavoring to correct his assumption. His *presumption,* really."

The knife went deeper on the second jab, drawing out a rill of blood that dribbled all the way to Alonzo's clavicle.

"Extraordinary thing, the neck," said Bernard Styles. "Powerful and fragile in somewhat equal measure. I fully believe, if we let evolution take its course, the carotid artery and trachea will very sensibly retreat an inch or two. So as not to be so fearfully exposed."

As if to demonstrate, Halldor drew a circle around the exposed area. And by now the blood was no longer a dribble.

"Just tell the bastard where it is!" I cried.

Alonzo's chest heaved and swelled. A gurgle rose from his larynx. A single tear rolled down his white cheek. But the expression in his eyes, that didn't change.

And I was helpless to save him. One move from me, and Halldor's knife would strike home.

"I know where it is!" I shouted.

Styles's head glided in my direction.

"Is that so, Mr. Cavendish? Where?"

"In his room."

"*Which* room?"

"At our hotel. The Dragon's Tongue. It's the — fuck, it's — the *Disraeli* room."

Styles gave me a sad smile.

"How kind of you to jog Alonzo's memory. I hope you'll understand, though, that in a case of this urgency I will need to hear it from the *horse's* mouth."

One more rake of the knife, straight down. And now the blood was washing like finger paint across Alonzo's neck.

"Technically speaking," mused Bernard Styles, "I'm not certain that killing a legally dead man even qualifies as murder."

What happened next still strikes me as something beyond the reach of physics. One moment Halldor was standing there, his arm coiled around Alonzo. The next moment he was on his knees — then on all fours — and his knife was skittering into the darkness. And there, where he had once been, stood Clarissa, swinging Thomas Harriot's age-hardened perspective trunk like a truncheon.

Released from Halldor's grip, Alonzo staggered toward me. I yanked off my Earl of Essex cloak and wrapped it around his neck.

"Just hold it there, okay?"

"Mr. Cavendish."

Bernard Styles's position had not changed a fraction. The one difference was that he was now holding a Webley 38, antique in its own way but primed for modern use.

With his other hand, he swung the light toward us, illuminating us one by one. First Alonzo . . . then me . . . finally, lingering with special relish on Clarissa.

"Oh, my dear," he said. "You appear to have come down with a nasty case of Stockholm syndrome. Too much time with the enemy, I expect."

Her eyes were as hard as his pistol.

"The enemy was right, Bernard."

"The enemy is never right."

"You're a killer."

"Pish, I'm a businessman. *Entirely* a businessman."

"Well, you'd better shoot clean then," she said. "Because you won't get all of us."

"I won't?"

And here is where I plead guilty to underestimating Alonzo Wax. He was not simply tending to his wounds, as I'd first assumed, he was awaiting his moment. The exact moment when his captor's eyes ticked away. At which point he flung his cloak-bandage straight at Styles.

The strategy was better than the aim, for the cloak only brushed Styles's temple and settled on his shoulder. It was the blood, I think, that made the difference — *Alonzo's* blood, smearing the old man's skin and clothes and hair, unsettling him just long enough for Alonzo to fling his entire bulk at him.

The flashlight fell to the floor, and Styles followed right after, with the force of a felled maple. But Styles's right hand, though pinioned, kept a firm grip on the revolver and fired two quick rounds into the nearest wall. To my bruised skull, the sound was like a summons from hell. I clapped my hands over my ears and waited until the ringing had passed, and it was in the act of recovering my senses that something massive and undeniable caught me in my midsection and flattened me to the ground.

Stunned, I stared up into the panther eyes of Halldor. And read my own destiny.

For, as he pressed his thumbs against my trachea (*Extraordinary thing, the neck*) he showed not the slightest uncertainty. He *would* kill me. In the swiftest and, all things considered, the most humane manner possible.

He worked on me as if I were a bellows, squeezing out the last reserves of oxygen. And just when I thought I had none left to give, another weight piled on top. It was Clarissa, pummeling Halldor's back and shoulders, clawing his skin, pulling his hair . . . and all it took for him to resolve the problem was a single backward crack of his fist. Clarissa flew off, and as my vision faded into half-light, I saw her subside into the square of floor next to me.

Halldor now was perfectly free to carry on his work. He bore *down,* and to my surprise, my blood thrummed not with panic but peace. My brain, half extinguished, explained the whole process to me:

This is how it feels, Henry. To die.

I suppose I would have, too, if some small

part of me hadn't still been burrowing down to essentials. How else would I have remembered the knife?

The knife Alonzo had handed me at the wedding. The knife that lay even now sheathed against my right flank. Not a rapier but not a bad substitute, either. Easy enough to lay hands on, if my hands had been free. If my limbs weren't flopping against the cold stone.

But whatever force remained in my body was concentrating itself in the fingers of my right hand. And these fingers were crawling now down my hip . . . pausing briefly at the upper thigh . . . straining with all their might toward the knife's hasp . . . teasing it out of its holster, millimeter by millimeter. . . .

And it was this, the simple act of freeing the blade, that emboldened me now to take the next step. To wrap my fingers around it and redirect it toward Halldor's thigh.

I heard him grunt. I felt his leg pull away. Two inches, no more, but enough to let me draw the blade out and drive it still higher.

And now Halldor's upper extremities could no longer ignore the tumult from below. The barest slackening of fingers against my throat, and still the lights inside me were fast dimming. I had one chance left. And so, with all the strength left me, I plunged the blade into his groin.

Halldor howled and snapped his spine back. And as his fingers sprang away, the inrushing air gave me the last impetus I needed to drive the blade one more time — straight into his solar plexus.

Not a fierce thrust, to be sure, but this time I had gravity working for me. The faster the life drained from Halldor, the deeper his body sank onto that blade. I was helpless now to do anything but observe it: the fine trail of blood curdling from his lip, the irises rolling higher and higher in their eye sockets.

He fought all the way to the end. His teeth ground out inaudible oaths, his hands flailed at me, his whole being grew radiant with hatred. If anything, it was the desire to do me harm that helped him stay alive as long as he did. God knows how much time passed — two minutes? twenty? I can only say that, just when I had about despaired of ever rising from that floor, Halldor's eyes went still and his breath squeaked to a stop and his hands twitched their last.

I was beyond celebrating: the pain in me was too extraordinary. The influx of air, which I had thought would be a relief, was a worse agony than what had preceded it. *Like a baby*, I remember thinking, *being born.* Only no sound came out. I didn't even have the strength to push the dead man's body off me.

And so I lay there — *we* lay there — until the act of breathing became slightly less unnatural, until my lungs could draw down enough fuel to awaken the rest of me. I gave Halldor one shove, another, a third . . . and at last had the satisfaction of seeing his long, ponderous frame roll away.

With nothing to hold on to but the air itself, I staggered to my feet. To my right lay Clarissa, facedown. To my left, the prone figures of Bernard Styles and Alonzo Wax, splayed across the floor, half in light, half in shadow.

Another minute passed. And then one of the men opened his eyes and blinked up toward the ceiling. He gazed at the Webley resting in his hand, at the widening circle of blood on the other man's chest. He groaned and wheezed and, with great effort, raised himself to a sitting position.

"Henry," said Alonzo. "You can't say I didn't warn you."

47

A black pool had formed around Clarissa's eye, and blood was spilling from each nostril . . . but she was still breathing and, as I knelt alongside her, her eyes quivered open, then winced shut again.

"God," she murmured, gingerly touching her nose.

"Broken?"

"Mm."

I gave her my hand and pulled her to a sitting position. She looked first at Styles, then at Halldor, finally at me. Unable to credit, probably, that I would be the one still standing.

"Jesus," she said at last.

With a whir of petticoat, she rose to her feet. Stumbled over to the patch of floor where the remains of Thomas Harriot's perspective trunk lay bathed in the glow of Halldor's flashlight. Bending down, she gathered up the shards of glass, arranged them against the canvas of her palm.

"It died in a good cause," I suggested.

The white mask of absorption, the unseeing eyes. She was channeling her visions again. Only she was wide awake.

"Forgive me for intruding," said Alonzo. "But I think now might be a good time to take a powder."

"Clarissa," I said. "Are you coming?"

She shook her head.

"You can't stay here," I said.

"Henry . . ."

"Yes?"

"Goodbye."

A weirdly singsong delivery, and yet it carried such a finality that it stopped me in my tracks. It took an ungentle push from Alonzo to get me moving again, and even as I left the room, I was waiting for her to call after us, to offer a loophole or an escape clause . . . but in that one word she had said all she had to say.

We had this much to thank Bernard Styles for. He'd left us a perfect blueprint for leaving. We just had to reverse the path he and Halldor had forged. Walk up the basement steps, through the great hall, and out the front door that Halldor had so cunningly jimmied open. The only thing that made us

507

pause in our tracks was the reappearance of Seamus the mountaineer, grim and unsurprisable, his rucksack affixed like a vestigial muscle to his back.

In our absence, he had simply rappelled down the tower and waited. And if he was the slightest bit curious about what had befallen us, he gave no sign.

" 'S late, innit?"

Yes. It was. Nearly five in the morning by the time we hustled our way back to London Road. The 237 bus wasn't running, and the more we thought about piling our battered bodies and Tudor garb into a cab, the more it struck us as the wrong kind of publicity. In the end, we walked the mile back to Brentford, and Alonzo, after sending Seamus on his way with a hundred pounds (and promises of much more down the road), led the way back to the hotel.

With the help of peroxide and Band-Aids from my shaving kit, we performed triage on Alonzo's neck, and to ease the throb in my head we stole ice from the gastro-pub. After which there was nothing to do but repair to our separate rooms.

Even after I'd downed four Advils, sleep was hard to come by. I lay on that hard bed, watching the first insinuations of sunlight through the shutters. Then I got up and took a shower and, with my one functioning credit card, booked two tickets on the one P.M. Virgin Atlantic flight for Washington. Then I knocked on Alonzo's door.

An hour later, we were downstairs, picking around sausages and stuffed tomatoes. A whole morning lay before us, and what were we to fill it with? Words? Acts? Neither seemed appropriate in light of what had just happened. So this is what we did: We put on our coats and went for a stroll.

The morning was cold and unusually bright — rain-scrubbed — and each time I met a blade of wind, I couldn't help longing for the Earl of Essex's hat and finery, the unbreathing wool with which Elizabethans had met the elements.

"They'll be found," I said.

"Our late friends, you mean? My guess is they *have* been found."

"Should we be worried?"

"Ehh." His mouth folded down. "By the time the police get all their ducks in order, we should be long gone."

"But extraditable."

"Henry."

"I don't know, there's fibers. Fingerprints . . ."

"Please, this isn't *CSI*. No one's peering into a microscope in a shadowy room. We'll be fine."

We'll be fine.

A good enough mantra, but at the sight of Kew Bridge, it died away completely. I couldn't cross that span without recalling Clarissa. Shivering in her red car coat. Her lips even redder from the wind. The memory was exactly like a wound.

"Starkers," I murmured.

"Sorry?"

"It was a word Clarissa used. An English word, only she said she'd never been in England before."

Alonzo gave me a searching look.

"You figured her out, too, didn't you, Henry?"

I rested my hands against the bridge's balustrade.

"Not with empirical certitude. It's just . . . she came in that room with Styles and Halldor, and she wasn't a victim, she was a ghost. She was *haunted.*"

"As well she should be. I can't understand why you're not angrier about it."

"I don't know," I said, with a wan smile. "When you're forty-four years old, you're disposed to overlook things. However inconveniencing."

A tapering hiss came out of Alonzo's

mouth as he squared himself toward the river.

"I'd be the last person to tell you how to feel, Henry, but please keep in mind she was deceiving us from the very start. *And* using us. And at the risk of being tasteless, she was an accomplice to theft and murder."

"Oh. Actually, she wasn't, Alonzo."

He crossed one hand over the other.

"And why is that?"

"Because Bernard Styles wasn't guilty of theft. Or murder. At least not Lily Pentzler's murder. And maybe not Amory's, either."

I made a special point of keeping my eyes fixed westward.

"Last night," I said. "Detective Acree called."

"The policeman you mentioned."

"Seems they found something interesting when they were reviewing the security tapes for your old building. The day of Lily's death."

"Oh?"

"Walking up the southeastern steps was someone — well, he was a good deal younger than the widows who live there. Larger, too."

I paused.

"From a certain angle he resembled you,

Alonzo."

I wouldn't look at him now. Not even if I could.

"Now, of course, Detective Acree couldn't be *sure* because — okay, he's never met you. And then there was the problem of your being dead. By court order. And, all right, let's say you weren't dead . . . why would you run the risk of being spotted by that camera?"

"Why indeed?"

"Well, here's an interesting wrinkle. This particular camera had been broken for more than a year, and it was only, oh, three weeks ago that management finally got around to fixing it. But you wouldn't have known that, would you, Alonzo?"

He folded his arms across his chest.

"Security cameras," he sneered. "I can't even find words, Henry, to — I mean, why do I need words? I was in North Carolina when Lily died. Which you know perfectly well."

"Oh, you know what? I don't. Know that."

"Well, then, Amory could tell you."

"Except he can't. It's funny, when we were hanging out last night in the Syon Park woods, I got to thinking about something. Something you said to me back at the Outer Banks. You asked me how Lily could possibly have dropped a lit cigarette in a book vault. *Lily,* with her ungodly command of detail."

"That was my point exactly."

"My point is something else. My point is how did you know about the cigarette?"

From the edge of my vision, I saw his mouth cinch into a bud.

"Jesus, Henry, it was in the papers. *The Washington Post* —"

"See, I read the *Post* article. I even looked it up online just now to be sure. It mentions your books being stolen, but it doesn't breathe a single word about how Lily died. Not the cigarette, not the vault — nothing. *Suspicious circumstances,* that's as far as it goes, because that's as much as the police were willing to say."

And now, at last, I shifted my gaze from the river to him.

"Such a dumb mistake, Alonzo. And me, how dumb was *I* not to pick up on it? Encyclopedia Brown would've kicked me out of his tree house."

His voice never wavered.

"You're quite right, Henry. I didn't read it at all."

"Then how did you know?"

"Someone told me."

"Who?"

"I hate to betray confidences, Henry. . . ."

"Could you please? Just this once?"

I closed my eyes. And then I heard him say:

"Joanna."

I opened my eyes.

"Joanna?"

"Lily's stepsister. Lord, Henry, she called in a perfect frenzy. *Slow down,* I said. *I can't hear a thing you say.* I should have been nicer, it's true. She was distraught, although I'm not sure why, she and Lily were never close."

"Yeah," I said, nodding ruminatively. "Except, according to you, Joanna was in Cinque Terre when Lily died. With her new neck. The one you paid for."

Under ordinary circumstances, I would have taken great pleasure in rendering Alonzo Wax speechless. But I wasn't savoring this: the sag of his face and shoulders, the constriction in his hands.

"I know," I said, soothingly. "The confessional mode, that's not your bag. But we don't have a lot of time here, so how's about I take a run at it?"

I looked back upriver, across the water meadows, to the point where Syon House's towers rose.

"Start with this," I said. "You were drowning in debt. I know because, as your executor, I had the privilege of going through your books. You were maxed out on five credit cards. You were being dragged through small-claims courts. You were running tabs everywhere you went — the liquor store, the corner grocery, the dry cleaner. You hadn't paid your rent in something like a year. All told, I'd say you were at least a million in the hole, and maybe more.

"You know what, Alonzo? I'm guessing those two goons at the airport — Officers Mooney and Milberg, remember them? — I'm guessing they weren't working for Styles at all. More like your garden-variety loan-shark collectors, demanding their boss's money. Debt has a way of following a man around, doesn't it?"

Alonzo was silent.

"But the thing is," I said, "you had one big asset. Your library, as we all know, was worth a *lot* more than a million. And you wouldn't even have to sell it off if you could just make it disappear.

"Of course, you'd have been the prime suspect — insurance companies get a little weird about that stuff — so you had to do something else first. You had to make *yourself* disappear. Because a dead man can't steal his own books, can he? Or collect on them, which meant you needed an insurance beneficiary. Someone you could depend on to keep the money safe until it was needed. That would be — well, *me,* apparently. Though you didn't get around to telling me.

"As for the rest, well, I'm guessing it was Lily who shipped the books to a safe house, God knows where. And you — hell, you had all the freedom you could want now. You could slip on down to North Carolina and hang out in Amory's shack and chase your dream. Your million-to-one, shoot-the-moon gambit.

"It's true no one ever accused you of thinking small, Alonzo. Or getting outsmarted. You had to know Bernard Styles would be on to you. He'd want his document back, wouldn't he? And sooner or later, he *would* come calling, and being a really smart fella, you saw how you could use that to your advantage. By making him your very own scapegoat."

Nothing had changed about Alonzo but the angle of his head, which was very slowly tilting to one side.

"That's where Clarissa came in," I said. "You saw through her early on, but you let her go on making her reports to Styles because you knew they'd bring him running. And you knew how well he'd fill the part — the part *you* created for him. Come on, all you have to do is spend a minute with the guy and the shades of death start creeping in.

"No, you cast him very well, Alonzo, and better still, he played along, and me, I ate up the whole show. When those two thugs showed up at Heathrow, I figured it had to be Styles who sent them. When Amory was killed, I ignored the most salient fact, which was that *you* were the only one in that house with him. The only one who would have had complete liberty to . . . well, come to think of it, how *did* you kill him, Alonzo? Poison? Suffocation?"

His mouth pulled down at the corners.

"Well," I said, "I can at least guess *why* you did it. Amory needed money, that much was clear. He was easily bought. Maybe you caught him trying to cut a deal with another collector. Maybe even Styles. Don't misunderstand me, Alonzo, I can't approve of what you did, but I can — I can *get* it at some level."

I paused.

"*Lily,* though."

I moved a step closer.

"The woman who served you all those years, Alonzo. How could you do that?"

And here was the truest measure of the change between us: He couldn't scoff me into submission. The Waxian high-handedness would no longer fly, so he had to grope for new registers.

"It wasn't Lily's fault," he murmured. "She was just weak."

I stared at him. For a very long time.

"What does that even mean, Alonzo?"

"It *means* she couldn't carry it off."

And now his entire two-hundred-and-forty-pound frame was shaking with rage.

"She *told* me, Henry! How close she came to blabbing the whole works to you. And that was just after a couple of drinks! You think she'd have made it through a police interrogation? No. Patently no." He shook his head to underscore the verdict. "I needed more time. She couldn't give me that."

I pressed my hands against my head.

"Oh, God. Alonzo."

Somewhere, I suppose, the world was still turning on its spit. Here, it wasn't moving at all.

"Okay," I said. "One thing more. What were you going to do about *me*?"

He gave me a look of pure, I might even say unfeigned, astonishment.

"You can't blame me for wondering," I

said. "I mean, once the treasure was found, I'd have outlived my usefulness, too. No reason to keep me around."

The thing is I wasn't even angry; I just wanted to know. But Alonzo's reaction was outside the realm of curiosity. His face sprang open, and the voice that came out of him was so violent that a couple of passersby actually flinched.

"How?" he shouted. *"How can you even begin to say that?"*

For a few seconds, his agitation actually got the better of him.

"Henry, do you — *unghhh* — do you honestly think I've kept you around — all these years! — out of *kindness?*"

Fists cocked like a tavern brawler's, he advanced on me.

"Do you think I didn't have better things to do than — bail you out of your fucking career, your fucking *marriages?* And your funks and your *benders,* you think people didn't wonder why I bothered? You think *I* didn't wonder? If I could've found a way not to — not to give a shit — believe me, if I could've found a *way,* Henry, I would have. I couldn't pry myself clear. From that first moment in fucking *Freshman* Week, I lost — I lost *me,* I lost the ability to conceive of myself without *you* — being somewhere near. And if that's not my life's greatest fucking *tragedy,* Henry —"

A gasp caught him mid-sentence.

"And its greatest joy . . ."

I will always remember how terrifyingly young he looked as he stared into my face, waiting for something. What? I was no longer capable of thought. I can only say he started laughing. And it was the saddest laugh I've ever heard.

"I didn't even *mind,* you know, all my money going in the crapper. I thought, Well, that just levels the field, doesn't it? Henry and I are in the same goddamned fix, we can meet on the same *ground* now. And then Styles showed me that letter — just the second page, that's all I saw — and I thought, What better gift for Henry? Thomas Harriot's own words? What better way to bring back all the . . ."

He slammed his palms against my chest.

"All that *passion* and *brightness* you used to have, Henry, and you pissed it away, and I hated you for that, and it *still* didn't matter."

His face seemed to collapse before my very eyes, and something appeared there I had never seen before. Bitter helpless tears.

He backed away. Gave his face a furious swipe.

"Listen to me, Henry. It was never about the treasure, it was about what it *brings*. There are *other* treasures. The world is lousy with 'em! Sooner or later, that insurance money *will* come through. No, it will, believe me. And that's all the seed capital we need to —"

"What?"

For a second, he floundered.

"Christ, to *go*. Somewhere, *any*where. Wherever we can *be*, Henry, be the people we wanted to be all along. The life of the mind. I'm not asking for the physical — *thing*. You know I'm not. That's not how I . . ."

With a stifled roar, he cried:

"If you want a woman, *take* a woman! I've never complained, have I? Hell, bring Clarissa, see if I care. All I ask is — all I've *ever* asked is — just stick *around*. That shouldn't be so hard, should it? There are harder things, aren't there?"

The river was moving again: slowly, very slowly. Two seagulls were bending toward us, and a solitary jogger was picking his way along the river trail. From nowhere, church bells rang out.

Sunday.

I ran my hands through my hair.

"Alonzo," I said, "I can't believe you did

all these terrible things for me."

"For *us*," he corrected.

"Then I'm sorry. I'm sorry those people had to die for us. I'm sorry I couldn't be more worthy of them. I wish I could forget about them, but I can't."

His face didn't look quite so young now.

"So what are you saying, Henry? After all we've been through together, you're going to — what, a citizen's *arrest?* Cuffs and all?"

I took a step back.

"I'm flying home this afternoon," I said. "On the one o'clock plane. Tomorrow morning, I'm going to call Detective Acree. I'm going to tell him everything I know."

"And while you're exorcising all that nasty guilt of yours, Henry, just what do you expect me to do?"

"I don't know," I said. "I don't care."

If I had taken a hatpin and driven it straight into his skull, I don't think I could have made him flinch as he did then.

"There's no sunset to head into, Alonzo. The School of Night is closed."

He nodded, twice. His head dropped. Then he reached into the pocket of his coat and pulled out a rolled-up sheet of paper.

"What's that?" I asked.

"Harriot's map, what else?"

"Not the original."

"Of course the original."

My finger vibrated toward it, then stopped an inch short.

"Don't be a goose, Henry. Styles can't use it anymore. If someone's going to keep it safe, it might as well be you."

And then, with a giggle of profound strangeness, Alonzo added:

"I'd just lose it."

Two impulses warred within me as I took that paper in my hands. One was to thank him for the gesture. The other was to tear the thing up on the spot. And because neither impulse prevailed, I just stood there dumbly, staring at the piece of paper that had made all this trouble.

"You've got a plane to catch," Alonzo said.

I nodded, briefly. I started to speak.

"Goodbye, Henry."

A strange resonance to his words. For, of course, this was the second goodbye I'd received that day.

And as I walked north along Kew Bridge, it was part of my pathetic fallacy that England itself was saying goodbye. Thomas Harriot and Margaret Crookenshanks and Walter Ralegh and Henry Percy . . . all those figures of the past sailing off to haunt someone new.

I shivered in the wind and pulled my coat

more tightly around my neck. All the exhaustion of the past twenty-four hours was sweeping over me at last, and I wanted nothing more than to be inside, in a warm bed. My *own* bed, pathetic as that sounded. I had a very clear vision of it, in all its disarray.

And so I was utterly unprepared for the vision that actually greeted me on the northern side of the bridge: Agents Mooney and Milberg.

Wearing the same bespoke suits they'd worn at Heathrow but looking decidedly less affable. Striding toward me with intractable purpose.

And there I stood, watching them come, every last protest frozen inside me. They could have hoisted me in a single swoop and carried me off, and I wouldn't have made a peep.

But, as it turned out, I didn't need to. They swept past me without so much as a sidelong glance and kept walking in the same hard, sweet, implacable rhythm. And I remembered then what Agent Mooney had been trying to tell me earlier. *You're not even in this,* he'd said.

Alonzo had been their quarry all along. And this time there would be no escape. The high-wire leveraging act he'd been carrying off all these years — borrowing piled upon borrowing, creditor played off against creditor — it was all about to come crashing down.

And the thought of Alonzo underneath that rubble was enough, in the end, to rouse me. I wheeled around. A warning cry rose up from within me and forced my mouth open. . . .

Only there was no one to warn. Alonzo wasn't there.

Which is to say he wasn't where I'd just left him. I had to shift the angle of my vision to find the large man, surprisingly nimble in his trench coat, clambering onto the bridge's parapet. A man with not a second to waste.

Even as I sprinted toward him, I knew it was too late. He jumped without a word, without a sign, without a backward glance. By the time I got there, he'd vanished beneath the river's surface.

On the occasion of his second death, Alonzo Wax had plenty of witnesses. A mother pushing her young daughter in a pram. An Anglican priest, pausing briefly to adjust his iPod shuffle. Two teenage girls with shaved heads, pushing their skateboards. An old gentleman in an ascot, dragging his knotted-wood cane behind him like a leash.

I heard a scream, a pair of answering cries. I saw strangers rushing to the parapet, squinting down with a philanthropic zeal as though they might coax the jumper back to the surface.

I saw Agents Mooney and Milberg pause for the barest second and keep walking.

None of it mattered now, for Alonzo was beyond all care. He had sunk as truly as a meteorite, and the pewter-colored water had folded around its newest freight and carried it toward sea.

■ ■ ■ ■

PART FOUR

■ ■ ■ ■

O eloquent, just, and mightie Death!
whom none could advise, thou have
perswaded; what none hath dared, thou
have done; and whom all the world hath
flattered, thou only have cast out of the
world and despised. Thou have drawne
together all the farre stretchèd
greatnesse, all the pride, crueltie, and
ambition of man, and covered it all over
with these two narrow words, *Hic jacet!*
— SIR WALTER RALEGH,
Preface to *Historie of the World*

48

Harriot is up at dawn. Dressing quickly, he hurries down to the Syon landing and tries to flag a boat. But there's not a waterman alive who will consent to travel to London now. It is an insult even to ask them.

— What do you take me for?

— There's *death* that way.

This, then, is what Thomas Harriot is forced to do on this September morning. Digging deep in his purse, he must purchase an entire wherry, climb into it unaided, and row himself downriver.

His mission is urgent but the tide is against him, and rather than fight it he forces himself to relax into the river's rhythm. An hour and a half later, he sees Westminster's roofs clawing through the midmorning fog. All the old sights pass by in their accustomed order: the Abbey, the Star Chamber, the gates of Whitehall, the marble upswelling of Charing Cross. It takes

Harriot upward of a minute to realize what's missing.

Boats.

The Thames is empty.

Downriver fleets and upriver farmers are holding themselves free of contagion, and so Harriot, much as he did in the old days in Virginia, drives his oars through untraveled waters, hearing only the slap of waves against his hull.

No one hails him from the jetties. The Old Swan stairs have not a single welcoming torch. No horses are to be had for love or charity. If Harriot is to find St. Helen's Bishopsgate, he will have to do it on foot.

He takes a reading from his compass. Pulls his cloak around him — the air is still cool — and takes the first long strides up Fish Street.

Less than a year has passed since Harriot had last wandered through London, but it could be another city altogether. Not a single whore waylays him. All feasts and assemblies have been canceled; all fairs have been banned within fifty miles. Inns are boarded up, guildhalls sit idle. There are no ballad singers, no street cryers. Not even a barking dog, for city officials, believing dogs to be the main agents of infection, have slaughtered them by the thousands.

How uncanny it is, how ungodly, to hear *wind* in a London street. Wind rattling through the abandoned houses, browsing through alleys. Wind and church bells, which ring out at punctual intervals from every parish, tolling more and more souls to heaven.

On he walks, through the webs of damp air, sipping from a flask of Devon cider, breaking open walnuts and tossing the shells behind him, pausing only when something actually blocks his path: an abandoned dray, a dead horse (its nostrils still stuffed with herb-grace). Just past the Cross Keys Inn, he nearly stumbles over a human skull, its eye sockets fixed on the sky. Hurrying on, he finds a human thighbone, split down the middle, its marrow sucked out.

Near the corner of Grace Church and Aldgate Street, a beggar staggers past him. The first human being Harriot has seen in blocks — and just a few steps shy of being bones himself.

— Alms, sir.

But when Harriot offers him a shilling, the man stumbles on, unseeing.

— Alms . . . alms . . .

The sun is just past its meridian when Harriot comes, heavy-legged, to St. Helen's

Bishopsgate. No bells are ringing here. The parallel naves are empty and dark, and Harriot is about to sit in one of the pews and grab a few minutes' rest when he sees a corona of light around the sacristy door.

A young vicar is there. His sleeves are rolled up, as though he were on the verge of polishing the thuribles that lie all around him, but his hands sit idle in his lap. His beard is long, his surplice sodden and gray, and there is a kind of wild hollowness in his eyes that dissipates slowly at the sound of another voice.

— Crookenshanks?

— That is the name.

— Bless me, she was buried some four days past. We reported it to the parish clerk.

— I know. Her daughter has asked me to see to her belongings.

— Not many of those, I can assure you.

His mouth creases as he studies Harriot.

— You are newly arrived in London?

— This very morning.

— Then you will pardon me speaking so openly with you, sir. If the Lord has seen fit so far to spare you, He would wish you to quit this place at once.

And then, as if he has been guilty of some intolerable rudeness, the vicar hastens to add:

— Notwithstanding I should be glad of the company.

— You are most kind. As is He. I fear, however, that my duty calls me, and I am bidden to answer. If you would be so good as to tell me where I might find the Crookenshanks house?

A tiny swell of rage blossoms from the vicar's red-rimmed eyes, just before they go hollow again.

— Bevismarks. East of St. Mary Axe.

— I thank you.

Harriot is just leaving the sacristy when he hears the vicar's voice trailing after him.

— Would you be so good as to close the door after you? I am not at all sure I can bear another visitor.

It is a fitting symbol of how things have turned. The London wall, built by the Romans to keep strangers out, is now performing the task of keeping citizens in. Bevismarks runs just south of that wall: a small age-worn street, no more than a few feet wide in places, with garrets that lurch toward one another like drunken lovers. Yet on a normal summer afternoon, this cramped channel would be full of children carrying water from the cistern and women emptying pots and hanging clothes, jakes-men and draymen, leather sellers and rat catchers, the occasional Jew, walking past with head down.

Today there is but a single boy, no more than eight or nine, sitting on a calico blanket, nearly naked but for the dogskin wrapped around his waist and — small touch of heresy — the St. Christopher medallion around his neck. His bones are like blades beneath his skin. His mouth is a black-gummed crater.

Harriot fishes out a handful of shillings and drops them in the boy's inert palm.

— Crookenshanks?

The boy's fingers close around the coins. His head tips slowly back, as though he were dropping off to sleep.

In fact, he is gesturing. And there, six doors down on the southern side, stands a three-story oak-frame house. Sere and peeling, it would bleed entirely into its surroundings were it not for the foot-long cross painted in cardinal red on its door. And the bill posted just above it.

LORD HAVE MERCY UPON US

Leaning his chair against the front door is a man of twenty-some years, bootless, shaggy, mysteriously entitled, like a freeholder gloating over his fifty acres. He is a watcher. One of the men engaged by the Lord Mayor to keep vigil on infected houses and arrest anyone who tries to escape.

Harriot draws himself behind a bow-front window. Listens very carefully to the sound of his breathing.

Act with no rashness. One wrong step will be your last.

So chastened, he reconfigures the man he has just seen into a symbol of hope. For a watcher does not waste his time on a house of dead people, does he? There must be a living soul inside.

And sure enough, when Harriot lifts his eyes to those boarded-up windows, he can make out a dim, flat ocher light, trapped like a moth in the house's interior.

She's there. Margaret is there.

And even this joy he resists. For it pales before the improbability of ever freeing her.

Watchers can be bribed, they say. But *this* one is large-boned, with swelled nostrils and a truculence in his very stillness and, at his side, an evil-looking halberd, hook and ax and bayonet all conjoined, waiting to be thrust or thrown at anyone who gets in his way.

The halberd is not a thing to be gainsaid, and even if its owner were open to overtures,

Harriot has but a few coins left in his purse. And should the man prove cruel or capricious, Harriot might well be clapped in irons and sent to Newgate, carrying with him Margaret's last hope of liberty.

Something else. Another way . . .

And here is where, much to his chagrin, his body takes over. His eyes first: spotting a break in the building fronts. His legs: sidewinding around privies and empty stables and dead gardens. His *arms:* pushing aside pile after pile of discarded linen and platters and candlesticks — all the items that scavengers should have made off with long ago — hacking his way through to the alley that once lay here.

With a stagger of surprise, his brain understands what the rest of him is doing: finding a new route.

He feels a tiny lilt in his heart . . . followed by a sharp contraction. For as he circles to the back of the Crookenshanks house, he realizes nothing has become any easier. The rear is every bit as impassive as the front. Solid timber. Layer after layer of clay and plaster. A lone door, resolutely locked. A cruciform of boards across every window.

The heels of his hands spring to his face, gouge at his temples. And from the dazzle that fills his vision, something emerges.

A window.

He looks again.

Yes. Yes.

Through haste or oversight or maybe even by design, the rightmost window on the third floor has been left unboarded in its upper half. No more than six feet square, but a way *in.* Or out.

For a moment, he thinks he might climb to her. But no amount of leaping or scrambling can give him a purchase on these beams. And how impotent and childlike he feels, thrusting himself against this barren surface. Not daring to shout her name. Able to do nothing more than hammer the plaster with his fists.

So hard does he pound that he actually breaks away a chunk of mortar. At first his care is reserved solely for the divot. He measures it . . . tries his boot in it . . . assesses how easily he can make it into a toehold . . . and from there another toehold . . . scaling the whole edifice.

Then his eyes light on the chunk itself, resting by his feet. He picks it up, weighs it in his palm. Then, drawing a sight line, heaves it straight toward the window.

It lands a foot short and clatters back to earth. Again he picks it up, again he throws.

And this time his aim is truer. The thump of stone against glass seems to reverberate all the way into the ground beneath him. He waits. Ten seconds, twenty. But no one comes running.

Undaunted, he throws the mortar chunk again. Again. He is lifting it for the fifth time when, like a note of music, a light wafts from the darkness, narrowing and concentrating as it approaches the window.

He holds his breath. And in the next second the pale oval of her face is pressed to the glass.

It is a feeling he could never have imagined before. Seeing *her* see him.

In the next instant, his hands have grown mad with speech.

Open the window. Open the window.

She makes a show of pushing the sash up, but it is only a show, for she knows something he is only rising to. The window is nailed shut.

Whatever joy had filled the space between them vanishes in a breath. Haggard, he presses his hands to his brows and stares up at that window, beseeching.

She does nothing more than look back at him. Then she raises a single finger.

Her right index finger, he has enough presence of mind to note that. She holds it there, then lets it fall to one side . . . until it is pointing in the exact direction from which he has just come.

Go back?

She can't mean it.

But in answer, she makes a slow declarative nod. And so vehemently now does she jab her finger that he falls back as before an actual shove and, with deep unwillingness, retraces his steps down the alley, past all those heaps of ash and ordure, silently calling her, already mourning her. . . .

Margaret. Margaret.

There is no sense in him of larger plans, only of private and excruciating duty. So that her scream, when it finally comes, is more than he can bear. His arms flop to his side. His lungs squeeze into silence.

And then he is running.

Running with a fleetness that only terror could grant him, and up ahead he can see the watcher, baffled from torpor, rising slowly from his chair, less alarmed by the cry, perhaps, than by the sight of Thomas Harriot running toward him like a Bedlamite, filling the street with famished croaks.

— You must open the door! A woman is dying!

The watcher scowls.

— I know she's dying, don't I?

— No! No, I mean she is *dead.* . . .

They are three feet apart now: Harriot panting and wheezing, the watcher squinting him down. Then, with an air of great umbrage, the man takes the key from his pocket and sets it in the lock.

A good twenty seconds pass while he struggles with the door. Then at last it grinds open, inch by inch, to reveal a stark pallid figure. A supine woman, wearing nothing but a shift, her mouth ajar, her eyes staring sightlessly at the ceiling.

Margaret.

He hears the watcher shouting:

— Stay away!

But there are no proprieties now. He folds like paper, collapses onto Margaret's dead body, presses his face against hers, shrouds her with his breath.

And then he watches one of those staring eyes slowly — slowly — *shut.* To form what can only be called a wink.

Is it a sob or a laugh that breaks from him now? No matter. He knows all he needs to know.

— I was right, he announces.

— She is quite dead.

— Let me see, then.

Gently Harriot rakes his hand over Margaret's face, draws the eyelids shut.

— As you wish. I cannot be held to account for —

He need not finish. The warder, as indifferent as he is to fear, is proud of his own rude health, *jealous* of it, cannot bear its being tainted. So he stands there, grudging and sullen, while Harriot passes through the motions of feeling for breath, pulse, life.

— It is most unfortunate. So young.

The watcher says nothing. And Harriot, feeling the pressure of that silence, hastens to add:

— I am a physician, of course.

He hears the falsity in his voice, but he presses on.

— Naturally, I shall see to the body. I happen to know of a — I believe there is a cemetery — not so very far from here. . . .

— A *cemetery.*

An ominous tone to the watcher's voice. His eyes burn with tidings. His lips part to reveal a black-gummed smile.

— That is *most* Christian of you, sir. But it appears you shall be relieved of your burden.

Harriot doesn't take his meaning at first. Then he hears the sound of a bell, followed by another man's voice — high and occluded — calling down the street.

— *Cast out your dead. . . . Cast out your*

dead. . . .

Glancing through the open door, Harriot sees a three-wheeled wagon trundling through the street mud, drawn by a straw-haired giant with a bright red wand.

Like a scene from mythology, Harriot thinks, benumbed. But what catches his eye is not the man or the vehicle but the cargo. A tangled weave of human limbs. Body piled upon body upon body.

The dead cart.

49

It is because she is so wholly bent on muffling every pulse, every sense, that Margaret is so slow to understand her fate. She hears Harriot cry:

— There is no call! This is monstrous. I forbid it.

She hears the watcher's cool reply.

— And who are *you* to be forbidding? Have *you* been deputized by the Lord Mayor? No? Well, then. Edgar!

Who is Edgar? Eyes shut, she listens now with a new level of discernment. The squeak of cart wheels. The friction of a man's coarse wool trousers. The watcher's pandering grunt.

— Got one for you.

— Age?

— You tell me.

— Name?

— Crookenshanks.

— Christian name?

And then she hears it: the name she hasn't heard in nearly fifteen years, the name she's forgotten she ever had. Dragged from the old baptismal records.

— How long dead?

— This very minute. As this Christian gentleman can tell you.

There is nothing to fear, she tells herself. Edgar is a parish clerk. He is recording her demise, just as he must have done with her mother. Closing the books on her. It is almost a relief to hear how thoroughly she has gulled them.

Why, then, is Harriot so agitated?

—You cannot!

— It's none of your concern, sir.

—You have no right!

—You would be warranted in retiring, sir.

Is Harriot listening? Can it be he is going to leave?

Again, it is her skin, growing incrementally colder, that senses the change. And would cry out if it could.

Stay . . .

But as soon as she hears the watcher's voice, she knows it is no good. For he is speaking out loud, as he never would if the gentleman in question were close by.

— Body snatcher, if you ask me.

— All sorts, answers Edgar the cartman.

— Lucky I didn't clout him.

Why do you not cry out, Margaret? Why do you let them take you?

The answer comes back with cool clarity.

Because if you do not carry out this pretense, you will be sent back to this terrible house. And the house will finish the work it has already begun.

Stay here, and you are as good at dead. In the open air, you have a chance.

Or so she tells herself. The promise of liberty, though, fades in the few seconds it takes them to wind the sheet around her. She can be grateful not to feel their skin against hers. But then they lift her from the ground . . . swing her once, twice . . . release . . . and with a spasm of horror, she realizes she is flying.

Not upward, as for a second she could almost believe, but parallel to earth. Landing finally on a heap of cruelly pointed objects.

Her capacity for self-preservation extends this far: She imagines herself to be lying on vegetables. Knobby turnips and carrots and beets. Her bed for the night.

But the frond of hair that settles across her lips, this is not vegetative. This belongs to something animal.

And with that, the illusion is gone. The

vegetables become elbows, knees, toes, chins. And before she can think to protest, the cart is shuddering into motion, and the cartman's bell is once again ringing.

— *Cast out your dead! Cast out your dead!*

She knows now exactly where she is bound. To the pest-pit.

She scarcely notices now when the cart stumbles on a high cobble or lurches into a hole. She does not even wince when three more bodies are flung atop her; she is even grateful for the cover they provide. For now, at last, she can relax her pretense. She can open her eyes.

Only she is staring straight into a human mouth.

Male or female, she cannot say. All she can see is a small universe of tongue and palate and gray teeth. Coming for her.

She would scream, but the pressure of the other bodies stops the cry in her chest. Moving is impossible, breathing a trial. Enduring is all. For, in the performance of his duty, the cartman is strong, patient, inexhaustible. He travels for blocks on end, shouting to the empty house fronts. A man wedded to his trade.

Pressed among all these ulcerous bodies, Margaret finds herself praying not for release but for . . . liturgy. In extremis, she wants nothing more than the full retinue of God's servants — reader, clerk, sexton, priest — shepherding her toward her lodgings.

And then, as if in answer to her wish, comes the sound of church bells, chiming out in fat chords. A message meant strictly for her.

We will miss you, Margaret. We will be sad when you're gone.

For several minutes altogether, she loses consciousness. A flat gray dreamless sleep from which she is prodded by . . . stillness.

The cart has stopped.

How far have they traveled? Where *are* they? The crush against her is dissipating, a rivulet of sun is traveling down to her. It is still day. Day somewhere.

To feel the air once more in her lungs! She doesn't pause to ask why. Only when the body just above her rises toward the sky does she understand the work that is under way. The cartman has reached his terminus, and he is carrying out the last part of his contract. Disposal.

It takes no more than a minute to consign a body to eternity. Which makes it only a matter of computation to see how much time *she* has left. Three bodies followed her into this cart; three bodies will precede her to the pit.

And when her time comes, it is no great difficulty to play dead, not with all the practice she has had. How weightless she is in the cartman's arms. How sad he must be to part with her, for he leans into her ear and whispers:

— Heave ho and up we go.

But not up at all. Down. *Down.*

Perhaps six feet, perhaps ten, she cannot be sure. But she knows what company she keeps. For they lie all about her and beneath her, and new ones are following hard on: body after body, dropping like meteorites from the heavens.

And when it is over, when they have stopped coming, she lies there a long while, utterly still, her breath coming in thin streams, her senses more aflame than ever.

The cartman is gone — mark the tapering squeak of his cart's wheels. The bodies lie uncovered — too late in the plague season to bother with burial. The time of her deliverance is come.

Her eyes spring open, and it is some relief to know her squeamishness has gone. All these rotting husks that lie about her — their rictus grins, their lidded eyes, their bare blue limbs, still running with sores — impediments, nothing more. Keeping her from the light.

The only trick is finding some still place from which she can launch herself. For these bodies are shy in her presence, they slide from her touch. She must set her foot on some wretch's midsection without regard to his comfort and gouge in and push *up.*

The smell is enough to extinguish her, but this she pushes away, too, as she pushes away the identity of everyone she meets. Not a mother or grandmother or son but an elbow, a shoulder, a hip. This long flaxen hair never belonged to anyone's daughter. It is simply the ideal vine for climbing.

Her groans are terrible, but they are her fuel, too. They give her the strength to find the air pockets, the crevices, to do what must be done to reach the next terrace and contemplate the prospect of the next.

And as she labors, the world's axis seems to tilt, so that she is no longer climbing up but *out. Swimming* through this sea of flesh . . .

And all the more astonished to find, at the far end, *another* swimmer, likewise parting the waters. His arms groping toward hers, his mouth an oval. Her own mouth opening

in reply, calling out with what may be her
last breath.

    — Tom . . .

50

They move ponderously, the both of them, as they make their way to the river. Their mouths are dry, their eyes fixed straight ahead. It comes as something of a shock to find Harriot's boat still waiting at the Old Swan stairs.

He helps her in. Pauses a moment, as if he were either committing or erasing the city from his memory. Then he digs the oars in.

The whole way back they are silent. And, to speak plain, there is nothing about the Syon House landing that should loosen their tongues. Not a single torch to light their way, for the Earl of Northumberland and the rest of his household fled hours ago. No hope of finding Harriot's cottage in the dark. The two travelers must take their lodging where they stand. Where they *fall.* Straight into the cool, wet, waiting grass.

From there it is a matter of seconds until

they fall into each other. And is that not both meet and right? Have they not rolled the dice against death and won?

In their elation, they lie newly revealed to each other. All the thrill of their first meetings comes back trebled. The subsiding is as exquisite as the joining. The world has left them alone.

— Virginia, he murmurs.

Even in the dark, he can see the color rising to her skin.

— Don't, Tom.

— But I love it.

— It was my father's notion. He dreamed of presenting me to the queen one day. It was silly of him. . . .

He puts a finger to her lips. Kisses the hollow just above her collarbone.

— Virginia.

He wakes to find the dew on his face. A butterfly is descending in spirals. In the meadows, a rabbit is chewing blackberries. Swans rock on the water. From the west comes the sound of a lute. She is sleeping on his arm. Harriot envies no one.

With the Gollivers discharged, the cottage is now entirely theirs. They plunge into bed, doze on and off through the morning. After lunch, Margaret gets up and draws water from the well, heats it in the kitchen hearth. She tears off her shift and, with a glad heart, sets to scrubbing London off her.

One thing won't scrub away: a smudge of soot on her left shoulder, about the width of a silver penny. Weirdly resilient, no matter how hard she goes at it.

She touches it with her finger. Not soot at all, but something rising up within. Something that wasn't there last night.

Her skin runs cold all the way down to the feet. But the cry she hears is not her own. Harriot is standing at the kitchen door, staring at the token on her shoulder.

In the next second, he has dropped straight to his knees, and the sobs are exploding from him in an unbroken sequence. She has to wrap herself around him for fear he will burst.

The fever comes on that night. Comes on hard and breaks just as hard. She alternates between hugging the coverlet to her and throwing it off in a fury. And he . . . what more can he do than moisten or dry her brow, as needed, coo in her ear, assure her she will be well . . . soon . . . *soon.* . . .

And when her entire body begins to buck and thrash like a demoniac's, he holds her until she is spent, then lays her back on her pillow.

Her neck and groin and underarms are wells of agony now. Knives rasp beneath her skin. His most glancing touch has become a torture. Everything he would do, he cannot. Even the syrup of poppy he gives her for pain is vomited up in short measure. She writhes and wails, she wets her garments, she tears holes in the linen . . . his helplessness only thickens around him.

If only it had been me, he thinks. *How much stronger she would have been.*

He used to have closely reasoned theories on the plague. While at Oxford, he concluded that dust-laden wind, coupled with field smoke and putrefying earth, created an unwholesome atmosphere that, under the impress of severe heat, erupted into poison.

In later years, struck by the cyclical nature of the pestilence, he began to turn his attention to astrological causes. The previous January, he spent three days attempting to link plague outbreaks to conjunctions of Saturn and Jupiter in Sagittarius.

How arid and useless these abstractions prove in the hour of need. Theory gives way before practice: the changing of dressings, the washing of sheets, the mopping up of vomit and bile and blood.

How little he has ever known.

The black tokens spread across her body like tiny footprints. He tries every remedy he has ever heard of: peeled onions around the bed; oranges and cloves; garlic, butter, and salt. He mops her skin with rosewater. He burns treacle, tar, old shoes. He dips a red-hot brick in a basin of vinegar. He makes a small pyre of juniper and bay leaves and carries it in a chafing dish from room to room.

There is no suggestion he wouldn't entertain. If a quack were to stop by with armfuls of dragon water and angelica root, Harriot would buy up every last vial. And when his supplies ran dry, he would take up a musket and hunt down the nearest unicorn.

She screams without any awareness of being watched. And when she is done, she doesn't fall asleep as he hopes but waits, glassy and shivering and impatient, for the next round.

One night, she mistakes him for the cartman, actually makes a wall with her hands and shoves him out of the bed. When he tries to get back in, she rises up, whitefaced, and begs him:

— Drive on . . . Not yet . . .

On the morning of the third day, her delirium fades enough that she is able to sit up and take sips of purging beer. Her face is a burnished blue-white, like a block of marble hammered on through the night.

— Paper . . .

He grabs the sheet closest to hand. The letter that has lain atop his papers all these days, still waiting to be packed. He never looks to see who the author is. He simply turns it over and places it in her lap and dips the quill in the ink. . . .

And waits.

Her hand hovers over the page. And then, as though she were taking the letters straight out of the air, she scrawls a single word:

pneuma

The pen falls to the floor. She will write no more, but she has told him all he needs to know.

Strange to imagine that their thoughts, under cover of darkness, should have been migrating in the same direction. Or is it that, with this single ray of light, she has managed to align their courses?

The *pneuma*. The spark of original creation that lies at the heart of all things and

556

can never be extinguished. Surely, in the moment of dying, that spark, freed of its clay, will hang suspended — if only for a second. Surely, a skilled alchemist can lay hands on it, claim it, *transmute* it into the pure and true and eternal, cheating death of its prize.

Surely, if a man is to save a woman, that is the way to do it.

He kneels by her bed. He presses his wet, wet cheek against her hand.

— I am not ready to send you on, Margaret. I would have you here. With me.

Speaking is an ordeal for her, but he needs her to speak. One last time. And so she opens her parched lips and whispers:

— Tom . . . you must. . . .

The apparatus is much as she left it. The racks. The pans and pots. The clay-luted glass. The coals, the stones.

One last survey he makes. Then, with sinking steps, he goes to her.

He lifts her from the bed, groaning not at her weight but at the truly terrible lightness of her. Carries her to the laboratory and sets her on the straw mattress. Her old pallet, smuggled down from the attic.

He takes his position by the brazier. He lights the coals, watches the flame gather and rise. Much as he has seen her do, much as he himself was wont to do.

His brain heaves with terror. Streaks of sweat have formed across his brow and neck. He has wandered out of his province; he feels that now. A transformation like this cannot be effected by a natural philosopher. He must make himself a priest.

Reflexively he bows his head . . . only to hear Ralegh's jesting voice circle back to him.

And to whom are you praying, Tom?

I don't know.

What, then, is your prayer?

I don't know.

The only words that come to him, finally, are the ones he printed on her ring. The ring that wobbles now like a loose wheel on the fifth finger of her left hand. It was his assurance that nothing could ever be fully lost. Whatever was, is. Whatever is, will be.

A lie! For, with each second, she is more lost to him. He kneels alongside her. Feels the pulse fading, beat by beat, from her wrists. Watches the eyes subside into an enameled glaze. Listens to the intervals of silence, longer and longer, between each rasp.

— Margaret . . .

She is silent.

— *Margaret!*

Stunned, he lurches to his feet, gazes wildly about him. She is *here.* All around him. Waiting for him.

Hurriedly, he throws the lapis stones in the copper pan.

"Ex nihilo . . ."

He lights the tallow flame beneath the copper.

". . . nihil . . ."

He listens to the stones crackle into life.

". . . fit."

A pewter mist billows up, then resolves into a powder. The air grows heavy with current. Harriot thrusts up his hands and roars. Four centuries later, he is roaring. . . .

51

This is what I saw.

A large man with rounded shoulders walking up the back stairs of the Cathedral Arms. Wearing sunglasses and, unusual for a summer day, a knit stocking cap. Moving slowly, almost ruminatively, his left hand trailing after him on the stair rail.

All in all, he took up no more than three seconds of the jerky, shadow-swamped security-camera footage. Detective August Acree, by contrast, was a far more substantial figure. He wasn't going anywhere.

"Now I never had the pleasure of meeting Mr. Wax," he said, pushing his laptop across the desk to me. "So I want you to take another look and let me know what you think."

"What I think?"

"I'd like to know if this particular gentleman resembles Alonzo Wax."

I pursed my lips. Leaned forward and

made a show of studying that shape-shifting form.

"Oh, you know what?" I said. "I can see why you thought it might be."

"You *can,* right?"

"He's roughly the same size."

"My thoughts exactly."

"As for the rest . . ."

"Yeah?"

"Well, looking at the various particulars, I'd have to say definitely no."

"Particulars."

"See, I'm looking at his face right now. I mean, what you can see of it. It's a little rounder than Alonzo's. And he just — he *moves* differently, too. More of a rolling gait."

"Rolling."

"And the *hands* and a lot of little things, really. I don't know what to tell you, Detective, I've known Alonzo a long time, and this isn't him."

"Best you can tell."

"Given the — you know, quality of the image."

"Would you mind looking again?"

"Sure, I'd be happy to, it's just . . . yeah . . . no. I really don't think so."

Detective Acree leaned back in his chair. Steepled his hands under his chin.

"Mr. Wax's sister," he said, off handedly. "We showed it to her, too."

"Is that so?" I was conscious now of entering a slightly steeper gradient. Conscious, too, of the three beta blockers I'd swallowed before coming here.

"What did she tell you?" I asked.

"She took one look and said, *Don't be ridiculous*. Said, *My brother's dead.*"

"Ah."

Detective Acree stroked that luxuriant mustache of his, so at odds with the small-gauge eyes.

"Do you want to take one more look, Mr. Cavendish?"

"No. Really. I'm sure."

"Well, okay."

We stood up. I half extended my hand. His arm didn't budge.

"Appreciate your time," he said.

"Happy to do it."

"How was your trip?"

"My trip."

"England, I think it was."

"That's right."

"It went well?"

"Yes, thanks."

"Good." No nod. No formal dismissal. One second, he was looking at me; the next, he was turning away.

I watched him open his desk drawer and pull out a pack of unfiltered Lucky Strikes. He didn't light them, just weighed them in his palm, like a bag of gold dust. A window, I thought, into August Acree's shitty job.

"Detective," I said.

He raised his unsurprisable eyes to mine.

"If you want to know what I believe," I said, "I believe Alonzo Wax drowned. I don't believe he's coming back."

Being intelligent and occupationally suspicious, Detective Acree might have made a point of calling up that day's London papers. But would he have paused over the accounts of an unidentified man throwing himself from Kew Bridge? Would he have guessed Alonzo Wax would use the same exit strategy twice?

The body had yet to be found, according to police reports, and the eyewitness details were contradictory enough to leave the reporter with no more than two hundred words for his efforts.

As for the *other* story — well, this, too, took up far fewer column inches than I would have guessed. Syon House had been broken into, no question, but the building staff made a point of declaring that nothing had been taken. All that was left to write about was the dismantling of the alarm system and the hole in the northwest tower and a mysterious crater blown in the old abbey wall — not a word about who had done any of this or why. Or the dead bodies that had been left behind.

Which left two possibilities: Either the London police were deliberately withholding any mention of homicides . . . or, to the list of Clarissa's talents, I would now have to add corpse disposal.

And if that were the case, *how did she manage it?* Moving Halldor alone would have taken half a day. Despite a broken nose and possible concussion, she had somehow wiped the crime scene clean and spirited herself away. So cleanly that when the news of Bernard Styles's disappearance broke three days later, Clarissa Gordon was among the very first to be interviewed.

The news stories identified her variously as aide, assistant, and consultant, but whatever the job title, she struck the same note. "It's completely baffling" (*The Guardian*). "We're obviously very concerned" (*The Times*). "We haven't given up hope" (*The Telegraph*). She was politic to the end, but the real proof of her delicacy lay in the sentence that uniformly concluded each article: "Police still have no leads."

It was more than I had dared to imagine. After everything had transpired, could I really have escaped without so much as a traffic citation?

By now, I figured, Clarissa would have gone through Styles's electronic files, erased any mentions of the School of Night or the Ralegh letter, deleted incriminating phone records . . . wiped the history clean. There were times I wished she could wipe me clean, too. The ghosts in my head — Styles and Halldor and Amory and Lily and Alonzo — all made for pretty thoughtless tenants. Some nights, it was a real racket. And no one but me to hear it.

In late October, I received a special-delivery envelope from Dominion Guaranty. Inside was a check, made out in my name. In the amount of $3,400,062.

I set it on my side table and stepped away, as though it were actually ticking. Then I took out my cell phone and called the Dominion help line.

"You *are* Henry Cavendish, are you not?"

"Yes."

"And this is your Social Security number?"

"Yes."

"Then there can be no mistake, sir. You

are the designated insurance beneficiary for Mr. Alonzo Wax. The lump sum in question is the estimated fair-market value of Mr. Wax's collection."

Mr. Wax's collection.

Alonzo's missing books. Missing, too, from my thoughts all these days and weeks. Coming home at last to roost.

"So this is for real?" I asked.

"Yes, sir."

I had gone so far as to place the check in my hand. I could actually feel the numerals pressing through the paper.

"Will there be anything else, Mr. Cavendish?"

"No."

I slept poorly that night. The next morning, I went to Peregrine Coffee and, feeling slightly extravagant, ordered a three-shot latte with a fleur-de-lis of scalded milk on top and sat outside in my sweater, hunched over my mug, listing all the reasons I had for keeping the money.

1. Alonzo was dead. For real this time.

2. I had never asked to be his beneficiary.

3. I had played no part in the disappearance of his collection. Had known nothing of it. Had never once imagined I would benefit from it.

4. I had no idea where the collection currently was and no idea of how to find it. The only people who did know were dead.

Seen strictly in legal terms, my claim seemed secure. As for *extra*legal considerations . . . wouldn't Alonzo have wanted me to have the money? Me above all others?

Which is where my house of ethics came crumbling down. For if this was truly what Alonzo had wished, how could I square it with what was good and just?

I emptied my cup, set it on the table a little harder than I should have. And then I watched as the chair on the other side of the table moved away.

Moved by itself, or so I thought, until I saw the small hand resting on top of it.

Clarissa Gordon — *Dale,* as was — in her car coat. Pale and drawn but also quickened by autumn, her lips redder, the black of her eyes richer.

"Is this seat taken?" she asked.

52

But the sitting part didn't work too well: We didn't have enough shelter from each other. So we got up and took a walk.

The weather was much cooler than the last time we'd strolled across Capitol Hill. The sun was small and mellow; only the maples were blazing. And yet, just as before, Clarissa stopped after a couple of blocks.

"Mind if we sit down now, Henry?"

She didn't seem remotely tired.

"Um . . . I don't see any . . ."

"How about there?"

She pointed to a tiny stone bench with carved animal curlicues, sitting in front of an old farmhouse. It was one of those benches you picture your kids sitting on during long July afternoons, laughing, drinking lemonade, forming memories. Only you know they never will.

"That's someone's yard," I pointed out.

"Bet they're not home."

The only way to fit on the bench was to lower ourselves in tandem and draw our knees straight to our chests. It would have been altogether impossible to feel adult . . . were there not adult feelings stirring inside me. Prompted by nothing more than her mint-and-clove smell.

"I've been thinking," she said. "About all the reasons you might hate me. So how about I go through my list, and you can tell me if there are any left over?"

"Okay."

"There's, first of all, the lying. Which I grant you, except not as much as you might think. I really *am* a dumb business major. Bernard liked me that way, he didn't want me to be an expert."

"Or you'd break your dumb-business-major cover."

"Something like that. My point is . . . all those questions I was asking you about Harriot and Ralegh, they were all sincere. I really wanted to know. And being with you and Alonzo — it was a real education."

"You've been an education, too."

"Huh. Really?" Her knees rose to her chin. "I won't explore that. So *another* reason you might hate me is you think I was lying about the visions. Which is not true because that really is how I met Bernard in the first place. I was living in London then, and these damned visions were coming every night, and they were — killing me, basically — and Bernard was giving a lecture at the Humanities and Arts Research Centre. On, what do you know, the School of Night.

"So I went. And afterward, I went up to him — just like I did with Alonzo a few weeks later — and I told him I have this problem, and he said, 'Funny, I have a problem, too. And *you've* got this security background, so how about we join forces? *You'll* learn all you need to know about the School, and *I'll* get my document back.' Seemed like a win-win all around."

She paused to interrogate herself.

"And I needed money, and this was a job. At least it was supposed to be."

She picked up a Bradford pear leaf and very carefully began to shred it. The margins first, then the veins and the midrib. When it was nothing more than a petiole, she flung it away.

"At the wedding, Henry. When I told you —"

"Yeah."

"I mean when I said I loved you."

"Right."

"Well, that wasn't a lie, either. It was just — you know, it was lousy timing. So anyway, for the things I *did* lie about, I apologize. Truly. And for putting you in danger, too, which I never meant to do but still. And . . ." She exhaled, shook her shoulders. "What else?"

"I don't know." I shrugged. "It's not like I kept a spreadsheet."

"Well, that's good."

"I'm glad you came."

"Well. I'm unemployed again, so . . ."

We sat for some minutes. Alone, except for a single tricycle, rolling mysteriously past, unattached to any child.

"It wasn't lousy timing," I said. "To say those words."

"No?"

"See, the thing is — I mean, you have to understand, I have a very fraught relationship with those words, all right? I used them with the first girl who had sex with me. I was so — immoderately grateful, they just came out. And since then — God, is it a dozen? *More* than a dozen women, probably, have heard me say those words and I was, frankly, most of the time, mistaken, though never exactly insincere, but the problem is I can't speak them anymore without thinking it's more bullshit. Which is the last thing I want in my life, even though I'm not exactly sure what's left — after the bullshit leaves."

"Okay. I get that."

"No. *No . . .*"

And now I could no longer sit on that tiny unbearable bench, but my legs, under compression, had nodded off, and when I tried to stand, they folded under me and left me . . . on my knees, yes, in the cool grass. Staring up at Clarissa. Very conscious of my humiliation, but conscious, too, that this was the best attitude to take when everything comes rising up.

"I love you," I said. "I love you, Clarissa Dale . . . Gordon . . . *Borgia,* whatever your name is. Whatever your infamy. I love you more than is good for me. More than may be good for you. I love you for the duration. Five acts, plus epilogue, plus curtain call. I love you without refund."

A single tear vibrated on the corner of her eye. She angrily brushed it away.

"Henry."

"I'm only sorry —"

"What?"

"That it's going to be so hard to stand up again."

She laughed.

"You don't know the half of it, Henry."

She helped me to my feet, and then she drew my arms around her and pulled me tight. And she was *there,* suddenly, all of her, scent and touch and heart and soul, ravishingly concentrated, her dark eyes shining like tomorrow. *No face is fair that is not full so black . . .*

"Glad we cleared things up," she said.

Just then, an ancient dog-walking woman in a wearable-art sweater walked past us. Her face lit up with a yenta's smile, and we grinned back, delighted to be exactly the people she assumed us to be.

"Let's walk," Clarissa suggested.

And so we did. Down blocks innumerable, toward every point of the compass. Past bird baths, azalea bushes, corner stores, abandoned middle schools. The breeze laid a chill on our skin, and the sun scorched it off. I envied no one.

"Henry, can I ask you something?"

"Of course."

"Alonzo. Did he . . . was he the man who jumped from Kew Bridge?"

I nodded.

"Well, I'm sorry," she said. "I'll miss him, if that doesn't sound strange."

"It doesn't. I don't know if — see, I found out Alonzo was —"

"Lily and Amory, yeah. I was getting around to that conclusion myself. Lord knows, Bernard *could've* done it, it wouldn't have shocked me, I just couldn't see why he *would*. There was no motive."

"What about the treasure? Wasn't that an incentive?"

She shook her head. "Bernard never put much store in that. He was willing to hold off for a little, see what came of it, but he was after another prize."

"Which was?"

She gave me a puzzled look. "The document, Henry."

"But that . . ."

I frowned, jerked my head away.

"It doesn't make sense. Why would he care so much about a few lines of Walter Ralegh's? I mean, sure, it'd be worth *some* money, but not *that* much. Nothing worth dying for, that's for sure."

"For *him* it was."

"Why?"

"Because without the letter's second page — without that signature from Ralegh — the first page loses most of its value. All of it, really."

I stared at her.

"There's a *first* page?"

"Yep."

"But Alonzo —"

"Never saw it. See? Bernard wasn't as much a fool as Alonzo thought. He might flash you a card or two, but he'd never tip his whole hand."

"So all along Styles had this first page. In his possession."

"Yep."

"And all he wanted to do was . . . reunite it with the second."

"Yep."

"So what makes the first page so special?"

Clarissa smiled then: slow and lippy. She unsnapped her cordovan handbag and pulled out a folded sheet of paper.

"See for yourself."

It was a digitalized copy. Written in the same hand as the other document. Written at the same time by the same man. But breaking a hole in everything.

"It can't be," I murmured.

"Keep reading."

To my verie loving frende and master Thomas Harryott of London, gent,

Yew were goode enough to ask after our healthe.

The Queene lyes now at White Hall dead. Shee came in with the fall of the leafe, and went away in the Spring, and neuer, I thinke, has the English Nation been so robed in black as youreself. In spite of the generall terror her death has occasioned, you shall perceiue that I haue more cause to mourne than most. The wheele of Fate turns, a new Sun rises vp out of the North, and no more shall the Truth bee my warrante.

All ready are slaunderous and shamefull speeches bruited abroade. I doe not knowe when I myself shalbe arayned, al-thoughe I must confess that my hearte is not heavy but of singuler lightness, I knowe not how. Besse and I haue taken ouersels to the Innes of Court, there to behold the latest fancy of master Shaxper. Yt was titled Alls wele thatt ends wele, and a more curious and straunge play haue I neuer seen. I was most forceibly strucke by the epithet resarved for ovr Hero, hight Bertram. Towit, foolish idle boye and for all thatt verie ruttish.

Was this not, in all its particulars, howe Kit used to speke of Shaxper? You recall ful wele, I hope, that night at Sherburne, whene Kit brought his louer there to mingle at lengthe with our Schollers. Wordes came but sparingly to the younge wight's lips, and though wee scanned the remot-est Orbs for their deepeste Misteries, there was for him no misterie, no glorie greter than his well-loved Kit. Howe little wee regarded him then, Warwickshire stripling, except when he had bene reduced most to tears by Kits gibes and japes.

I read it again and again. The words didn't scatter, as I kept expecting, but remained stubbornly, surreally in place. And how neatly they segued into that second page, which rose now from memory.

Hee wold not be the first louer so to be served by Kit, who wold burn Hotte and Cold in the space of but one breth and who cold conjure up proofs for the Deuil or our Savior, howsoever the winde tourned him.

The one figure I'd never given a second thought to — Marlowe's lover — was the Colossus that had been squatting over us the whole time.

I laughed so hard I actually fell down. Sprawled there in a tree box, with a row of liriope.

"Henry?"

In my defense: It's not every day the entire field of Shakespearean scholarship bursts open. Violence like that can make a fellow shaky.

"Breathe, Henry."

But if anything, it was a case of too much

oxygen. Too much possibility.

Where even to begin? If this was a genuine letter, it would be the most exciting find since — Jesus, the plays themselves.

It would fill in the seven-year historical gap between the birth of Shakespeare's twins in Stratford and his first emergence in the London theater scene.

It would give the School of Night new and global renown as the incubator of some of England's greatest masterworks.

It would tie Shakespeare to Ralegh, to Harriot, to Chapman . . . and, most thrillingly, to Marlowe, who was not just Shakespeare's colleague or rival or associate but his *intimate.*

And here was the point I was still groping toward. It would give Shakespeare's career an entirely new trajectory: an arc of revenge.

"Sit up," said Clarissa. "And explain that last part."

"If we're to believe this letter," I said, "the young Shakespeare was mad, *crazy* in love with Christopher Marlowe. *No mysterie, no glorie greter than his well-loved Kit.*"

"Okay."

"But it wasn't a romance of equals. They were the same age, sure, they both had fathers in trade, but Marlowe went to

578

university, he read Machiavelli, he was full of that 'new philosophy,' it shows in all his plays. Compared to Marlowe, Shakespeare was less learned, less accomplished. A real *rube*."

"And Marlowe made him suffer for it."

"From the sounds of it. And not just Marlowe. It sounds like the whole School found young Will a bit wanting. *Warwickshire stripling. Howe little wee regarded him.* I'm guessing they never asked him back, and I'm guessing, too, that Marlowe discarded him before long. Which, when you're an infatuated young man —"

"Ambitious."

"— is going to sting like a million lashes."

The sun was out in full strength now, bringing the white paper to full dazzle.

"So what does Shakespeare do?" I asked. "He builds a life — a life's *work* — in direct opposition to the School of Night. He mocks their pretensions in his plays. He plants his flag in the camp of Essex, their enemy. And maybe he doesn't stop there. Maybe he testifies against Marlowe, maybe he slanders Harriot."

"You're speculating."

"But *someone* leaks word about what the School was up to. Who has a better reason? The jilted lover. Think about what happens when Ralegh gets in trouble with King James. Out of nowhere comes a poem, 'The Hellish Verses,' attributed to Ralegh, full of atheistic sentiments. Pretty much the stake in Ralegh's heart. Who's likely to leak such a damaging document? Someone with a serious grudge. And someone with firsthand knowledge of what the School was up to."

Clarissa frowned into her hands. "Suddenly, Shakespeare doesn't sound like such a nice guy anymore."

"Nice or not, it doesn't matter. He's a *different* guy. Not just a survivor, a *player*. Avenging himself on the men who rejected him."

The fire in my brain was almost too much now. I had to bury my face in my hands. I had to . . . *Breathe, Henry.*

But I was thinking of the last ten years of my life. My little wasteland of self-unemployment. My amassed debts, financial and spiritual. And now, with the help of Alonzo Wax and Bernard Styles, all that was on the verge of changing. A single two-page letter was going to be — how had Styles put it? — *the springboard for quite a splendid academic treatise. Such as might restore a man's career.*

"Christ!" I wheeled toward Clarissa. "Do you have the original?"

"I didn't handle Bernard's security for nothing. I've got the original, and it's tucked away. How about you? Do you have the other one?"

"I do."

"Then we're good to go."

She said it so simply that I almost let the momentum take me. But sadly it is part of my nature always to look beyond the verb to the entire predicate. Good to go . . . *where?*

"We can't," I said, gritting my teeth. "We *can't*. This is not even legal."

"Why not?"

"The letter belongs to the Styles estate."

Like a tightrope walker, Clarissa raised one of her jeaned legs. Angled her face toward dogwood overhead.

"In theory, I'd agree with you, Henry. Except I'm pretty sure Bernard didn't come by the letter innocently. That whole story about finding it in some law firm's archives? I checked it out; it doesn't hold up. And think about it. If he came by the document legally, why didn't he call in the police when it went missing? He could have saved himself a lot of trouble."

"So . . . is there anything left to tie the letter to Styles?"

She gave it some thought. Then shook her head.

"Not anymore."

"Does anybody else know about it?"

"Far as I know, only dead people."

But dead people can still fuck you up. My career had been derailed by an eighteenth-century dilettante. The whole thing could be —

"A forgery," I said, dismally. "Likely as not."

"Could be," she said. "I guess that's for you to figure out."

"Me?"

"Who else?"

And then she smiled. Just enough to break my heart.

"Because ideally, Henry? It should be someone who's still alive a year from now."

53

Every doctor agreed: It was the damnedest thing.

At thirty-six, Clarissa Gordon had the biological indicators of a woman of seventy: shortened telomeres, progressively failing homeodynamics, drastic reductions in cell division. She was aging at twice the normal rate, but her symptoms didn't align with any of the defined pathologies (Hutchinson-Gilford progeria, Werner's syndrome, Cockayne's syndrome, ataxia telangi-ectasia), and parts of her body — her skin, her hair, her bones — seemed strangely impervious to the senescence that afflicted the rest of her.

"It's like Hollywood aging," she told me. "Very glamorous all the way to the end. I couldn't have arranged it better. And you *know* they're gonna have to name it after me."

Before we were done, we would see more than a dozen specialists — physiologists, gerontologists, geneticists, evolutionary biologists, embryologists. She would be subjected to microarray analysis, bioinformatics, full genome sequencing. Her hair and saliva would be pored over like entrails. So would her entrails. So would her epithelial cells and bone marrow. A researcher in Bethesda would attempt to give her an entire wing at the National Institutes of Health. A professor from the University of Oklahoma would beg her to leave him her organs.

No one from any field or discipline would be able to explain exactly what was happening or why. The only thing everyone could agree on was the end point.

But I'll say this for her. Clarissa's mission was never just to fold up like an old chair. She had a story to tell.

From the moment she held that old perspective trunk in her hands, the fragments that had been haunting her all these months began to gather into something like a narrative. There were missing chunks, to be sure, holes in the continuity, but as I set it all down on paper, the gaps somehow filled themselves in, and the story began to tell itself. Clarissa talked; I wrote; and if what we ended up with is as much fiction as fact, I know it's true at least to us.

"You know what this means, don't you, Henry?"

I had just printed out our final draft, and Clarissa was holding it rather shyly to her breast.

"It means you're just as crazy as me now."

I'm not so sure. Of course, I'm no medical specialist, I'm not even a licensed metaphysician, but in those moments when the walls of my empiricism soften, I fall back on a theory of my own. Thomas Harriot did not stand by helplessly while his beloved lay on the verge of death. By luck or by design or some combination of the two, he cupped his hands around her essence and sent it spinning into the future. Never guessing where it would land.

Naturally, we couldn't expect him to get it perfect his first time out. And so, with each incarnation, the spark has been gradually reduced, and maybe it will finally die with Clarissa. Or maybe it will never die.

This much I know. Being with her is a rare and good thing, and the rareness and goodness would be impossible without the shortness. We have vaulted past all the normal stages — exploration, evolution, devolution — and landed right in the home stretch. Our golden *year,* Clarissa calls it.

And so, like any old couple, we spend a

lot of time on benches. Quiet as snow. Our history speaks for us, I guess. A history we just happen to share with two people who lived and died centuries before you were born. Among the four of us, I'd wager, we've lived a good long life.

The money? For now, we're skimming interest off Alonzo's principal. Clarissa has drawn up a list of charities she wants to have remembered in her will. And I have my own ideas on the subject, which I'll keep to myself for now.

Ralegh's letter? I had to ponder that for a while, but once I'd decided, it was the easiest thing in the world to drop those two pieces of aged rag paper in a padded manila envelope and mail them, anonymously, to the Folger Shakespeare Library. Let the experts sort out the truth. Grant them the glory, too, if they want it. To my great surprise, my career is here. On park benches.

Once I asked her, "Why did you dress like that?"

"Like what?"

"The day of Alonzo's funeral. The day I first saw you. You didn't wear mourning. You wore a summer dress. Scarlet."

"Oh."

She closed her eyes, and for a moment I thought she'd nodded off. (She does that a lot.) But she was just parsing her words.

"I suppose it's because I don't believe in death," she said. "The capital D part."

Which, to my mind, is the best kind of apostasy. In my strongest moments, or maybe my weakest ones, I choose not to believe, either. And if that doesn't earn me a diploma from the School of Night, nothing will.

54

Syon Park is silent. The cuckoos, the swallows, the blackbirds, the thrushes have all moved on, leaving behind the season's last roses and scarlet oaks and pools of elm and beech leaves . . . and now and then a heron calling across the river. Just to see if anyone's listening. It's a fine time to die.

But death, it seems, has washed its hands of him. Why else did it keep him from following Margaret into the grave? Why, in the intervening weeks, has his health taken not a single turn for the worse? Is he merely being dared to take events into his own hands?

The Earl of Northumberland's steward, returning in early November, is astonished to find Harriot still in his cottage — and sporting, for the first time in memory, a beard. Nothing like the earl's fashionable profusion but weedy and gray and straggling, a perfect misery of a beard, repelling the questions it raises.

Barges are at last coming downriver in full sail. London is safe — though not for Ralegh. A widely bruited set of atheistic lines, attributed to him, has appalled even his most devoted supporters and tipped the balance of opinion against him. On his way to trial, London's citizens line the streets for the sole purpose of pelting him with curses — and tobacco pipes.

But in the course of defending his life, Ralegh carries himself so nobly that, despite his death sentence, he is a hero by the time he emerges. It is said that men who would have gone a hundred miles to see him hanged would now travel a thousand to save him. Rather than weather this sea change of opinion, King James chooses to commute Ralegh's death sentence — and then send him back to the Tower for perpetuity.

Harriot, never one to shirk duty, pays regular visits to his old friend and patron, bearing scientific instruments. But the words of cheer Harriot would normally bear alongside, these are missing. It is left to Ralegh to steer their conversations. One afternoon, as they are strolling past the pigeons on the high walk that overlooks the Thames, the great man offers his own words of cheer.

—The School of Night. It lives on, does it not?

■ ■ ■ ■

Back at Syon House, Harriot sleeps half the day, shuns all work, walks from room to room. The beard goes away (he hates the scratch of it) but the *hunger* for her, which is deeper than grief or perhaps grief's other face, this remains.

He lives, somehow, without living. The woman who schooled him in that art is no longer here, and how hard it is for the student to step away from the teacher. Perhaps the only thing that saves him is this. On a bright smoky April morning, the Earl of Northumberland pokes his head through Harriot's open window.

— Trout, Tom?

Midsummer's Eve is hardest, for he cannot help but recall that night with Margaret on the tower. Venus's phases . . . the swell of her lips . . . the stories she told of ghosts running abroad.

That night, he climbs the steps of the northwest tower. The sky is clouded but mistless. He peers into the rain and waits.

— Are you there, Margaret?

He wishes, often, that he had penned a love

lyric to her. Then again, how could he have vied with Astrophel and Stella?

So when he takes up the sheet of paper on which she scrawled her last message, he begins to inscribe . . . not verses, not even words, exactly, but codes, puzzles, indirections: the currency of their lives together. It pleases him, in fact, to imagine her standing over him as he composes, using a magnifying glass to write in the smallest possible grain.

Yes, I see, Tom. Well played.

It is not plague that comes for him after all but an angry red spot on his upper left nostril. He pays it no heed, and the spot, for its part, is in no large hurry to colonize the rest of his nose. Another thirteen years pass before it bothers to spread to his lip. And here at last it betrays a degree of impatience, spreading with economy to his palate, his tongue, his jaw.

By the end, speech comes with great difficulty. Breath itself is a vexation. He spends his last days in Threadneedle Street, the guest of a mercer who sailed with him to Virginia all those years ago. Physicians are brought in — one goes so far as to blame Harriot's troubles on tobacco — but his most constant nurse is visible only to him.

I know your pain, she says. *But soon you will get to the other side of it, and you will wonder what all the stir was about.*

Ralegh by now has gone to his reward. Northumberland is in the Tower. Three others are standing at Harriot's bedside when he passes, and each believes he is the one being addressed.

— Oh, you were right. Yes, I see. You were quite right.

ACKNOWLEDGMENTS

It's not quite a cast of thousands, but many kind people were tasked with making me less dumb. Among them: Jessica Berman, Steve Cymrot, Daniel De Simone, Teresa Grafton, Barry Meegan, Katherine Neville, George Pelecanos, John Riley, Jonathan Simon, Francis Slakey, and Dan Traister. I particularly want to thank the patient souls at the Folger Shakespeare Library, especially Georgianna Ziegler, Richard Kuhta, Betsy Walsh, Heather Wolfe, and Karen Lyon.

My Library of Congress research angel, Abby Yochelson, fielded every bizarre question I could throw at her. Gary Krist provided, with his book *Extravagance,* a useful structural template. James Reese offered invaluable feedback and encouragement. Leslie Feore and the staff of Syon House were so kind in responding to queries that I felt quite churlish devising a fictional burglary of their property. I hope they will pardon me for my make-believe crimes and for any real-world offenses against fact.

Thanks, finally, to Marjorie Braman and Christopher Schelling, who've been riding this train from day one. And to Montuori, who is absolved, of course, from reading a word of this.

ABOUT THE AUTHOR

Louis Bayard is the author of the critically acclaimed *The Black Tower*, the national bestseller *The Pale Blue Eye*, and *Mr. Timothy*, a New York Times Notable Book. A former staff writer for Salon.com, Bayard has written articles and reviews for *The New York Times*, *The Washington Post*, Nerve .com, and *Preservation*, among others. He lives in Washington, D.C.

We hope you have enjoyed this Large Print book. Other Thorndike, Wheeler, Kennebec, and Chivers Press Large Print books are available at your library or directly from the publishers.

For information about current and upcoming titles, please call or write, without obligation, to:

Publisher
Thorndike Press
10 Water St., Suite 310
Waterville, ME 04901
Tel. (800) 223-1244

or visit our Web site at:

http://gale.cengage.com/thorndike

OR

Chivers Large Print
published by AudioGO Ltd
St James House, The Square
Lower Bristol Road
Bath BA2 3SB
England
Tel. +44(0) 800 136919
email: info@audiogo.co.uk
www.audiogo.co.uk

All our Large Print titles are designed for easy reading, and all our books are made to last.